Colorworld

Book 1 of the Colorworld Series

To Sivi
Welcome to the Colorworld!

Rachel E Kelly

Edited by Jamie Walton

Published by Rachel E Kelly, Williston, North Dakota, USA

Published by Rachel E Kelly, Williston, North Dakota, USA.
Web Site: http://www.colorworldbooks.com

ISBN-13: 978-1480153639

Cover Photograph by Richard J Heeks

Cover Design by Beth Weatherly

Colorworld

For Bradley Kelly—

Who has inspired every word I have ever written.

Some colors are visible; others are not. But all colors are of arcane significance. Only by fully comprehending the visible can one grasp the mere existence of the higher colors—those that are hidden and invisible. But Human kind has not even mastered the colors they can see. Therefore, sight of the higher colors has never been given to Humanity.

–The Zohar

1

*"G*eez, Ezra, could you be any *less* ready to go?" I grumble as I look from the clock on the microwave to my 15-year-old brother's disheveled blond hair and Spider-Man pajama pants.

"I don't know, maybe you could have waited a little longer to get me up... Yeah, then I would definitely have been *less* ready," Ezra replies flippantly as he pushes past me into the bathroom. "You didn't tell me we had to leave early," he says after he shuts the door, knowing perfectly well I can hear him. "What am I? A mind-reader? If you weren't going to bother telling me, you could have at least set my alarm for the right time."

I roll my eyes at the door but can't think of a good retort. My diabetes demands I put something in my stomach before I leave so I search the cabinets for something quick. Finding some nut-free granola bars behind a half-full box of pasta, I rejoice. Trying to stretch my grocery budget this week, I've lived on the dregs of dry cereal for breakfast; this will be a nice change.

The time on the microwave sends me into a fresh panic so I dump the entire box of bars into my bag without thinking. I immediately curse under my breath. The clock is ten minutes fast. It's *supposed* to help me be on time, but instead it makes me frantic. Then I do dumb things like throw ten granola bars into my overfull shoulder bag when I know I still have to search its cluttered contents for my keys.

Groaning, I plop down on the floor so I can paw through the mess more easily. Of course my keys aren't there. I crawl over to Ezra's twin-sized bed, which is shoved into one corner of our studio apartment. I peek underneath it, behind it, and in between his sheets. I yank the blanket and cushions off the couch where I slept last night.

Nothing.

I consider pulling the hide-a-bed out to search it but decide against it; I don't have time and I didn't use it last night anyway. I rarely do because I always jam my shin into the corner of the metal frame. Our apartment is too small and the cushions are more comfortable anyway.

I turn around to check the small kitchen countertop. It's piled high with paper, textbooks, Ezra's backpack, dirty dishes, unopened mail, and a laptop computer. The disorderly pile leans precariously toward the edge, so I shove the whole thing to the back of the counter and attempt to pluck out the collection of mail without disturbing the integrity of the stack. I probably put my keys down along with the mail last night.

Gingerly, I ease the small bulk out, but an envelope slips to the floor anyway. There's no return address on it, and *my* name and address are both handwritten. Forgetting my hurry, I pick it up and begin tearing into it.

"Looking for these?" Ezra says from behind me. I turn to see him swinging my keys from one finger.

"Where were they this time?" I ask, snatching them away. Remembering that I have no time to examine the mysterious envelope, I shove it into my bag.

"In your jeans pocket on the bathroom floor," he intones obnoxiously. "You know, Wen, you really should—"

"Thank you very much, *little* brother!" I snap, turning on my heel. "Let's go!"

I don't have shoes on. *Crap.*

Ezra sniggers and grabs his schoolbag from the precarious Mount St. Countertop disturbing nothing in the process. He moves over to the door, waiting for me. He crosses his arms and taps his foot like he's been standing there all morning.

Once my shoes are in place, I bound past him and through the door, tearing down the stairs and praying that the traffic will be kind this morning. In my car, I relax a little when I see the clock on the dash—which is accurate. If there haven't been any accidents on the freeway, I should be right on time. I glance at Ezra. "I'm going to have to be late to work unless you can find a ride from school—or I could pull you out a half-hour early?" I sigh. Ezra could probably teach his last period calculus class himself so thirty minutes won't matter. The kid is smart.

"Nate will give me a ride," replies Ezra, unconcerned as he stares out the window.

Nate is Ezra's 18-year-old friend who shares his interest in comic books. He's probably Ezra's *only* friend to share that interest. I wrinkle my nose in distaste as I remember my last encounter with him. I was picking up Ezra from Nate's place and waiting for Ezra to get his things while Nate stood there in his filthy kitchen letting his eyes roam the length of me. He could have at least been discreet about it.

"Don't worry," Ezra teases, catching my expression, "I won't let him sniff your underwear drawer."

I scowl at him. "He'd better not. I swear I know exactly where everything is in my underwear drawer. If even one thing is out of place I'm going to kick him in the nads and rip one of his comic books until he cries."

Ezra gives me a mock fearful look before saying, "Yeah, right. The Hulk himself could be in our apartment and you'd never know the difference. Anyway," he adds, looking serious again, "I won't even let him in the door. I have an English paper to get done."

I give him a withering look as I pull up to the curb in front of the school. We're at least thirty minutes early so the lot is virtually empty. "English paper?" I say before Ezra can get out. "And when was *that* assigned? Yesterday?"

Ezra stares at me blankly.

"I knew it!" I accuse. "I bet that paper isn't due for another week at least. *Why* do you have the sudden urge to stay on top of your least favorite subject?"

Ezra looks at me with confusion now. "You're mad that I'm *not* procrastinating?"

"No," I huff. "I'm mad that you're always trying to please me. It's annoying. So just do what *you* want for once, okay? Have Nate come over. He might not be a credit to the male species but he's pretty much harmless. I trust you guys won't be doing anything more than drooling over superhero chicks and their ginormous breasts in cartoon spandex." I grin. Ezra rolls his eyes.

"Maybe I should go to high school and you should go to work if you're interested in being all *responsible* and *grown up*," I add. Then I furrow my brow. "Come to think of it, if you were taking *my* classes, you'd probably have a four-point-oh and already be graduating."

I can't help sighing. It really would be easier if it were possible for us to exchange places. Shame constricts my throat as I think about our disorganized lives. Mom would never have stood for this. Ezra knows it too, or he would act less responsible—more like a teenager. I swallow to stifle the irritation bubbling in my chest. I want to yell at him right now and tell him to leave the effing parenting to me. But I bite my tongue. I can't justify being upset at him over something so silly.

He looks down at his hands, deliberating for a moment before looking at me and smirking, "Okay. But just remember you asked for it. Nate will take me home and then we'll leave all our dirty dishes on the counter. I'll be sure to put my shoes in your study spot and shove your books under the bed along with my dirty socks. I think I might even pee on the toilet seat for good measure. Sound rebellious enough?"

"Only if you promise to tell me you hate me when I yell at you for it," I reply, laughing, genuinely grateful that he's going to while away an afternoon being unburdened. Maybe one of these days he'll skip school and make me *really* proud.

I am so screwed up.

He rolls his eyes again but then unexpectedly leans over, grabs my arm, and kisses my cheek. My own self-doubt is replaced by such a warmth of affection that I catch my breath. My heart melts right into my stomach. I know these are not *my* emotions though; these are Ezra's. He has disarmed me completely by touching me and letting me feel what he feels. Ezra lets go of my arm then, unlatches the door, and moves to get out.

He stops before shutting the door, leans back in, and says, "Oh yeah, I almost forgot." He reaches into his pocket and pulls out a handful of bills. Putting the small wad firmly in my hand, he says, "One of Nate's friends has been paying me to tutor him in math."

Before I can protest, Ezra shuts the door. He turns to wave goodbye. I think I might cry. I also imagine rolling down the window and throwing the bills out. Settling for something in the middle, I stick my tongue out at him as I drive away.

When he's out of sight, I peek down at my hand. It isn't much. Maybe twenty-five dollars. The scent of the bills wafts into my nose; I have always hated the smell of money. It reminds me of dirty laundry—another smell I can't stand. In fact, just last week my laundry got out of control in our apartment. Every day I kept meaning to do it, but I was being swamped by review homework since exams are coming up. The laundry got staler until one day I came home from work late at night to the faint smell of detergent. Ezra had done the laundry—*my* laundry. Folded it. Put it away. I struggled between grateful and pissed off. Ezra has been doing little things like that for months. And now he's actually giving me *money*? It isn't right. Ezra should not feel like he needs to help keep us afloat.

Yet I can't deny his gesture just now. Ezra knows I can discern the emotions of others when their skin touches mine. He let me in on *his* so I would accept the gift. How do I deny him when his feelings speak his regard for me so clearly?

The change in him still bugs me though. I remember the last time he got in trouble at school; it was when Mom was still alive. Ezra had mouthed off to his science teacher who was lecturing about how things with enough mass create their own gravity. Ezra had flippantly remarked to the overweight man, "Does that mean *you* have your own gravity, Mr. Burkwith?"

I can't help cracking a smile at the memory; I'm a sucker for Ezra's irreverent humor. And I miss that carefree side of him. He used to skip class a lot because he was bored with it. But not anymore. Now, no matter how I shelter him, he's burdened with *my* mounting bills, *my* full-time job, and *my* full course-load. He's being forced to mature because I can't keep my crap together.

And now this touching thing… Ezra used to avoid it—he didn't like the breach in privacy. But lately he's been doing it as a precursor to doing little things for me. I have to give it to him: he has me figured out.

So did my mom before she died.

"Wendy, you don't need the responsibility. It's not healthy for you," she told me when I asked her for custody of Ezra. With no extended family, she had planned to put him in the care of her one and only long-time friend.

What she really meant was that I couldn't handle it. I was only eighteen. I had a history of 'not handling it.' So I couldn't blame her. But I pleaded with her over and over anyway because if I didn't have Ezra, I would be alone once she died—on my own completely. It was exactly what I had wanted in the years leading up to Mom's death. But once that dream started materializing into reality, I was terrified of it.

Mom finally conceded. But she told me I had to finish college. It would be so much easier if I could quit school and get a second job. It's not like she'll know the difference now, but my hope is that she made me promise because she believed in me. The alternative is that she knew if I took a break, I might never finish. But that is *not* going to happen. I *will* make this work with Ezra, one way or another.

I groan and grip the wheel harder. Ezra must have gotten his hands on my banking password and learned that I'm going to have to put the electric bill on a credit card again. I need to actually *memorize* my password so I don't have to write it down for him to find.

As I ease onto freeway, I wish for the umpteenth time that my job would just pay a little more. A regular income doesn't matter if it doesn't cover all the bills. I've been slowly but surely accruing a credit balance to make up the difference. I'm slated to complete my computer engineering degree in only two more years, but even at my breakneck pace I'm digging myself into a financial hole. I need to supplement my income.

Maybe today is the day.

The traffic begins to swell and I check my mirrors anxiously for a more open lane. I'm still on time but southern California freeways are always one fender bender away from a standstill. I do *not* need to be late today. I don't want Pneumatikon, LLC to have any reason to refuse my application to be part of their study.

I feel like a loser doing something like a drug study to earn money. But I'm desperate. If this doesn't work out I might have to sink to a sleazier level and sell my plasma or something. This study, at least, claims natural methods.

But I'm almost convinced that this opportunity was a sign of the gods finally taking pity on me. Something drew me to the job postings board that day even though I had no time for a second job. I guess I was dreaming I had the power to extend the days to 28 hours.

I found no time machines for rent. No free money. Nothing beyond pleas for tutor work and roommates.

I looked down at the floor in defeat. "*Got food allergies?*" said the flyer at my feet. "*Looking for some extra cash this semester?*"

I did my research and the offer turned out to be just as real as the company. I can already taste the peace of mind that would come from a little extra money in my pocket.

I finally escape the congested freeway with relief. The broad, quiet, palm-tree-lined street is nicer than I expected. It whispers legitimacy.

Pneumatikon, LLC, the purveyor of the promising flyer, specializes in treating autoimmune disorders. They run their own drug trials and develop their own treatments. Their website claims that they use a non-invasive approach, although they don't disclose

6

the specifics. They are seeking willing participants to validate their methods.

If there's money involved, I'm willing.

After several suspenseful blocks the sign for Pneumatikon appears, settling a good portion of my doubts. It adorns an unremarkable single-story building. The sign itself is white with black serif letters. Beneath the words is a logo: a circle divided into six triangles like a game piece from Trivial Pursuit.

Once I'm parked, I instinctively check my reflection in the rearview mirror. My pale blue eyes framed in dark lashes always manage to make me look less tired than I actually am, so my late night of work and then homework doesn't show much. I do have faint circles under my eyes that have persisted this past semester, so I dig in my bag for some concealer and apply it lightly. I put on some clear lip gloss for good measure.

My hair looks decent. This morning I actually gelled my unruly auburn waves and they've sprung into genuine curls. It looks nice. I should really do that more often instead of putting it into a ponytail all the time.

I imagine the person I see in the mirror is the girl of a year and a half ago: long, sleek, copper tresses that took an hour to blow dry; green eye shadow—my calling card; flirtatious pink lip stick; and mascara that turned my already full lashes outrageously long. Add an outfit that was just enough but not too much, a group of friends, and an endless supply of nights to do whatever I wanted. That was my life for over a year.

I shirk away from that image. It doesn't look beautiful or exciting anymore. It now looks overdone. Wasteful. The last time I blow dried my hair was at my Mom's funeral fourteen months ago. I threw out my collection of green eye shadow; I now think mascara looks dumb on me; lipstick is too expensive; and I sold my nightlife clothes to a second-hand store only six months ago to drum up some cash.

I might be struggling, but the girl in the mirror finally looks like an adult to me.

2

*T*he generic furnishings of the waiting room I step into remind me of the cancer clinic my mom used to frequent: floral upholstered loveseats mingled with padded chairs, fake potted plants, grey-toned wallpaper. I hold my breath automatically to avoid the stale, rancid odor of sickness I expect. But I finally inhale and pick up only the manufactured scent of new industrial carpeting and the glue used to apply it—I have a discerning nose.

As I wait for the receptionist to come back to her window, I notice a framed quote to the left that says, '*A body is essentially spiritual. A spirit is essentially temporal.*' Company motto?

"Can I help you?" a voice says in front of me.

I turn to the woman at the window. "Wendy Whitley?" I question stupidly. I'm obviously expected; I have an appointment.

The tubby blond girl offers a bored smile without even a moment of eye contact. She looks at her computer screen. After a few mouse clicks, she slides an empty clipboard closer to herself, attaches a few forms. "Ms. Whitley, if you could fill these out first, someone will be with you shortly."

She holds the clipboard out to me and indicates a bead-filled vase on the counter. It has several pens taped to the stems of plastic flowers. I hate those things. I guess they're supposed to make you feel cheery and welcome, but their giant daisies are too distracting as I write.

Ignoring the flower pens, I plop down on a chair near the corner of the room and dig in my bag for something else to write with.

The first thing my hand touches is the mysterious letter I didn't have time to read this morning. Impatient once more to have my curiosity satisfied, I place the letter on my lap, redoubling my efforts to unearth a pen from the abyss of my bag so I can fill out the forms and get back to the mystery. My irritation mounts as I wade through granola bars for the third time this morning, but I finally find something to write with.

I hope the paperwork will reveal more about Pneumatikon, but it only contains standard questions like contact information and medical history. There *is* one interesting thing though: a consent page that reveals the sum of money to be allotted for participation. It should pay somewhere in the neighborhood of... *$500 each month I'm enrolled*? That's *far* more than I'd hoped for. With this happy outlook, I return the clipboard to the disinterested receptionist and get back to the letter.

It's type-written on a single sheet of paper:

Dear Miss Wendy Whitley,

I understand your mother, Leena Whitley, passed away fairly recently. I want to convey my condolences for your loss. I had the opportunity to know Leena earlier in her life, and she was a generous and honest woman whose friendship I appreciated for too short a time.

You must be confused as to why you are only just now receiving word from me, an uncle who has been estranged to you for most of your life. It was not my idea to be absent, but keeping my distance from your family was a request your mother made years ago, and I made a promise to her then which I never broke. I may have been absent from your life, but I can assure you that you have not been absent from mine. I have wrestled with whether to make contact with you for months now and decided that in light of your newly orphaned state, even your mother would not argue with allowing you to associate with the last remaining member of your more immediate family.

I'd enjoy meeting you and your brother, and I hope you'll allow me to help you out with your responsibilities as your parents would have, were they still alive. It cannot be easy for a young lady to support herself as well as a minor while attending both school and a job full-time. I hope only to make that burden lighter.

Please take the opportunity to call me and arrange a time to get together. I would provide travel means for both you and your brother. I know the urgency of your situation and the obstacles you face. We should meet soon. If I don't hear from you, you can most certainly expect me on your doorstep at some point in the very near future. However, I wanted to give you the courtesy of allowing you to arrange the terms of our meeting at your convenience before imposing on you.

9

I can be reached on my personal cell phone: 408-608-4221 or by e-mail: RobertHaricott@QualSoft.com

My Fondest Regards,

Your Uncle,

Robert Lee Haricott

I blink in disbelief, turning the paper over to examine the blank backside. I don't know what I hope to find there, maybe some indication that this is a joke. I just now realize I'm gritting my teeth; what a presumptuous bastard! About a hundred different scenarios float through my head, some slightly feasible and most completely ridiculous. But all I can manage to feel is afraid that whatever has prompted my uncle to write to me, it cannot be a good thing.

My uncle. It's weird to even think that. He's never been part of my life. I knew he was out there, but my mom never knew or cared where. I don't know much about him, but the story is he had a falling out with my dad, his brother, shortly before he died in a car accident when I was three and a half.

The lack of information I have and my mom's indifference about my uncle would seem odd to me except I don't know much about my dad either. I didn't even know what he looked like until I was a preteen. Mom had to dig through a couple boxes before she found it: the *one* photo she kept of him. And I'm in the picture, too. There isn't much to see of his face—both our backs are to the camera—but the setting of the photo itself tells more about him. Both of us have crayons in our hands and we are drawing on a pristine wall inside the house—something I did a lot of until the age of seven, to my mom's disappointment. At our feet are crayons strewn about. I'm happily scribbling away, oblivious, and Dad's looking slightly behind him to the camera with a guilty smile on his face. My mom told me she caught us like that when she came home one day.

Despite the sweetness of that picture, I always suspected that Mom and Dad's relationship was on the rocks around the time he died. They never married and when I asked her about him, her answers were always straightforward, lacking nostalgia. He was a doctor, but he was terrible with managing his money. Mom was pregnant with Ezra when my dad died, but she never spoke of it as bitter-sweet or even hard. Instead, to me anyway, she always came across as *triumphant* about it. Relieved? I don't know for sure. She never welcomed me touching her during the few times she spoke of him. Knowing that I could sense emotions with touch, she was always aware of what she passed to me, sheltering me I suppose. Like always. Mom never wanted us to worry, but I know my dad's debts ruined her financially for years.

I wonder if what my uncle says is true, and if it is, why did Mom deny him contact? She must have had a good reason, and I bet it had something to do with my dad.

Aside from the shock of hearing from him, I don't know what to make of his cryptic remarks. He has not been absent from my life? He knows the *urgency* of my situation? Does the guy have a tap on my bank account or something? That is so weird. And stalkerish. He's going to show up at my door if I don't consent to meet him? What is *that* about? I don't like this at all.

"Miss Whitley?" says a voice from directly in front of me. I jump slightly, and look up into the face of a tall woman with shoulder-length silvering hair.

"Hi," says the woman. "I called your name from the door, but you looked engrossed so I came over to get your attention."

Remembering where I am, I recover quickly. "Sorry," I say, "I must have totally zoned out." I stand up and shove the letter into my bag.

"No problem," she replies. "Right this way." She beams at me.

I inhale deeply and try to box up all my growing internal questions about the letter for later. But my focus scatters in a hundred different directions and I barely notice the hall we pass through or the décor of the room she leads me into. When we reach our destination however, and she turns to face me, I focus.

My unusual emotional sensitivity has been a crutch in the past so I try not to touch people except when I'm uncertain about a person. This is definitely one of those scenarios so I thrust my hand out to take a read on the woman.

"Dina Gregor," she says, smiling at me as she takes my hand. "You can call me Dina."

"Nice to meet you," I reply, sensing slight falseness in her words, a practiced façade, but before I can get any more, she releases my hand and excitement dissipates which I only recognize as hers once it's gone. I'm left with my own slight apprehension.

"Would you like to have a seat?" she asks, indicating one of two chairs in the small room. It's then that I notice an unusual cushioned table that looks kind of like a massage table. There's also a small desk but that's about it.

I don't like her guarded greeting, but I know from experience that most people have some kind of pretense built-in when they first meet someone. Dina's inauthenticity is in normal range for a first meeting. She passes.

I've had plenty of time in my 19 years to wonder about the origins of my weird empathic skill but I've yet to come to any conclusions. Ezra says it's a supernatural ability that I evolved—but Ezra reads too many comic books. My mom always downplayed it to being just an unusual talent. 'Uniquely perceptive' was the phrase she used to describe it. She pointed out that the possibility of other people possessing such idiosyncratic gifts and never making it public knowledge was pretty likely. After all, I don't broadcast my ability either.

I've adopted my mom's lackadaisical attitude because I don't know any different—I've been reading people this way for as long as I can remember. Mom's explanation sounds reasonable to me. I know that it's unique though, and if I could figure out a way to make money from it I would, but being emotionally in-tune isn't a riveting circus act.

I sit down, ready to give this my best shot. "So, are you a doctor?" I ask. "I didn't see anything on your website."

Dina crosses her legs and clasps her hands over her knees casually like we're about to exchange gossip. She definitely doesn't come across as 'doctorly' even though she's wearing a white coat and dress slacks. "You checked us out. Good," she says. "You're certainly not the first to question my credentials. No, I am not a doctor, but I *am* a naturopath specializing in energy healing. At Pneumatikon we handle all kinds of mild autoimmune diseases—not just food allergies. As for our methods, have you heard of energy medicine like Therapeutic Touch or Reiki?"

Naturopath specializing in energy healing? "Um, energy treatment?" I say, taken aback. "Is that like laying on of hands and stuff? My religion professor was really into that. He showed us a demonstration last semester but I don't really understand it." My religion instructor was kind of a nut. I wonder what a bunch of hand-waving mumbo jumbo has to do with food allergies.

"Yes, laying on of hands is definitely a large part of many methods," Dina explains, "And the theory is the same no matter what method you use. The human body has an energy field running around and through it. Some call it an aura. We call it a life force. Anyway, the body holds or centers this energy field. Conversely, the field can also center the body. When there is something physically wrong with the body, energy healing attempts to utilize the energy field outside of the body to heal what's wrong within it. Does that make sense?" she asks, tilting her head to one side and examining my face.

I nod. Is this energy treatment the actual trial itself? They want to pay me $500 a month to massage my energy? I keep my mouth shut, afraid that my unwillingness to accept this as a treatment will exclude me as a subject. Then I won't get the money I desperately need. I look at her with an expression that I hope conveys interest instead and wait for her to continue.

She knows exactly what I'm thinking though and, with a bit of smugness, says, "Don't worry, energy medicine doesn't rely on the subject's willingness to believe in it. You have a life force around your body whether you believe it or not. It can be manipulated without your conscious consent."

She pauses briefly to let that soak in and then continues, "I hope skepticism won't keep you from participating—that would certainly be our loss as well as yours. The premise behind our research is that the physical manifestation of your food allergy can not only be observed through energy manipulation but can also be healed this same way. We believe that autoimmune disorders like food allergies indicate a larger problem in the life force that requires establishing a balance within it to cure."

I find her reference to me participating in the trial far more interesting than the rest of her explanation. Apparently I'm in. I passed the litmus test, whatever it was.

"So what exactly will this involve?" I ask, relieved and excited that I will see some monetary gain after such agonizing stress. She can do whatever she wants to my life force.

"We use our own brand of energy touch," Dina explains. "But in experience, it's similar to others in that it doesn't require physical contact. A practitioner merely has to have their hands within your life force, which extends several inches from your body. We believe in manipulating energy *only*, and contact of our physical bodies distracts the life force from healing the body. Physical touch is its own kind of therapy and we want to ensure that the life force is what we focus on. You won't need to do anything more than lie down and cooperate in achieving a level of relaxation similar to a light hypnotic state. It keeps your energy pliable."

Dina talks fast and the authoritatively, making me wonder if she gets paid to make energy medicine sound more legitimate or if she really does believe what she's saying.

"I'll then use my own energy field to detect the source of the problem and treat it," she explains further. "There'll be approximately five sessions spaced one week apart. Afterward, we'll run some tests. You have a nut allergy, and allergen tests are fairly noninvasive—a couple skin tests to measure the success of our methods. And that's it!" She smiles widely at me. I guess she's waiting on my answer.

I can't believe that no drugs will be involved. Their website said 'natural methods,' but I never would have guessed at *this* method of treatment. Maybe this is some kind of psychology experiment instead, only they can't let on for fear of skewing the data. I'd like to laugh and say, "No, you're kidding right?" Then maybe I'd follow up with, "Well I'm fine with imaginary treatments as long as the *money* isn't imaginary."

I bite my lip to keep from laughing at my own joke. I must not let this woman know what I suspect. It might disqualify me. How silly to have ever worried about the credentials of Pneumatikon. Even if this *isn't* a head game, there obviously isn't any risk anyway with something that doesn't involve drugs or even contact.

Dina watches me expectantly. I manage to croak out, "Sounds good to me," while trying not to smile too widely.

14

3

*D*ina familiarizes herself with the severity of my tree nut allergy with a catalogue of questions. When she asks about my most recent reaction, remorse over that day is still fresh.

A couple of years ago at a wedding reception for one of my mom's coworkers, I decided I would have carrot cake even though I knew there were walnuts in it. I hadn't had an incident in so long I halfway believed I wasn't susceptible anymore, but mostly I was angry at Mom and wanted to get back at her. I don't even remember what I was so ticked off about. I didn't have an EpiPen with me despite the number of times Mom bugged me to carry one, but I knew she had one. She always did. I did it expecting the risk to be minimal.

Once I swallowed the first bite, I figured I had prevailed, but after a few minutes I felt hot all over and couldn't get enough air in my lungs. I woke up later in the hospital and learned that I had chosen the one time my mom *didn't* have a pen with her to exercise stupidity. I immediately begged forgiveness. Considering that I rarely apologized for *anything,* I assumed it would earn me a pardon.

But instead of clemency, her eyes searched out every inch of my face. It felt like they were spotlighting all my ugly parts. I even caught a flash of my reflection in her eyes for a second, so I saw the blunder of a daughter I'd become, too. She didn't invite me to touch her, but her disappointment found me anyway through her eyes and scorched me like a brand.

She seemed to be telling me something with her expression, but I didn't know the language. All I could think about was melting into the floor.

When she finally spoke, she said just one sentence: "I won't always be here to carry a pen for you."

After Mom died, I started exchanging the words "carry a pen" for any number of things I hadn't had to do before she died. I took it upon myself to finally start carrying a pen. The day I did that was the worst in all of the time I spent mourning her loss.

"I see here that you have Type 1 Diabetes as well?" Dina says, looking over my paperwork. "I don't recall you mentioning that on the phone."

"Uh, is that all right?" I reply, worried. "I mean, will it cause a problem with participating in the trial?" *Stupid! Why did I write that down?*

"Oh no, of course not," Dina says, not looking up. She stares at her notes unseeingly for a moment, pensive. Then, to my surprise, she says, "Actually, I'm excited to deal with your case. We don't get to work with people with multiple autoimmune conditions usually. It should present... a unique challenge." Dina's face is intent and focused as she contemplates it.

"Okay..." I say, having no idea what a 'unique challenge' entails in the realm of energy medicine—if, in fact, that's what this trial is actually about.

"Well!" Dina says, putting the clipboard on her knees with a satisfied slap. "Today we aren't going to do any energy manipulation, but I do want to test your senses. We'll also do a comprehensive personality test and a memory test. We want to get a general idea of your 'before state,' and then we'll do it all again after the treatments are done. It's simply a side note, not really pertinent to the treatment, but we are still experimenting with energy medicine. We still don't fully recognize all of the benefits. I'll have you sign these release forms and we can get started."

A personality test? This has *got* to be some kind of social experiment.

I focus on the forms, reading the fine print because I don't have time to waste on social experiments that don't pay money. I do find a compensation agreement, which quells that concern. But then I read an extensive explanation about patent protections for their research. One particular part stands out: I can't publicly share the origin of any benefits directly achieved from energy touch treatments. That's confusing. They want to legitimize their methods but they don't want the benefits made public?

I ask Dina about this, and she says that they must first have the data to back up and protect their patents before revealing any findings. That sounds reasonable. Despite not knowing if this is 'real' research or not, everything seems to be in order. I can't imagine anything I *should* be worried about.

Dina leads me into a large room with a short wall of filing cabinets next to scales and other medical diagnostic tools on wheels. A treadmill takes up a large corner space. A couple of computers sit next to what looks like a switchboard on a desk under a single window connecting this room to another presumably soundproofed room. A vision test poster hangs from the wall directly in front of me. Standing in the midst of so many technical-looking things, I'm as confused as ever about what this actually *is*. I let it go though; I don't really care as long as I get a check.

"Okay, first we'll take care of the sight test," Dina says, flipping a couple pages on her clipboard. "You'll want to stand at that yellow line just behind you and cover one eye while looking at the poster on the wall. Read to me the first line, please."

Doing as she asks, I recite every line on the poster and then she has me do the same thing while covering my other eye.

Dina looks at me with slight surprise but says, "Back up to the next line, please, and repeat."

She flips the poster to a new set of characters as I step back. I complete the process again. I've never had a vision test before, but I know I have excellent vision, so my ease is no surprise to me.

As I finish reciting the last line in rapid-fire succession, Dina's surprise turns into amazement. She recovers it though and takes the poster off the wall again, revealing yet another set of letters and symbols.

"Back up about five more feet, if you will. We're going to see just how good your eyesight really is. Do you wear contacts?"

"No," I answer as I guesstimate five feet behind me.

I repeat the exercise, and wait for Dina again. Her puzzlement is clear as she writes something hastily on her clipboard.

"Back up to the end of the hall please," Dina instructs, flipping the poster once more.

I must be around 40 feet away now with my back against the wall. I see every line but the last clearly. I squint and focus. Dina notices my trouble and asks, "So you are just starting to have difficulty?"

"Yeah, I think another five feet would probably make the last line impossible to read."

I wonder how impressed she actually is. I watch her face carefully but she doesn't give anything away.

"Has your eyesight always been this good?" she asks, slightly demanding.

I shrug. "I guess I've always been able to see well. Why, is it really good?" Maybe I sound a little naïve, but I've never had bad vision to compare it to, so how should I know what's considered good eyesight?

Dina watches me incredulously for only a moment before saying carefully, "Yes. It's good. Better than I've ever seen demonstrated with the naked eye."

She looks down at her notes while I mull over the new information. Why does she even care? Maybe I should start doing a little less well on these tests. Her interest unnerves me.

"So," she beams at me, returning to the cheery, take-charge attitude I'm used to, "shall we see if your hearing is as good as your eyesight?"

Sitting in the sound room, awaiting her instructions, I make the decision to lie on this test. My hearing, in Ezra's words, is "scary-good." I've never received an official hearing test, but I can hear conversations clearly from over fifty yards away as long as no interim noise, like lawn mowers or screaming crowds, blocks me. I can hear through the insulated walls of a house with no problem. Ezra considers it a pain in the butt. He claims he has no privacy. He's right.

My problem at the moment is that I don't know how to feign "normal" hearing. What's normal? How do I know when to stop hearing at the right time?

This is stupid. What's she going to do? Ship you off for experiments? I've watched too many comic book movies with Ezra. Still, Dina's reactions have me on edge.

"Just raise your hand when you hear the sound," she instructs through my headphones.

I do my best at hearing what I guess to be normal. By playing a song in my head and humming it with closed lips I manage to only respond to the sounds that break through my concentration on the music.

Every time I look through the window, Dina's eyes watch me like she's trying to decipher more than just my raised hand. I grip the headphones and lean forward slightly in order to complete my act. I can't say whether she buys it.

"So you're sure you didn't hear anything that time?" her voice sounds through the headphones.

I shake my head, affixing indifference to my face. She frowns and writes something down.

"You have excellent hearing," she says simply after I come out of the sound room.

"Like how excellent?" I ask. *Is she being evasive now?* I eye the bare skin on her hand, wishing I could find some way to touch her and find out exactly how honest she's being.

"Certainly exceptional," she replies disinterestedly. Yes, she is definitely dodging me. It's like she knows I lied and doesn't want me to know that she knows.

Defiance boils to the surface. I don't like that I now have to hide my apparent exceptional senses from her. I cross my arms, sighing heavily while relishing the fact that Dina has no idea what my other *real* talent is. She likely thinks I'm some kind of freak. Well, she doesn't know the half of it.

She continues taking notes while I stew, and eventually I realize that a large part of my indignation is at myself for being so naively oblivious to my extraordinary senses. *What am I, and how in hades did I end up with hawk-like vision and cat-like hearing?*

Dina finally stops writing and sits me in front of a machine the size and shape of a screen projector. "Hold your nose here," she instructs me, indicating an opening in the device with a mesh concave. "The machine will emit certain smells that you should be able to identify at potent enough levels. The point is to see how low the levels have to be before you can no longer smell them."

I nod in assent. I'm probably going to prove myself a bloodhound now, too. I smell things I know other people can't and eventually have stopped saying, "Do you smell something?" Because I know exactly when a smell is strong enough to be detected by others, I'm an excellent cook. But I'm an incredibly picky eater, too, able to taste the preservatives, additives, and chemicals so commonly found in food.

Dina runs through the smells, and I lie about smelling them just shy of what I think would be considered too acute. Dina doesn't react, but writes things down now without asking me anything or even looking at me. I give up trying to figure out how much she believes me. She can't prove it one way or another.

More troubling and consuming is how oblivious I have been to myself for my whole life…

But does it really matter? Nobody cares that I can sniff out processed lunch meat. And it's not like super-senses could have paid my bills if I'd known about them earlier.

Dina interrupts my internal justification, "Are you ready for your personality test?"

"No. I wasn't given any study materials," I reply drily.

Dina chuckles and, bringing a computer monitor to life next to the smell machine, begins entering my info into the program.

***

A long personality test, memory test, bottle of orange juice, and granola bar later, Dina hands me the fruits of my efforts in the shape of a white unmarked envelope.

"This is your check for today," she explains. "You'll get one after each session. We can do your next session as early as tomorrow, but I'd prefer it if we meet no later than a week from today."

I happily make another appointment. With this unexpected money in my pocket, my stress is about a hundred pounds lighter.

"It was nice to work with you, Wendy. I'll see you next week." She extends her hand with a smile, and I take it.

She definitely has some anticipation. And then... a twinge of envy? I don't have time to absorb her more fully as she quickly lets go of my hand. She turns and exits the waiting room, taking her emotions with her.

Dina's strange mix of feelings confuses me, but the more I try to remember what she felt, the more shrouded the memory becomes. Emotions are difficult to hold onto after they dissipate, so I give up, deciding instead to do a happy dance in the parking lot to celebrate my new-found wealth.

4

"*C*an you believe that all this time I've had superhuman senses and I didn't even realize it? I mean, I guess it's easy to overlook, what with my emotional violation being especially weird, but I don't get how it never occurred to me even once."

I sit on the floor in front of the couch, waiting for Ezra's response as he shovels Oreos into his mouth. Eating dinner together on a Saturday night is a rare occasion, but I also made homemade mac and cheese and salad with a dressing Ezra raved about. Cooking things from scratch is practically unheard of with my work and school schedule, but I've been so upbeat since I got the small check from Pneumatikon that I decided to exhale for a night.

Ezra snorts. "I realize you're a little unobservant, but in your defense, you've only really had the super *duper* senses in the last year or so."

"What do you mean?" I ask, confused.

Ezra gives me a derisive look. "Really?"

When I don't reply, he says, "Wow. Okay, so make that *exceptionally* unobservant. You haven't noticed how much more you can hear now than you used to? All these years I thought I pretty much had your range figured out, but seriously Wen, your hearing ability has increased. Remember that day I was talking with Nate outside, and you heard him tell me to hook him up with you? I was sure that you hadn't heard him, but then I came inside and you were all like '*Eeew Ezra, keep that geeky loser away from me!*'"

I roll my eyes, making a face at his mimicry. "I *know* I didn't say it like that."

"Yeah, that's not the point. We were standing outside and down the stairs, not outside the door." Ezra gives me an expectant look.

"On the second floor landing?"

"Negatory. I mean the *base* of the stairs, the first floor. That's through a door and down two flights of stairs. *And* I was standing beside Nate's car while it was running, and that piece of junk is *not* quiet."

I narrow my eyes. "Are you sure? And I haven't always heard that well? Maybe the window was open."

"No, Wen. I've had it down like a science. I could always be sure that if there were at least three insulated walls between us, or two walls and loud music, you wouldn't overhear me. That day rewrote the rules. Trust me, you hear things now that I never would have thought you could."

"So what about my vision?" I ask.

"I wouldn't know as well, but in the few times I've thought about it, you've seen farther away than ever. Remember that day when you picked me up from the mall and you pointed out that girl coming out of the other department store entrance? It was way over a football field away and you were telling me how cute she was? I couldn't see squat but you just went on and on about every detail of what she was wearing, including the words on her shirt? I've been pretty aware of what you could see, but that blew me away. You have *never* been able to see *that* well. You've always had good vision, good hearing, but not *that* good."

"So a year then? I've only been hearing and seeing this well for a year?"

"I started noticing sometime after Mom got sick. A year and a half maybe? But who knows how long before then it started improving."

"I am so dense," is all I can think of to say. I stand up and head over to start the dishes. Ezra picks up one of his comic books.

The improved eyesight is definitely weird. Having Type 1 Diabetes has had me expecting that my vision would eventually deteriorate, but to think it has gotten better is just... bizarre "Why didn't you say anything?" I ask after a minute.

"You never made a big deal out of it before, and I thought maybe you had always heard that well and were holding out on me. Plus, there were other things going on..."

There certainly *were* other things going on. Like Mom dying. Like gaining guardianship of Ezra.

"Why would it improve?" I ask, intending the question rhetorically but hoping Ezra has some insight anyway. *How have I not noticed?*

"You got me."

I look behind me at Ezra absorbed in his comic book. Sometimes he can make connections so quickly it boggles my mind, but he's pretty selective about engaging his brain. Maybe it's an overabundance of comic books or maybe it's just the curse of being a teenager, but he isn't naturally inquisitive about most things. Even the origin of superhuman abilities, apparently.

I lean over the sink, absentmindedly scrubbing and pondering the possibilities. The problem is I don't know where to start. I go over the last couple years in my head to pinpoint times I should have caught on to changes in my senses. But you just don't notice stuff like that, at least not right off, not without someone pointing it out like Ezra just has.

Furthermore, when I think about the past, all I can remember are a few poignant details along a timeline of blended moments: the smell of Ezra's hair—he'd lay his head on my shoulder while we watched a movie together after getting news from the doctor; the pattern of the pastel, multi-colored, one-inch tiles of the bathroom wall in the old apartment we had when Mom was still alive; the weight of the hospital room door in my hand; the tempo of Mom's labored breathing that was always the same speed whenever I visited; and her face that changed completely as the cancer faded the life from her features... It upsets me still that when I think of her I remember most readily the frail face rather than the healthy one from my childhood. It's like the cancer also infected the memory I have of her.

Since her death, I literally have not stopped at all to think about anything but how to pay my next bill. How can I possibly be upset at myself for not doing a systems check?

I wipe my eyes, dry my hands, and retrieve the *other* white envelope that I've been meaning to talk to Ezra about.

I'm nervous. I've *been* nervous about showing the letter to Ezra since this past Tuesday when I first read it, which is probably why I've put it off this long. "So you are never going to believe who I got a letter from," I say, sitting on the couch next to him, the paper clutched in my hand.

I notice just now that the comic book he's reading is an issue of *Superman-Batman*. I snort. Ezra picked that one out on purpose. When I told him all about the vision and hearing tests Dina gave me, we kind of got off on a superhero tangent. Ezra said I was like Superman, and he's like Batman with all the smarts.

"Batgirl?" he answers from behind the pages.

I snort with laughter. Then I grab his comic book away and punch him in the gut.

"C'mon! I'm serious! Aren't you even a little curious?" I taunt, holding the letter up with two fingers and waving it in the air.

Ezra snatches his comic book back and gives me a bored look, but his eyes shift to the paper in my hand. "Only if some long lost relative left us a big inheritance."

His answer is so close to the truth that I examine the paper in my fingers like maybe I missed the part about the inheritance. "You got half of it right."

"What?" Ezra sits up abruptly and grabs the letter from me before I can react.

I watch his eyes move across the page and then narrow, widen, and finally stop moving as he reaches the end of the letter.

"So what do you think? You want to meet this guy?" I ask.

Ezra scans the page again. "Is there actually a choice? Looks like he's pretty serious."

"Well, we could always move under cover of night into a cash-only motel and change our names," I say, grinning. "Isn't that what superheroes do? Get secret identities?" I pause a moment when a new, more serious possibility comes to me. "You don't have superpowers, do you? I mean, maybe this is genetic or something and you have some kind of ability? Like being super genius," I say, remembering how brilliant he is in math.

Ezra rolls his eyes. "Being a math genius isn't considered a superpower."

I roll my eyes back at him. "You would know, I suppose, since you've done such in-depth research."

"Yeah, yeah. Anyway. Yes, I think we should meet him. Maybe he's not trustworthy, but maybe he's serious. Maybe he just wants to help. Mom didn't say much about him, and I would think that if he was a real danger she would have said so before she died. Like, 'Stay away from your uncle' or something." Ezra stares at the paper. "I'm really curious."

"Yeah," I say as casually as possible, propping my elbow on the back of the worn blue couch. "You probably haven't considered the fact that we're barely scraping by... and I can hardly afford to buy you new clothes. He seems to have some bizarre interest in us already. What if...?" I don't want to say it out loud for fear of making it a more real possibility.

Ezra's eyes flash with quick recognition. Of course. Genius that he is. "You think he wants me to live with him? He wouldn't!"

he says, distressed. "I wouldn't go! He can't make me; I would stay here with you!"

I scoot next to him and deliberately link my arm in his. Ezra's angst jars my chest uncomfortably but it relieves my worry.

Then I say exactly what I decided earlier when this possibility occurred to me, "We don't know what he wants, but it doesn't matter. We're staying together. The guy hasn't been around our whole lives. That's got to count for something, right?"

Ezra becomes a bit more hopeful. He struggles to gain a hold of his worry and think about it.

"Besides," I say soothingly, "If that's actually his goal, and the worst happens, I'm going wherever you are; he won't be able to get rid of me."

He calms finally, and relief that emanates through his skin invigorates me. I exhale as he relaxes. I don't deserve a brother like Ezra. He is so loyal. His immediate change of mood jives exactly with his personality. He gets riled up easily like me but he is more forgiving of people—he can let things go. I hold grudges. And I love to be angry.

Ezra wants to live with me, not someone else. Until now, I hadn't realized how much I worried that he would choose this other, better-off family member over me. That's why I touched his skin; I wanted to be sure of what he wanted.

I should have known. Ezra just isn't me. I probably would have wished for a long lost uncle to take me in at his age. Ezra doesn't complain. Only I do that. I wonder with trepidation what my life would be like if I didn't have Ezra counting on me and believing in me. I would fail. I would fail miserably. I've been so close to failing already. Losing Ezra would launch me into the deep end.

I am going to be royally pissed if this guy tries to take away the one person that matters to me.

"Let's get this over with," I say after a moment, getting up to retrieve my cell phone.

I punch in the number, put it on speaker, and sit next to Ezra again. I can tell he's nervous, but so am I. The phone rings only twice, and then a pleasant male voice answers brightly, "Robert here."

Determined not to sound concerned, I delve in, "Hi, this is Wendy Whitley. I got a letter from you saying you wanted to talk to me?" Straight to the point.

"Yes! Wendy! It's so good to hear from you," Robert says. "I hope I didn't startle you too much when you received my letter. I can understand if it was a bit... odd."

"Oh, no, we're accustomed to getting cryptic letters," I reply.

Robert chuckles. "So then you'll allow me to meet you?"

I want to say no, he's not *allowed,* but that probably won't go over well. "Sure, Ezra and I are open to whatever you have in mind—you know, as far as meeting you, that is," I add, worried he might take 'whatever you have in mind' too literally. "Family is family, right?"

"Absolutely," he says enthusiastically. My eyes narrow. I don't know why, but I don't like this guy. "I understand you're in school, and I don't want to interrupt your studies. I would be glad to come to you if that would work out better for your schedule."

"No, no," I say, looking around my sparse and messy apartment. "We can come to you. Monterey isn't that far of a drive. And this semester is over in a week anyway." The whole thing is actually pretty convenient. I had already requested a week's vacation from work after the Spring semester—I planned it that way to give me some time to recharge before summer classes start. Besides, I am *not* having this man visit me in my apartment, making judgments about my ability to care for Ezra.

"Smart girl," he adds appreciatively. I don't know how to translate the meaning behind that. Hopefully it's because he knows I figured out where he lives based on his phone number and place of business. He continues, "I won't hear of it though. I'll book a flight for you and your brother. Would a week from today be okay then? What day would you need to return?"

"That's fine. And we can fly back on Sunday. Ezra will still have school," I reply, grateful for Robert's offer. He must have money. I don't want to think about what gas would cost me to get all the way up to Monterey and back.

"Wonderful! I'll e-mail you the itinerary when I have it if you will give me your e-mail address," he replies pleasantly.

I relay it to him and we hang up with cordial goodbyes. I look over at Ezra who looks back at me anxiously.

"Well?" he says.

"I don't like him."

Ezra exhales tediously. "Of course you don't. He's too excited. Too nice. Too old. Too rich. Too generous. He probably drives a car you don't like. Wears the wrong color tie. Plus, everyone knows Monterey is full of cocky rich people, right?"

"Hmph. Like *you* would know."

"What *would* you like him to be? Rude?"

"At least if he was rude I'd know where I stand."

"Yes... And all our questions would be answered then?"

I scoot back to the floor and sigh, letting my head fall back on the seat of the couch. "No, I'd probably dislike him then, too."

5

*T*uesday morning arrives, and despite the sudden strangeness of my life, I'm in high spirits as I set off for Pneumatikon for my first installment of energy mumbo jumbo. I'm kind of excited about it. I'm always so consumed with studying, work, and money problems that a little weirdness offers a nice change. Plus, I have exams this week, and from what I've read about energy healing since my last meeting with Dina, it's supposed to be relaxing. That sounds perfect.

I don't sit in the waiting room for long before Dina arrives to lead me back to the same consultation room of my previous visit. She looks friendly and excited, and a shake of her hand reveals her enthusiasm is honest. But I've experienced Dina's mental state three times now and I decide she is definitely hiding something. Instead of being *more* comfortable around me, letting her hair down so to speak, she seems to hold even more in reserve. It's a subtle thing, and if I didn't have years of practice, I'd have a hard time picking up on it. In fact, it feels like she's even working to stifle her own thoughts as if she's worried that whatever she's holding back from me is going to come out accidentally. After all the strange tests, however, I'm more convinced than ever that this song and dance about energy medicine is just the prop for some kind of psychological research. Dina's attitude confirms it.

She asks about my weekend and I mention studying for various exams when she exclaims, "Computer engineering? You must be a very bright girl!"

"Well, I'm not super smart. Just a hard worker. The smart one is really my—" I start but then remember I haven't mentioned having a brother and want to keep it that way. "—mom," I finish. "I mean, *was* my mom. Before she died, that is."

"She passed away? Oh, I'm so sorry," Dina says with pity. She looks at my chart, flipping a couple pages and stopping. "Cancer? That must have been terrible for you. How long ago?" she asks.

"A little over a year," I reply, annoyed at having to discuss my mom's death with a stranger. "So what's the plan for today?" I change the subject.

Dina doesn't miss a beat. "We can get started actually. You'll need to lie down on the table. I have a pillow for you as well," she says, pulling one from a cabinet. "You'll be more comfortable if you use it. The session will take at least a half-hour, but could be as long as an hour if conditions aren't optimal."

I don't know what determines 'optimal' conditions, but she has the same look Mom used when she was giving me a nonverbal warning. What does she think I'm going to do? *Not* relax?

"An attendant will be with us while I work, and the session will also be video-taped for teaching purposes." Dina leans around the door and calls out to someone named Derek.

I adjust myself comfortably face-up on the cushioned table and stare at the unusual shade of blue on the ceiling when a man in probably his early forties—most likely Derek—enters with a small stereo. He wears blue jeans and a white polo shirt. His features are mostly unremarkable, but the easiness of his movements makes me like him immediately. Derek offers me a smile and then plugs in the device.

The lights dim a little and the resonance of a harp dissolves the silence. I'm already sinking heavily into relaxation. Odd, since they haven't started the hypnotism process yet, but I'm too at ease to care. Probably exhaustion from another late night is catching up to me.

"Okay, Wendy," Dina says softly, standing over me with her silver hair pulled back out of her face in a low ponytail. She has nice features, I notice, long and graceful. "You look quite comfortable already, but we're going to go through some relaxation techniques to get your energy really pliable. Keep your eyes open, but I want you to focus on your breathing, concentrating on in and out." Her voice takes on a rhythmic musical note, like she's reading a poem but the words don't rhyme.

Her face disappears from my view, but her voice continues, "In... and out... in... and out. Try to breathe slowly... and evenly. Enjoy the sound... and the feel... and the sensation of air moving in... and out."

Tranquility moves into me with every breath.

"Now I want you to concentrate on the sound of my voice while you watch my pen," her musical voice continues. A pen appears directly in front of me, about fifteen inches from my face, and I train my eyes on it, letting the ceiling and my peripheral vision blur.

"Concentrate your visual efforts on the pen; keep your focus on it as I move it closer, not letting your attention waver. The pen is the only thing you care about right now. Release every other focus. You care only about the pen and the sound of my voice."

The pen moves closer slowly; watching it isn't a challenge. I think maybe I'm going cross-eyed, but before focusing becomes uncomfortable, the pen vanishes. *What a neat trick.*

"Now you can go back to breathing. In... and out... Close your eyes," her voice commands quietly.

I obey. Now that my eyes are closed, I feel an inexplicable security, like all the burdens I usually carry are so trivial that it's funny.

"I want you to focus on your breathing. Feel it. In... and out. I'm going to be silent now and let you enjoy the relaxation."

Cool air rushes into my nostrils and warm air expels the same way, a lovely contrast of cool to warm, cool to warm. I even become preoccupied with the rise and fall of my chest, the fresh air in, the used air out. For a long time I focus on nothing but my own breathing, amazed how each inhale renews some important part of me. It leaves me refreshed with every breath.

Eventually, other sounds start to tickle the background of my awareness. The music, which was once pleasantly soothing, now sounds louder than before. The roar of the freeway interrupts that sound; engines drone from far away. Cars honk, dogs bark, a woman laughs. The louder noises jar the serenity of the moment until I become fully distracted by them and everything else I can hear.

There are quieter sounds: the tapping of a pen, pages turning with a whispering *whoosh*, the hum of electrical devices. Those sounds are much more pleasant, and I contemplate them, noticing even quieter ones, like breathing and heartbeats. Aside from the one I recognize as my own, one heart beats excitedly, the other more slowly and evenly.

Mingling with the sounds comes naturally for a long time until I notice smells: new concrete and carpet, my hair gel and deodorant, perspiration, soap, and the metallic burn of electricity—a familiar smell from work.

With so much to take in, I spend what could be hours or minutes absorbing the miracle of sound and being amazed that it's not overwhelming. I think it's because I have a bit of practice already. The walls of my apartment always allowed conversations, television shows, and music to invade my ears just when I was studying or working on a project. I learned to focus on one and move the others to the background like flipping through a photo album. But I don't have to do that now. I'm able to rifle through the sounds easily and avoid them becoming a cacophonous roar.

A new sensation has been materializing though: a strange vibration against my skin. It tingles, like static electricity when you hold a charged balloon close to your arm hair. The sensation starts at my chest and moves out to my arms and legs. It energizes me, continuing to pulse across my skin in pleasant waves. I have no idea how long this continues. I don't care.

The tingling fades and my mind is subdued, leaving more room for my thoughts. I hadn't realized they had retreated until they begin to ease into my consciousness once more. The first thing I think about is the sound of Dina's heartbeat. At least I assume it's hers, because it sounds the closest. I wonder why it's so erratic. She pulls in deliberate breaths to steady it. Derek's heart beats at a fast pace too, and because I don't understand why, my own heart accelerates.

I smell newly-shed perspiration; I think it's the smell of anxiety or stressful anticipation until I realize I don't just smell it. I *feel* it. Emotions. Excitement washes over me, but experience tells me it's not my own. My own confusion over this begins to pull me out of my relaxed trance and the complex array of feelings, sounds, smells, and sensations burst forth all at once.

What is this?! Stop! It's too loud!

I surface further, and the slight bubbling of foreign anticipation begins to boil more violently, making my efforts to keep the cacophony of sounds at bay agonizing. Painstakingly, I look at each one and then tuck it behind my focus. But it's not as easy as before. The unfamiliar eagerness I feel is too distracting. I want to sit up, to move my twitching legs and release the tension, but I can't move. I can't find the right buttons with so much sensation swirling around and through me.

Dina's voice barrels into the middle of my fight for coherency. "Wendy," she says firmly.

"Yes," I reply immediately; I guess I knew where my voice was after all.

I hope she will keep talking. It gives me something to concentrate on. Excitement nips at me again, and I cry out softly, afraid of it.

Curiosity stills the giddiness, unfamiliar and unfounded. I don't like not knowing who is touching me, so I open my eyes to see.

Something is in front of my face. It retreats farther away, becomes the pen, and I wonder if it has been there all this time. With this recognition, the sensations of earlier slam back into me all at once. With the throbbing of unfamiliar anxiety also demanding my attention, I find it hard, if not impossible, to gain control of my senses. I move my hands to my ears instinctively, trying to remember how I managed to put the sounds in their place before.

Like an album. I visualize it in my brain.

Working hard to breathe through the unfounded emotions, I concentrate on the task of controlling the sounds while my attention is pulled in every direction at once. The noise finally subsides until I hear only the room around me and I exhale with relief. I make a move to sit up.

"Lie still and allow yourself time to adjust," Dina says from across the room.

I turn my head toward her. She's leaning over the desk and writing something down on her clipboard. I remember what just happened. "That's a 'light hypnotic state'?" I say with skeptical sarcasm. It could be. I don't know much about hypnotism, but instinct tells me I was hypnotized as heavily as a person can be and still be conscious.

Dina's face appears a little older, her pores more visible, her wrinkles deeper. Her makeup looks untidily distributed over blatant blemishes. I can see the rise and fall of her pulse at her temple in time with the sound of her heart. Maybe the residual hyper-alert state of hypnosis hasn't worn off yet.

She stands up fully and crosses her arms. She shrugs dismissively while Derek stands at her elbow taking his own notes intently. "The point is to get you relaxed. Some people require a deeper hypnotism than others to do that." She says the words casually, but there's a hint of insult there.

I ignore it. I can't decide whether I'm upset by the deception. I'm too busy marveling at how the entire session felt like a trip into an alternate reality. Except my eyesight. It seems... improved? And my hearing... I test it again, cringing a little when the sounds explode forth with clarity. I shove back at them. Yeah, my hearing is definitely improved.

"Are you all right?" Dina asks.

I don't answer. How long are these enhanced senses going to continue? I turn my eyes to the ceiling. The texture of the panels moves into focus, and I trace the pits and valleys with my eyes. Blue color brushes the pocked surface haphazardly; it looks like bubbles of air escaped during the drying process. The detail surprises me, and I'm less convinced that this is a temporary side-effect.

I look back at Derek, noting the irregular pattern of the blue irises around his pupils. I retract my focus and brush at a piece of dust in my face. Something has happened to my eyes and ears. I never could see this level of detail before. I'm ten feet away from Derek and should not see the dilation of his pupils, the intricate arrangement of the blood vessels on the whites of his eyes, or each individual eyelash with this kind of distinction.

I must have gasped, because Dina moves forward in front of my view and says, "Is everything okay, Wendy? What are you experiencing?"

I'm jittery with a sudden pulse of impatience now that Dina is next to me. I wince away from her.

"Um…" I'm unsure of what to say.

"How are you feeling?" Dina asks as jealousy flares up hotly in the background of my unease.

I look down to my feet. *No one is touching me!* But I'm certain these are not my feelings.

I move my arms to sit up again, and Dina puts her hand on my wrist, maybe to help me, maybe to make me lie back down. I don't have a chance to find out.

6

*D*ina's touch drains me of energy nearly instantly. With it, my limbs weaken and my intellect slows. The swiftness is disorienting and I don't have the presence of mind to question it.

Blindness falls over my eyes, which rouses me from shock for a moment. I blink but see not even a shadow, no particle of light. I reach out, but I can't perceive my hands. Being unable to move, the black abyss surrounding me shrinks into a box.

I look for the walls. But darkness doesn't allow me to see them or anything else. Not knowing where the walls are leads me to the terrifying conclusion that they must be moving toward me, closing in. I can't perceive it with my senses, but I imagine it. And the more I imagine it, the more certain I am that this is reality. And nothing compares to the utter horror of standing in a pitch black room and knowing the walls are collapsing.

Unable to find my mouth, I can't even scream.

With no air passing my lips, I begin to suffocate. I think I might be coughing, but I can't tell. I try again to lash out but I still can't find my body. I'm not even sure I *have* a body anymore. The darkness has erased it and is now trying to erase my mind.

I feel the walls now, and they have sprouted obsidian hands that twist like vines through what's left of my mind. Squeezing. Obliterating every iota of thought.

Except one remains: I am inside a single, unmoving moment of torment.

That moment shifts as I acknowledge it, changing my perception in an instant. An inkling of awareness offers a pinprick of enlightenment: if I can feel agony, I still exist. And if I am existing, then I can fight. And if I can fight, then the darkness has *not* eradicated me as I thought. So I thrash and kick, scrambling for air.

The darkness retreats the tiniest bit and I finally realize what's going on:

This is not *me*. This is… *someone else.*

No sooner have I recognized this than the walls fall away and the terror that once had control of me now feels like liquid as it drains away, leaving me empty. Emptiness is a relief, so I curl up in the indentation. The sensations of awareness start to fill up the concave where I've retreated, buoying me up.

Finally able to perceive something other than my thoughts, I feel my heart beating erratically. I shiver with cold. My vision returns in time to see Dina's hand on my arm, her eyes staring blankly at my face, and her mouth formed in a petrified 'O.'

I struggle to get my mouth to work. "Dee-ah?" I slur. My mouth feels full of cotton. I search her face. Something is wrong. And then I hear it: her silent body. Only two heart patterns sound in this room and neither of them belong to her.

She crumples to the floor.

My eyes follow her as she falls and panic rejuvenates me enough that I find words. "Oh my God! Her heart! Help her! Her heart! Help me!" I shout, frantically searching the room but failing to process anything or anyone I see. I half-leap, half-fall off the table to start CPR. My body moves clumsily though, and I have trouble remembering how to use it.

Closing my eyes to concentrate and fighting for strength, I finally roll her over by digging my shoulder into hers. Putting my hands on her chest, I pump with barely any force. I'm too weak, I realize, to exert my muscles enough for compressions.

I look around for someone and see Derek at the door, shouting the name Lisa. He's telling her to bring paddles. He finally leans down beside me to take Dina's pulse.

"It stopped. Her heart stopped!" I yell at him, aggravated with his need to confirm what I already know. Instead of helping me, he gets up to go to the door again, yelling for Lisa more loudly this time. I continue trying to pump life into Dina's chest. Despite my desperate efforts, I'm becoming less agitated and more resigned. Dina is dead; I feel none of her presence. Even unconscious people think on a rudimentary level; their minds have a vibration I can sense when I touch them. Mom was there with me right until her heart stopped beating. In fact, I felt her leave right through her skin. Only an eerie emptiness remained and it was quickly occupied by my grief.

Finally, I hear footsteps pound the hall toward us. I have stopped pumping, resting one hand on her chest, the other against her wrist, searching for any sign of life, any promise that she can come back. I *need* her to come back.

Derek is nearby again; his shock pumps ice water into my chest. He grabs my wrist to push me out of the way. As soon as he does, I freeze as every reserve of energy I have left is leeched from my body. I fall forward. I think. My vision has gone dark once more. Where are my hands?

"Noooo!" I scream at Nothing, at myself, at Derek, at anyone who will listen.

With the last remaining awareness I have of my body, I gather every bit of will I possess and push it into my muscles, launching myself away. I don't know where I end up, but I keep clambering away until the strangling darkness retreats like smoke in a draft. I finally feel the solidity of the floor under my knees. Light filters into my unseeing eyes.

I see people. I see Dina on the floor several feet away. And I see someone else fallen on top of her. At my back is a wall—a corner actually.

I need to get away from here. But there are too many people and the door is blocked. But at least my mind is alone. I'm trembling and gasping for breath but the discomfort is nothing compared to what I felt when Dina and Derek touched me. That was... like nothing I've ever felt. The strangling terror... it should have taken the life out of me. I gingerly test my thoughts again to make sure my mind is my own. It is.

Shivers travel the length of my body several times as weakness sets decidedly into my muscles. I would like to press into the wall behind me—solid surfaces always help me gain control of myself—but I just don't have the strength. As a result, I start to hyperventilate even though I'm so drained. At least *this* is familiar. Uncomfortable but familiar. I started having fits like this the day Mom told me she had cancer. It happened several times after that whenever there was bad news. I overcame it for a while until the first month my paycheck failed to cover all of my bills. Occasionally anxiety gets the best of me.

I grasp at my knees, tucking my head down to collapse in on myself, giving my lungs less room to gulp at the air so I don't pass out.

With my breathing under control, I lean back just enough to test the wall. Inhale. Exhale. I lift my head a little to rest my chin on my knees and look around again. What I see—what I now process—causes my heart to skip a painful beat. Derek's body lies near Dina's, too still to be conscious. I listen, relieved only slightly to hear the steady beat of his heart. Someone is taking his pulse.

I struggle to think linearly so I can understand what's going on. A woman, maybe Lisa, sits back on her heels beside Dina, defibrillator paddles in her hands, amazed disbelief on her face as she looks from Dina to Derek. I guess I missed the resuscitation attempts. I don't look at her long, but glance back to Derek. There are a couple other people in the room as well, but I don't comprehend them. I watch Derek's body: the slight rise of his chest.

For a second I allow the memory of what I just felt to resurface. My heart races. My mind lurches this way and that nauseatingly. Bile rises in my throat. My eyes water and I turn my head to the side and vomit on the floor. I cough and gag, hoping to purge out the memory. But it's oily and the foul taste clings to the inside of my mouth. Knowing they weren't really *my* emotions doesn't seem to make them any easier to bear.

For several moments I resist thinking, instead listening to the rhythm of respirations that fill the room as they mingle with heartbeats. I hear Derek's as well, and I listen with bated breath as if each beat of his heart will be his last.

Something tickles my cheek, and I reach up to find that I'm crying silently. I'm calm enough to rationalize now, probably because I've pushed every particle of emotion either current or remembered aside out of necessity.

Dina touched me. She felt… awful. And then she died. Derek felt it too, only he fainted, I think. I don't want to accept this, but what other explanation is there? I force my lips to say it, hoping the words will sound false out loud. "They touched me," I whisper, "And I felt…" I look at Derek again. He is still alive. "I felt Dina die," I finish. Actually, that *does* sound wrong. Mom didn't feel that way when she died. She felt calm, completely serene. Dina's death was… calamitous. Reason tells me that *I* did that to Dina, that whatever she felt, *I* made her experience it. And maybe *because* she felt it, she died.

But the walls… they squeezed the life out of me, too. So why am I still breathing?

I shake my head, too addled for impossible questions. All I know is something happened to them when they touched me.

I glare at the people surrounding Dina and Derek. This is *not* my fault. *They* did this to me, those liars who claim to be researching allergies. They must have injected me with something while I was hypnotized. I wouldn't have known any better. Didn't something tingle on my skin? That must have been the drug, whatever it was.

If they knew, why would Dina have touched you?

"I don't know!" I wail. "I don't know!"

This captures the attention of the people in the room, and a broad woman with blond hair and crowded features moves toward me slowly, squatting down to make her eyes level with mine. She's not touching me, but the insistent throb of her wariness makes my overwrought chest hurt.

"What happened?" she asks just barely above a whisper. Her eyes, which are close anyway, crinkle together even more, making her look angry rather than frightened.

I don't know how to answer the question to myself let alone her. I blow out several breaths through pursed lips and try again to figure out what exactly *did* happen, and why. Maybe energy healing counteracted with my bizarre superhuman talents. Maybe if I had told Dina what I could do, she would have known the side-effects and been able to prevent this... this... whatever it is. What am I supposed to say? *Should* I say anything? What if this wasn't them at all? It's more likely this is me and my emotion-sensing touch and weird super-senses gone crazy.

"All *I* know is that you shouldn't touch me," I reply finally with more venom than I intended. Granted, I don't know *whose* fault this is yet, but I know I don't trust these people. I've got a pretty clear before and after picture, and right now blame is leaning its way in their direction.

"Oh believe me," the woman says with wide eyes now, "I have *no* intention of touching you."

My body starts shivering again. I'm so utterly drained, and my head doesn't want to remain upright so I rest it against my knees, slumping into the corner, struggling to get as close to the wall as possible. I want to be on the other side of it so badly. Beyond this space are people who lived the same minutes of time that I just did, who are living *these* minutes right *now*. Only instead of utter terror and crippling uncertainty, theirs have probably been full of laughter or maybe a little stress. I want to see them so I can believe that sane moments will find me again. If I can just move *these* moments along I can get to the other side of this faster. I need to get out of here.

All of a sudden, the implications of what I've done hit me in a new light. Probably they won't *let* me leave. Dina is dead. Derek is unconscious. I just killed one person and maimed another—who knows if he'll survive? There's a word for that: *manslaughter.* And it's punishable by law.

Dread paralyzes me. Where will I go? What will happen to me? What will happen to *Ezra*? Just thinking about how this will affect him sends me into a fit of sobs. I press my eyes into my knees to stop up the tears. All I can think is that I do *not* want to be separated from Ezra. So I make up my mind: this is *their* fault, and everything I say to them from now on will be to that effect. They don't have to know anything about my unusual talents previous to this.

This is not my fault. This is not my fault.

I'm so desperate to prove it that I entertain flashes of the last half hour to search for clues to support my claim. But I can't find any, which keeps my conviction in flux. The fragments of memory do nothing but immobilize my thoughts again until I can only beg earnestly for this to be a nightmare. But I don't wake up.

"What happened?" a male voice asks. The question is not directed at me.

A female voice answers, "Dina grabbed her arm and then she collapsed. So did Derek... What the hell did you *do*?" I can only assume she's talking to me now.

I don't like her tone. I want to open my eyes and accuse her and everyone here of making me a killer. I want to scream at them, but I'm too weak and afraid.

But they couldn't have known.

Whatever they might have expected, surely it was not this. The logic only makes me angry at myself for defending them though. Anger is a relief, however. If I can just stay this way, I won't fall apart.

I look up and ground my eyes into the first person I see: a man with blond hair and brown eyes which seem to exude something softer, maybe compassion. I don't feel him like I did the blond woman. He's too far away, I guess, or maybe my new long-range empathic skills are intermittent. "I don't know what happened," I snap. "They just touched me and collapsed."

I turn my body fully, pressing my forehead into the corner. Talking is cracking my sanity. I want them to leave me alone instead. I don't want to look at them or answer any more questions. I don't want to say anything that might implicate me. I can't make sense of anything long enough to know what to do. I just need time to process what happened.

"Can you tell me anything else?" he asks.

I don't look at him. What does he mean? What else is there to tell? I close my eyes. *Just go away. Just go away.* I can't talk right now. I don't know the right things to say. All I know...

I see Dina's eyes. I ground my palms into my own eyes to force out the image. But the memory conjures itself again anyway: the walls hell-bent on eradicating me moving ever closer...

My breaths are ragged and I gulp at the air as I labor against the memory. I just want to forget. I hold my head in my hands and grind my teeth until it hurts. A close-mouthed scream escapes my throat but it doesn't give me relief. *Please let me forget it.* But the more I resist, the more the darkness constricts. I put my arm in my mouth and bite down, grateful for the physical pain to distract me.

I taste blood. I pull my arm from my teeth and see two red arcs. My vision blurs with tears and I begin hyperventilating again, only this time I can't control it. Sobs have joined the chorus of my gasping inhalations. I sink into despair; the memories of having my soul smothered will never leave me. If I ever get away from here, how will I bear the weight of carrying them around?

Unable to cling to any hope of moving past this moment, I retreat into the only place I can find: sound. I lie down with my cheek to the floor, closing my eyes to draw in the roar of a thousand noises playing a bedlam symphony. No coherent arrangement. Just... a lullaby of chaos. But the volume is too loud to shut my brain down. It's like trying to sleep with ten movies blaring at once. I wish someone would just knock me out.

Then, as if I said it aloud, something pricks my arm, and within minutes sweet unconscious deliverance reaches out for me comfortingly and pulls me into slumber.

***

Sleep is no sanctuary. Horrific dreams torment me. As if omniscient but powerless, I watch and experience Dina and Derek blindly fight walls of nothingness. I see their mouths scream silently. I watch their eyes dart frantically, searching for light. The lack of sight, sound, taste, smell, or feel erases them from the inside out. I watch them dissolve when they finally feel Nothing. And I feel Nothing with them. And even though I scream at them, telling them

40

they're real, they don't hear me. I run for them, but some transparent wall separates us.

And then I watch the same thing happen to Ezra, to my mom, and to other people I've known. As I watch them fight for existence, I sob out screams until my voice and my breath both run out. But they have no way of discerning me. They don't even discern themselves. I cannot endure it. I beg the invisible wall for death.

It doesn't grant my wish so I begin biting at my wrists to drain my life away. But invisible hands restrain me.

Sometimes I think I see faces and lights, only to be pushed back against the crystal-clear glass wall—I'm now pressed up against it, unable to move. I can only turn my head from side to side as people are deposited beyond the glass, only feet from me, slated to battle against themselves.

And then it finally ends, but I'm not aware enough to be relieved. I fall into a dreamless sleep.

7

$\mathcal{M}$y first thought when I wake up is that I need to check my blood sugar—that's my habitual thought *every* time I wake. It's dark. I try to sit up, but I can't move. I look from my right to my left and see restraints on my arms and legs. My breathing accelerates and my heart pounds loudly.

Memories start surfacing: remnants of soul-clenching darkness. I catch my breath, stopping my thoughts where they are, but one fact pushes forward insistently: *I killed Dina.*

I heave in several breaths, trying to absorb that reality, but it doesn't settle. I turn my attention back to my surroundings and hear a heartbeat and even breathing nearby.

Who's here!?

Snapping my head in the direction of the sounds, my eyes nearly bug out of my head at who is lounged on the couch across the room.

"Ezra!" I exclaim.

He shifts groggily for a moment and then bolts up. "Wen?" he says. "You're awake! Thank God. I thought they were lying to me when they said you weren't in a coma." He gets up and switches on a lamp that's on the table next to the couch.

I squint away from the light and look around the space that resembles a large hospital room. "Where am I?" I ask.

"That crack-pot energy place in Pasadena. Pneuma-whatever-it's-called." Ezra moves closer to the bedside and looks me over with sharp worry. I flinch with incredulity that he's not touching me, yet I know the concern belongs to him. It shouldn't surprise me, but I had momentarily forgotten I can read people at a distance. My recent memories are still too terrifyingly fresh to explore—like waking up in the middle of a nightmare with your chest throbbing as you fight to rid your head of heinous images that are too clear.

But the gravity of my situation demands answers. I clench my teeth and reach into the toxic fog for the few concrete moments I can get my hands on: I can feel others' emotions outside of touch now, but my senses have also noticeably improved…

Anxiety bubbles like acid in my stomach. I feel sick.

"Freak, Wen," Ezra says, rubbing a hand through his mop of hair. "You've had me so worried. They said you tried to kill yourself which is why you're strung up like some nut job in an insane asylum. What the hell happened?"

"Has anyone checked my blood sugar?" I ask. As a life-long diabetic, glucose-testing takes precedence over everything; it's like breathing.

"Yeah, yeah. Of course. They tested you like an hour ago."

"How long have I been out?" I ask, struggling to adjust my position. My butt is numb and I desperately want to bend my knees, but with my hands and feet restrained I can't do much more than shift weight from one hip to the other and turn my head.

Ezra looks at the clock, which reads ten-fifteen. I assume P.M. since the sky is dark through the one small window in the room. "Well it's Wednesday. You went crazy and turned into Rogue from the X-men yesterday morning. So over twenty-four hours. You know, I can't decide if you're more like Rogue or Wither. I wonder if you kill plants too..." He notices me wiggling against the restraints then, and his painful indecision twists my insides as he watches, unsure of what to do. "I want to get those off of you but... they said I should call them when you woke up and they'd handle it."

"I'm not interested in killing myself right now, Ezra," I say with indignation. "But I'm going to have bedsores if I stay in this position much longer."

Ezra looks unsure. I'm about to ask him why he won't help me when I remember what he was just saying. He compared me to Rogue from the X-men...

"I can't believe I almost forgot," I breathe. "I can't believe they let you... You *cannot* touch me. Do they know...? I mean did they figure out why—*how* I killed Dina? Is Derek all right?" I cringe at the words that sound so ridiculous. If I weren't restrained and the memories so available, I'd seriously question my sanity. But the horror is as real as anything else right now. And Dina's eyes... those blank, unseeing, empty eyes are ingrained permanently on my psyche.

Ezra's disbelief funnels up from my chest. "Yeah... They told me about what happened. I can't believe... That's just crazy, Wen! Are you sure it was you?" Ezra looks down. "Okay, never mind. Stupid question. But nobody's told me anything useful except that I shouldn't touch you and that you'd wake up eventually."

43

"Wait, wait," I say, getting frustrated with the lack of information. "Can you just start at the beginning? I'm still at Pneumatikon, which makes no sense. I *killed* a person, and they didn't turn me over to the police or something? What's going on?"

Ezra sighs and rubs his face, gathering his thoughts. "I knew you'd gone straight from here to school to work yesterday. I didn't expect to see you last night because I knew you had a late shift, but when I woke up this morning and you still weren't home, I freaked out. I started calling around and found out you hadn't made it to work. So I looked up the number to this place since I knew you'd had an appointment with them. I told them I was your brother and that I hadn't heard from you. They told me you'd had an accident, but you were fine and I should come in. I didn't understand why you were here and not in a hospital, but I was so worried I didn't question it. I just had Nate drive me over. They said they would've called me but they didn't know you had a brother."

Ezra moves to sit on the couch again. I notice the twitching of his worry left me as soon as he retreated, and I estimate the distance: at least several feet.

"They told me you had energy therapy done," Ezra continues, "and that afterward you touched this Dina chick, and she died. Then they said you touched Derek, but he survived after being unconscious for a while. They said you were kind of hysterical in your sleep—that you started biting at yourself? That's when they put the restraints on you. But since *I've* been here, you haven't stirred much. Hopefully that was just a bad dream or something?" Ezra eyes me questioningly.

I don't answer even though Ezra has paused. I don't want to relive any part of my 'bad dreams' right now. I just want any information Ezra can give me.

Nonplussed by my silence, Ezra adds, "The gist I got for why you're here instead of... somewhere else, was that they realize whatever happened to you resulted from their energy hoodoo, and they feel responsible. Plus, they said nobody else would know how to help you. I wasn't in a mood to argue. I was more concerned about you waking up. But Randy seemed like she knew what she was doing—she's an actual doctor apparently. And so here we are. I'm just glad you're awake finally. So do you remember anything? Did you really kill that lady?"

This isn't any more information than *I* have—except the part about them feeling responsible. That's a relief, and it implies that they know more than they've told me. "Yes. I did," I reply quietly. "I don't know how, but..." I look around like someone might be listening in. I don't know if I should say anything out loud. I definitely don't trust Pneumatikon. "We'll talk about it later. Maybe you should call someone in here now?"

Ezra looks at me for a long moment and then nods. He moves for the door, but doesn't open it. Instead, he picks up a phone on the wall next to it and presses a button.

From where I am I hear the ringing, the click, and then the feminine voice that answers, "What do you need, Ezra? Is she awake?"

"Yeah, she just woke up," Ezra replies.

"I'll be there in a minute."

He hangs up and turns to me. "So what do you think happens next?"

I shrug. "I have no clue. Your guess is as good as mine as to why I'm here, but whatever the reason, I'm pretty sure they haven't been honest with me about this supposed drug trial, or energy medicine or anything else. Which *does* make them responsible. But just let me handle it, okay?"

"I can't believe how calm you are," Ezra says. "I've been expecting you to start yelling and demanding answers."

"I'm getting to that," I say. "But my guess is the more hysterical I am, the less likely they are to take these restraints off me." What I've told Ezra is partly true, but mostly I'm calm because I know I killed someone. I don't know how dangerous I am, and having Ezra in the room this close to me stretches my nerves excruciatingly. Just how far away does a person have to be from me to avoid getting knocked out like Derek? Why did they even let Ezra in here? I *desperately* need answers. Dina's empty face won't leave me; it floats like a ghostly apparition through my rattled mind, suspending me over an abyss of uncertainty. I don't want to lose it, and I think the only reason I'm not crying is because I'm on my back and gravity is keeping the tears from overflowing.

"Hey," Ezra says quietly, looking at my stricken face. "It's gonna be okay."

I realize I'm biting my lip. I definitely *look* like I'm going to cry. What is going to happen to me? What if I'm permanently lethal?

What if I shouldn't be anywhere near living, breathing people for their own safety? What will happen to Ezra then? I have so much worry weaving in and out of my cramped stomach that I'm afraid I might start hyperventilating again. This hysterical Wendy has *got* to stop.

I pinch my stinging eyes together for a moment until I hear the door unlatch. A woman of perhaps forty enters, carrying a clipboard and wearing a lab coat. Her honey-colored hair winds in a classy twist at the base of her neck, and fashionably discreet glasses perch on her nose. I smell her perfume: an understated, tasteful musk. Every aspect of her appearance is put together crisply and elegantly. I don't see a single wrinkle in her clothes.

Her eyes scan my body from a distance, and I only just now notice I'm clad in a hospital gown.

They took my clothes off?

That disturbs me until I remember how long I've been unconscious. It was probably necessary, but it's still weird. Although if they removed my clothes, that must mean they weren't afraid to come close to me. That gives me a bit of hope.

After her quick, visual assessment, she looks at my face and says pleasantly, "Hello, Ms. Whitley. How nice to see you awake and yourself." She offers a smile.

I choose to be quiet because I don't know what to say to get the answers I need. Maybe I should have mulled it over before having Ezra call her in here.

"How are you feeling?" she asks.

The question is so ridiculous that I can't help myself. "Are you serious?" I reply. "How am I feeling? I would think that'd be obvious, and if you actually cared about how I feel you would have made sure the first thing you did when you walked in was to take these restraints off me and given me a little dignity. Holy hell, lady, I'm wearing a hospital gown. My hair probably looks like a rat's nest. How do I feel? I feel like a damn animal science experiment!"

I hear laughter from the hall, and I glance at the door briefly, wondering who is out there listening to my tirade. I turn back to the woman—Randy, I assume. She smiles mildly and moves closer to get a better look at me. Apprehension grips me—*her* fear—with a tentative softening of compassion. I get sidelined once again by this phenomenon of sensing people at a distance. From four or five feet maybe? I can't get used to it.

"You're afraid of me," I say. "I get why, but are you afraid I'll hurt you on purpose? I'm not a killer. At least not until *you* people made me one."

A breeze of surprised recognition moves through her as she scans my body. "Ms. Whitley—" she starts.

"Wendy," I correct her.

"Okay then, Wendy," she says, backing up and finding a stool to sit on. "You possess the ability to drain others of their life force when you touch them. You are a danger to others for this reason. You could very well kill me without even intending to. And you were endangering *yourself*—I'm sure you can feel your wrists, so that should be evidence enough."

My mouth falls open. *Drain* others of their life force?

"Wen isn't going to hurt you or anyone else," Ezra says, stepping forward and crossing his arms. "And she's awake and aware, so she's not going to hurt *herself* either."

Randy looks at Ezra and then back at me. "Do you remember what happened?"

"Yes," I say, recovering from my shock over Randy's pitiless explanation. "So Ezra tells me Derek is okay?"

"He is recovered."

"Just how lethal *am* I?" I force the question out because I need to know right here and now what exactly 'drain others of their life force' means.

"Your ability only goes into effect with direct skin-on-skin contact," Randy replies efficiently.

"What did you people do to me?" I demand. How do I stop my skin from… killing people? *Can* I stop it?

Her face changes to indecision. "We'll get to that. I just want to be sure you understand what you're capable of before you're free to act of your own volition."

"I think if *anyone* gets what I'm capable of, that person is me," I snap, enraged by her detachment. "I don't recall *you* being there. So who are *you* to decide whether I'm free to *act of my own volition*? I was right there when Dina was standing over me, and I remember exactly what her face looked like before she collapsed on the floor. I just spent a day having nightmares about it. All I want right now is to understand why and how. So do me a favor and cut to the chase."

Randy nods just slightly. One edge of her mouth turns up a little like she's amused. I'm pretty sure I got my message of sanity across sufficiently. She gets up, walks over to the door, and opens it.

Two men enter and their clothing is the first thing I notice. They're wearing gloves, turtle-necks, and long pants. I'm horrified at the possibility that the head-to-toe clothing is a precaution for being around me. The weather doesn't justify their bundled-up appearance. Just seeing them dressed like that shatters the calm I just found with imaginings of an unknown future awaiting me. My eyes flash in fear.

Randy nods at them, and they approach me while I train my eyes back on her. Their emotions come into range at some point, however, distracting me. Curiosity and an edge of concern bluster through my own tense apprehension. They each take a foot, and I turn to the one on my left as he concentrates on removing the buckle. He has dark brown, almost black hair, light brown eyes, heavy brows, and a tanned complexion. A soul patch adorns his lower lip, but other than that, he's clean-shaven. His features hint at Latin roots but they are still angular enough to have some Caucasian descent. He's exotically dashing and I think he might be the most handsome man I have ever seen.

His eyes sparkle at my focused interest in his face. The corners of his lips are turned slightly upward. He moves to my arm. The nagging of his curiosity tells me he has many questions he'd like to ask. I don't know how I know it's him wondering and not the other guy at my other arm, but I think it's because I'm experiencing the supple interplay of his interest and concentration in context with his actions. His thoughts are so clear, they could be written across his face, which is also expressive and open. I swear if he stood there long enough, I might be able to decipher exactly what his questions are; that's how certain and focused he is.

Removing myself from the wonder of his mind, I glare at him first, and then at Randy. But I can't keep my attention away from him for long. My eyes keep drifting back on their own.

When my hands are finally free, I sit up, testing my arms and legs, grateful for the freedom of movement. I eye the man to my left again suspiciously, and he looks back at me with equal intensity. His brown eyes regard mine without an iota of shyness. His pure, unapologetic eagerness surprises me.

I snort and look away, noting once again that I'm dressed in a hospital gown. I clutch it around me and pull my legs under the sheets. But then I sigh in annoyance. I hate that I suddenly care about my modesty in this most bizarre situation.

The magnetic Latin man's scent reaches my nose then: musky alpine.

I want to look at him again, but I try desperately not to. He can't possibly be that good-looking, and his eyes can't possibly be that engaging...

Ugh, Wendy. You act like he's the first hot guy you've ever seen. Get a grip.

To prove my indifference, I glance over briefly to find him still staring at me with delight and expectant interest. A nearly irresistible grin appears on his face when he sees me look at him. Meanwhile, he backs up a little to maintain a sentry position near the head of the bed.

Yep. Gorgeous. I was wrong.

I fight the need to frantically and girlishly look away and instead try to shoot daggers at him from my eyes. I glom onto his thoughts automatically though. His amusement at my attempt to intimidate him skips to center-stage like a quickstep dance. But sadness breaks up the gliding movement. I wonder why. I *long* to know why. And he wants to speak, but remains silent. I can tell it's really bugging him to keep quiet. In turn, it bugs *me* that he won't talk. He resigns himself to silence then, and I think he's reminding himself to be patient.

I push through the feeling, exploring it, wondering at my discernment of his thoughts. It usually takes me a lot longer to decipher a person's emotional patterns like this. I wonder if it's just him or yet another improvement to my unique talent. Maybe my attraction puts me in-tune.

I search for the other man on the opposite side of the bed whom I've completely forgotten about until now. He's a sullen-looking older guy with hands clasped clinically behind his back. His interest is much more subdued. I haven't noticed his quiet fascination until now because I've been so consumed with the more expressive nature of the other man's.

Randy pulls a stool closer to my bedside. I'm surrounded now, and their various mental states jostle one another in my head until I can't tell which belongs to whom. I twitch restlessly as I struggle to take them in all at once. The confusing haze is new to me since in the past I rarely touched more than one person at a time, and certainly not for so long.

The three of them watch me. I think they're waiting for me to say something, but I'm too busy wrestling *their* feelings to know exactly how *I* feel. I want them to move away, but I can't think long enough to know if telling them that is a good idea.

I don't speak, focusing on Ezra instead, who looks worried. He gets up to move closer, making the atmosphere in my head *really* uncomfortable.

"Can you guys just give me some space?" I say finally, thinking this ought to be seen as a normal request and not a suspect one. My mind is so crowded I have to resist the urge to brace my head in my hands.

Some shuffling takes place around me, and the dense cloud dissipates somewhat. I look up to see that the two men have stepped back several paces. The Latin man stands by the door and the other guy near the corner. But Randy remains in place. Ezra sits at the foot of the bed still, which annoys me because I was talking to him, too. Randy's expression, however, immediately steals my attention from Ezra. She's scrutinizing me coolly. Her eyes take in every nuance of my countenance, and suspicion—*her* suspicion—constricts my muscles, setting me on edge.

"What?" I snap, glaring at her.

She raises one delicately-groomed eyebrow, and then casually but deliberately eases her stool backward. She clicks her pen and writes something down. I can only guess what she finds noteworthy about my behavior.

Randy raises her chin just slightly and I swear she's looking down her nose at me. "So is this far enough?"

Oh damn. She knows?!

I stare back at Randy with equal intensity. "Yes."

Randy clicks her pen annoyingly again and scrawls something else. I look from the clipboard to her face, wondering if I'm right. But how can I be? I must be reading into her words.

"So some type of telepathic ability... You can sense the emotions of those around you. Is that correct?" Randy asks, somewhat smugly.

Ezra jumps up, and I catch his slack-jawed expression. "What?" he asks.

I gape at Randy astonishment. "Just what in the hell is going on?! How could you possibly know that?"

"Hmm," she says, observing my reaction like it's some kind of spectacle for scientific study. "So you must have had some empathic ability beforehand, right?"

More shock. More fury. "*How do you know that?*" I seethe.

"An educated guess," she replies airily. Then she softens her tone just a bit, "And we only want to help you. But *you* are going to have to be honest with us if you want help for your condition."

I blink in disbelief, incredulous. I cannot believe this woman's nerve! *Demanding* that I be truthful when they've obviously been lying to me from the very beginning? I heave in outraged breaths as she watches me with infuriating patience.

"You should probably start explaining things, Randy," Ezra cuts in, looking between Randy and me. "Unless your goal actually *is* to royally piss Wen off... In that case, good job on that so far."

"Maybe *you* ought to sit closer," I growl at Randy.

"Why is that?" she asks, unruffled.

"So I can tell if *you're* lying," I spit at her. I cross my arms over my chest. "You know, since you're so interested in *honesty*."

Randy ignores my request. "I can understand your frustration—"

"Oh look, *another* lie," I interject. "Tell me, Randy, when was the last time *you* killed someone?"

"Ohhh damn," Ezra says. "Randy, can I get you a tissue?"

Curious Eyes chuckles under his breath, and I shoot him a glare. He looks like he's stifling a grin. I guess he finds this about as funny as Ezra apparently does. Ezra gets especially snarky when he's unsure.

Randy, on the other hand, ignores the jibe, but watches me patiently and expectantly as if waiting for me to finish my temper tantrum—which only makes me angrier. I look around for my things. I spot the bag I came with on the couch. I don't actually intend to leave without answers, but I'm so pissed off that I do *not* want Randy to think I'm falling for her bribe of 'help' even though I likely need it. "Where are my clothes?" I demand.

"Randy," Ezra says loudly, his eyes darting from me to Randy again. "For real. Stop being such a robot. You quacks are the ones that did this to her and you act like she *shouldn't* be upset. Wen just wants answers. We *both* want answers."

"Let's start over," Randy concedes when I put my legs over the side of the bed to get up.

I stop and grip the edge of the mattress, waiting.

"My name is Miranda DeLange," she says, crossing her legs elegantly as she perches on her stool, "but everyone calls me Randy. I work for Pneumatikon, which *is* committed to studying energy medicine, but it is not limited to treating auto-immune disorders. We study the interaction of the life force with the body. Louise–she runs this organization—will explain more about that to you later."

Randy pauses but I just stare at her with unmoving expectation.

"As I said earlier," she continues, "you have the ability to absorb the life forces of others. My understanding is that you evolved this ability when you underwent a hypnosis and energy touch session. We refer to our method as hypno-touch, and it was discovered and developed by Louise. We've found that in certain people it can bring out latent abilities. You appear to have developed an ability that is incredibly powerful, one that we could not have foreseen."

Ezra laughs. "So what, you create superheroes by messing with their life force? Is that what you're saying?"

"So, what *did* you foresee then?" I ask, thinking Ezra's question is rhetorical. "And how did you know about my ability to read emotions?"

Randy sighs.

"And *how* in *hell* do you get a death-touch from being hypnotized?" I cry, an edge of fury creeping back into my voice. But her hesitation provokes me so easily. "So is this some kind of experiment gone awry? Tell me what you *really* did. You injected me with something? You've obviously lied to me before. How do I know what you're saying is true?"

"I did tell you," Randy replies calmly. "We hypnotized you. Then we performed energy touch on you. It's non-invasive. You were aware of everything that happened. Hypnosis doesn't allow us to do things against your will. That's movie nonsense. No one touched you, at least not until Dina did. You know exactly what happened. You were aware of everything."

"Come closer when you say that," I order.

Randy obeys, at ease as she rises fluidly and stands near the foot of the bed. "Wendy, we did not imagine this would happen.

What we do… it has never manifested such a strangely powerful ability. We didn't do anything different with you. Dina followed hypno-touch protocol exactly. No one laid a hand on you while you were hypnotized. You would have been aware of it. You would remember it."

She is telling the truth. But this still doesn't make sense.

I place my head in my hands, feeling the weight of what this may mean for my future. And it grows with every passing moment. "So you experimented on me without my consent. You made me believe you were trying to cure my food allergies so that you could get your hands on my *energy*?" I look up. "Why me? What do food allergies have to do with these latent abilities you're talking about? It's ludicrous!"

"I know you're confused," Randy replies with the first signs of empathy in her voice. "Louise will explain all those things to you. My job right now is to make sure that you at least believe that you can be dangerous. The hows and whys will do you no good unless you accept that."

"Yeah, I do. I got it. I'm dangerous. What next?" I reply.

"Okay," Randy says with a kind of relief. "Will, Gabe, I think Wendy has a handle on herself. Could you go let Louise know for me?"

I watch the two sentries move toward the door. The curious-eyed Latin man pauses before he reaches it though, turns around, and walks toward a sink that's on the other side of the room. He reaches into the cabinet below it and pulls out a plastic cup. He fills it with water and walks over to me. "I can only imagine such a long bout of unconsciousness would make a body thirsty," he says, holding it out to me. His voice is rich and articulate, and I can tell he wants to say more. He settles for an apologetic smile as his mental presence seems to reach out to me—a bit of guilty indecision nags at him.

A body? I move my hand slowly to take the cup from him. I actually really *am* thirsty now that he mentions it.

"Thank you," I say, tipping the cup and gulping as I look at him over the top of it.

He stands there for a few more moments and it occurs to me that he's purposely keeping himself in-range so I will pick up his remorse—this is what he wants to say. And while I do process that, mostly I'm enthralled with the nature of his thoughts. They flow forcefully but dynamically as they skip from one thing to the next.

Their persistence relaxes my frustration over Randy. Before the man's attention becomes awkward to the room—and to my disappointment—he turns and follows the other guy out, shutting the door behind them. I can't help looking at the door after he's gone and wishing he would come back.

"You're probably wondering why you're here with us and not elsewhere, under government care and testing," Randy says, interrupting my ill-timed whimsy. "The reason is that we are the only ones in the world that practice hypno-touch; Louise does not publicize our findings. No one understands life force abilities like us."

"But *you* are the ones that did this to me," I say with measured control.

"We do share a portion of responsibility for what happened to you," she replies. "But we are also the only ones that can help you."

I narrow my eyes at her. "How am I supposed to accept help from people I can't trust?"

Randy weighs my words as she looks at me. "Who you trust is *your* business, not ours," she points out. "But surely you can appreciate that someone with your ability should not be unleashed on the public without proper restraints in place."

My mouth falls open in disbelief once again. The woman's sanitized attitude continues to amaze. "*Restraints?*" I ask. "You already gifted me with those, thank you. I'm not interested."

Randy rolls her eyes. "You know I don't mean those kind of restraints."

"*No,*" I say. "I *don't* know that. Considering my situation right now, I don't know *what* to expect."

"What I meant was, don't you want to find out about your ability? Figure out how to control it? What future is there for you if you don't allow us to help you? You would never be able to touch anyone; you might very well kill someone accidentally. If the wrong person finds out what you can do, they will lock you up and dissect you. You can't want that?"

"You never asked me what I wanted. Ever," I reply scathingly. I heave in several angry breaths. I hate that she has a point. I hate that I know she's telling the truth.

Randy doesn't reply.

"What do you want from me? How is it you think you can help anyway?" I ask, determined to *act* calm even if I can't *feel* calm. "You keep saying you're the only ones that can help me, but what does that involve?"

"It's an amazing thing, this ability you have," Randy says more animatedly now that I sound open to her offer. "Don't be discouraged. I am sure there's a way to regulate what you can do and also that there's a purpose to it; we just don't know what it is yet. We—"

"A purpose?" I interject, throwing my hands up. "I kill people when I touch them. How does that have *any* purpose other than murder?"

Randy exhales with deliberate patience. "Life force abilities are never inherently evil, Wendy. Don't limit your expectations just because it *looks* that way. We want to study your ability more. You are not the only person with talents beyond the norm. Gabe and Will, whom you've just met, are both people who have such abilities. Pneumatikon has worked with hundreds of people just like you— well not *just* like you. Your case is unique."

That's what Dina said, too: *unique.* Apparently she discounted how dangerous 'unique' could really be... "How do you study someone's ability?" I ask.

"We run a compound that is a collection of individuals who are alike in that they each have special talents. There we practice methods to help gifted people develop their life force abilities."

Ezra, who has been silent for a while, laughs and says, "What, so like an X-men style gifted school?"

Randy looks at him like she's insulted. "No. We are about research, not spandex and secret identities."

"Bummer," Ezra says. "So no stealth jet under your basketball court then?"

I shoot Ezra a look but can't help giggling a little anyway. My brother is the anchor of reality I need right now.

Randy finally gets that Ezra's not being serious so she turns back to me. "Through hypno-touch we have seen individuals grow their abilities to more efficiently use them. I believe you can do the same. What you can do may first seem wrong and unnatural, but it represents a powerful untapped ability you possess, and there is more to it than we now see. Our mission is to help you discover it." Randy watches my face for a reaction. I can tell she's confident.

I draw my knees up and wrap my arms around them. "So... you're saying you want me to come live at this facility and participate in *hypno-touch* so I can figure out how to control my ability to kill people? Is that right? And you all are cool with me killing your pal, Dina? It's pretty weird that you'd be so excited to 'work with me' if you haven't seen an ability like mine before. I still don't get how. If hypno-touch made me like this, why would I want to continue doing it? I want to get *rid* of it, not *develop* it."

"Wendy." Randy inches a bit closer to my bedside. "It is not bad." She annunciates each word. "You have an extraordinary gift. Nobody blames you, and we are beyond excited to begin working with you despite our sadness over Dina's loss. That was not your fault, and you shouldn't spend unnecessary time thinking about it. I believe strongly that you can figure out how to control what you do. Once you understand the hypno-touch theory, it will make more sense. I'm not asking you to make up your mind right now. I'm only making the offer. Just listen to Louise, then decide."

Randy's matter-of-factness might drive me nuts but it also makes all this sound... reasonable. To think that I don't have to figure this out alone is a relief even if I'm apprehensive about what lies ahead. Randy's nonchalance makes me feel... less freakish.

"Are you going to tell me why you knew about my ability to read emotions?" I ask.

Randy smiles and stands up. "Well first you have to understand that life force abilities are what we do. And second, Dina had an ability that made her like a polygraph. So we knew you were lying about your exceptional senses, for one thing, and also that you were hiding something else. Because you manifested such a powerful ability after only one session indicated that you might have had some talent beforehand anyway. Usually it takes several sessions to see enough progress to notice a life force talent. We are trained to watch for clues of emerging abilities. And your behavior indicated some kind of telepathy, although we doubted it was straightforward telepathy. So yes, it was a guess. And you confirmed it."

"Oh," I reply, feeling sheepish about lying even though I shouldn't. They've lied to *me* plenty.

"Now, I think it's time you met Louise," Randy says.

8

*P*acing the length of the small bathroom, I dry my hands until the paper towel is nearly shredded. Then I sit down on the floor next to the wall for the third time since I came in here. I'm waiting to meet Louise, who should arrive any minute, but that's not what has me so nervous. It's *after* I talk with Louise that I'm not ready to face. Because I will have to leave Pneumatikon finally.

Now that my aggravation with Randy has worn off, a solid lump of debilitating fear has weighted me to this spot. I can't think about being outside of this building without anxiety building in my chest to the point of making it hard to breathe—that kind of thing can send me into hyperventilation. Even the bathroom seems like dangerous, uncharted territory. That's why I keep searching out the wall as a familiar landmark.

I hold up my hands in front of me like they're a new instrument that I have to learn how to use, which is frighteningly close to the truth. Randy has assured me that I'm only lethal with direct skin contact; she said she even used latex gloves when she checked my blood sugar. I can't fathom how she had that kind of daring. That daring, however, makes me believe that Randy's right when she says they have the right skills to be able to help me. They seem to know more about my condition than I do.

As for how I feel about Randy's offer, I'm wavering between anger and desperation. Things still don't line up and I'm unsatisfied with the lack of information. Out there, however, back in my old life, in the world of normal, regular people, there are crowds oblivious to the danger of my flesh moving among them.

My body feels so far out of my control. Sure, I can flex my elbows, turn my head, extend my legs, but to think that my skin *kills* people and I have no control over that whatsoever... I shudder, repulsed by my own body. It has betrayed me, which makes me feel inexplicably bereft for reasons outside of simply being cut off from physical contact with others. My eyes begin to water.

The perpendicular surfaces at my back move into focus as I close my eyes and exhale. Walls will always be vertical and floors will always be horizontal. These are facts that remain no matter how crazy life gets. What *does* change are people, *especially* their emotions. They cycle as long as people remain within the clockwork of life. But they don't change unless you're moving. And that's what I need to do now.

After taking several calming breaths I open my eyes and stand up.

Randy gave me an elastic band for my hair, and I stand in front of the mirror now, piling the disheveled mess on my head and securing it. I'm getting sick of being in a hospital gown, not just for practical reasons, but also because it makes me feel like I've just been checked into a mental hospital. I made Ezra take a bus home a while ago because he has school in the morning and I don't need him to babysit me. He protested of course, but I insisted. I'm starting to rethink that idea though; now that he's gone, I realize that Ezra's presence was the only thing keeping me grounded.

A knock sounds, startling me. I put my hands on the counter in front of me and look at the door. "Yes?"

"Wendy, it's Louise. I've brought some clothes for you," a female voice replies.

I haven't met Louise yet, but I'm already warming toward her. It's like she read my mind—wait, maybe someone here can? I don't know anything about the other people with abilities that Randy mentioned, so probably at least one of them can, right?

I open the door carefully, standing back to avoid the risk of contact. An older woman with straight, silvered hair that must be two feet long smiles serenely at me through the crack in the door.

"Thanks," I say, eying the bundle in Louise's hands but not knowing the best way to take it from her. My stomach bubbles with discomfort at this simple but telling conundrum.

She doesn't miss my expression, and she sets the bag of clothing on the floor and steps back. I can now see that she has latex gloves on. Of *course* any idiot would have considered how to deliver the package to me safely beforehand.

I pick up the bag. "I'll be out in a minute," I say, shutting the door.

The green mock turtleneck and grey yoga pants aren't unusual articles of clothing, but it's mid-May in southern California, I'm going to look silly just like the two men who removed my restraints earlier. I try not to process that this is going to be the norm for me for a while and put them on anyway. At the bottom of the bag are two pairs of gloves. Both are flesh-colored, and one set should come far past my elbow, nearly to the shoulder. I lay both pairs on the sink countertop and examine my hands again. I don't know why I keep looking at them. Randy says my ability probably isn't confined to my hands, but to me, it doesn't really matter. I don't intend to test it out.

Once I'm fully-clad, I open the door to a pleasant smell: maple syrup and pancakes. I take another sniff. Some kind of melon and orange juice as well. It must be way after eleven P.M. by now, but after being unconscious for so long, I'm starving. Louise must have brought it with her. Yet again she proves to have thought things through. It makes it hard for me to stay resentful at her and the organization she represents.

Louise is curled up on the couch, her legs tucked under her and her chin propped up on the couch arm. She's exotic in a beatnik kind of way. A blue linen scarf sweeps her long silvered hair from her face, and a purple ribbon winds into a small braided section. She wears trim jeans, a loose eyelet sweater over a fitted t-shirt, and moccasins. Several strings of beads wreath her neck but she wears no make-up.

"Eat," she says, pointing to a table on wheels that must have been brought in while I was in the bathroom. The food I smell is arranged there.

No fuss. No formalities. I like her.

Not needing any further invitation, I pull the rolling stool Randy used earlier over to the table and dig in. The pancakes are whole wheat, and the syrup is the real stuff, I can tell. I don't know where Louise conjured such a meal at this hour, but it's heavenly and warms the inside of me until I begin to feel somewhat normal again.

After a few hasty mouthfuls, I surface to see Louise looking toward the window with her chin propped on her hand like she's pondering some great life question. Not only is this odd because it's dark outside and I don't think she can see much out there, but the ease she demonstrates here in the middle of the night with me, a girl who can easily kill people, is unexpected. Dina and Randy especially were both more professional, and I assumed Louise would be similar. Instead, she's just weird.

What do you expect from someone who collects people with special abilities and deals with energy, auras, and hypnotism? On second thought, she kind of looks the part.

"I started studying energy healing some thirty years ago," Louise says without introduction and in a sing-song kind of way, but also like she's giving a narrative that she's delivered many times before. Probably she has. "I've always found the idea of a life force fascinating... The animating force of a body—it's a great mystery. It's my passion to understand them. I've always been a spiritual woman so energy healing just made sense when I was introduced to it. I wholeheartedly believed that if we could better understand a life force, we could utilize it more fully. Initially, though, I studied energy medicine as a way to treat sickness. My work in manifesting supernatural abilities came about entirely by accident."

After a brief interval of staring out of the window during which I wonder if I should respond already, Louise continues, "I have spent many years doing what I do. I've tested thousands of energy manipulation methods, but one thing is certain: no matter what school of energy healing theory you ascribe to, the life force surrounding a sick body feels different than the life force surrounding a healthy body. The flow feels... disrupted... disjointed. Sometimes it feels loose or the temperature varies from one area to the next. Energy medicine influences those disruptions. We use our own healthy energy to do it, soaking in the heat from diseased areas or administering cool relief... coaxing the flow... smoothing it."

I balk in confusion. It sounds so harmless... "Is what you did with me different from that?"

Louise laughs lightly. "I know. It sounds too simple to be real. But it's more about the right conditions than it is about methods. That's the secret."

"And what are those conditions?"

"I'm getting there," she says, her voice petitioning patience. "Years ago I decided to take on a client with Multiple Sclerosis to help him manage his symptoms. I normally didn't work with individuals that were as ill as he was but I wanted to better understand the relationship between the life force and disease. His life force had what I now term an 'energy kink,' and I'd never worked with such a defined variance in the flow a field—not surprising considering his illness.

"I spent countless hours with him, trying to manipulate the energy kink. I smoothed it, pulled it, tried different techniques to coax it into the normal flow that I knew it was supposed to be. But nothing worked. The flaw in his energy flow seemed irreversible."

She looks at me. "Have you ever tried to hold a balloon or inflatable under water?"

"Uh, yeah," I reply after taking a sip of juice.

"Well that's what it was like when I tried to smooth this kink. It perpetually resurfaced. But I did notice that when the man fell asleep while I was working, I could more easily discern his life force. The kink was more relaxed and open as he slept. I could better feel it then, but it didn't change the effect I had—or *didn't* have as it were. But I worked at it. I figured that maybe a life force was like a muscle. Physical therapy allows weak muscles to be exercised into working order."

Louise pauses for what I think is dramatic effect. She looks like she's reminiscing. A smile comes to her face. "While we were discussing his case one day," she says, "the man joked that I needed to hypnotize his energy to get it to do what I wanted."

She looks over at me now with a gleam in her eye. She's not close enough for me to pick up her emotions, but her face states clearly how excited she is. It makes her look more youthful I notice. "As you might guess," Louise says, "the idea was intriguing to me. The two pieces connected right then. I knew enough about hypnotism to know that it put the patient in a highly suggestible state. Suggestions given while under hypnotism can endure even after the hypnotism is over. That's why people seek it out as a means to cure addiction. Our life force energy is connected to our minds, and our minds are connected to our life force. You can't do something to one without doing it to the other. This most basic of energy healing beliefs brought about my hypothesis that if our minds were suggestible under hypnotism, then our energy might be too."

Louise's eyes are on fire; her fervor peaks, stealing every bit of my attention, and I anxiously wait for her to continue.

"I tried it out right away," she says. "A hypnotist and I engaged in three sessions with this patient. So you can guess then, how I ended up naming the method 'hypno-touch.' After the very first session, the kink was far less pronounced. After the third session, the kink was gone. In its place was a different flow of energy: free and loose. I was sure I was on the right track."

She pauses momentarily to get a grip on her enthusiasm. She swallows and then continues in a more serene voice, "Even though I was confident I'd accomplished *something*, I never would have guessed that my patient would come back to me a week later and tell me that, after our latest hypno-touch session, he had discovered that he could project hallucinations on others."

I have stopped eating, completely caught up in her story. I never expected her to tell me the whole story of how Pneumatikon came about. She could have just told me she discovered you could give people superpowers through hypnosis and energy medicine. The more she shares, however, the more I want to know. The idea is fascinating. She has a lot of ardor for what she does, and it sets my foreboding to rest for the moment. *Here* is someone who can help me.

"I started looking for more patients," Louise says, looking at the window once more. "The more terminal their ailments, the more likely it was that I could feel their energy variances. I worked with lots of people under hypnotism, and they developed abilities that would have been groundbreaking to modern science. But the problem was that these individuals died from their illnesses anyway. Sadly, the energy healing methods I used would manifest abilities but had no effect on the body's affliction.

"I tried working hypno-touch with healthier individuals, but they had no kink to smooth. There was no ability to manifest. I eventually discovered that autoimmune diseases held the most promise. Severe food allergies were encouraging, as well as a few others like Celiac's disease, presenting enough of a kink to work with but ensuring that my patients would remain alive and healthy for me to study and work with them years into the future."

Louise looks over at me again. Solemnly she says, "The more terminal, the stronger the ability I can manifest in an individual. I've been frustrated time and again with this reality, but I'm still hopeful that we'll discover how to save them from disease as well as give them incredible talents. And your case is extraordinary. You have diabetes, an allergy, *and* natural gifts. Powerful indeed."

"Wait," I say nervously. "So does that mean I'm really sick? Like more sick than just a diabetic with a nut allergy?"

"Oh no, I don't believe so," Louise says dismissively. "For one thing, the energy kink doesn't manifest strongly enough to be manipulated until a disease has progressed enough to be noticed. In other words, you'd *know* you were ill by now. Another reason is that you already have a natural-born ability—two apparently since you had enhanced senses and an empathic talent *before* hypno-touch. You aren't the first person we've worked with to have a life force ability already present, although it *is* rare. The world is full of people with hidden extraordinary talents. Hypno-touch works for naturally gifted people as well because their life force is already somehow freed from the natural inhibitions of the body. Any disconnect between body and life force like this is what allows us to tap into a person's talents through hypno-touch."

She is the third person to talk about the rarity of my situation. It makes me uncomfortable. Obviously having a food allergy would make me of interest to her, but what are the chances that someone has two auto-immune conditions *and* already developed special abilities? The coincidental nature is intriguing and suspect at the same time. They've concealed the truth from me since I began coming to Pneumatikon, and it starts to rub uncomfortably inside my head. I wonder how things would have gone if they *had* told me the truth from the beginning. If they'd been up front about what they were up to, would I have agreed anyway?

Probably. Even though being *uniquely perceptive* is something I've taken in stride, having little regard for its impact on my life, I've still always wondered if there were other people out there like me. I would have liked to meet them. I probably would have jumped at the chance to work with Pneumatikon—especially with compensation. I just never would have guessed at the outcome. I'm sure I have a right to be angry here; I'd even *like* to be so I can have someone to blame. But even if full disclosure had been in place, the outcome would still be the same. And I need help. That much is clear.

"So how rare *are* natural life force abilities?" I ask. "I've never heard of anyone *else* out there who can read emotions when they touch people."

"Well they'd hardly announce it," Louise replies. "But I've worked with a few in the past. Savants are an unacknowledged example of the life force ability phenomenon. Brain-damage stimulates a life force to function more fully and that's why we see such incredible mental skill in them. Where a body lacks, the life force will automatically make up the difference. Think about someone who is blind. It's proven that they will likely develop exceptional hearing to compensate. This is the body's life force at work. But we've discovered a shortcut with hypno-touch. It's really not so fantastical if you think about it."

"I guess not," I reply. "But doesn't that mean that every sick person should automatically discover hidden talents?"

"Well, I would say that everyone, sick or not, has talents that seem to defy science. But they are usually so subtle that they wouldn't be noticed and can hardly be studied and quantified. Most abilities we see are mental and there's simply no way to measure what is and is not supernatural in nature—although I reject the term supernatural. Life force abilities are very much natural. We just bring them to the surface with hypno-touch."

"That's... really interesting," I say genuinely. Louise definitely sounds like she's on to something.

Louise nods. "See, it's not the allergy that's the thing, or even the sickness. It's the disconnect between the body and life force *because* of those things that allows manipulation, manifesting abilities like telepathy or a pain alleviating touch. Given the right conditions, everyone has access to their life force abilities. You've surely heard of individuals claiming to have had spiritual experiences before death. The same disconnect exists in a life force before the death of a body. We just never truly notice life force abilities in the dying because these people are usually suffering and are often unconscious. It takes an attitude of self-discovery to recognize talents like these. Death isn't usually a time that a person experiments that way."

Louise looks at me expectantly. I guess it's my turn to talk. "So what's to study then?" I ask. "You manifest the abilities and then what?"

She smiles. "The energy field powers these gifts. Most individuals undergo daily hypno-touch sessions to progress their ability. We record the improvement. We test different methods of hypno-touch and gauge their effectiveness."

"So how does this help my problem?" I ask.

"Simple," she replies. "The life force abilities we currently see are only the tip of the iceberg. What you and everyone else we work with can now do is only part of what you are capable of. We want you to work with your ability and discover what exactly it is so you can learn to control it. I'll give you an example. We have someone currently who can heat water at will. That was all he could do when his ability was first discovered, but after a while he began to be able to cool it as well. We uncovered an opposite side to his ability. Do you catch my drift?"

"What's the opposite of killing someone when you touch them? Bringing them back to life?" I scoff.

She looks at me with serene patience. "Perhaps. But I think that's probably a bit overgeneralized. If we know you absorb life forces, then maybe you can feed them also. You may be able to do it already and don't realize it. There are many possibilities. We can help you explore them."

I believe Louise knows what she's talking about and I can't handle hopelessness. There *has* to be a way to undo this.

I turn to find Louise staring directly into my eyes for the first time. Hers are emerald green, so striking that I'm surprised I haven't noticed them before. This is the first time I think I really *see* her face. The rest of her has been interesting enough to hold my attention. I like Louise. I like her passion and down-to-earth attitude about my condition. I have nowhere else to turn. To know that Louise is prepared and ready to help me makes things seem a lot less dire.

The worst part of this is how it will affect Ezra. All I've wanted since Mom died is for Ezra to have his needs met and to feel secure. Right now I can't give him any of that. I can't even hug him. I know I need to talk to him before I make a decision though. And I need time to think and have the shock wear off.

"What are you offering, exactly?" I ask.

"To come stay at our compound," she replies. "We'll provide for your needs there, study your energy, teach you about hypno-touch, and help you acclimate to living with your ability. There are a few things I'd like to try that will hopefully allow us and you to better understand how your talent works more precisely. Once we understand that, control should come naturally."

I nod. "I need to think about it. Right now, I just want to go home and sleep in my own bed. I'll let you know in a few days." I get up to grab my bag from the bed.

"Take your time," Louise says, unconcerned. "But do be careful, Wendy. You are still very much lethal. I know you may be hoping that this was just temporary—that it will fade away. Let me be the first to tell you that I have never seen that happen."

I stop where I am and look at Louise with alarm, but she's looking out of the window again.

What is with *her and that window?*

I don't know if she meant to, but her words hit me with a pang of fear. I have finally begun to feel comfortable with going outside, but it strikes me that even this comfort can be dangerous. I ought to remember that I'm lethal. I *have* to remember that or I'm going to accidentally hurt someone. Louise, as comfortable as she seems around me, hasn't forgotten this. And it makes me like her even more. She gets what I'm going through and she knows what I need.

I think the decision to go with her has already been made for me, but I don't like feeling like I'm being forced into this. I need to prove that I can function in the real world first. If I go to Pneumatikon it will be *my* choice. I'm an adult. I have a little brother who needs me. And Ezra is all that matters.

9

If I were old enough to buy alcohol, a shot of liquor would be just perfect right now. My nerves have never been so on edge; I just narrowly escaped being enveloped by a gaggle of twenty-somethings coming away from the parking lot.

I stop for a minute to recover from the near-miss, resting my palms on the warm hood of a small, white SUV, noting that it takes a while for the heat to penetrate my gloves—I'm wearing the shoulder-length ones today even though I also have a long-sleeved shirt on. This is insanity. I can't live like this. Once again, I'm sucked into daydreaming about the compound Louise described, which has now become more like a haven to me rather than the research facility she claims it is.

Once my breathing slows—enough—I continue walking toward the math building where I'm set to take my statistics exam this morning. I try to focus on remembering the content I know I'll find on the test, but instead I'm looking from left to right to spot anyone who seems like they aren't paying attention. Someone might be in a hurry—as students always are on a college campus—and bump into me by accident. Any number of scenarios could result in another count of manslaughter on my record.

I swallow slowly and look skyward for just a moment. I'm being too overcautious. I should relax. I know from experience how rarely people actually make skin contact—in fact they tend to avoid it. And the only exposed part of me is my face. I'm safe. Or rather, *they're* safe.

Just as I reach out to open the door to the math building, a pair of hands grasp my arms from behind.

I jerk away, yanking my arms from the grip of whoever is holding me.

"Ay yi, Wen. It's just me," a familiar feminine voice with a Hispanic lilt says. I take a few steps away from her before turning and collapsing against the wall of the building, heaving while she holds up her hands in surrender, her eyes wide with bewilderment.

"Holy crap, Letty. You scared me," I gasp.

"I'll say," she replies. "Who'd you think it was?"

It's a valid question. Letty is my closest friend, and there aren't any other people on campus who would sneak up on me for a hug. Of course it would be her. She just doesn't realize how close I was to killing her. She doesn't understand why I'm now shaking like a leaf, propped up against the cool brick wall which, thankfully, is facing the shade. My clothing is stifling, and today it's probably at least 85 degrees.

"Why are you dressed like that?" she asks, giving my head-to-toe getup a once-over. "A scarf? Gloves? Is that a fashion statement or something?"

"No," I say once I stop quaking. "Some kind of weird rash."

Letty takes a step back. "Eeew. What from?"

I shrug. "The doctor says it's some kind of allergic reaction. It should clear up in a couple days. But it looks really gross so I didn't want to freak people out."

"Well, that was considerate," Letty says, smiling. "So no more studying this weekend, right? Want to hang out?"

Since she's been talking, Letty has come back into my empathic range, and I can tell she's hopeful I'll say yes. Her request is so genuine that her blatant display of friendship wrenches my heart. "Oh, sorry," I reply. "Ezra and I are going to Monterey this weekend. I actually found out I have an uncle living there."

Letty's full lips move into a pout. "Then next week. We can go to the beach. I am *sooo* pale and it's supposed to be in the nineties. I need my good luck bruja. Te extraño. I miss you."

Beach? Swimsuit? I think it's enough to send me into hyperventilation again if I think about that much skin exposure too long. But I hate disappointing her. *Again.* Letty and I aren't very close anymore. In the last year we've barely seen each other. We sometimes pass each other in the hall at school but that's about it. I haven't had the time to nurture friendships outside of my responsibilities. Every other person I used to hang out with pretty much forgot about me. But Letty, knowing my circumstances, has never held my neglect against me despite the number of times I've turned her down. She continues to ask. She probably won't hold my rejection against me now, but what kind of excuse can I give her for why I'm not going to be able to see her at all next week?

An idea pops in my head. Lightening the mood, I roll my eyes. "Letty, you are Hispanic. How can you possibly be pale? If you're pale, I'm albino. And anyway, I got an internship in San Diego for the summer. So I'm doing that instead of taking classes. I start Monday."

Letty's buoyant hopefulness moves to slight annoyance with my rejection. She sighs. "I don't know how you do it, Wen. But hey, this uncle sounds promising. Maybe you can get some help and stop running yourself ragged all the time. I think you're going to go grey before you're twenty-one. Is Ezra going to stay with him while you're in San Diego?"

I blink at the question. I've been stressing over the situation with Ezra since yesterday when I woke up in my own bed for the first time since being at Pneumatikon. I haven't been able to figure out how I'm going to get help while still taking care of him. Letty's got a decent idea. I mean, if my uncle is serious about helping out... Well, why not? It would be a legitimate excuse for why I'd need a place for Ezra to stay all summer.

"Um, yeah, I'm thinking about it," I reply. "I've gotta meet this guy first."

Letty nods. "Okay, well I better go." She smiles at me with warmth. "It's good to see you, Wen. Take care of yourself, okay? I mean that."

"You too, Letty," I reply, nervous suddenly. The custom for Letty and me would be a goodbye hug, and she moves in. I'm sweating bullets, and I worry Letty can hear my heart trying to beat out of my chest. I briefly consider hugging her while keeping my skin at a distance, but the risk is just too great. I leap to the side at the last minute, surprising her. "Sorry," I say. "I'm just suffocating in this outfit. I think a hug might put my temperature over the edge."

It's a lame excuse, and Letty eyes me with disbelief. But she doesn't push it, thankfully. Instead, we part ways without physical contact.

Once inside the cool building, I collapse in the corner bathroom stall, whimpering as tears escape down my beet-red, overheated face. All I can think is that I almost killed my friend. Twice. Within a 15 minute window.

***

"Are you sure about this?" Ezra asks.

I've just told him about my idea for him to stay with Robert while I go to Louise's compound. But it's hard to answer in the affirmative with Ezra's indecision plunking around in my head. "No," I reply. "And apparently neither are you. But what's the alternative?"

69

Ezra looks out the airplane window, his intellect cycling through possibilities. Probably none of them feasible. I'm facing him at a diagonal, as close as I dare: close enough to sense his emotions and far enough away to not touch him accidentally.

When Robert said he'd fly us up, he didn't mention it would be in his private jet. Obviously the guy is loaded, and I can't be anything but grateful that I didn't have to navigate any airport crowds. I even looked up Qual-Soft yesterday. It's a software development consulting firm. And it's *very* successful.

"What if he won't do it?" Ezra asks finally.

I exhale heavily. "I don't know," I say, trying not to let my voice quaver. "I guess I'm hoping it's just going to work out." That's the truth. I don't have a backup plan if Robert doesn't agree to this.

I consider again taking Ezra with me to the compound. But that idea dissipates quickly. I've already been through this. I'm dangerous. Ezra, no matter how much he knows about my condition, doesn't take it as seriously as I'd like. He has breezed around me in our small apartment just like before, not taking any precautions.

Last night he came out of the bathroom when I was just outside of it and nearly walked into me. I yelled at him for several minutes, and it ended with me saying, "That's it! I'm going, Ezra, or one of these days I'm going to kill you!" And then I cried in the bathroom while Ezra kept apologizing over and over outside of it. I didn't come out until he went to bed. Then I called Louise this morning to make arrangements to meet her in a week—right after Ezra's last day of school. I don't like the idea of Ezra being with Robert without me. But I like him with *me* even less.

"Wen, you're just freaked out because you aren't used to it," Ezra says.

I glare at him. "So you expect me to get *used* to having lethal skin? And then what?"

Ezra's shoulders slump. "I don't know. I just think that if these Pneumatikon people were willing to lie to you from the get-go, they shouldn't have any more information about life force abilities than they already have. It just seems like... going to the enemy for help."

"I don't disagree," I say. "But again, if I don't go to the compound, what am I supposed to do?"

I look out of my own window, impressed at how well I can see the buildings and cars and people below. Everything is so clear and crisp yet at the same time overwhelming. It would be nice if I could have some clarity about the future. Instead, all I get are a bunch of useless details. Only one truth is clear: I am literally terrified of my own self.

Going to school these past few days to take my exams was like traversing a mine field. People are so careless with their bodies. I also went to work on Thursday and Friday at the retail electronics store where I fix computers. I begged my supervisor to let me work on machines in the back, but he made me man the counter among my coworkers instead—probably because I was already in the doghouse from missing two days of work without calling. I left work each day with trembling hands and my nerves in an upheaval. I almost called out, but I need to earn every last penny. Money is weighing on me heavily since I can't expect to keep my job if I go to the Pneumatikon compound. In fact, I called to have my power and internet turned off starting the week I leave. I paid my rent for June with no idea what I'll do if this extends into July.

Life is dissolving into chaos. I need to work and earn a living… I need to look after my brother and finish school… The two exhausted halves of me have bickered over the particulars more times than I can count. The internal argument has always ended with memories of blank eyes that cause my hands to tremble and hellish heaviness to settle achingly into my bones. My dreams have also welcomed shadows of the unseeing, unhearing, unfeeling Nothing. I've hardly slept, waking up in a sweat not only because of the nightmares, but also because I refuse to share a space with Ezra without being clothed from my neck down, gloves included. My apartment has no air conditioning.

"But you don't even *like* Robert," Ezra points out finally. "I thought you were worried he might separate us. And now you're asking him to do exactly that."

I put my face in my hands.

Don't cry. Don't cry. I take several trembling breaths but the guilt is stifling. I just don't have the mental defense I should right now. Things have progressed to a point where I'm on the edge of my own sanity. Exhaustion, both mental and physical, has seeped into every particle of my body. The strangling darkness I keep dreaming about has spilled over into my reality.

"Wen, I didn't mean it that way…" Ezra says gently.

"Then how *did* you mean it?" I say, looking up at him. I take a couple more calming breaths, but Ezra's words are just too hurtful. I struggle to speak without anger. "I'm doing my best here, Ezra. You think I haven't *already* considered everything you're saying? You think I don't *hate* everything I'm being forced to do? I don't want this. But I'm too dangerous to continue things like I have the last few days. I'm going to lose it."

"I know," Ezra says, running a frustrated hand through his hair. "I'm sure you have. But I don't like seeing you so afraid like this. And I'm pissed about what they did to you. It's not fair that they should benefit from it."

"Life's not fair," I sigh. "You and I could come up with a laundry list of reasons why that's true. But it won't help the situation. I can't let the pride of principles get in the way of what needs to be done."

Ezra nods, reassuring himself. "So we're going to tell Robert you have an internship in San Diego and that you want me to stay with him. Is that right?"

"Yes," I reply. I don't like the idea of such a massive lie. But it seems innocuous compared to the truth. Which I'm not sharing with Robert.

"If this is what you think you need."

My heart sinks again. "Ezra," I plead. "If I have my way, it'll be a really short stay. I won't be gone long. This isn't permanent. You know that, don't you?"

Ezra looks at my stricken face with regret. "Wen, this isn't about me. Will you stop mothering me? I'll be fine. I'm only worried about you. The way this whole thing has gone down with them…" Ezra shakes his head. "It just makes me uneasy."

"I need to learn everything I can about this hypno-touch thing," I reply. "Going to the source is actually really smart if you think about it. I'm not an idiot and I'm obviously not helpless. So really, Ezra, I'll be fine."

It's clear that Ezra is telling the truth about not feeling abandoned. That's really all I care about. The rest is just him being overprotective. Once again, he's confused about who exactly needs protection around here.

$\mathcal{R}$obert's mind moves like the turtle who won the race against the hare in that fairy tale. Methodically, he plots a course from one thought to the next. I piggyback the whole trip, fidgeting as I wait for him to arrive wherever it is he's going.

My impatience may be due in part to the improved scope of my ability though—I'm still getting used to foreign feelings bombarding me all the time. I've come to term it 'emodar' because it operates like radar. I can pick up emotions within a range of around five feet. The distance varies a little from one person to the next, but only by a few inches. Robert, for instance, has to be about six inches closer than Ezra for me to pick up on him. Either way, what I got from people before was the blog entry state of mind—the catalog of intimate moments experienced only during touch. What I get now is the novel-length version. And Robert is Moby Dick.

My impression is that he's well-intentioned though. His emotional trek has none of the erratic movement of deception. I wonder at times if he's unintelligent, but he's wealthy enough that I doubt he's a dimwit. I think Robert doesn't have the mental agility to be dangerously deceiving, which is comforting.

One thing does niggle at me. As I nervously shook his hand when we met, my gloves were not lost on him. He gave them a long look. And I mean *long*. Shoulder-length gloves in mid-May *are* a strange sight, but not worth that kind of scrutiny, I think. Moby Dick launched into systematic litigation with himself. It ended five minutes later with a resigned, unanimous jury. It's had me in a fix since then because Robert's painstakingly ordered emotions don't weave enough for me to decipher specifics.

Ezra seems to take to Robert right away, which is both a heartache and a relief. When Robert is done expressing his excitement over meeting us—which frankly isn't *that* exciting even though Robert is genuine about it—awkwardness climaxes in the eat-in kitchen of his massive Monterey home. We're all seated defensively around the space: Robert on a bar stool with a mug of tea to occupy his hands, Ezra sitting behind the table, and me leaning against a wall by the kitchen entryway.

Robert, taking the hint that the ball is in his court, says, "What questions do you have?"

After the week I've had, interrogating Robert is not something that interests me. A strangely absent uncle that suddenly reappears is the least of my problems. And Robert seems like a nice enough guy. A nice guy that I hope will take my brother in for a little while. But the questions need answers so I get to the point. "Why did my mom not want you to have contact with us?"

I would have expected Robert to be ready to answer that right away—it being the most obvious question I'd ask—but a pensive look settles his features as if the query isn't something he's ever considered and he needs time to think about it.

In the middle of Robert's mental exposition, I glance at Ezra, dropping my jaw slightly and jutting my chin in amazement. He shrugs in reply, clearly not as bothered by the hesitation as I am.

"Your father was in trouble around the time he died," Robert says finally. "Most likely financial. Gambling maybe. He asked for money and I gave it to him. But he didn't manage it properly and asked for more. I refused, which resulted in some hard feelings, so we didn't have much contact before his car accident." The words come out of Robert's mouth uncomfortably and I can see the wrinkles of regret at the corners of his mouth.

"Your mother... well I don't think she knew the entirety of what he was up to until it was too late," he continues. "When he died she wanted to start over. Whatever your father's problems were, they didn't die with him. Your mother asked me to have your names changed and your paper trail erased so you could remain under the radar."

I recoil in surprise.

"You're saying Mom was like, *on the run?*" Ezra asks, leaning forward, agape.

I move to one of the other barstools so I can put Robert back in-range. Immediately, my mouth sours with his remorse.

"She was," Robert sighs, turning his mug around in his hands. "And she asked that I stay out of your lives so that whoever was after your father would not be able to track you through me. It was a reasonable request, and even though I offered to take care of her and you, to protect you, she refused. She wanted you to have unburdened lives. She and your father were definitely at-odds when he died. And I think that also influenced her to want to disconnect herself from his family at all costs."

Robert's story poses more questions than it answers. He isn't looking at us, but into his tea. I can feel that this is a touchy memory for him. But he's resigned to the discomfort.

Ezra gets up and moves to the remaining free stool. He brings with him a wave of incredulity. Moby Dick is lost to the sea.

"Do you have any idea who she was trying to get away from?" Ezra asks impatiently. "Are they still out there?"

"I don't know who," Robert says quietly, looking from Ezra to me. "But as to your second question, I believe so. That's my reason for wanting to get in contact with you. Your mom was careful to cover her tracks. That's why she always dealt in cash, never took out a debt, never sought after a reputable career. She didn't want to draw attention to herself. I don't know if she told you, but she was a math prodigy like you, Ezra. She could have held any number of distinguished positions, made good money. But she didn't, to protect you two."

"Mom was a math prodigy?" I ask, propping an arm on the counter. I knew she was smart. She never had problems helping me with homework, but her skills never drew my attention—not that I was *paying* attention. But his story does make sense anyway. Mom *did* do funny things that came across as paranoid.

Robert nods. "Yes. She was brilliant with geometry. She had a kind of instinct for geometric patterns and angles." He smiles. "She was excellent at pool. Beat me every time in one or two turns."

Ezra's swelling astonishment hasn't given me a chance to read Robert. I should have told Ezra to steer clear of my emodar while we're with Robert, but I haven't had enough experience with multiple people in my range at once to have foreseen this problem ahead of time. I need more one-on-one experience with the flavor of Robert's tedious emotional discourse to be able to find it amid Ezra's more glaring pop fiction. So I give up searching for it.

I'd think the news of my mom's hidden talent would bother me more, but I've had so many shocking epiphanies in the last week that this latest one registers only as a minor blip. After all, Ezra had to have gotten his smarts from *somewhere.* However, I *am* trying to connect the dots to explain this supposed secret life of my parents. Mom kept me in the dark about a lot of things.

"Anyway, I just wanted you to be aware of it, now that you're on your own," Robert says, watching our reactions. "I wouldn't have made an issue of it except that I've always had an eye on your family. Someone has been looking for you. Only I don't know who. They are very careful."

"What do you mean?" I ask. "Looking for us how?"

"Well your birth name is Wendy Haricott. Leena changed your last name to Whitley, but someone's been pulling credit records for Wendy Haricott. Since you're nineteen, probably they assume you'll be old enough to start a credit record which would flag your location. Fortunately they don't seem to have caught on to your name change."

Starting to accept that my mom was living a sort of double-life, I ask, "If Mom's last name wasn't Whitley, what was it?"

"Rowan," Robert replies. "And her first name was Sara."

"What the heck would they want from us?" Ezra asks.

"Most likely money. Maybe they suspect your father left the money with your mom when he died and they think they can extract it from you. Or maybe it's information. It could be anything. But it was a big enough deal that Leena felt the need to hide you."

In retrospect, I can see that. We *did* move around a lot, sometimes randomly and without warning. Mom always claimed she got bored sitting still. But that was clearly a lie. *Why* didn't my mom tell me any of this? "But I don't *have* any money," I say, my aggravation with her growing. "So why not *let* them find us and figure out that my bank account hovers above zero all the time?"

"It's too risky. Especially when we don't know *what* they're after or *who* we're dealing with. Leena was smart. She wouldn't have hid you if it were as easy as that. What's more, I *am* wealthy. If they are sure you have something they are entitled to, they know I'd be a way to get it one way or another. As I said, I wouldn't have contacted you if I wasn't worried. Let me do some digging to figure out who it is."

I lean back on my stool, crossing my arms. I have *had* it with this week. I've undergone energy treatments that made me lethal, I've learned my parents had another side to them, I've met a long lost uncle, and I've found out somebody with possibly sinister motives is trying to find me.

I lay it all out so I can figure out my next move. This is proving to be the *worst* time to leave Ezra. But it's either that or spilling everything to my uncle and begging him to let me mooch off of him indefinitely. That is *not* happening. I need a cure for my lethal skin more than anything else right now. And Ezra should be pretty safe with Robert, who, strangely, has been looking out for us. I initially thought that was creepy, but in person, Robert doesn't come across that way.

"Okay, that all sounds fine... and necessary. But I do have a favor to ask," I say, accepting that Robert is a good guy. He's strangely aloof but it doesn't seem deliberate. Instead it comes across as automatic. Moby Dick is just intrinsic to who he is.

"Anything," Robert says. The whale lunges from the water slightly and I can tell he's both surprised and pleased by my warming toward him enough to ask him for something.

"I just found out I got accepted to an internship program in San Diego for the summer," I explain. "So I'm hoping Ezra can stay with you while I'm gone."

Robert's jaw slackens and he blinks a few times before his forehead creases. I can only assume it's a bad sign. Maybe when he said he wanted to help, he only meant to keep us safe. Probably he wasn't expecting to be a babysitter. My heart sinks. "I'm sorry," I say in a rush. "That was too much to ask when we've barely met. I just thought—"

"Oh no, no, no," Robert says. "*I'm* sorry. You just surprised me. I didn't expect you'd feel comfortable with me so quickly. I'm honored by the request. Of course I'd be happy to help. An internship? Wonderful. Your mother would be so proud, Wendy." Moby Dick's pleasure crests right out of the water.

I feel Ezra's eyes boring into my face. I look at him and realize that I'm not smiling. I just got an internship, didn't I? I should be grinning ear-to-ear. So I pull up the corners of my mouth to infuse my expression with as much enthusiasm as I can find. But I can't stand that it's a bold-faced lie, *especially* when Robert is so gratified by it. "Yeah, thanks," I say blandly. "I'm just worried about Ezra. I wasn't going to take it, but then your letter came, and I thought..."

"Perfect timing," Robert says, smiling, unperturbed by my lack of zeal. "Ezra will be in good hands. In fact, I'll give him a summer job at my office. What do you say, Ezra?"

Ezra does *not* have to act. "That'd be great!" he exclaims.

"Well it's set then. Thank you for letting me help you," Robert says. "It's a relief after all these years of having to watch from a distance."

I consider telling him the truth. It would be nice to have an ally and confidant other than Ezra. And Robert seems to be what he claims… But his story is lacking a lot of detail. There has to be more to it. If Robert doesn't trust me enough to tell me then I probably shouldn't trust him enough to bare my own story. Robert might be helping me out for a month or so, but he's still mostly a stranger. I might think he's a nice guy, but there's no telling how he'll react to his niece being able to kill people she touches. Even nice people can do bad things when they are afraid. And people have every right to be afraid of me.

11

"*H*ere's your room," Randy says, holding a door open. Careful to skirt around her at a comfortable distance, I step into a bedroom that seems cavernous because of the vaulted ceiling. There's nothing remarkable about the furnishings: a bed, desk, chair, night stand, dresser, mirror. And my own bathroom.

The compound's residential building is of log construction. I kind of felt like I was on vacation at a ski lodge as soon as we pulled up to it. This was quite a change of attitude for me from when we reached Running Springs—located in the San Bernardino mountains—and was told I'd have to be blindfolded the rest of the way. I didn't expect that, but Randy assured me that it was only a precaution to protect the people participating in their research. She said the compound was in the vicinity of Big Bear Lake, but that's all she could tell me. It was downright suspicious, but that feeling didn't last long. It wasn't *so* odd. What's *really* odd about the whole thing is that I'm going to be among a bunch of people with superpowers. What's more, I actually *do* feel more secure knowing that *my* location isn't broadcasted. So I let it go.

I place my suitcase on the bed and Randy says, "I'll give you some time to get settled, then you'll want to come to the kitchen for lunch."

I nod, and Randy closes the door behind her. I walk around the room, testing the walls with my hands, tracing the bevels on the door. I don't know why, but checking out all the hard surfaces in a new space makes me feel more at home. Ezra jokes that I was meant to be born blind.

I wonder who lives next to me and what they think about living so close to a genuine grim-reaper. People can be pretty superstitious. I know if I had told Letty, for example, what I could do, she'd probably have sent an exorcist over.

I go into the bathroom, running my hand along the counter and seeing a collection of yellow daffodils in full bloom arranged in a vase. I wonder who put them in here. Louise? They're lovely, and I take a sniff, pleased that I can smell them so strongly. They're almost overpowering. Most smells are that way now. If Randy didn't have such good taste in understated perfumes, her cologne would have given me a headache on the way here.

I spend some time unpacking my belongings, which are meager. I had to leave behind all of my tank tops, shorts, and flip-flops. Instead, I had to purchase some new shirts with my last paycheck. I was really picky about what I bought, balancing coverage and breathability. It's nearly June, and I'm grateful this place is in the mountains; it will be a bit cooler here than in the valley. I did bring one tank top though. I'm still fighting that decision because while I had hoped it would be an incentive, it seems more like an item of torture—something I want but can't have.

I hang it up and look at it. It's a really cute shirt; yellow linen with embroidery on the neckline. The rest of the closet consists of mostly long-sleeved shirts. I have stretchy cotton shirts in several colors and the four new blouses I bought, all peasant smocks which I hope will keep me cool enough. I also brought jeans, yoga pants, and tennis shoes. The yellow tank top sticks out like a sore thumb.

And then there are the gloves. I sigh as I unpack the spare ones and place them in my top drawer. I'm nearing a week and a half of having to wear them, and putting them on has become as automatic as underwear already. I just stand there for a full minute and stare at them, amazed that a simple piece of cloth like that manages to keep me from killing people. And also amazed that a simple piece of cloth like that can so fully stifle me at the same time.

When I reach the bottom of the suitcase I find a paper bag folded up. I don't remember packing it. There's something inside. I open it, peer in, and pull out the plastic package. As soon as I see what it is, I burst out laughing.

It's a Superwoman costume.

"Ezra!" I shout to the empty room, knowing this was definitely his doing. To prove it, there's a sticky note on the back:

I looked everywhere for a Rogue costume, or at least some kind of silver hair extension like hers, but I couldn't find one. Superwoman seemed to be the next best thing. Or maybe they give you your own spandex there? Enjoy! Love you.

Ezra

I shake my head, a wide grin plastered to my face. I'm genuinely smiling for the first time in days thanks to Ezra. I miss him already even though I saw him only this morning when I said goodbye to him at the airport—Robert's jet was waiting to take him up to Monterey.

I take the costume out and hang it in my closet next to the yellow tank-top—emblems of my old life which I'm determined to get back. Then I look at my door, nervous already about going out there. We didn't see a soul when we arrived, which was strange, but Randy told me they'd all be at the research building at this time of day. I'm far more comfortable here, however, than I was while on campus at school with so many unwitting people around. Here everyone knows the extent of what I can do. They'll stay well away; I don't have to worry about carelessness so much.

As soon as I open the door, I immediately become distracted by the floor. I noticed it when I came in but didn't have time to stop and appreciate it. It's solid wood—like most things in this building—a rich mahogany with mesmerizing grains and grooves. I stand on the threshold of my door, enthralled with the beauty and amazed at my ability to see things that regular people would never be capable of observing. I guess that it's stained oak, probably nothing particularly special to anyone else, but to me, each swirl and knot is hand-painted by nature exquisitely. I reach down to touch it, halfway expecting it to feel different simply because of how beautiful it is. I notice my gloves again and wrinkle my nose, annoyed at them for keeping me from satisfying my desire to connect with the floor.

"What are you looking at?" a chirpy female voice asks from down the hall.

I snap my head up. A teenage girl stands about ten feet away.

"Uh, nothing," I reply as I stand back up. "You live on this hall?"

"Just next door," she says, folding her arms and raising her eyebrows, cocking her hip into a more permanent stance.

She's a moderately attractive girl. She wears tights and a short jean skirt. Her hair is dark brown, substantial and heavy-looking. I've always coveted thick hair like that. She uncrosses her arms and sweeps the mass forward over her shoulder in what I guess is a nervous habit. Then she places her hands on her hips.

After giving her a once-over, I say, "They're recruiting young aren't they?"

She rolls her eyes. "My dad makes me stay here. So you're the new one everyone's talking about."

She eyes my clothes and hair like she's deciding whether I'm cool or not. Teenage girls are so predictable. I bet if there are any cute boys here, she sees me as some kind of competition. *Stupid.* It doesn't matter if my would-be future husband is here. I can't touch anyone, so what does it matter?

As we size each other up, I'm grateful to have left the pettiness of teen drama behind when my mom died. Still, I don't want to make enemies with the first person I meet, especially someone that doesn't seem too afraid of me.

"Your Dad *made* you come here?" I ask, genuinely curious.

Her face relaxes instantly and she strides over until she's only a couple of feet—and the thickness of my gloves—away from death. She leans against the wall, crosses her arms, and sighs.

Now that she's in my emodar, I falter in surprise; she's strikingly lonely, and disappointed about something. For a moment I worry that she's upset about me, but after a bit more time I realize it's directed at someone else.

"Yeah, I guess it's a little weird when you can move things by thinking about it," she huffs. "He figures I should 'be with my own kind' or something. 'Realizing my potential' or whatever they like to call it here." She says it flippantly, like being abandoned at a compound of supernatural humans is an everyday occurrence. Her dejection reveals that her tone is not genuine though. I'd wager her feelings are so fresh because she's recently communicated with the person she's upset with.

So this must be the telekinetic Randy mentioned on the way. She told me about some of the abilities people have here: telekinesis, especial charisma, temperature and light wave manipulation, exceptional memory, analgesic touch, and Randy's own ability of magnetic field creation. Derek, I learned, has the ability to put people at ease. Not surprising when I recall what it was like when he came in the room before my hypnotism. This girl, supposedly with the talent of moving things with her mind, seems like an ill-suited package for such a big talent.

"Hey, you want me to show you around? I am *sooo* bored!" she says energetically, making a genuine effort to rid herself of melancholy.

I smile at her. "Sure, that'd be great."

She bounds forward with a twinge of relief, leading me down the hall. For a brief moment, and to my alarm, I almost link arms with her in comfort. It's been a long time since I did that to anyone. Because of my talent, I was always a hands-on person. But I stifled that tendency after my mom died. For Ezra's sake.

Mom was the last person I spent a lot of time touching. She was committed to being conscious for Ezra and me when we would come to visit her. She refused the heavy medication even though I knew she must need it. When I realized what she was doing for us, I touched her every chance I got. I couldn't feel her physical pain, but I knew its effect on her mind: stressful, nagging desperation to escape. Touching her was a penance I sought.

I sigh. The girl's voice has fully faded into the background as I think about my mom. She sacrificed so much for Ezra and me for so long and I never appreciated any of it until she got *really* sick.

I had spent so much time being addicted to the emotions of others to numb myself. I knew I needed to escape that cycle. I turned to masochism instead, hoping it would help me quit the habit. I went to the children's ward under the guise of volunteering to do a story time. I thought if I could only have the memories of their suffering and the needless injustice of it, I could stop looking at my own hardship as unbearable. I *knew* that the unfairness of my life was nothing compared to theirs, but I just needed to experience it personally. I needed it ground into my brain.

But they schooled me in a completely unexpected way: they were happy. They didn't waste time on asking why. They lived for newness, for excitement. They thrived on *moments*. I would come in with a book, a puppet, a little game, and *that* moment became the most *important* moment to them. No matter what life brought, they were game. In a word, they were fickle. But that fickleness is what made them brave. It was a strength, and I needed to learn it.

That's why I insisted I could take care of Ezra. I needed to fill my moments so I wouldn't have time to dwell on doubt over whether I could do it. Without questioning when my long-standing guilt and heartache would go away. I had to treat my emotions like moments instead of realities.

So I put my nose to the grindstone and maniacally focused on providing for him. And somehow I have made it a year and a half without once being tempted to seek out emotional highs. In fact, I hadn't even acknowledged my sobriety until this moment. It puts a smile on my face to realize how well I've done. What's more, it's profoundly ironic that emotions are now being shoved in my face whether I like it or not. Yet I haven't once sought them out or been tempted to dwell on them...

My smile grows.

"—and she lives three doors down from you, but I wouldn't bother with her. She has a—" The girl stops talking abruptly, noticing my expression. "Something funny?" she asks.

I shake my head. "This whole situation is just ridiculous. Still trying to wrap my head around it." I furrow my brow thoughtfully, feeling that my words apply beyond simply the strangeness of being at the compound. I can't quite articulate it...

"What's your name anyway?" I ask with a renewed determination to make being here work in my favor.

"Oh right. Kaylen," she replies as she pulls open a set of double doors.

"I'm Wendy."

She smiles. "Nice to meet you, Wendy." She waves her hand at the space before us. "This is the kitchen."

The room is empty, and I'm relieved that I don't have to face any crowds. Kaylen, however, is close to me, and getting nearer by the moment. This girl is definitely not afraid of me, even a little. "So... do you know anything about my... condition?" I ask apprehensively.

"Yeah, Randy told us you can't touch people. They pass out or something." She looks like she's trying to recall the information. "Oh, and you can read emotions."

"Yeah, well it's more like they die or something," I correct her, cringing at my own words and wondering if Randy really did water down what I do. That would be frightening. "So, just be careful, okay? You seem pretty comfortable around me. I don't want to accidentally bump into you. If some part of my skin touches you... it wouldn't go well for either of us. Just keep that in mind."

Based on my encounter with Derek, it probably takes more than a light brush to drain someone of their life force. But I'm not taking any chances.

"Are you threatening me?" Kaylen asks. Her playfulness flits through me and I know she's joking.

I roll my eyes. "Funny."

She sniggers. "I think I can manage to keep my hands off you." She pulls herself up to sit on the long, stainless-steel counter that separates the kitchen from the dining area.

"Whatever," I reply, exasperated. If she chooses not to take me seriously, that's her right. I walk over to the counter as well and admire the shiny length of it, leaning against it and propping my elbows on it, my chin in my hand.

"Sorry," she laughs. "I'm sure that totally sucks. I shouldn't be so insensitive. Just trying to lighten the mood from talking about morbid stuff."

"It's okay," I say. "Probably a little humor will go a long way toward maintaining my grip on reality. Hey, maybe when your dad finds out there's a person with a death-touch here he'll think it's too dangerous for you to stay, and he'll let you come home." I try to joke, but I actually mean it seriously.

"Not likely," she says. "He'd just find somewhere else to send me." Her voice conveys flippancy, but she's quite close to me; smarting anger is behind her words.

I don't know how to handle being able to read people whether they like it or not. Something about people allowing me to touch them before always seemed to convey permission—a level of intimacy which would make the violation okay. But in this case, only distance can stop the emodar. Am I obligated to remind people of this?

"I'm really sorry for whatever is going on between you and your dad," I say, deciding to demonstrate my ability to make the point. "It's really awful that he's stranded you here. So I guess you just spoke to him?"

Kaylen is speechless for a moment, her jaw hanging open just slightly. "Wow, they weren't kidding about your abilities were they? You sure it's not telepathy?"

"I can't read your exact thoughts. But emotions follow them whether you're aware of it or not. It's really just an informed guess on my part. But I have years of practice." Kind of.

"That's awesome. Way better than what I can do. Wanna see?" she asks even though I pick up reluctance on her part.

"Well don't feel obligated," I reply, pushing away from the counter. "Is that standard practice around here? 'Hello, my name is Wendy, and I kill people when I touch them.' *Oh, cool, I'm Kaylen and I move things with my mind. Awesome, right?*"

Kaylen giggles. "Yeah, it kind of is like that."

I shrug. "Well I don't know the protocol, so you're free to rudely withhold a demonstration of your ability from me. I won't know any different." I smile at her.

More at ease, Kaylen concentrates on the stove across from her, focusing intently. Then, as if on a heavy but directed gust of wind, the towel that was hanging on the stove flutters to life. It blows over to my shoulder where I catch it.

"Nice," I say, definitely impressed. *Ezra would love this.* I can't wait to tell him about my friend Kaylen, the telekinetic.

My friend.

I've made my first friend. Even though there's no plausible reason, it lightens my mood. For the first time since I woke up at Pneumatikon a week ago, I'm being *normal.* Making friends. Having a conversation. I would not have thought it were possible in my current state. But I should know better. Life goes on. It *always* goes on, whether you're ready or not.

12

"That's about all I can do," Kaylen says when I ask her how much she can move telepathically. She grabs a bottle of water from a drink cooler and then looks at me. "Do you want one?" she asks.

"No thanks," I reply, noticing Kaylen's more inflexible expression and uncomfortable movements as I walk over to what I think is a walk-in fridge. I don't need her in-range to tell that she *really* doesn't like talking about her ability. I'm a little miffed by her attitude only because I wish my own ability was as harmless as hers. But then again, she's got some awful father that abandoned her here, so she has a right to be upset about it.

I run my hand over the stainless surface of the door of the fridge, even pulling it open to check out the inside of the well-stocked refrigerated space.

Kaylen begins pointing out different parts of the kitchen, including a counter and set of cabinets at the far end of the room, intended, she says, for separate food prep when they have people with gluten issues. "But we don't have anyone here with wheat allergies right now," she says.

"None *now*? How long do people stay here? They get different people all the time?"

Kaylen nods. "Sometimes they're here for a month. Sometimes a year. It varies. New people come in about every month."

"And how long have *you* been here?" I ask, thinking the only way she would know how often people rotate is if she's been here for a while.

"Way too long," she replies, not offering anything more.

She then explains the cooking schedule which is taken on, surprisingly, by the residents. They use a pre-determined menu, but supplementation is allowed as long as it follows the allergy guidelines which are printed up on a poster on one wall. Examining it, I note that I'm not the only one allergic to tree nuts, nor am I the only diabetic. The poster indicates there are 18 people staying here.

I spot the names 'Gabe' and 'Will' and my heart skips a beat, unbidden. Randy didn't say they were staying here currently and it hadn't even crossed my mind until now. In fact, I'd all but forgotten the attractive Latin man who helped remove my restraints and gave me a glass of water. I still don't know what his name is. The poster says Will has an allergy to peanuts and Gabe doesn't have anything listed at all… What does that mean?

I hate my automatic fascination with the man. I don't need girlish crushes right now. What is wrong with me? I sigh and turn away from the poster.

The kitchen is industrial and brightly lit contrasting the rest of the common areas I've seen thus far that are more homey. Two long tables fill this room cafeteria-style, probably enough seating for thirty or so.

"You wanna see the rest of this place or what?" Kaylen says, standing at the door.

I hang up the towel and follow her out. She shows me through the large but efficiently constructed lodge which includes a recreation room and a separate men's wing.

Finally, Kaylen leads me to the huge wooden door in the foyer. She pushes it open and the sun hits me. I blink against its brightness. I shade my eyes with a hand and my body relaxes as I drink in the fragrant peacefulness of nature. Every blade of grass, every leaf, every tree, and every flower begs for closer examination of its intricacy. It's not as if this is the first time I've been outside today—or even in the last week—but any kind of natural beauty I find especially distracting. I can't get enough of *seeing*.

Randy brought me in another entrance on the opposite side of the building that was shaded and hardly noteworthy as far as landscaping. But this entrance spills into a huge flower garden, and the sun casts brilliant rays across the field of color, spotlighting the amazing detail of each flower: gentle curved petals, some ruffled, some smooth; delicate filaments with furry stamens; the weaving vascular systems of each leaf. I'm impressed with the individual life embodied by each singular plant. Each is noticeably different in a way that makes them more alive to my perception and it fills me with wonder.

Just then a breeze picks up some of the dust from the concrete walkway and I watch a million particles swirl up and travel through the air as the sun glitters off their surfaces. The very air is sparkling. I gasp at the sight that's dazzling and mysterious, yet it must have been happening invisibly since the dawn of time.

Kaylen watches my reverie with confusion.

"Sorry," I say sheepishly when I notice her. "This is just really beautiful, and with my eyesight, being outside is like having ADD or something. Everything demands my attention."

"Your eyesight?" Kaylen asks.

"Uh, yeah," I say. "I have really good eyesight. *Really* good."

"Hmm, Randy didn't tell us that part," Kaylen says as she leads me down the steps and toward a path that cuts through the woods. Trees surround the residential building on all sides; we are definitely in the middle of a mountain forest.

The natural wonder everywhere preoccupies my attention enough that I don't notice the people walking toward us until their footsteps reach my ears. I look up to see a woman with short, spikey blond hair, possibly in her thirties, walking next to a lanky man with glasses and sharply angled features. Too far away from them for a greeting, I take in their reactions from a distance. The woman hesitates, but the man raises his eyebrows enthusiastically.

"Kaylen!" the man exclaims when we reach them. "Randy's going to broil you for skipping out again." He glances at me before looking back at Kaylen.

She gives him a mock-defensive look. "Well I *do* have a good excuse. Wendy needed someone to show her around."

"Hi, I'm Wendy," I say, looking from the man to the woman, actively restraining my instinct to hold out my hand. It makes my greeting feel incomplete.

My words do the trick anyway. The woman offers a tentative smile. "Corinne," she says. "It looks like you found the right person for a tour."

I glance at Kaylen and say, "Yeah. She's totally fine with associating with someone who can suck out her life force."

Wow, Wendy. Wow. I nearly shake my head at myself. Sometimes I could swear I *want* people to hate me.

Corinne raises her eyebrows. "I see that. But you'll probably find more acceptance than you expect."

"I hope you're right," I reply, although based on my greeting, I have to question the honesty of that statement.

"I'm Jimmy," says the lanky man beside her with a big grin. They haven't closed the distance enough for me to pick up on what they might make of me, but Jimmy's interest communicates clearly through his tone and expression. "Glad to have you here," he says cordially. He steps forward into my emodar and holds out his hand.

I look at it and then his face, unsure what I should do or say. I can't believe all I'm getting from him is interest. He's an analytical thinker, I can tell. And he doesn't seem to excite easily. I think about saying *"Boo!"* to see if I can get a reaction, but decide against it. Maybe next time. I don't care how comfortable he is with shaking my hand. I've got gloves on of course, but I am *not* comfortable.

When Jimmy sees me eye his hand with incredulity, he catches on. "Oh! Sorry!" he says, pulling it back. "I just thought with your gloves on... Well, never mind."

I wonder if everyone here is like Kaylen, misinformed that I just 'knock people out' with my touch. Did Louise or Randy not communicate that I killed someone?

I also wonder what Jimmy's ability is. Blind enthusiasm? Death-touch resistance? Reckless abandon?

"It's okay. It's good to meet you." I say, managing a smile. I've been really worried about how to act around people here, thinking my dangerous ability would scare them off. I'd decided that if I was extra nice and friendly, they wouldn't be so on edge about being around me. Either my method is working, or these people are sadly ignorant of my true capability. Or maybe they are just as dangerous as I am, and *I* am the ignorant one.

"Well, I'm sure we'll see you at lunch," says Corinne. "We're headed over to get it ready. See you later."

"Don't worry. People are used to weirdness around here," Kaylen says, noticing my expression as they walk away.

While Kaylen leads me down a wide dirt path shaded by heavy tree cover, she tells me about life here, about the rules of communication, about the extreme precautions they take for anyone leaving or coming onto the compound.

I got that impression from Randy already, but mostly in the form of going back over the patent protection forms I signed—not to mention the odd blindfolding episode. The way Kaylen puts it however, my impression of the place changes from 'summer camp for special people' to 'top-secret energy voodoo ashram.' It's a nice facility though, and considering what they're harboring here, I can see why they protect it.

Kaylen shows me the stables where I admit to her that I have always wanted to ride a horse and she promises to take me out. I especially like the inside of the barn; the worn edges of the space make it inviting. It also appears old—much older than the residential building. With my eyesight it's easy to see how filthy everything is, but that adds to the appeal. The building could have sprouted right out of the dirt.

Kaylen is definitely more comfortable here, too. It's the first place we've been where she is completely relaxed. It's obviously her favorite place. She introduces me to Morgan, her horse, who smells like sun baked earth, tangy grass, and sweat. I ask Kaylen how long the barn has been here and she tells me Louise bought the property six years ago with the old barn as part of it. Kaylen has always been into horses though, and she insisted on having her own horse on the compound. And Louise liked the idea of keeping a few more, so now there are four total.

"So, how old are you anyway?" I ask after Kaylen points down another path which leads to tennis and basketball courts. We have one last destination: the research building.

"Sixteen," she answers. "Just turned, actually."

"My brother Ezra's fifteen," I say.

"I wish I had a brother—or a sister. But it's just me and Dad. And Morgan, of course," she replies.

I want to ask her about her mom, but I don't. It sounds like she doesn't have one which means it's probably a story for another time after we know each other better.

After lots of uphill and downhill grades on a path that weaves gently through the woods, we finally reach the research building. It's a large, square, cement structure shrouded by tree cover. The architecture isn't impressive; it's simple and economical. Upon seeing its science lab-looking mundaneness, this Pneumatikon compound seems more legitimate and less like I've been inducted into a superhero cult.

I say as much to Kaylen who laughs and says, "You're pretty much it as far as useful superhero talents go."

"Well, I don't think so," I reply, "Every superhero team needs someone to manage the hand towels."

Kaylen giggles. "Oh yeah. I get hand towel duty on every mission."

We enter through an unobtrusive door on the side of the building. It's just as boring inside as it was on the outside: tiles, white walls, industrial doors, and absolutely no décor.

"So this is where the action happens," says Kaylen in a bored voice. Boredom is hardly her true sentiment, however. Her resentment flares up and makes me clench my own fists in response. I feel what people feel, and while I can usually differentiate it as not my own, if strong emotions hit me without warning—as has happened a few times since my transformation—I automatically react without meaning to. Kaylen's pain-ridden bitterness toward this place is definitely not what I expected.

"The lower floor is for running tests, doing research, classes, meetings... pretty much everything but the actual hypno-touch sessions," she instructs. "Those happen upstairs. It's way nicer up there. Mornings are usually when they do that. Afternoons, most people are down here, or outside, or at the lodge."

I hear voices coming from upstairs, and I take a moment to listen, amazed at how clearly I can understand them.

"We'll work on it some more..." a male voice says.

"—thought I could try with a lower wattage," says a bubbly female voice.

"I feel the variance right here..." Louise says. I concentrate on her voice. "I can't seem to get a hold of it, but I'm going to pull it some more and see if we can get a response." She falls silent then, so I move on to the other voices, probably in other rooms.

"—really can't imagine what it must have been like to wake up from that," says a smooth and refined male voice. "But she sure was full of fiery indignation. So *together* despite how events transpired." I know that voice. It belongs to the hunk of Hispanic hotness I met: Gabe or Will.

A woman's voice answers him, "She must have been in shock. Still must be. How do you cope with not being able to touch people without killing them? Too bad there's no psych here anymore. She could probably use one."

A gruff man's voice, different from the first, chimes in, "Her ability is incredible. I just can't believe a life force ability would manifest that way... so *powerful* after only the first session. It has me a little worried. We still don't understand the energy-body relationship fully, and there's no telling how her life force has been affected after absorbing someone else's energy like that. I'd be afraid to touch it. I can't believe Louise is going to do it."

"That's true," says the woman's voice thoughtfully. "Energy can't be destroyed. It has to go somewhere, transferred or transformed. I wonder which it is."

"She seems wholly ignorant of any facts to explain it," the first man's voice says. "Gloves are effective in preventing the transfer of energy. That's odd given that abilities are supposedly life force manifested and the field extends out from the body several inches. One would think that you shouldn't be able to get within a foot of her without getting hamstrung. That indicates that it's stemming directly from the body rather than the field, like it's biologically driven... I'm fascinated."

"Gabe, when have you ever *not* been fascinated?" the woman chuckles.

Kaylen's voice sounds behind me, "You coming?" I raise one hand to indicate I need a moment.

"—tested to see if it extended from her body?" says the woman.

"Louise of course," says the gruff voice. "That woman's got chutzpah. She's the one that figured it was energy absorption."

"What are you doing?" Kaylen demands.

"—going to speak with Randy if we're done here," says the first male voice—I now know it belongs to Gabe, the Latin Adonis.

"Where to next?" I say, withdrawing my attention from the conversations above.

Kaylen crosses her arms and raises her eyebrows. "You have super-hearing, too, don't you?"

I nod.

Kaylen's eyes flutter in surprise. "Seriously? Oh, man. You sure are talented, aren't you? Louise must be beside herself." She shakes her head in wonder.

I don't reply and she says, "Well, that's all there is to see. Lunch will be starting soon, so we might want to get back." She turns on her heel, and my body relaxes when we reach the door—*her* reaction at finally leaving.

"You don't like it here, I get it," I remark. "But you act like they subject you to medieval torture. What gives?"

"If you'd been here for as long as I have, you'd feel the same way," she says. I can tell she's not inviting discussion so I let it go.

On our walk back to the dormitory I ask Kaylen who has the most powerful abilities here, if there's anyone as dangerous as me, anyone I should be careful of.

Kaylen laughs. "No way. I told you, you're it, Wendy. I can probably poke you in the eye with a pencil if I wanted to, but I could

93

probably do it better with my hand. Corrine's ability is to make you want to impress her, and I guess that could be dangerous if you were really naïve and impressionable, but for the most part, everyone's talents are pretty weak. Will can only heat a glass of water a couple of degrees. Randy can't make anything more than a few keys magnetize to her hand, and Chloe can diminish your pain—that's the exact opposite of hazardous. There's Marcus' fire manipulation, but all he does is make a flame grow a couple centimeters. Jimmy can memorize every detail from a picture. Big whoop."

I put my hands on my hips and cock my head to the side in confusion. "So let me get this straight. The people here came because they went through some kind of energy healing hypnotism thing and now they have special talents. But none of them can actually *do* anything that would change humanity like take down a terrorist cell or blow up an enemy tank? I'm sorry, but what's the point? And why do they care about keeping something like that so secret?"

Kaylen stops and sits down on a log that lines the path while I face her. "Well Louise would give you some spiel about bettering humanity and all, but I think it's totally pointless. We hardly get anywhere with improving people's abilities. I'm going to be dead and in the ground before I can move anything really big. And the secrecy?" Kaylen shrugs. "I think Louise thinks she's on to something big and doesn't want anyone moving in on her *big find*."

I snort. "So what, she thinks she's got some kind of patent on human potential?"

I intend it rhetorically, but Kaylen sighs heavily. "I don't know, but my dad sure believes all her hype. My guess is she thinks she can sell what she does... I bet she thinks people will eventually pay her to unlock their abilities. Just think how she could market it if she figures out how to manifest that stuff in healthy people. They'd pay even if it was something as insignificant as what everyone *here* does. We had this one guy about a year ago who actually spilled a little bit to someone about how he came to have his abilities after he left. Louise sued him into oblivion from what I heard. She is *dead* set on keeping this place and what she does here hidden."

Kaylen is obviously a smart girl. Behind her youthful exterior lies a thoughtful human being. I've underestimated her.

"I hadn't thought about that," I say. We start walking again and I ask, "So does everyone eat at the same time?"

"More or less."

"Great," I reply. "I guess this is the part where I learn how to *cope* with my ability." I roll my eyes. "This is going to give me such a good excuse to avoid people."

Kaylen giggles. "Lucky you."

I've noticed quite a few flowers on the paths Kaylen and I have been walking on. Since they aren't wild, I'm sure someone plants them.

"Do the residents do any of the grounds work?" I ask, thinking how truly huge such a task would be. The trails alone, which connect the buildings, are pretty long. At a bare minimum each one requires routine brush control to keep the forest from taking over.

"No. But the flowers are mine. The place felt like a military camp before. So I convinced Louise that flowers would make it more inviting. It would help put people in a better frame of mind for more effective energy manipulation. She agreed to foot the bill if I would plant the flowers."

"I bet she did," I reply. *The better to hypnotize you with, my dears.*

"I get people to help me every now and then with the mulching and stuff, and I took a few bulbs and planted them on the paths to the barn and courts to grow wild. I obviously can't take care of *that* many flowers without help. So bulbs seemed like the best solution."

"Wow," I say in astonishment. This girl is more surprising by the moment. "I'll help you if you need it. What are you going to do with those?" I ask, indicating the huge bunch she's been accumulating in her hands.

"Put them around the lodge. I just threw the old ones out this morning. I think people really like them, and I have so many that cutting some every few days won't be too noticeable. Plus, it's the end of bulb season. Gotta enjoy them while I can!" Kaylen exhales serenity as she talks about her flowers.

"So was that you who put flowers in my room?"

Kaylen smiles. "Yeah. Kind of a welcome gesture I guess. I'd hate to have gone through what you did... This place is weird enough without having that kind of experience."

I have to control my incredulity. Every time she opens her mouth, she changes my impression of her. She's utterly likeable in every way.

"Sorry, Kaylen," I say after a moment.

"For what?" she asks.

"That you're stuck here," I reply. "And for thinking you were an ignorant teenager."

She looks at me and smiles. "It's okay. I *am* a teenager. Everyone is allowed a first impression." We reach the front doors of the lodge again and she says, "Are you ready for lunch?"

"Are you kidding? I ingested an entire energy field. I'm set for at least a month," I reply.

Kaylen stares at me open-mouthed.

"Kidding," I say, laughing at her expression.

"I know. I just can't believe you're... okay talking like that about it already."

I look down, fighting the sadness threatening my composure. I think about making an emotional deposit with Kaylen about this most completely *not* okay subject. Since I like her, and since I'll probably spend more time with her in the future, she should know so that there aren't more awkward moments like this in need of explanation.

"If I don't joke about it, I'll cry," I reply softly. And then I exhale heavily now that it's out there.

Kaylen senses that I'm only explaining my words, not looking for a shoulder to cry on. She grabs the handle, holds the door open for me, and we walk inside.

13

After going to my room to check my glucose before lunch, I return to the kitchen to find it full already. Spotting me, Kaylen immediately takes charge of introductions. She handles the task like a natural, grabbing people by the arm and pulling them over to me. She tells me some interesting tidbit about them, like how Marianne can beat *anyone* at Rummy or how Gina, who is Italian, actually *hates* pasta. Everyone goes along with it as if acclimating new recruits is Kaylen's official job. Maybe it is.

The group is nothing like the band of superheroes I imagined. They are all ages and personality types just like anyone else you'd meet on the street. And they all have regular, everyday careers from which they've taken leave to come here. Kaylen wasn't kidding that sharing your supernatural ability is standard protocol, so I learn that information along with names and faces. Gina is a short, exuberant lady who manipulates light by dimming and brightening a light bulb just by thinking about it. Jimmy's gift is an exceptional photographic memory. Celine is jealous. That's her emotion, not her ability. I don't connect her jealousy to a source right away, but she offers a brief greeting and goes to sit at the far end of the room. It's then that I realize she's jealous of *me*. I don't bother trying to understand that one.

To my pleasant surprise, no one skirts a conspicuous perimeter around me and no one seems afraid to be in the same space as me. I guess I managed such an easy transition because every one of these people agreed to live on an anonymously located compound and participate in daily hypnotism and energy therapy to develop superpowers. I nearly laugh when I think of that. I guess if *anyone* will accept me, this group of misfits ought to.

As Kaylen chats with anyone in earshot, I'm starting to understand that she is the darling here. Her interest in making me feel welcome now seems like an offshoot of her personality. She clearly has rapport with everyone—except Louise, I notice. Kaylen unapologetically ignores Louise.

With my plate finally in hand, I make a beeline for a chair at the end of one of the tables so I won't have to feel jilted if nobody sits by me, or afraid if somebody *does*. But Kaylen doesn't hesitate

to plop down next to me. Jimmy grabs a chair across from me...
Well at least I'm not *completely* surrounded.

"What does it feel like to absorb a life force?" Jimmy asks
after I take the first bite of my sandwich.

I stop chewing, shocked that he feels at liberty to ask me
something so morbid *and* personal. If my mouth wasn't full, I'm
positive I'd be telling him it's none of his damn business. The
memory of exactly what it *does* feel like is still, after an entire week
and a half, frighteningly fresh. Next to me, Kaylen is taken aback as
well, and I can tell she's trying to work out some response on my
behalf but coming up blank.

I draw out chewing and swallowing so I can think of a better
reply. I don't want to give the impression of a girl whose temper too
easily vomits from her mouth.

I realize the room is quiet and it occurs to me that Jimmy
might as well have yelled the question considering how loudly he
spoke it. Now everyone is hanging on the edge of *my* silence. Jimmy
isn't alone in his macabre curiosity, which doesn't surprise me, but
he ought to have more common sense. He doesn't strike me as
stupid, so apparently he really is that much of an ass.

"Like dying," I reply coolly. And then I give him a quizzical
look. "Or were you asking for a demonstration?"

My words translate differently on each person's face. Some
get that I'm shutting the inquiry down. Others wonder if they are
missing intended humor. Jimmy doesn't even acknowledge the jibe,
instead trying to actually *imagine* what dying might feel like. I know
this for a fact since he's in my emodar. *What a freak.*

As I look around surreptitiously to take note of peoples'
expressions, I notice, sitting at the other end of my table near a
vacant-eyed and disinterested Louise, is Mr. Hispanic Hotness
himself: Gabe. *When did* ***he*** *get here?* I didn't notice him when I
came in earlier—and I am *sure* I would have.

He wears a knowing smile as he watches me intently. It's like
he heard the 'none of your damn business' when it first crossed my
mind rather than what actually came out of my mouth. Even though
he's probably fifteen feet away, his presence emanates outward like
he's right next to me and examining the contents of my head.

I glance away to keep any more of my thoughts from spilling
out. I wonder if he's some kind of mind-reader. Did Kaylen or
Randy mention someone else could do that other than me?

The weight of his eyes on me is still apparent though, and I try to ignore the sensation while another man sitting next to Jimmy, whom I recognize as my *other* guard from Pneumatikon, introduces himself as Will. I barely register what he's saying to me as I work on remembering any ability I've heard of that might explain Gabe's... discerning presence. At least I manage to smile at Will and say, "Nice to meet you."

Kaylen, I notice, has been distracting Jimmy from asking anything more about what it's like to kill people by shooting the nearly empty salt shaker across the table at him with her mind. So far her efforts are working. I send her a grateful look. I love Kaylen already.

I turn carefully in my chair to get up and return my empty plate to the pile of dirty dishes next to the sink. But Gabe sweeps in out of nowhere and takes it from me. "Allow me," he says. I'm left staring at his momentarily retreating back in surprise.

He returns seconds later and flashes an alluring grin. He gets down on one knee in front of me, takes my gloved hand, (which instantly feels less like a hindrance and more like the fashionable vestures of a high-class lady), and kisses the top of it like a chivalrous knight.

As if his lips on my hand aren't shocking enough, he actually rests them there for a few moments. His eyes linger on mine from under thick eyelashes, imploring my attention. Now that he's so close, my own eyes seem to have gained autonomy. They reach out for his automatically as if they've simply been waiting for an invitation.

His mouth finally leaves my hand but I can't now recall how long his lips rested there. I just know the moments felt full of movement even though our bodies were still.

"Gabe Dumas. A pleasure, Miss," he says boldly and eloquently.

Spellbound by the way his eyes lead mine and the timbre of his voice so near, I can't even register alarm at this invasion of my personal space. Instead, I feel compelled to meet his unusual choreography with a move of my own. I push my chair back, stand up, and curtsy delicately. I bow my head, and say, "Dear me. Thank you kindly, good sir!"

Laughter explodes around me. I hadn't noticed that the entire room was watching our interaction until this moment. I look back at him with an expectant smile, waiting to match his next step.

Gabe beams up at me. Again his eyes seek mine out, and when they make contact, it is the release of touching hands during a Minuet. The tenderness of it evokes a surge of warmth that loosens my body and incites a rush of abandonment and the desire for the moment to not end.

I catch someone shifting in my periphery and I remember that we are not alone. My insecurity jars the dance of our eyes so that they pause in their step. Gabe concedes submissively to my hesitation, finally releasing my hand and standing up.

"You are such a goob, Gabe," Kaylen says, pulling me further out of… whatever that was.

"And that's why you like me, Kaylee-girl. But it wouldn't have been nearly as fun without someone to play along," he replies, glancing at me with audacious invitation.

I take a few inconspicuous deep breaths to calm the frolicking feet pounding my chest. I have the urge to do something spontaneous like hop up and twirl around with my hands outstretched.

"Scoot over, Jimbo," he orders Jimmy. With Gabe's attention momentarily off of me, I finally get what just happened: those were *Gabe's* emotions. I didn't realize it because they were unlike anyone I have ever felt. His mind is not like the dark closet most people have. The opening to his closet has no door.

"Will just left so there's a chair on the other side of me. Why should I scoot over?" Jimmy asks, annoyed.

"Yes, there is, but clearly you don't possess the tact necessary to make new arrivals feel welcome," Gabe says in a wearied way as if his answer should have been obvious. "You ought to let someone else manage it."

Jimmy looks confused, glancing at me before moving grudgingly over to the next chair.

Gabe exudes charm as easily as someone does the scent of cologne. He's a flirt as well, but his magnetism is something he carries naturally. He radiates it inside and out. I'm automatically drawn to focusing on his thoughts alone because they move so vibrantly, striking a rhythm that reverberates within me. It's far more dynamic than anyone else.

"Don't mind Jimmy. He wasn't raised properly. It's no fault of his own," Gabe says, looking at me with his hands folded under his chin. His expression is somewhat dreamy, and slightly disconcerting to me, the object of his attention. Jimmy glares at Gabe who doesn't even look his way.

"I'll make a note of that," I say, completely taken by the dance of his emotions. They execute a series of grand jetés and pirouettes in my stomach. "And what should I note about you? Obnoxious honesty?" It's abundantly clear that Gabe is taken with me. I can even hear the rapid beat of his heart. He must know I can tell, and I have no idea how to handle it other than to pretend like I'm oblivious.

Gabe laughs deeply. "Most indubitably."

"Don't forget annoying grasp of antiquated English," Jimmy says.

"Jimbo. We've been over this. It's not antiquated. It's underused. And I take offense to the term 'annoying' as a descriptor. That's subjective," Gabe says, looking at me the entire time. His eagerness pounds out a beat of vigorous leg throws in my stomach like a battement in a ballet. And then, another pirouette any time my eyes touch his for even the briefest moment.

"And the term 'obnoxious' *isn't* subjective? That's biased," Jimmy replies.

Gabe shrugs. "She asked what *she* should keep in mind. If she considers my honesty obnoxious, that's her prerogative. I have no right to correct a person's opinion. You, on the other hand, wish to mar my character in front of the lady."

"You are impossible," Jimmy huffs, getting up and leaving.

Kaylen giggles next to me, and Gabe sighs with exaggerated relief. "And he says *I'm* impossible. What say you? Impossible or tons of fun?"

Gabe watches me with far too much unapologetic interest.

"I haven't decided," I reply, wishing he would look at someone or some*thing* else. His attention makes me feel as if every eye in the room has shifted to me suddenly. Maybe they have. I'm afraid to check.

"Would it help if I apologized for playing a part in violating your trust not so long ago? I've been feeling ghastly about the whole event all this time, just itching to get in front of you and make amends, as well as find out if you truly are as spirited as you seemed that day—I'd say that question has been answered. But I *am* sorry. You won't hold it against me, will you?" Remorse slows his exuberance into a painstaking waltz, sealing the genuineness of his apology as he awaits my answer.

"Probably not," I reply. "I'll let you know once I decide what to make of you."

He mulls that over, faltering a bit more in his confidence. My instinct is to reassure him that no, I don't hold it against him even a little bit. His personality makes disliking him impossible. I wish all these people would leave and let me be alone with him. I want to see what else will come out of his mouth without me having to be self-conscious about it.

"And how can I help you decide it faster?" he asks in a lower voice, leaning toward me as if we really *are* the only ones in the room.

I blink, trying to unlock myself from the need to look at him, but his unwavering fascination with my every word has me spellbound. "I don't know. But I'm pretty sure it takes more than five minutes to get an accurate impression of someone."

"Not in your case, I would think," he replies, tilting his head a little. "I could be wrong, but I'd think your unusual powers of perception would allow you to glean quite a bit of depth about a person, just by being around them."

I'm starting to get that Gabe is not in the least bit ashamed of his captivation. In fact, it seems like he's practically shouting it at me without *actually* shouting it at me. I suppress what was going to be a drawn-out sigh and put my hands under my thighs to keep from moving closer. "Yes. But you're kind of unusual. I don't think I've encountered anyone before who was quite so... forthcoming with his thoughts."

He smiles, thrilled by my answer. "I'm curious," he says, propping his chin on one hand. "Just how much of a person's thoughts *can* you read?"

I glance up and away, knowing for certain that Gabe is not just asking for informational purposes. He's practically calling out his own attraction to me. He must wonder what I think of it.

"When I know someone well, quite a bit," I reply, hoping I can keep the conversation from moving to a place I am *not* ready to explore. "You'd be surprised how much your emotions can say."

"Hmm, that sounds fascinating. How does that work?"

"Well, everyone has undercurrents of emotion. Only they're too accustomed to them to notice," I explain, wanting to satisfy his insatiable need to know. Plus, I need to talk so his stare doesn't expose my feelings—not that I'm entirely sure of what those are yet. "It's kind of like smells. You can spend all day in a room that smells like Lilacs never noticing the scent yourself because your nose adapted to it. But if someone else walks in, they'll pick up on it immediately because they aren't used to it. The emotional patterns your mind usually runs on are too familiar to you for you to realize them. But when they hit *me*, I pick up on their tenor immediately because they're so different from my own."

As he considers my explanation from different angles, he leaps from one idea to the next buoyantly. He may twirl or flip between each leap, but the movement is gracefully controlled as he analyzes the significance of my every word. The elegant acrobatics are mesmerizing.

"Brilliant!" he says after several moments. "That does make sense."

I smile at him again because that just comes naturally. I glance around and realize that we are the only two people at our table. Everyone else has left, just as I wanted. Except now that we're virtually alone, (a few more people linger at the other table), his presence gathers in force, intoxicating me further so that I can't do much more than stare at him. Even though he's on the other side of the table, it feels like we're occupying a more intimate vicinity. Or maybe it's just his bliss leading me through another dance of revelry. My heart hammers out the beat.

As the pull between us intensifies, it startles me and I resist. My sudden and forceful attraction frightens me. Before I have to figure out how handle it, someone appears next to me. It's Randy.

"Wendy, I'd like to meet with you now if that's okay," she says, looking from Gabe to my face.

"Yeah, of course." I slide my chair back. "Nice to meet you, Gabe," I say, disliking how false it feels to say that. It was definitely more than nice.

Gabe looks up at me wistfully, begging with his thoughts that I not go—and as a result *I* don't want to go.

"That conversation was far too short," he complains. Then he smiles. "But every moment was delightful to say the least."

Another surge of warmth twirls dizzily in my stomach. As I retreat from him, I notice that the taste of him in my head takes a lot longer to dissipate than I expected. With my back to him, I can't be sure, but it seems like my emodar range might be a lot wider for him. I don't turn to verify. I just sigh with relief when I finally escape his gravity.

14

$\mathcal{R}$andy takes me to the research building and then upstairs to her office, which is designed with contemporary taste. Everything flows in neat lines accented with bright, solid colors. I especially admire her desk: iron legs welded into box patterns with a glass top. I move to the nearest chair, which looks uncomfortably minimalist but actually turns out to be surprisingly ergonomic.

Settling herself behind her desk, Randy retrieves a file from a discreet cabinet. She is either meticulously tidy or she never uses her office, because until she pulls out the file, not a single shred of paper can be found anywhere.

"So, we're going to start out with describing events until now. I want to know how you felt during hypno-touch—any odd sensations. Then I want to document your other abilities. I suggest, Miss Whitley, that if you want us to help you, you don't lie about what you can do."

I groan with annoyance. Randy is supposedly a doctor—a career that ought to make her more personable—but she's about as relatable as an android. Crossing my arms defiantly, I say, "Well excuse me for not trusting people as soon as I meet them. You actually expected me to just lay it all out there for Dina? I'd like to see *you* grow up having a weird talent like sensing emotions when you touch people and see if *you* tell everyone you come in contact with. And besides, *you* weren't honest with *me* at all. You want trust? You give it first."

Randy watches my rant with exhaustion and says, "Are we ever going to move past that, Wendy? We're trying to help you. If you don't believe that, why are you here? I simply meant it as caution, not an accusation."

I roll my eyes. She obviously doesn't get it. "Whatever, Randy. So what is it you want to know?"

She begins probing me about Dina's hypno-touch which I recall as strangely wonderful, although I doubt I can truly look back on any part of that day with an accurate perception of how it really was. I give a longwinded description, afraid of getting to the gut-wrenching, panic-stricken state I always succumb to whenever I even *begin* to remember what Dina felt.

"And can you be more specific about what it felt like after Dina touched you?" Randy asks, writing something down as if she just asked me if I'd like fries with that.

Sweat gathers on my forehead as anxiety pulses into my limbs. I eye the grey wall to my left, wishing I was next to it right now. Why do people always have to put chairs in the middle of the room in an office? It puts you on the spot, and nobody likes that. A chair next to a wall, on the other hand, invites the comfort of the people visiting.

I close my eyes briefly and work to dislodge the residual terror of that day. I'd like to scrape it off and hand it over to Randy so maybe it won't torment me anymore. But getting so close to it is making my heart palpitate so I have to stop. I flex my fingers to be sure that they haven't been erased.

"When she touched me I kind of blacked out and it was scary," I say when Randy looks up at me expectantly. "I was really confused, but then when I came around I couldn't hear her heart anymore."

Randy nods just barely, scrawling notes across her clipboard, unaware of my discomfort.

"Was my hypno-touch experience typical?" I ask, hoping she isn't going to ask any more questions about Dina. I can't relive it. I'm surprised I even survived the torture intact.

"Yes," she says when she's done writing. "I'd say so. The sensation you felt was over your entire body, which indicates that your ability is not limited to just your hands. That's what we found for the most part when we tested it."

"You—you tested it out? How?" I ask, shocked.

"Relax. We were very careful. Louise simply felt your energy to determine if more of it was gathered in your hands—sometimes abilities are only concentrated in the hands... like mine. When it wasn't, she hypothesized that it was in effect over your whole body.

"Based on Derek and Lisa's accounts, she assumed that death only results when the touch is prolonged. She believed brief touch would only cause a person to faint, at worst. So she tapped your foot with her finger. Sure enough, she experienced only disorientation, and she sat down to recover herself."

Randy's voice is so clinical and detached that I wonder if she's reading the words from her clipboard.

"Um, is Louise okay in the head? I just can't imagine what would prompt her to take a risk like that."

"Louise is driven," Randy says somewhat defensively, "and like I said, she has a sense about these things. I trust her judgment implicitly."

I wonder how implicit your trust would have been if she'd asked you *to tap my foot.*

A phrase comes to me... something about insanity breeding genius. I probably *need* an insane genius like Louise to help me if I'm going to figure this out.

"What's Louise's ability?" I ask, wondering if supernatural talents have something to do with Louise's daring.

"She has many talents, but she doesn't have any manifest latent abilities," she replies nonchalantly.

"Say what?"

"Manifest latent abilities. That's what we call abilities that manifest during hypno-touch which are above normal human capability," she explains.

"No, I mean, she doesn't have *any* above-average ability?" I say, stunned.

"Not the kind you're thinking of. She is the most skilled at hypno-touch, and her insight into the state of one's energy is like no other practitioner here. Our research would be stopped without her."

"But... why?" It doesn't make sense that the leader and founder of a group of people with supernatural abilities wouldn't have any special ability herself. What have these people been *doing* all this time?

"So far, Wendy," Randy explains patiently, "we have only been able to broaden the abilities of those who already possess them and stimulate the emergence of latent abilities in those who have energy kinks. Louise fits neither of those categories even though she was the founder of the entire movement and has more experience with hypno-touch than all of us put together."

Randy thinks I'm ignorant, and when she puts it that way, I suppose I am. Louise *did* tell me the same thing. I just figured that if you had been participating in hypno-touch long enough, you would see *some* results, even if they were hardly noticeable. Plus, couldn't she like... give herself an allergy or something? Eat too much sugar and give herself Type II Diabetes? I don't know. That's probably silly. But someone as motivated as Louise surely could have found some way to give herself one of those energy kinks she talks about.

I realize I unconsciously placed a lot more hope in this place than they deserve. I accepted they were a lot further along in this process than they actually are. The reality-check, although necessary, hurts.

"Wow, that must be tough for her," I say with feigned pity. "Surrounded by all these exceptional people and stuck with the same mundane human abilities."

"Louise believes in the cause too much to overly concern herself with her own progress in that respect. She is the driving force, and everyone looks to her for guidance," says Randy, disregarding my tone.

"So when you work with people with allergies, it doesn't even come close to curing the allergy, does it?"

"No."

"Well, that sucks," I snort. "I would have at least liked to have gotten *something* positive out of this whole thing."

"Your attitude will hardly help to accomplish what you came here for."

Randy is so irritating. Why does Louise have me deal with her?

"Okay then, Wendy," Randy continues. "We'll do a more calibrated test this week, but I need to get an idea of whether our tests will even register your senses accurately. First up: sight. Just how good is it now?" she asks, pen held at the ready to record my response.

"Mind-blowingly good," I answer, pulling my feet up onto the chair to get more comfortable—and to annoy Randy with my dirty shoes on her stylish digs.

I think she glares at me a little, but she asks, "Maybe you could give me an example?"

"Well, sitting here, I can see that you have a layer of dust on your windowsill. The curtains are nice but cheaply made—unless rough cheap cotton is your thing. You've been biting your pen a little, although not enough that regular people can see it I bet. I can see where you've rested your teeth on it though. You have a mole under your obviously heavy makeup below your bottom lip. You have a zit just barely coming in on the left side of your nose."

That was probably a bit much, but I really don't like Randy.

I look around the room some more. "There's a hairline crack in the drywall under the paint above the window. The walls could actually use an extra coat of paint… it's splotchy in some places… And an ant is crawling on the floor over there by the filing cabinet— I'd say that's pretty impressive since your flooring is almost black." I feel slightly guilty for being so snide, but I get over it quickly.

"Hmmm," says Randy, definitely impressed. I wonder if the dust and ant comments bug her. The organized nature of her office indicates she may be a neat-freak, and I'm not close enough to her to tell. I almost smile when I think about her running to the bathroom after this to check her nose for incoming acne.

"Besides detail, I can see pretty far…" I add. "Maybe several hundred yards and still be clear? I'm not sure. It's mostly the detail that I've experimented with."

"How about your ears? How much can you hear?" she asks after a moment of writing.

I pause, listening. Even though my hearing is excellent, I still have to focus in order to interpret any one sound individually, otherwise the combination of unlimited and ongoing sounds forms a deafening roar. Aside from nightmares this past week, which made the insomnia bad enough, I've had a hard time sleeping through the incessant noise in my apartment complex and from the surrounding buildings.

"Your breathing, heartbeats. Your stomach digesting," I reply. "Farther out I can hear the horses on the move. I hear birds in the trees—I don't know how far away. Leaves rustling in the wind… I hear people talking downstairs. Gina's going on about light wavelengths. Gosh she's a talkative one, huh? Celine doesn't like me—What is *her* deal? Kaylen is complaining about an assignment she has coming up in chemistry. That enough? I can find out if they're gossiping about you…" I say smugly.

"No, that's fine," says Randy. "Smell?"

"Starched cotton. Sweat. Don't worry though, I can smell that on everybody." I glance at Randy. She probably wouldn't like the idea of someone smelling sweat on her. She probably thinks she doesn't sweat at all.

I close my eyes to concentrate. "Paper, electricity, upholstery… Let's see, did you change fragrances a while back? I smell a perfume lingering in the furniture that's a bit sweeter than I'm used to from you, but it's kind of stale. Your newer fragrance is better, I think. You know, I don't smell many other people in here. Do you not entertain much?" I open an eye to look at her, but she doesn't respond, only writes. "I also smell some horse manure. I think maybe that's from my shoes. And it smells like you added pesto to your sandwich at lunch and then you brushed right after. Good?" I bite my bottom lip to keep from smirking about my comments on her breath.

"Yes, thank you," Randy replies, only glancing at me briefly between notes. "And would you say this is the same or improved over your senses prior to your hypno-touch?"

"Improved."

Randy then asks questions about my emodar, even getting out a tape measure to calculate the range exactly—which we measure at sixty-two inches for her. I find I actually can sense her a bit beyond that, but she fades at the five-foot range. I tell her it varies a little from one person to the next.

"Interesting," says Randy after writing down the numbers. "Empathic ability with a radius. We originally wondered if your ability was pheromone-driven, but since it has such a clear boundary radius, it most certainly is not. Do you ever pick up anything more than just pure emotion?"

"Well, if I've felt a person enough, I can get the gist of the motivation behind the feeling, but it seems more like just 'knowing them,' you know? I don't think I'm reading their mind, but I make assumptions based on what I know about them. Now that I don't have to be touching people to read them, I'll probably get even better at that."

I imagine for a minute what it might be like to be an *actual* telepath. I wonder if I would even understand what I was reading if I *could* read a person's mind. They aren't linear like books.

"Well, here's what we know," Randy says, leaning forward and crossing her arms in front of her on her desk. "Your energy-absorption cannot occur without skin contact. You should have no problem touching people with your gloves on—Gabe demonstrated that fairly well, I'd say. Also, you don't seem to affect animals or other living things—we tested a cat and it was fine. Your energy field is whole and normal, so I am unsure about what happens to the energy you take in. It may just be that you channel it into the atmosphere, but I can't really say for sure. Maybe you used it up somehow between touching Dina and when Louise felt your life force." Randy shrugs.

"You tested it on a cat?" I ask sadly.

Randy nods. "There was no other way to find out. Animals and plants have life forces as well, but they are weaker, different, in a vaguely discernible way. We'll be trying some different hypno-touch techniques to see if we can encourage your latent ability to develop a little more."

"Wouldn't it *not* be a good idea to develop it? I mean, what if it develops into something worse like killing people if they come within ten feet of me?" I ask, dismayed that I didn't consider this danger when Louise suggested just such a thing.

"What if it develops into something else?" she asks. "Life forces are made up of positive energy. Since gifts are powered by that force, I find it hard to believe that positive energy could be feeding something intended solely to detract. Personally, I think there's a flip-side to it that's underdeveloped. Another possibility is that regular hypno-touch sessions will bring you a measure of control, or at least awareness of your own life force."

Randy notes my heavy skepticism and continues, "If you prefer, you can learn the techniques of energy medicine first before you decide to develop your gift. It can be a last resort. I'm more curious about your abilities in hypno-touch. It's very possible you're especially sensitive to energy. Learning hypno-touch may actually allow you to become aware of it when you're around people and eventually be able to control how you interact with it. I think that's where your best bet is."

"Agreed," I reply shuddering at the possibility of morphing my ability into a death *presence*. "So when do I start?"

"Louise has volunteered for at least your initial training. She's busy at the moment, but she'll be available later this evening after dinner."

Randy and I make an appointment for eight o'clock. I'm elated that already, at day one, I'm *doing* something. I should be able to see Ezra again in no time.

15

$\mathcal{A}$s I walk down the stairs, I make plans to find someone, Kaylen probably, to ask about hypno-touch and how it's done so I can be prepared to get as much out of tonight's meeting as possible. I would have asked Randy, but I don't like her. And they might *claim* that their only interest is in helping me, but I know that what they really want is to dissect my ability.

Mental exhaustion nags me despite my drive. I had a number of terror-filled dreams last night, and anticipating coming here had me on edge as well. I barely slept. I think I'm going to need a nap.

As I push open the exit door I hear a pleasant and articulate voice behind me, "Wendy! Wait up!"

Gabe. My heart skips.

"It's Wen," I say, turning. I wish I could stifle my words, but they're already out there. Why did I tell him that? I don't know him. Only people who know me well call me Wen. I also notice, now that I'm paying attention, that I was right: Gabe's range is *much* farther than anyone else's. By several feet at *least*; his eagerness bounds lightly through my fatigue much sooner than expected.

"When what?" Gabe asks with a mischievous smile, coming up beside me.

"Ha, ha," I say turning away from him as I walk through the door and onto the path. "That wasn't all that clever, you know. Given your introduction earlier, I'd expect more." I inhale the scent of the coniferous trees and decaying needles around me and find his evergreen-like scent mingled pleasantly with them.

"Sorry to disappoint, but I couldn't help myself. I was hoping to catch you smile so I was already desperately looking for an opening. I had to try. I'm sure you understand."

I swallow, intentionally avoiding his face so I don't ogle his refined good-looks. He walks quite close to me; his proximity magnetizes the small space between us.

"Oh yeah, I get it," I say, ambling down the gently sloping path. "But you obviously strive to rile the natives just because you can. I don't think you *find* openings. I think you *make* openings. So I doubt you were that desperate. I think you just like to hear yourself talk."

Gabe cocks his head slightly and sighs with gratified adoration. "You're spectacular, you know that?"

The image of reaching out for his hand floats through my head and I have to stifle my own sigh. But then I visualize what it would be like to stop in the middle of the path and move tantalizingly close to him, just enough to convey the invitation for a kiss. The idea warms me over.

"Uh, thanks?" I say to interrupt my wandering fantasies. "So what's up?" Maybe his ripples of attraction are making me incoherent. I can't tell. I become too easily caught up with whatever dazzling performance is happening in his head.

"You're welcome?" he questions and then grins. "Anyway, 'What's up' is that everyone was monopolizing you at lunch and I didn't get much of a turn."

"Really? It looked like you had no trouble angling yourself in there. You practically chased everyone off," I reply, putting some space between us. I'd like to find out how much of my breathless desire is my own. But he keeps closing the distance.

A smile overtakes his features, reaching all the way to those ridiculously captivating eyes of his. I can't resist smiling back. He closes the distance between us again, and I settle for working through everything I'm feeling right now, verifying what's mine.

At that moment, the pulsing electricity between us moves more to the background, and more buoyant curiosity takes its place.

"What did you want a turn to do?" I ask, perplexed that my feelings seem to follow Gabe's wherever they go. "Ask me about death and what it's like to suck out someone's soul?"

He pauses mid-stride to look at me directly. At first he's confused, but it's followed by a light of recognition. "I suppose my eagerness could be misconstrued as morbid interest... But no, I wasn't kidding when I told Jimmy he was a lout. I certainly don't want a turn to ask you something so crass."

"Then what *do* you want?" I ask. *A lout? Who **says** that?*

"To find out your secrets, of course, seeing as you know mine already. Sólo es justo, mi amor." His hands find their way into the back pockets of his jeans, and he kicks a stone idly. He watches me while I wonder what he's talking about.

Did he just speak Spanish to me?

Most of the Spanish I know consists of Letty's expletives. I might have been able to figure out something if he'd said it slower. I *think* the last part was 'mi amor.' I think it means, 'my love.' I must have misheard him.

Meanwhile, his eyes lure me in again, just as they have every time I've seen him: a lively shade of brown, and probing like they want to launch into orbit around my soul.

"I know your secrets?" I ask finally, failing to decipher his meaning. *Or* his Spanish.

He tilts his head to look at me. He squints his eyes a little like he's trying to see better into mine. And then he laughs.

"I don't get the joke," I say, frustrated.

"I just find it funny that you choose to avoid something so blatantly obvious."

"What's that?" I ask hesitantly because I think I'm starting to get where this is going... though I can't believe his nerve. I only really just met him *today.*

He straightens up and looks at me directly. "That I'm enraptured by you and you very well know it."

Though I expected him to divulge some facet of his feelings, I didn't expect it to come out quite so... bluntly. My eyes widen and I look away. My cheeks flush. I don't understand why he would lay it all out like that when we've only known each other a few hours.

"You act like this is news to you..." he says pensively, transitioning to some new idea. "Unless you were lying about your ability to read emotions... That *would* explain your discomfort." He is not in the least bit embarrassed by that possibility.

"No. I didn't lie," I say, backing up slowly to get him out of my emodar. At six or so feet, I still feel him, but I stop because he's going to notice. "I picked up on it but I barely know you so I wasn't sure *who* it was directed at. I'm not a mind-reader." *Such a lie.* I could pick Gabe's thoughts out of any crowd. My deceit irritates me, but at least my aggravation grounds me enough that I don't get completely flustered and start stumbling over my words.

His eyes narrow in suspicion. "You expect me to believe that? I don't think it's possible for you to mistake who they were directed at. I couldn't have been any more straightforward if I'd announced it out loud. And I would have, but as you know I'm crazy about you so I didn't want to make you uncomfortable in front of everyone. Which is why I'm standing here now instead."

How do I even respond to that?

"Look, I was just going to ignore it, okay?" I say, taken aback by his continual unapologetic declarations. I have no experience in dealing with a strategy like that. And I can't even *think* about how to deal with it while my heart is fluttering so rapidly.

I back up curiously now. Just how far away from him do I need to be? I'm amazed that as I keep backing up, his mental presence is still there. I try to calculate the distance. Six? Seven? *Eight* feet? I sigh with relief when he finally begins to fade. I estimate at nine feet I can no longer pick up on him at all. I'm finally alone in my head but it's in chaos: a hurricane of awe and euphoria and annoyance and distress.

"Ignore it?" he asks after a few pondering moments "Why would you do that?" But then he sees the distance between us. He glances back up to my face. "Oh. My apologies." He straightens and grins half-heartedly. "I'll do my best to contain myself." And then even his diffident smile deflates.

"No!" I say, interrupting his dejection and stepping toward him again, putting him back in-range. He's so acutely distraught that it feels like someone sucked the life out of me. "I didn't mean that. I just meant for your sake I would ignore it, not that I didn't like you... Not that I'm attracted to you... You know what? I don't even know why we're talking about this." I sigh heavily.

Why can't I just let him believe I'm not interested?

"Hijo de un sacerdote casto! Eres una mujer cruel! Jugando con los sentimientos de un hombre!" Gabe exclaims, his exuberance soaring once more and leaving his disappointment behind like it never was. The swiftness of the flight leaves me a little short of breath. "If you can detect my feelings and decipher what I'm thinking, then you ought to at least give me the courtesy of knowing yours as well. It's only fair." He crosses his arms with an expectant and self-satisfied look.

"Uh, excuse me? I don't speak Spanish. What does that mean?"

"And I can't sniff your emotional waves out of the air and translate them. So I suppose we're even," he says smugly, his flirtatiousness mocking me. "Besides, some of that wasn't polite. Can't very well say *that* around a lady, now can I?"

I giggle—something I hate doing. Nothing makes a girl sound more trivial than giggling around a boy. "A *lady*? Are you some kind of time-traveler from nineteen-hundred or something?"

"No," he says, looking down his nose at me with his arms still crossed. "My mother just raised me right is all."

"She sounds like quite a woman to have raised the likes of *you*."

He smiles delightedly. "So, are you going to tell me?" he asks, easing himself directly in my line of sight. His elation has recovered fully and starts leaping in grand jetés again. When it touches back down, it melts into heated attraction. I have trouble stilling my hands. I think they're going to reach out to him on their own at any moment. He's just so *intense* mentally. I swear it's like he can take control of my body with his mind. And now my eyes find his because the distraction of his yearning for me has my guard down. They're so bright and inquisitive, and his anticipation is electric. My body may be almost completely covered right now, but I still feel naked under his piercing gaze.

"Tell you what?" I ask in an attempt to get control of *some* part of myself, if only my mouth. Enduring him is like running a marathon. Maybe that's why I sense him so far out—his emotions are just so *extreme.*

"You are so exasperating!" He throws his hands up. "What you make of me! How you feel about it! I deserve to know!" he demands, planting himself squarely in front of me, ready and willing to block any retreat. Not that I think I *can* retreat at this point.

"*Deserve* to know? How do you figure that? I don't even know you," I protest. I'm stalling, I know, but I don't want to answer his question. My thoughts are under assault; I don't know *what* I feel.

"Will you answer the confounded question, woman!" he insists. He fights to look serious, but a smirk threatens the corners of his mouth. He definitely gets a kick out of making me uncomfortable.

That's definitely something I know how to handle. I mirror his crossed arms and say, "And if I don't?"

He smiles devilishly. His attraction then bounds forward and sweeps me up so fast I think I left my stomach behind. My eyes flutter in astonishment at what feels almost exactly like being touched that way physically. But he's still several feet away... I have no idea how he does that. And I like him *so* much that I don't pause to marvel, only rest without protest in the warm cradle of his eyes.

He analyzes my face carefully for a period, searching me out. I don't resist. He's ecstatic about what he finds. Then, releasing me of his gentleness delicately, he says in a lower voice with a self-assured smile, "No matter. I have your answer I believe."

Then he turns and starts walking down the path again.

"But I didn't say anything!" I protest, rushing to keep up with him. "Do you have telepathic abilities or something?" That must be it. I've never felt a person connect to me like he does.

"Of course not!" he says indignantly, stopping again and turning to me, gratified that I've rushed after him so readily—I regret that move already. "But you, mi encantadora doncella, are smitten with me!"

"What the—? I didn't say that!"

He bellows out a laugh, delighted. Then he bites his lip and crosses his arms for several moments, thinking. "I suppose... considering your distress... I could make an allowance... Let you set the record straight? You could tell me what you *really* think, or I will just have to assume. I would take the opportunity if I were you. I can't keep my mouth shut about anything, as I'm sure you can tell. And rumors can be such a vicious thing."

He's blackmailing me?

"You!" I say, aghast. "You are thoroughly despicable!" I grit my teeth to keep from grinning though. Oh my gosh, I could talk to him *all* day.

"Who's using early twentieth century idioms now, hmm?" he mocks, grinning slyly.

"I'm having a hard time recalling my previous impressions in the face of my feelings now," I reply confidently. He doesn't know who he's messing with.

"Oh do try," he implores sweetly, *still* grinning. *Does he ever stop smiling?*

"If memory serves me," I say, lifting my chin haughtily, "my first impression was that you were a total charming hottie. But I'd say in light of your obvious arrogance I have no choice but to change my—"

"Tut, tut, tut," he says, holding his finger in front of, but not touching, my mouth, startling me. "I don't need additional commentary."

I shrug, unconcerned. "Fine," I reply matter-of-factly, "be delusional. The arrogant ones always are. I know better than to trust first impressions. Especially physical attraction. Hotties are a dime a dozen." My heart beats loudly in my chest though, threatening to give away my real feelings.

"A valid point," Gabe replies thoughtfully. Then he looks back at me. "Arrogant? Really?"

I don't answer.

After working to decipher my expression, he settles on confidence. "I can redeem myself. Never fear. I have plenty of experience wooing beautiful women, and I'm certain I can win over one who has a history of being attracted to me."

With his looks, I don't doubt it. "Oooh, more cockiness," I reply, crossing my arms. "Every girl's dream is an ego with a pretty face."

Gabe chuckles. "Wendy, Wendy," he says. "I think you're mistaking arrogance with audacity. There is a distinct difference."

"Yeah. And in my book, blackmail is on the arrogant side of the line."

"Tilly-vally! If you were as distraught about that as you claim, you would hardly be standing here giving me the opportunity to charm you further."

"Wait, what? Tilly-vally? What in the world does that mean?" I ask, knowing full-well that I *am* consciously giving him the opportunity to charm me. But in my defense, every word he says is charming. Who *doesn't* like being charmed?

He rolls his eyes and says, "Really, what are they teaching in schools these days? It means 'balderdash,' 'bananas,' 'baloney,' or, more commonly, 'nonsense.'"

"Okay, you can't be *that* much older than me, so I find it hard to believe that your generation uses 'Tilly-vally' either."

"Why, are you worried I might be too old for you?" he asks, one side of his mouth curled up teasingly.

I roll my own eyes now. "No. Actually, I think it's more likely that you're some kind of bizarre incarnation of a Charles Dickens character."

Gabe laughs delightedly, "Really? Which one? And would you date them?"

"I don't know which one. I hate Charles Dickens."

"Harsh," Gabe says, wincing but undeterred. "I know better though. Your repartee is just your way of showing you care. You like me. I can tell."

"You're like an unruly child," I say, shaking my head. Jimmy was right. You *are* impossible."

He laughs joyously. "You like me, and soon enough, you'll admit it," he says in a sing-song voice.

He stands there a bit longer, his affection for me building with every moment. Like stepping into the hot shower when you're cold, the warmth infiltrating your body little-by-little. I have no desire to leave. But still it builds until it becomes sensual; the heat of it has me panting. I blink my eyes several times and shove my hands in my jeans pockets to endure it. I think he felt it to deliberately disarm me.

Then he turns abruptly and heads off at a jog toward the stables and courts. I watch him with my mouth open. He's wearing a fitted t-shirt, and it pulls flatteringly against his shoulders as he moves. I shake my head to interrupt my own gawking just as he turns, still within earshot—my earshot anyway—and says, "Oh Wendy? As always, our conversation was *such* a delight. Until next time!"

I force my eyes away from his retreating form, wondering what on earth I'm going to do about him.

16

Butterflies have invaded my stomach for the last hour and a half. They are in such a flurry that I'm starting to feel nauseated with the intensity. I cannot calm down. Not with *his* face on my mind.

Intuitively I know this sudden infatuation is a *very* bad thing. Yet I can't quite articulate the whys anymore. Instead I wonder about other things. I wonder if his name is short for Gabriel—Would he let me call him that? I wonder what it would be like to kiss him with our emotions entwined like they were earlier… I wonder if he's thinking about me right now… Where would the curve of his arms rest if he were to put them around me…?

I hop up from where I've been lying on the carpeted floor and throw myself on the bed. I pull a pillow over my face. This is useless. Louise left a case file under my door with a note to read over it, and I've been trying ever since my encounter with Gabe. I've really tried. But Gabe is up there and won't go away. I had hoped that once I finally got away from him, I'd discover that it was just *his* emotions that were making my stomach flip-flop. But that's not the case at all.

I can't get a grip on my romantic imaginations. My head has detached from my body and is floating away. I have *no* control over it. I imagine all kinds of impossible things that involve touching him as well as the sound of his voice as he tells me again how he feels about me with more ridiculously old-fashioned words. In my recollection he really *does* call me 'mi amor.' I'm annoyed and indignant that I'm getting so carried away. But I keep reverting back to a daydream.

I groan loudly. How can I feel so ready and willing to ignore every single obstacle that's sure to make this kind of pursuit end in complete heartbreak?

I have fallen in love with him.

To my surprise, the admission isn't hard. What's hard is imagining how it happened, how it's even *possible* after only two short conversations with him.

Not so hard, Wendy.

I guess it isn't. Because I've experienced *him.* I don't have to wonder if he is what he seems. I know he's *exactly* what he seems, both inside and out.

Acceptance finally eases my struggle and fills me with wonder as I remember what it was like to be around him: lighter than air, easy, like finding something precious I forgot I lost.

But in the aftermath is also sadness that grows as I imagine the reality my feelings will create. It doesn't matter if I love him. It can't work. It won't. No matter how refreshingly authentic he is, I can't have a relationship with someone I may never touch. I *know* this. But I remain indecisive.

Because he's perfect.

I don't want to think about why that's true, but the reasons come far too easily: memories of the revolving door of guys who have been attracted to me. I *always* had the upper hand because I knew where their mind was whenever they were around me. And I might have tried them out for a while on occasion, but I dismissed them as easily as wallpaper samples.

I've been in love before, at least I thought so. The infatuation is the same, but this is more swift and inevitable. Like an undertow. The possibility of a future with him is so *real* in my head. This is *not* superficial attraction. He has the one thing I have always wanted, and he has demonstrated that one quality in the two short encounters I've had with him:

Honesty.

I-don't-care-how-uncomfortable-it-makes-you truth comes out of his mouth. Every time. I want to make it out to be just his brand of flirting, but I know it's not. I don't think he's capable of shying away from truth, even if it makes him uncomfortable or vulnerable. Actually, truth doesn't make him uncomfortable at all which is even more unusual. I've felt the depth of him and I never imagined someone like him was actually out there. And now that I know he exists, I am positive I will never want anyone else.

Knowing that Gabe is real suddenly brings to light why I always failed at relationships: lying words, lying actions, lying thoughts—it was the exhaustion of putting up with lies. Even little ones. Like emotional avoidance. Like not letting me in on every facet of what they were thinking—a silly demand for an adolescent relationship—but even then I must have intuitively known what I wanted. I just hadn't conceived of it. And now that I think about it, I was always picking the fights and it was always about some stupid insignificant lie. Of course, none of them were ever aware that I knew the gist of their thoughts, but I couldn't turn off my talent.

It didn't matter if a guy was just trying to please me. If he so much as told me he wanted to see a movie I picked out even though his thoughts told me otherwise, I would jump down his throat like he had betrayed all semblance of trust. I just couldn't seem to help it. It became my justification for using and discarding guys like it was my right, for controlling them, and for traveling down a path of self-destruction for a long time before my mom died.

I sigh under the heavy guilt those memories always bring. I know I was unreasonable. I know my ensuing behavior was awful. That's why I have completely avoided all relationships or dating since taking care of Ezra. But that doesn't mean I value honesty any less. Honesty, to me, means truthfulness about even the most insignificant things. If that makes me too exacting, so be it. I doubt anyone in my shoes could ignore deception either when it's right in front of them. My ability has been a handicap in every relationship I've ever had, friendship or romantic. Inauthenticity: it's a plague. A plague even I suffer from.

And now I've met Gabriel... I can't imagine him telling me he doesn't care what movie we watch when he really does. I am falling like a rock into a well that has nothing but the waters of Gabe in it. Every daydream stages the soothing sincerity of his words: playful, obnoxious, kind, annoying, desirous, frustrating, intelligent. All his words are different, yet exactly the same because they're candid. I want to be near him so badly.

The thought sends my heart soaring until my body feels overcome with the intensity of my feelings. I hold up a hand and notice it's shaking.

And then I see the glove that covers it.

***

I wake up later to knocking at my door. I rub my eyes, feeling mentally lighter after a bit of unconscious down-time.

"Yeah?" I yell at the door. I look at the clock. I've been sleeping a couple of hours and I didn't have a single bad dream. That's a relief.

"Wendy?" says Kaylen, poking her head around the door. "I'm sorry, did I wake you?" She comes fully into the room.

"It's okay. I'll be awake all night if I sleep any longer." I sit up.

"I thought you might be hungry," she says. "They serve dinner around here right at six. I couldn't remember if I told you that, so I came to get you."

Kaylen stands in front of the door with her hands behind her back and a smile on her face. She's a lot prettier than I first thought. Her dark hair is pulled back in a low ponytail that falls over her right shoulder in a glossy wave, and her eyes are dark yet still soft and kind because they're so large and open. She reminds me of a porcelain doll, her cheeks slightly rosy and her skin smooth and youthful. I can't believe I didn't notice her beauty before, or that I thought she was shallow when I first met her.

"Yeah, I *am* hungry. Thank goodness you woke me up. Just let me test my glucose first." I pull my test kit from the nightstand.

Kaylen waits patiently while I stick myself and prepare an insulin injection.

"How often do you have to do that?" she asks.

I shrug. "It varies, depending on how I feel, my activity, and what I've eaten."

"That's awful. Death-touch and diabetes. You have an allergy, too?"

I nod. "Tree nuts. But my diabetes actually isn't that bad. I'm kind of lucky because I've never had much problem keeping it under control. My doctor is always amazed. And I only have to see him every six months or so…"

"Regardless, you're like the hypno-touch trifecta. Louise probably threw herself a party when she found *you*," Kaylen says. "Okay, well c'mon or we'll only get the leftovers."

That's the second time today that Kaylen has mentioned what an ideal subject I am for Louise to study. I can't decide if I should explore that… Kaylen has obviously been stuck in this place for a long time, so her perception is probably on the negative side. That won't help me right now.

"Did you just get back from riding?" I ask, standing up and noticing her outfit has changed since the last time I saw her. She wears fitted jeans and sturdy boots, both coated with a layer of dust. She smells like sweat and leather.

"Yep," she replies. "Just let me know when you want to come. I go almost every day."

I walk silently down the hall next to her, and to my surprise, I'm clear-headed enough to make a decision about Gabe. Actually, I *knew* what the right decision was before. But I now feel like I might be able to follow through. Gabe is a no-go. Definitely not until I've got my lethal skin under control. Once I've accomplished that, if he's still around, I can pursue it. And oh do I want to pursue it. I thought a tank top in my closet would be a good reminder to stay focused… Now I have the possibility of a Latin dream-boat to encourage me to fight for a normal life with even more vigor.

He seems really smart, so I'll spell it out. And he'll accept it because it makes sense, and he'll stop being so maddeningly charming. He'll leave things be and let me get to work on my problem—it's the only chance we have of ever being together.

I hang back near the doorway of the kitchen to avoid the crowd, leaning against the wall, waiting for everyone to serve themselves and find a seat. I automatically spot Gabe across the room talking with Will about energy transference, thermodynamic bodies, and latent energy; they're discussing Will's ability to heat and cool water.

Gabe catches my eye, sending my pulse into overdrive. He grins, winks, and then turns back to Will. I work meticulously to get my heart rate under control, smelling the dinner and testing whether I can name all the ingredients.

I close my eyes.

Chicken baked with chili powder, cinnamon, and lemon. Interesting...

Salad with spinach leaves… cranberries… oranges? No. Mandarin oranges? Or is that the dressing?

Something like fresh pine needles.

That's not dinner. Apparently my nose has already programmed itself to seek him out. I bite my tongue hard instead of kicking the wall, which is what I *want* to do.

Once the rush has dispersed I push off the wall, going to the counter to serve myself.

"Over here!" Kaylen says, having already gotten a plate. She sits at the end of the same table we sat at during lunch, and the two chairs across from her are vacant. She holds up a plate she's already filled for me and sets it down across from her.

"How did you end up so nice, Kaylen?" I ask, pulling the chair back and sitting down.

Kaylen shrugs meekly.

After a couple of minutes, Louise materializes next to me.

"Mind if I join you?" she asks.

"Suit yourself," I reply, spearing a forkful of salad into my mouth. I grimace at the preservative taste in the dressing but chew and swallow anyway. Chemicals in processed food are stronger than I remember. Since my transformation I've had a harder time ignoring them—which is what I used to do. I could never afford to be *that* picky.

Kaylen's face hardens, and her thoughts turn icy, but she distracts herself with a mouthful of potatoes.

Louise sits in the empty buffer chair to my right and leans forward, elbows propped on the table. "I am so looking forward to our appointment this evening. I can hardly contain myself." Her breathy voice and relaxed demeanor confuse me. She sure looks, sounds, and feels like she's having *no* trouble containing herself.

"Yeah," I say, smiling. "I hope I don't kill you. That'd be a shame."

I glance at her in my peripheral vision to see if I had any unnerving effect on her. I didn't.

"Me too," she replies wistfully. "But I'll be incredibly surprised if that happens," she adds matter-of-factly.

Incredibly surprised? Is she trying to be funny? I wonder if I simply haven't caught onto her brand of humor.

"You won't have a chance to be surprised if it happens," I point out.

No reaction. She stares at the wall past Kaylen; right now she seems a lot more excited about that wall than our meeting tonight. Now I wonder if she's blind and no one has told me. She sure stares at things a lot that have nothing to do with who she's talking to.

At the other end of the table, Gabe hops up from his spot and comes over to us. He sits down next to Kaylen and looks at Louise. I have to spend a few moments adjusting to the force of his presence.

"I know that look," he says to Louise. "What's cooking up there? Having a hunch again, Louise?" He glances at me and offers a secret smile.

Unfortunately, I can hear the effect our closeness is having on his heart patterns. Mine are having the same reaction.

He leans forward, mirroring Louise's body language while I battle the crowded climate created by the three people now in my range. I manage it more quickly than I expected. Maybe because I've felt them all before individually for extended time periods—they each have their own current.

I allow Gabe an audience. He has an agenda and whatever it is he's after, he expects to get it.

Louise looks at him with a penetrating but brief gaze. "I do not have *hunches*. Energy practitioners have *perceptions*. They operate on a higher plane."

Louise, who is definitely entertained, also expects something.

"Potato, potahto," he says. "Come on now, you know what I'm talking about. You're letting Wendy get a hold of your energy with hers. You aren't worried that in that heightened state, she'll soak up your life force instead of replenishing it? Sounds like quite a risk. What would we do without you if something happened?"

Louise lifts her head, letting her hands drift to the table gracefully. "You are such a charmer, Gabe. I suppose you have an alternative? Who have you conned into agreeing with that plan of their own volition, I wonder?" An amused smile plays on her lips. I can tell she knows *exactly* who he's going to suggest.

I lean in, drinking in Gabe's waves of thrilling anticipation, and only when he spares me a glance of brazen excitement do I think I get it. I catch my breath.

Gabe looks at Louise again and snorts. "Don't be ridiculous. I don't know whether to be more offended for myself that you doubt my moxie or for the individuals in this room who you think would allow themselves to be 'conned' as you so quaintly put it."

I want to laugh. *Moxie? Who even uses that word?* My humor doesn't last long though, and a knot of dread pulls my stomach inward even in the face of Gabe's thrilled expectation.

Louise chuckles and a half-grin forms on her face as she looks away from Gabe. She finds another wall of the room that's more engrossing. "I suppose I should have known," she breathes. "You're ever the inquisitive one. Don't sell yourself short. We need you as much as we need me, the anomaly that you are. What, my dear, would we do without you?"

"No!" I nearly shout as my suspicions are confirmed. "What are you thinking? You just said yourself it was stupid and risky. Why would you volunteer? I won't do it," I sputter.

My resolve to tell Gabe to back off sure hasn't lasted long, and I regret my words as soon as they leave my lips.

Louise and Gabe look at me at the same time, stunned by my outburst. And then, while sending as much warmth my way as he can summon, Gabe says quietly, "Louise is the best there is, Wendy. She will be able to guide you and make sure you don't make a mistake. She can tell the moment you start moving energy. I'll be perfectly fine. I wouldn't have volunteered if I didn't think so."

I cross my arms and sit back in my chair, biting back further protest. "Fine," I say. I'm determined to keep my cool and remain objective if it kills me. Even if it kills *him,* apparently.

"Well then!" Gabe says, rubbing his hands together expectantly. "That's settled! When's the party? I need to get my affairs in order."

I roll my eyes. "Don't forget to pick out your casket and make your final requests."

Gabe just grins delightedly as he tilts his head. In an instant the heat of sensuality pulses a steady beat through me. It feels like he's pulled me to him evocatively, as if the warmth of his breath is at my neck at this very moment. Then his thoughts strut lithely like a suggestive rhumba and I instantaneously want nothing but to bend to his rhythm as he leads me through gyrations and pivots.

The power of it takes me completely by surprise and I inhale sharply before holding my breath against the inertia of his ardor. When he finally releases me, I grip the table leg to steady myself as if I really *had* just danced a breathtakingly hot number with him and have fallen into a chair to recover. I look away, perturbed by his effect on me. I can't believe he's figured out how to manipulate me with my own ability. *Who would think to do that so quickly?*

"I have an appointment with Gina after dinner, but then we'll get started. Eight o'clock," says Louise, rising fluidly.

The room has slowly emptied except for Chloe and Marcus who sit far away at the other table.

"She's such a snake," Kaylen hisses, glaring at the doorway through which Louise disappeared. "That woman could get a widow to hand over her only child."

"Tsk, tsk, Kaylee," Gabe admonishes. "We both went into that with an agenda. *I* won't be trifled with, and she knows it. She also knows I like to be in on the action, so she made a correct assumption about my interest. That's why she brought it up."

Gabe looks pleased with himself. Then he turns to me. I realize I'm frowning.

"It will be all right, Wendy. She really does know what she's doing. I'll be in good hands." Then he laughs at his unintentional joke.

"So what did she mean, 'anomaly that you are'?" I ask, changing the subject. "Like more of an anomaly than everything else about this place?"

"I have a natural-born ability," he replies. "And despite having no health concerns, no allergies or otherwise, Louise was able to manifest a new ability in me. It was also done sans-hypnosis. I suppose you'd call it hypno-touch a la carte... or plain old energy touch. Which is fortunate. I don't take well to hypnosis."

"Oh, there's a surprise," I say, rolling my eyes.

Gabe *looks* affronted, but he *feels* amused. "Excuse me? And why isn't it?"

"You probably make jokes the whole time and won't shut up, telling the hypnotist what a 'jolly fine day it is' and how you're 'pleased to be of service' to them. Or something like that."

Gabe laughs, a bellowing laugh, and Kaylen follows suit.

"You're an absolute pleasure, Wendy, mi encantadora doncella," he says.

"It's rude to speak to people in a language they don't understand," I say.

"And it's rude to examine people's thoughts without their permission," he retorts.

"Well, she can't help that," Kaylen offers.

"And I can't help that she doesn't speak Spanish," he says, eyes on me. "Perhaps she'll teach me her language, and I'll teach her mine."

I worry where this is headed. His look is way too probing, and I am way too engaged in our banter. I'm still curious about his talents, though, so I decide that's a lighter topic of conversation. "You have two abilities?"

"I suppose it depends on how you look at it. They're mental abilities that enhance each other."

I expect him to expound a bit more, but he doesn't. "So are you going to tell me what they are?" I ask impatiently.

He looks at me quizzically. "Why would I do that? I have to keep you interested."

When I don't counter, he rises from his chair. "Well, lots to do before our date! Setting affairs in order reminds me I ought to call my mother and offer my final goodbyes." He chuckles and strolls from the room whistling.

I turn to Kaylen, conspiratorial. "So? What can he do?"

Kaylen giggles but doesn't answer my question. "He is so into you," she says instead.

I sigh. "Yeah, I know."

Kaylen gives me an expectant look, but when I don't answer, she says, "You don't like him?"

I consider the best response. "Does it matter? There's no future there. I have a lot bigger issues to worry about before I can even *think* about having a relationship with someone. It'd be like a romance in prison," I say, disgusted with fate's ugly sense of humor.

Kaylen softens with empathy. But then she says, "Well maybe so. But who knows? Maybe he's just what you need. You can't just be miserable the whole time, and Gabe is very fun. If he's that interested in you, I doubt you'll be able to ignore him. He's annoyingly persistent when he wants something."

"We'll see about that."

Kaylen laughs, leans back in her chair and crosses her arms. "It's going to be fun to see who wins *this* battle."

"Thanks for your confidence," I grumble.

"Sorry, I just know what Gabe's capable of. A few weeks ago, he started putting up a stink about the language in Pneumatikon's legal forms. He said they were meant to be deliberately deceiving, and it wasn't ethical to use them. Dina was a lawyer. She actually wrote the things, and the two of them would go at it all the time. She'd get all pissed off that he was criticizing her legalese, and he'd just spout off all kinds of court cases he'd read about that involved people getting sued for not having clear forms."

Kaylen grins as she remembers. "He said they might as well have been written in Russian, and to make his point he started *speaking* in Russian. To *everyone. All* the time. You'd ask him, 'Hey, Gabe, will you switch dinner duty with me?' and you wouldn't understand a word of his answer. It drove everyone crazy! He even wrote out the meal menu in Russian. I don't think he spoke a word of English for two weeks. Dina told him if he didn't stop he was going to get kicked off the compound. So he went to Louise and said if they kicked him out, he'd blab anything he wanted to about their research. And then he gave her his legal defense, which he'd written up himself. Supposedly it was so complicated that Louise didn't understand it so she gave it to Dina. Dina read it and from what I heard, she was furious, but she changed her forms after that—Guess he knew what he was talking about. Everyone thought Dina was pretty nasty. So it was nice to see her get knocked down a notch."

"Wow," I say, amazed. I would love to have witnessed that. "He speaks Russian?"

"Oh yeah. And a lot of other languages, too, I think."

"Geez," I say, definitely concerned now. I really need to know what his abilities are that make him so... intense. "So you're not going to tell me what he can do?"

"No way," she says. "For one thing, I don't want to get in between Gabe and what he wants. And for another, he's a really nice guy. You like him, and I think you need to at least give him a chance."

She sees my sullen look and holds her hands up in defense. "I'm out of it. Hey, you wanna help me with my chemistry homework instead? I went riding today instead of working on it." She wrinkles her nose. "I hate chemistry."

"I barely remember that stuff. That's Ezra's thing." I frown, reminded of how distant Ezra is right now.

"He's smart then?" asks Kaylen.

"He's the smartest person I know. He might be your age, but he's got a brain like a doctoral student. He would be able to help you with your chemistry with half his brain tied behind his back."

I smile at the memory of him working on a math problem: eyebrows crinkled together, leaning over the paper, his bottom lip in his teeth, his hand moving a pencil erratically across the page. Ezra is usually the one helping *me* with my homework.

"Wow," says Kaylen, thoughtfully. "Sounds like Faye—she was pretty brilliant too. But of course she wasn't born that way. Sounds like you and your brother are pretty rare."

"What do you mean?"

"Well you both have natural-born abilities, don't you? That's practically unheard of as far as this place is concerned."

"I wouldn't call him supernaturally smart. But what about Gabe?"

"Okay. Well in *my* experience, you and Gabe are the only ones who have had natural-born abilities. I guess there could have been more before this place, but two people in the *years* I've been around here makes natural abilities seem pretty scarce."

"Really?" I say. The numbers make me uncomfortable, too. Louise also said natural abilities were rare, but that sounds more like unheard of.

"Yeah. I'm surprised Louise didn't ask you to have your brother come here also. I'd have thought she'd be all over that. She was pretty ecstatic about having Gabe to dissect. She's always trying to figure out what's different about his life force."

"She is *not* getting her hands on Ezra."

"Yeah, well look out. She'll probably use you to get to him. She's relentless. She got you, didn't she?"

"She did *not* get me. I *chose* to be here," I say, even though it's only partly true.

"Uh huh. That's what she *wants* you to think."

17

The sun settles behind the trees, shooting hazy beams through pine needles and casting intricate straw patterns on the ground. I skirt leisurely around Kaylen's flower beds and toward the path that leads to the research building to meet with Louise for our appointment tonight. Admiring the fleeting illusions that precede dusk, like the way the yellowed light makes the tiny facets of each rock look like gold flecks, I'm caught up once more in the secret seduction of nature. I haven't been outside of greater Los Angeles in years. And I've been too busy or too caught up in myself to notice the things around me. My improved eyesight does help though.

The peacefulness of my surroundings amps up my senses to full attention. That's when I hear unexpected running footfalls. Jolted instinctively by the sound, I step off the path and into the trees, waiting.

The moment I spot Gabriel in sweat pants and a t-shirt with headphones in his ears, I feel foolish for my alarm. I can even hear his music: some kind of dated rock and roll. I watch him, knowing he can't possibly see me in the swiftly-departing light from this distance. He breathes heavily and sweat beads along his arms and forehead, glistening in his dark hair.

I sigh audibly. I think I could look at him all day.

His cologne is usually the first thing I detect when he's near, but his exertion brings out his human smell which is rich and poignant. This intrinsic scent reminds me of parched earth, begging for water.

He's moving quickly, getting close, so I step out from the trees and continue walking, expecting he'll catch up.

"What a lovely vision to come upon on a night such as this. I wonder if it speaks?" he says from much farther away than human ears would normally discern. I wonder how he knows I can hear him. Kaylen gave the impression that Randy didn't share all of my abilities.

I can't help myself; I smile and turn.

"Why do you go by Gabe?" I ask when he nears my side. "Is it short for Gabriel? Because I knew a boy in high school named Gabe with long stringy hair and a repulsive adolescent goatee. I think of him every time I say your name."

My words take him by surprise. He slows to a walk. "You don't like my name?" he asks, disappointed.

"I really like the name Gabriel, actually. I just don't like Gabe." I pause momentarily, thinking. "I could call you Gabby if you want." I chuckle to myself. "You do like to talk a lot."

He wrinkles his nose. "Please, no. If you'd rather, call me Gabriel. It *is* my given name, and I'm sure my mother would appreciate it. She tried calling me that for most of my childhood. But even she calls me Gabe now most of the time."

We continue walking. His questions bounce steadily in my head and it frustrates me that I can't gratify him; my inhibitions won't allow it. I wish I could link my mind with his and let him wander around, satisfying all those questions. Maybe then, after figuring me out, he'd understand why I can't give him what he seems to want. Instead, I'm stuck with my own logic and fears that can't reconcile with my heart, and words inadequate to the task of explaining to him what I know I need to. I'm immobilized, especially in the face of his pining for me.

"Is this because I won't call you Wen?" he asks after a while.

"No... But everyone calls me Wen in the end."

"Do you *like* Wen better?"

"No," I reply, knowing this is going to generate a whole line of questioning from him.

"Then why did you want me to call you that?" he asks, as expected.

"I don't know why I told you that. I don't know you from Adam. It just popped out."

He's silent as he ponders my answer. He moves in and out of ideas, finally settling on one. "I noticed your brother calls you Wen, and you two seem close, so it makes sense. How is he?"

I may have known he was going to ask me a question, but this line is unexpected. Random even. And how does Ezra calling me Wen make sense of anything?

"He was fine when I said goodbye to him this morning."

"No, I meant how's he doing with all of *this*—with you coming here?"

"Oh, he doesn't like it. But I think he's still getting a kick out of his big sister being at a superhero camp." I smile. "Ezra is totally into comic books."

"Can't say I've ever read one. But my brother did, so I'm familiar with the parallel."

"Well what *do* you read? Technical manuals? Legal briefs? Obscure dictionaries?"

He grins. "Certainly all of the above at one point or another. But mostly anything of a scientific or philosophical nature."

"So you have a brother?"

"Yes, a younger one. No other siblings." He smiles in the middle of a memory. "Mike and I are quite close."

"Two boys? Oh man, is he anything like you?"

"In some ways. Why? Thinking of trading me in already, are you?" he teases—although I pick up a hint of worry behind it.

"I didn't know I had you in the first place," I say, uncomfortable with how we've moved back to a heavy topic. "What I meant was if he's anything like you, your mother must have had her work cut out for her."

"My mother managed just fine, although I don't think she's ever really gotten me like you seem to have in such a short time."

"You give me too much credit. I only get people because of my talent. Reading you is as easy as reading anyone else." *That's* a lie. Gabriel is an anomaly.

"So I'm not special then, as far as you're concerned?" he wonders, agitated by my reply.

I know what he's asking, but I'm not going there. It's like he's sniffing out the contents of my heart, little by little. Every time I try to throw him off the scent, he circles back to it. "Oh you're special all right. You bring new meaning to the word authentic. So tell me, just how many people have you offended with your tenacious truth-telling?"

He smiles appreciatively, gleefully triumphant for a reason I can't figure out. "Let me take a count. But first, I have to know, have I offended *you* by speaking my mind?"

"No," I reply. *A thousand times, no.* I almost wish he *had* offended me. Then I would have a good reason to stop being madly in love with him.

"As I suspected. Well then," he says, as if completing a tedious count, "the answer is everyone but one person. Might I say that I'm in love with my thoughts being so transparent to another human being?"

My heart surges upward in my chest, elated. I lock my jaw in place to hold it down, struggling to ignore my burgeoning of happiness at his words. I look into the shadows of the forest as I try to inhale something else to clear my head of *him*. But he's in there like no one else ever has been: his affection, his adoration, his unrelenting pursuit. The depth of him so easily partners the depth of *me*. We've reached the research building, and we stop at the door. I will my heart to slow down, but it won't listen.

Gabriel reaches out and pulls my gloved hand from where I've tucked it across my chest. He's so close, only a couple feet from my face. My heart lurches in fear, but mostly with electricity. His heartbeat keeps pace with my own; their lub-dub beating out a poetic waltz. His tenderness glides through my thoughts as if it belongs there, twirling me around with care, pulling me in and leading me across the proverbial floor with the carriage of veneration. It's invigorating, like having some part of me I never knew existed brought to life and displayed for all the world to see.

"I don't call you Wen because Wendy is a beautiful name and shouldn't be shortened for convenience's or familiarity's sake," Gabriel says, pausing in our steps to just hold me with his eyes. "I don't want to be your brother."

The air between us is so charged it feels viscous. Everything he says douses me in warm water and I just want to soak in his fearless words. How does he do it? How does he put his whole self out there without fearing rejection even a little?

For the briefest moment I clutch his hand more firmly to pull myself nearer, but the sensation of my glove reminds me of why I'm here. The moment is twisted into an ugly eye-opening reality:

This is the closest we can ever come to each other.

The fever of the moment breaks and I shudder with the chill. I can't handle this constant disappointment. It's more than either of us should have to endure. And then it will end, leaving me desolate. Whatever he envisions, it's delusional.

I step back, pulling my hand from his grip.

"This will never work, Gabe." I heave in a breath to gather up what I need to say. "I have to focus now so I can get back to my brother. I can't begin to guess how long it will take... longer than either of us will have the patience for, I'm sure. I don't want to fight your emotions in my head all the time, so please stop manipulating me with them. Just let this go."

Gabriel's leaps of rapture lose air instantly, faltering as he stumbles, taken completely off-guard by my rejection. He inhales heavily, struggling through the hurt and frustration.

I back away to escape his pain; I already have my own to deal with and I'm on the verge of tears.

"Louise is probably waiting for us," I say evenly, focusing on making my heart work again so I can push my legs up the stairs.

Gabriel's footsteps follow me after another moment, and we ascend the stairs in silence. He moves past me wordlessly to take the lead—I don't know where Louise's office is. I hang back to keep him out of my range for as long as possible.

Louise gives me a sublime smile when we enter the room. "There you are. Let's get started."

She gives Gabriel a once-over. "Glad to see you prepared."

Anticipating my confusion, he explains, without looking at me, "Exercise releases endorphins. They are my pseudo-hypnosis; they help me achieve the necessary hyper-alert state."

He hops up on a table that appears to be some kind of a raised futon cushion. It's more plush than the one that Dina used with me.

"We'll give him a moment to go into meditation," Louise says.

As soon as I see him close his eyes I realize my mistake. Why did I choose to break the news to him right before our hypno-touch session? I'm already struggling to focus on what I have to do, but in a few minutes I'll have to be close to him, perhaps closer than I've ever been before. I'll have to touch his energy when all I want is to be as far away from him as possible. Not only that, but I'll feel him the entire time. If I could see any way to bow out of this gracefully, I would.

I sigh and allow my eyes to rest on Gabriel who is in the middle of timing his breathing. He starts with deliberate, slow breaths and gradually relaxes them into a more regular and even pace. It takes him a long five minutes, during which time I mirror my breaths with his in an attempt to relieve my agitation. How am I going to be able to focus with him this close? I was so rash and stupid. I should have just let our encounter end how it would have ended and dealt with him *afterward*.

Satisfied with Gabriel's meditation, Louise walks to the other side of his body. "Now you mirror me on your side. The hand motions are hardly difficult, but we need to get you energy aware. That's the hard part."

Tentatively, I step forward until I stand over him. I avoid looking at his face, though I want to.

"We start at the chest. Always," Louise instructs, placing her hands palm-side down, about four inches above his body.

Gabriel's chest is lean and subtly muscular. The scent of his musky perspiration invades my nose... *Ugh. This is going to be impossible.*

I stretch out my hands, but fear seizes the movement. *Why am I doing this? I could kill him!* My emotional instability will never allow me to concentrate on the subtleties of detecting a life force. And I won't be able to tell if anything goes wrong.

"I won't let anything happen," says Louise, observing my hesitation. "I'm adept at sensing the movement of energy."

"My gloves?" I ask. *Please, don't tell me I have to take them off.*

Louise smiles in understanding. "You can keep them on. Energy touch doesn't require contact. It's not really a tactile sense—it's more like a perception."

Relieved, I reach my hands out slowly, bringing them closer to Gabriel's chest. Unsure of what's supposed to happen next, I look over at Louise. She has her eyes closed.

I close mine, trying not to move my hands. Louise inhales. "Your imagination will help you if you'll allow it. Imagine dipping your hands in a rushing creek. What would that feel like?"

"C-can you just give me a minute?" I stutter, unable to control my thoughts enough to picture a creek.

Louise's silence answers the question, and I maintain my stance with my hands resting over Gabriel's chest, my eyes closed. I reach out for calm, but find that I can grab on to Louise's peaceful demeanor. Even Gabriel, I notice, has managed to exude tranquility despite my dismissal only a few minutes ago. I embrace their calm, letting the gentle waves wash over me to dissolve my agitation. I sigh.

I picture putting my hands in the creek, as Louise instructed.

"Soothing and cold," I answer.

"Yes, but that describes any body of water. What if the water is moving? Rushing by quickly? Describe that sensation."

I think, experiencing it in my head but wondering how I would describe it. "Like a massage. Not like a hand rub, more like... pressure. Like brushing your hand against silk. Less friction than a massage."

"Yes! Very good. Now I want you to imagine feeling that against your hands, but the water is warm. In fact, it's precisely the same temperature as your skin. You pause, letting your hands go limp in the water, allowing it to pass through your slack fingers."

Silently, I imagine that. It makes me kind of sleepy, but I'm still acutely aware of Gabriel's body, only inches from my hands, and the alertness and relaxation begin to reside at the same time within me, interweaving in the same space.

After several silent minutes, the sensory image of the water becomes stronger. In fact, it feels so real that I open my eyes to check, half expecting to see my hands in a creek. Instead, a light blinds me. I'm so shocked, so terrified this is the visual manifestation of my ability and I'm killing Gabriel that I gasp, snatch my hands away, and stumble backward. The light immediately disappears and Gabriel's body emerges from the brilliance, inert on the cushion in front of me. "Gabe!" I exclaim fearfully. "Are you okay?"

Relief floods me when I see his eyes open. They lock onto mine instantly.

"Wendy?" he says, concern drawing his eyebrows together while my chest inflates with his eagerness.

I look at Louise. She stares, not at my face, but down at my hands, a gleam in her eye. A *fiery* gleam. I half expect to see flames blazing behind her pupils.

"You felt it?" she says, looking into my face now. The question seems rhetorical until she continues, "The flow like water, the life force—you felt it?"

I nod.

If Louise was ablaze before, she now looks like she might hop right out of her skin. I retreat automatically from her fervor until I feel the wall behind me.

At that moment, Randy appears in my peripheral vision. Louise looks over at her and then reels in her zeal. She straightens and puts her hands behind her back, looking as disconnected and otherworldly as I'm used to seeing her. The dexterity she has with her emotions is just plain freaky, and if my head weren't elsewhere, I'd spend more time thinking about it. There are other things more awesome at this moment—namely the blinding light I just saw that I intuitively know was a life force. I wonder how I know that, but no answer comes.

"Absolutely astounding," says Louise in her usual breathy, detached voice. "And on the first try. Have we ever, Randy—? No, I'm certain we haven't. No one has ever felt it on the first try."

Louise only just notices my distance and open-mouthed shock. "Don't be alarmed, Dear. Most people are taken by surprise when they first feel it. And you did so incredibly quickly! Goodness. You must be exhausted. Gabe, be a dear and take her back to the lodge, would you?"

Gabriel, who has been watching us silently and with interest, moves to my side quickly, takes my hand, and looks intently into my eyes, pleading, willing me to come with him.

I allow him to lead me toward the door, too bewildered to argue.

18

Gabriel all but carries me down the stairs. His feet move too quickly for me to pull my wrist away—he only grips it harder. Once we burst outside, I yank away from him.

"What are you doing?" I hiss, exasperated.

"Shhh!" he whispers. "Do you hear anyone out here? Listen!"

I glare at him but obey, letting my ears stretch out to meet the encroaching forest. Crickets put up quite a racket, but I hear no sounds of human life other than our own. Gabriel's heart, I notice, beats fearfully. His worry puts me on edge.

I shake my head. "No one. Now will you tell me why you dragged me down the stairs?"

Gabriel walks to the edge of the woods out of the beam of the lights illuminating the path. He beckons me to follow him, and I cross my arms, trailing him cautiously into the darkness, hoping this isn't another ploy to get me to fall for him. I already have. I don't require any refreshers.

"You saw a light, didn't you?" he asks in a low voice.

I look at him through narrowed eyes. How does he know there *was* something to see? Even Louise didn't catch that. And Gabriel knows exactly *what* I saw? What's he been keeping from me, and is it just him, or is everyone withholding information? He must have telepathic abilities. There's no other explanation for his acute perception of my thoughts all day long. This proves it.

I'm not giving anything away anymore. I'm tired of being tricked. Lied to. And Louise doesn't want to cure me at all. She wants to *use* me; I could see that in her eyes. I'm not here to be used. I'm here to get my life back to normal.

My problem with Gabriel has just solved itself. I should thank him for making this easier than I expected.

"I'm done talking to you, Gabe." I turn on my heel and start walking down the path.

His footsteps don't follow for almost a minute. In that short time I'm both sad and gratified: sad because he doesn't care enough to follow, gratified because he is going to let me go without making it harder on me. Sadness wins. I cry silently.

When I do hear his footsteps, they're running. He literally sprints past me and throws his body in front of me, spreading his legs and crossing his arms, just daring me to get past him.

"Move," I order, stepping to the side. He changes his position to block me and I have to stop, afraid of harming him in his concerted efforts to bar me.

"You're going to stop telling me what to do," he says firmly. "And you're going to stop drawing your own conclusions."

I look down at the ground, willing my ears to stop working so he won't shake my resolve.

"Will you look at me!?" Gabriel nearly shouts.

I refuse.

He sighs. "Por favor, es justo," he pleads softly. "Please, it's only fair. I know you can feel what I feel. I need to at least *see* what *you* feel."

He's right; it's not fair. But it's not my fault either. He's standing only a few feet away, and the hurt he's suffering makes my own eyes sting.

I look up, clenching my fists at my sides like I can hold the tears at bay that way. It's working so far. "I don't owe you anything, Gabe. Can't you see what I'm trying to do? Why do you keep getting in my way? Why do you keep lying to me? Why does *everyone* keep lying to me?"

Gabriel thinks in uncharacteristic fits and starts. "You won't stop long enough to listen to me! You're just assuming things! I've not lied to you, not once, not about anything! Why are you acting like I already have when I *know* you can tell whether what I speak is truth?"

I close my eyes and a tear squeezes out. He's making this so hard. Why can't he just recognize what a dysfunctional relationship this would be and take the way out I'm offering him?

Give up, Gabriel. Please.

I temper my voice. "I've listened, and I've decided. This can't happen. I'm not interested. Whatever it is you're asking, the answer is no. Whatever you want to say, I don't want to hear it. Now please, move."

He reels in disbelief. Even in the silvery moonlight, I catch the blood moving to his face, invading his tiny capillaries. His heart picks up pace before he turns, spots a small rock on the ground, and kicks it toward the woods with all his might.

I take the opportunity to walk past him briskly, distancing myself as much as possible from the sharpness of his anger. With every foot that stretches behind me, the connection between us loosens, releasing its hold on me. I should be grateful, but of course, heartache doesn't care how practical or necessary the break was.

I must be fifty yards away, but I pause when I hear him speak to me quietly, "Don't tell them what you can see, Wendy. Please, if you can find a way to trust anything I've said, trust that. Esperaré por ti, mi amor. "

I know for sure he said it this time: mi amor. My love. I try to fling the words away from me, but my ailing heart grips them firmly. I have no strength to begrudge myself this small token, only the strength to move my legs away from here. I hear his footsteps move off the path and into the woods. I refuse to wonder what he's up to or when I'll see him again.

$\mathcal{E}$zra is on my mind when I wake up the next morning. It may be my heartbreak from last night, but I miss him more than ever and it's barely been a day. I test my glucose and then log onto the lodge Wi-Fi with my laptop computer so I can shoot him an email.

Ezra,

> The compound-issue spandex is actually way cooler than what you sent with me, although thank you for making sure I was prepared. Do you have any more tips on how to gain rapport with my teammates? I think not being able to participate in the secret handshake is hurting their trust in me. Anyway, I would take a picture of our team, (we call ourselves the Communal Cohorts), but our wise and fearless leader Louise thinks it expedient that we not reveal ourselves just yet. We're trying to uncover a secret government plot to experiment on handicapped people and we need to stay under the radar for now. I know you understand.

> I'll call you in a couple days, but meanwhile, be sure to protect my identity, just as we discussed. You know, as my brother, you may become a target in order to subdue me. Take care of yourself, Ezra, and be vigilant!

Wen

I read over the e-mail to be sure it complies with Randy's guidelines and chuckle as I click send. I bet Ezra's going to have a clever reply.

I wonder if Randy has any way of knowing whether people are following the rules in regard to communication. I don't suppose it matters. Not with their thorough patent law disclosures. And if Gabe had a hand in their making, I am *sure* they are iron-clad.

I sigh. *Gabriel.* Thoughts of our final words to each other kick up little cyclones of anxiety in my stomach. And a little bit of anticipation, which I smother with memories of his clenched jaw and inflamed eyes.

I don't want to look like I just had my heart squashed yesterday so I take a shower. I spend a little more time on my hair than usual, using a diffuser to dry it into soft, chestnut waves.

Donning a linen tunic in my favorite color—chartreuse—a twinge of happiness flutters within me. When I examine the origin, I'm sickened to realize that it has resulted from knowing that I look good. And the only reason I'm trying to look good is because of *him*.

Angrily, I start to take the shirt off, but then stop. It's just a shirt for goodness sake. I have three others just like it, but in different colors. Am I never going to wear them at all? Then I go to the bathroom for an elastic to put up my hair. I stop in the doorway. Should I cut off my hair just because I think it's pretty? I can look good without feeling guilty about it, can't I?

I decide that, as far as my hair goes, I'm safer with it down. The tunic has a lower neckline than the other shirts in my closet and presents greater chance of skin contact. My hair can make up the difference, at least a little.

I open the door only to realize I forgot my gloves. Spending so much time quibbling over my clothes and Gabriel and how he'll respond to them has made me forget this most basic precaution. I can't blame myself too much, though. When I was at home with Ezra this past week, I slept in my gloves because I was too afraid of touching him since we shared a room. Last night I decided that since I have my own room I can sleep without the gloves. I just have to form new habits. Glucose testing and glove checking will have to occur together.

When I start walking down the hall I realize the building is completely empty. No voices or footsteps or signs of life. When I reach the kitchen, I look at the time which says around 10 A.M. I guess I missed breakfast. After foraging for a few minutes, I jog to the research building where I think I'll find everyone.

Once I'm in front of the door, I hear Louise's voice from inside and upstairs, "I know this makes some of you uncomfortable, but I believe she's got a real talent, and without individuals to practice on, it will never fully develop. I'm asking for volunteers now, and I hope, as we prove to you skeptics out there that this is perfectly safe, all of you will choose to participate. I'm asking for your cooperation on this in the interest of your cause. Think about it, and get back to me. Enjoy your day off."

A bubbling of voices fills the room above as I examine Louise's words. Everything she said reveals that she only sees my ability as an opportunity for her own gain. She has no interest in curing or controlling it. My heart sinks in dismay; my trust seems to have, once again, been misplaced.

Chairs shift and footsteps fall in the stairwell. I decide to wait outside, leaning against the side of the building until most of the people have exited so that I don't have to maneuver my way through them.

I can't help listening for Gabriel's voice. It happens automatically.

"—don't think she'll concur," Gabriel says.

"I understand that, Gabe, but as of right now, you and Louise are the only subjects, and Louise needs to concentrate on instruction. You are just going to have to get past it. You have excellent control. I'm sure you can manage," Randy replies.

I guess Gabriel must be trying to get out of being my hypno-touch subject. I partly hope he succeeds, but it still stings.

People are about to come through the door, so I stop eavesdropping. Kaylen is the first one out and she spots me immediately.

"You're awake," she says, smiling.

"Yeah, I was making up for a semester of sleep deprivation, I guess," I reply. Actually, last night I didn't have any nightmares, which are the main reason I've been sleep deprived.

"I hope you don't mind, but I volunteered you for kitchen duty with me tomorrow night," she says, looking me over. "Cute shirt."

"Thanks," I say, self-conscious about my choice in apparel again. "Kitchen duty sounds fine," I agree, infusing my words with enthusiasm. Kaylen is possibly my only friend here.

"Great!" she says, smiling broadly.

The others file past us, offering various greetings. Jimmy stops briefly with his mouth open, considering asking me a question. But he decides against it, just says hello, and heads off with the group.

Louise follows last, and when she appears, Kaylen turns and leaves. Louise offers me a genial smile. "Nice to see you finally awake, Wendy. You had quite a busy day yesterday," she says conventionally as her long prairie skirt billows in the slight breeze.

"Yeah, so what's the plan from here?" I ask, even though I don't care what she wants right now. She just made it clear what *she* wants, and it's definitely not what *I* want.

"Well, Dear, as you can imagine, I am *so* pleased with your progress. I see no reason to delay allowing you to work on the others here alongside me. We may see results faster that way."

"Results for whom?" I challenge.

Louise regards me in the same unperturbed way I remember Letty's cat would when I'd come over. The tabby would lie on the back of the couch, twitching his tail as he people-watched, all the while with a self-satisfied expression—although I think *all* cats look that way. Just like a placid feline, Louise doesn't react to my bitterness in the slightest when she says, "For everyone involved, of course." She tilts her head at me. "Do you expect I shouldn't take advantage of the opportunity to understand your unusual ability?"

So she knows I was eavesdropping. "No, but I do question what your primary goal is in all of this. Would you, for example, cure me even if it meant I'd no longer have an ability to dissect?"

"My dear, if we learn how to reverse an ability, it would undoubtedly unlock the secret as to how abilities manifest in the first place. And that would benefit everyone. Our goals take the same path."

I don't miss that she didn't answer the question. And I don't think *she* missed that I caught that. What have I gotten myself into?

"Are you up for a session after lunch?" she asks. "I believe Randy has Gabe cornered. We can coordinate."

I look at her long and hard. "For now," I reply.

No reaction on her part other than to reply, "Have Randy collect me when you're ready to start."

I watch Louise's figure retreat. Her silver hair glistens in the sunlight at her back, making her look even more like some kind of mythical figure. Even though I think she's about as relatable as a whimsical phantom, and selfishly committed to her cause to boot, I wonder if I should tell her what I saw. She *does* know about life forces. If I'm right, and what I saw was a life force, this could make or break figuring out how to reverse my condition. But if Louise doesn't *want* that… I might be shooting myself in the foot by telling her. She may counter by lying to me again, and Louise's emotions never seem to reveal her true intentions. She's an enigma.

I sigh. I need to spend more time thinking about what seeing a life force means first. I was too anguished last night to invest my brain in it.

Randy and Gabriel push through the exit together.

"Wendy. You're finally up and about," Randy says. "Sundays are our day off, so you're free to take some leisure time."

I know Gabriel is watching me, but I don't look in his direction. And since he's in my emodar, I also have to exert all my effort to ignore his wounds, which are obviously still bleeding. "Ah, yeah... Louise wants to do a session this afternoon."

Randy raises her eyebrows apprehensively, glancing over at Gabriel who is looking at me. "Gabe?" she asks reluctantly when he doesn't readily offer anything. I grimace with her discomfort at being in between the two of us.

"You don't have to question *my* approbation," he says, looking squarely at me.

"It's not like I have a choice," I snap. "Everyone else is afraid I'll suck their soul out, including you, Randy."

Gabriel winces almost imperceptibly. His frustration throbs more insistently.

"Well, that's settled then," Randy blurts, her eyes flitting from me to Gabriel, and then back. "I'll meet the two of you here after lunch. Session room two, I think."

"Understood," Gabriel replies without sparing me another glance. He begins jogging lightly down the path.

Randy starts to retreat but I come up beside her. "Randy, has anyone ever been able to see a life force?"

She glances at me. "*See* a life force? Not that I know of. Why?"

"Just wondered." I shrug. "I just thought with all these talented people you've worked with, you might have had someone who could see life forces. Seems maybe someone like that could help me."

"Probably so," Randy says, amused. She thinks I'm naïve. "A person who could see life forces could probably help just about anyone. Life forces are the key to health. To spirituality. To death." Randy laughs. "Seeing life forces would change the world as we know it."

20

*N*eeding some time to think and process things, I decide against a session with Louise. I tell Randy I'm not feeling well during lunch and decide to spend the afternoon in my room.

I sit on the floor cross-legged as I try really hard to find a solid place in my head to organize my thoughts. But they remain tangled. And I keep fidgeting.

I go out for a quick jog instead and eventually end up in a secluded place behind the lodge. I sit on the cement, leaning against the building, but I don't like the log surface against my back. It's just not uniform enough and I also don't want to be in the shade. There are a couple of picnic tables back here that don't look like they've been used much, but I need the ground today.

Finding a spot right in the sun, I lie down with my knees bent. I love the warmth of concrete at my back and the sun on my face. The breeze has kicked up even more since this morning, and it tries to free my hair from beneath me.

I hold my gloved hands up. They look so normal and innocent; they can't possibly be capable of killing people.

After a night free from subconscious reminders of Dina's death, I feel more myself today than I have in over a week. And with it, I begin to flirt with disbelief. This moment is too normal for any part of my condition to be real. They've interpreted Dina's death wrongly. She died of cardiac arrest caused by some coincidental event. Derek fainted from the stress.

Without much effort, however, crippling memories wick the edges of my skepticism, soaking in until I cannot ignore them. I know what Dina and Derek felt. I felt it again when I was unconscious. And then whispers of it every night in my dreams. It was beyond words. No, I killed Dina. There is no other explanation that makes sense.

I clasp my hands over my stomach and groan in aggravation. I thought I had made the decision a week ago about coming here. And it had seemed such an automatic, easy answer. Louise made me this way. Louise knows how to put me back. But Louise *doesn't* know. Her motives are not mine. So is it possible that this is not where I should be?

If I go back out into the world, I truly believe I don't have hope of being able to hold a job, go to school, and take care of Ezra in my condition. It's just not safe. A week of trying to live normally proved that—I literally did not leave the apartment except to pick Ezra up from school. If I'd had to go to work for an entire *week* like this? No way I would have made it.

So after rounds of the same justification I began with when I was deciding whether or not to come here, I remind myself that it's only been a day. I need to stick it out and stop second-guessing my decisions. This is the place I need to be. At least as far as I know. I wouldn't know how to find anyone else who might be capable of helping me. You can't exactly Google 'cure my supernatural ability' and expect to get a legitimate hit.

But there has to be an answer, right?

What if there's not?

"Don't move," a voice whispers, directly next to my ear.

My eyes pop open in alarm at its closeness. I immediately see Gabriel's face suspended over mine.

"Oh, good," he says. "I was a little worried you had fainted or something." A parade of lively anticipation marches into my thoughts that doesn't belong to me.

"What are you doing, Gabe?" I demand, my jaw setting tightly, but I remain motionless on my back. His face is far too close.

My sharp words punish *me* just as surely as they punish *him*. His misery roils within me and I swallow back his pain.

"Making sure you don't run away," he says, a mere foot from my face. "So I can ask for a truce."

"What kind of truce?"

He sighs, not moving but looking somewhere beyond me. His nearness sends an involuntary thrill down my spine and the cells of my being feel drawn to him. I swallow in that moment that he's not looking at me. I have to inhale as well and I catch a big whiff of him. It's intoxicating.

He glances back to me, searching my eyes. I refuse to look back. "Friendship," he says. "I know why you rejected me. It has nothing to do with trust, and everything to do with misguided sacrificial altruism."

"I don't want to talk about this. I made my position clear." I search for a patch of blue sky in my line of sight to avoid his face. It looks like he's crouched down beside me, leaning over me so I can't get up to move away from him safely. But with the security of the concrete at my back, I'm just confident enough to keep him at bay. I'm also far less fearful of him being so close. I'm part of the earth beneath me right now, solid, immovable. Predictable.

"I know, I know," he replies. "I'm getting to my proposition, I promise. I just wanted *you* to know that *I* know."

"No you *don't* know," I seethe, glancing briefly at him. "If you knew *anything* that I was thinking, you wouldn't be holding me hostage right now."

A hollow gust of his misery cuts me like a frigid wind. I want to physically push him away. I hate that he's subjecting me to his injuries. Aren't I hurting enough without his to compound it? It's almost more than I can bear. I close my eyes, trying to dissolve into the ground.

He clears his throat deliberately, agitation blossoming from his bleeding heart. Geez... he even feels *negativity* stronger. The intensity of his pain physically hurts my chest. With my eyes closed I discern that the small space between his face and mine feels charged differently all of a sudden. Like two magnets meeting the wrong way. Our emotions resist each other, yet our skin yearns to be in contact, as if the simplest flip of the magnet will make the range too much to resist.

"I had to," he says. "You won't listen—but that's beside the point. Look, perhaps you can exculpate me from your accusations if I tell you that my questions about what you saw were merely based on a well-reasoned guess."

I open my eyes. "Bull."

"I'm not blind, woman. You were blinking like you'd just looked into the sun when I opened my eyes. What else would cause that but a very bright light?"

"Gabe, I hardly would have noticed that if *I* had been in your position, and my eyesight is beyond perfect. You're telling me the *very first* thing you looked at was my eyes? Don't you see how ridiculous that sounds?"

His heartache relaxes somewhat as he explains, "Yes, but your eyes are *always* the first thing I long to see. And yes, I understand your hang-up. But let me explain. The short version is that I had a theory. I've studied the idea of a soul and I'm convinced that the life force *is* the soul. Operating on that thesis, I have deduced that a soul should be visible, in some form or another. All branches of science agree with the idea that if there *is* such thing as a soul, it's made up of some kind of matter or energy. Those *are* the only two ultimate concepts discovered in the universe.

"I've studied physics, theology, philosophy... Plenty of sources believe the soul may very well be a form of light, not visible to the naked eye. I wasn't necessarily sold on that, but with your reaction, the idea fit. And evidently it's a light that's invisible to normal human vision."

I restrain the need to shake my head in amazement. He is obviously way out of my league in the smarts department.

"That's quite a leap," I reply skeptically. "I still don't understand why you would jump to the conclusion so quickly that I actually *saw* something, not just *felt* something."

Gabe's enthusiasm has grown so much that if our mutual heartache is still smarting, I can't tell. The conversation sends tingling thrills down my spine. And he's relieved beyond belief to be able to talk to me finally. And I can't be anything but happy to feel him so upbeat once more.

"I had a theory that you might be able to," he says, adjusting his position next to me, but not moving enough to allow me to get up. "Your incredible vision was the clue. I hypothesized that it might allow you to see things that are invisible to the rest of us, given the right circumstances."

His ability to make connections astounds me. I need him, I realize, to draw the conclusions I can't. I've been heavily leaning toward telling Louise what I saw because I need someone to translate it. But Gabriel has possibly even more insight than she would.

But you can't have him.

I sigh. Gabe looks down at me hopefully.

"Can you please stop endangering yourself now?" I say. "I'm not going to run away. And concrete *does* get uncomfortable after a while."

He smiles and sits back, but he doesn't really scoot away from me. I roll over a little to get up safely, sitting cross-legged on the concrete a few feet away from him. I exhale with relief that I'm no longer inches from killing him. Or maybe it's relief from the addictive tension between us that not only lingers but seems to have built even though I've rejected him multiple times.

"How do you know about my senses anyway?" I ask, trying to break up the electricity in the air.

"I read Randy's report."

"So does everyone here get to know the nitty-gritty of everyone else's abilities?"

"No."

I raise my eyebrows expectantly.

He shrugs like it's no big deal, but he spends a noticeable amount of time struggling with wanting to say something other than what eventually comes out of his mouth. "I know how to get what I want from Randy and Louise," he says. I almost tell him to spit out what he's really thinking because his distaste sits bitterly in my mouth.

Despite his malcontent, I can't help imagining just how Gabriel *can* worm his way into anyone's good graces with that incorrigible charm. I fight the smile that wants to form on my face as I reply, "I bet."

That was unfair.

Gabriel's heart melts a tiny bit. He squirms with unspoken words, but maintains his commitment to remain objective, at least on the outside. "Now, for my proposition."

I tense, and a frown turns the corners of my mouth down. There's only one other unaddressed topic, and it's the hardest one.

Gabriel closes his eyes, gathering resolve before opening them again. "I give you my word: I will exert every effort to restrain any manifestation of flirting or general romantic naughtiness. I will... even *try* to control my feelings around you, although I can't promise I'll succeed."

I frown, guilt-ridden over inflicting anything like *restraint* on Gabriel. It's not right. I like him *unrestrained.* But it's not something I can handle right now.

"Curtailing my thoughts and actions," he continues, wrinkling his nose, "does not come naturally to my character. It would be far easier to leave this place, with you in it, so that I wouldn't plague your efforts. But I cannot ignore that you are in need of help. I am here to offer it." He takes a laborious breath.

"Gabriel, I can't ask—" I begin.

He holds up a hand. "Wendy, if you would be so kind as to let me finish." And then he tilts his head a little at me and considers something as I close my mouth. I think he noticed I used his full name—the name I told him I liked. I can't decide if I regret doing that. It just popped out.

He works to not let my subtle show of affection excite him too much and instead settles back into discomfort at not being able to say what he really wants to. Then he continues, "If you won't let me do this simply because I want to help, perhaps you'll allow me to at least satisfy *some* part of my nature, which is an unquenchable interest in the unknown. Your case promises an agglomeration of new insights into the human soul. I ask that I be allowed to participate."

Why do I feel like I've just knocked the wind out of him, while at the same time having the fleeting sense that I've been hoodwinked? I should be elated that he has promised to do everything I need and nothing I don't. But the uneasiness of taking advantage of him fills me with familiar self-loathing. And knowing that I'm all but demanding Gabriel go against his nature just makes me ill. Knowing what I value about him, that is just so *wrong*. But then, nothing about the last two weeks has been right.

He's made it impossible to decline, however. I don't think taking anything from him is right, but he's claiming it's not a one-sided deal; I can give him something in return.

He's a manipulative genius.

"Accepted," I reply, defeated.

"Fantastic!" he exclaims. His exuberance feels good after so much constipated effort.

"One other thing," I say. "I have my own reasons, but why do you think I shouldn't trust Louise?"

"That's simple, but first let me preface my explanation. Whatever feelings you may or may not have for me, you should know that you *can* trust me. I have no designs to exploit you, and I will do everything in my power to help you reach your goals here." He relaxes finally. "I realized as soon as I witnessed your interaction with Randy after you woke up that you'd been deceived by Pneumatikon. And that was after I expressly pointed out the faulty nature of their disclosure forms." Gabriel shakes his head angrily.

"Everyone here that I know of had some inkling about what possible 'side-effects' they might experience as a result of hypno-touch, whether they believed it or not," he continues. "It looks like you had no idea. I can only guess that this was because they worried you might not participate if you knew. I can't say for sure. I feel badly that I inadvertently became a part of that deception. My initial decision was to leave, but I found myself too drawn to your—"

He struggles internally. I try to remove myself from it, but it's impossible. "Situation," he finishes, nearly gasping. "I won't allow them to deceive you again, at least not with my knowledge," he says more easily. "Which brings me to your question. My concern is what Louise might do if she knew what you saw. I haven't seen her that worked up since you first surfaced at Pneumatikon. Those are actually the only two times I've seen her that way. If she knew you could *see* a life force?" Gabriel shakes his head, a bit of apprehension burrowing into his thoughts. "No, it is definitely better that she doesn't know that. I had to get you out of there last night before you told her."

"You really think she would do that?" I ask, propping my elbow on my knee and putting my chin in my hand. "She doesn't seem… violent. Only weird and driven. Besides, I *can* defend myself which is probably the *only* benefit of this particular curse." I grimace as I look down at my free hand.

Gabriel turns solemn, changing positions and pulling his knees up. "Yes. Louise has been working at this for quite some time. It culminates her life's work. And I've been around her a lot longer than you have. I think in time you'll get with your ability more accurately what I mean, but her attitudes and behaviors are narcissistic. I don't believe she would ever allow the life and freedom of one person, namely you, to get in the way of her effort to uncover the mysteries of the life force. You may be able to handle yourself one-on-one, but if she wanted to hold you, she could figure it out."

"So why should I stay then?" I ask, uneasy with the idea that Louise is more than just a little underhanded.

"Because no one understands more about life forces than she does."

I frown. Well that's just not fair. How am I supposed to navigate that?

"Quite a sticky-wickett, isn't it?" Gabriel says, watching my expression.

I don't bother restraining my laughter. "Sticky-wickett? How do you come up with this stuff on the fly?"

"I have an excellent memory," Gabriel says dismissively, but I can tell he really likes making me laugh. "Now then, I'm grateful to discharge the previous unpleasant task from my to-do list and feel inclined to action. What would you say to a more private hypno-touch session so that you aren't caught off guard again when you're with Louise?"

The word 'private' makes me nervous, but I'm certain Gabriel will be true to his word. Furthermore, a private session is *exactly* what I need.

"You read my mind," I agree, trying not to be dismayed that he would consider me an 'unpleasant task.'

21

We stand at the base of a gently sloping hill. Large boulders litter the area prohibiting the trees from invading the space and offering an open view of the cloudless blue sky. I expected we'd perform the session in one of our private rooms at the lodge, but Gabriel insisted this was a better idea. He led me down one of the many unofficial trails that snake through the woods around the compound and then about fifty yards off of the trail into the thick of the forest.

"Will this suffice?" he asks, hopping up on a large, slightly uneven rock and extending his legs to lie on his back.

"It looks perfect," I reply as I approach him, thinking it's not the *rock* that looks perfect right now.

"Will you be able to reach your energy senses without help?" he asks, looking over at me. "Most people need prompting for a while before they can do it on their own."

"I'm not most people," I reply, remembering exactly what it felt like.

"You most certainly are not," Gabriel says, closing his eyes and adjusting his position slightly. He's still in my range—in-range for *him* anyway. I can tell he's daydreaming about something that's a bit sensual, the anticipation of which bounds higher and higher with every passing moment. It makes my face hot and I have to hold my hands behind my back to keep them still. But I can't help my breaths coming more quickly and adjusting my feet as his fantasy carries me along. I can't find the will to move farther away and out of range.

Maybe be hears my heavy breathing or the gravel shifting under my feet, but he opens his eyes and looks at me. He notes the distance between us—way over five feet—and speculates for a moment before drawing a conclusion. But it's not the right one. "Are you all right?" he asks. "I honestly believe you can't have an effect unless you're touching a person. It really should be fine."

"Um..." I say, unsure of how to broach this problem. Obviously Gabriel agreed to watch his thoughts around me, but he likely based that on the expectation that my range for him is the same as it is for everyone else—he *did* read my file after all. I would just ignore it, but I don't think I can handle it if *this* is what he's going to be thinking when he's around me.

He realizes he mistranslated my expression. "What is it?" he asks.

"I think I need to tell you something," I say uncomfortably, but there's no way around it.

"What?" he asks, getting excited for no other reason than he can't wait for me to say whatever it is I'm thinking. He's like a kid. I think Gabriel *loves* surprises. I think he loves learning new things simply *because* they're new.

I back up until he falls just out of range to demonstrate the distance. "Well… I have no idea why, but my emodar range for you is a lot farther out. I'm only just outside of it right now. So… uh, maybe you could remember that?"

He looks at me with amazement and then he's definitely smug. I may not be reading him right now but I just *know* he's drawing conclusions about what this new information means. Like that we belong together or something… That there really *is* a special connection between us like he was implying yesterday. I look up and away from him, letting the awkwardness settle—*my* awkwardness anyway. I doubt Gabriel knows the meaning of the word.

"I see," he chuckles finally. "My apologies. I didn't know, obviously. I certainly *will* remember that. Anything else I should know?"

I definitely don't miss the double meaning there but I ignore it. "No, that's it," I reply, looking into the trees. He doesn't need to know more about the effect he has on me, how *easy* it is to read him. I doubt it's anything he can control.

"Well then! Now that that's settled, give me about five minutes to achieve a trance," he says, closing his eyes and breathing a contented sigh.

I spend the entire five minutes examining all of his features. I know I shouldn't, but he's so good-looking and I've spent so much time stifling my overwhelming desire to be close to him. It won't affect *him* if I take a couple of minutes to gaze at him.

His deep-set eyes are what make his stare so irresistibly heady and it's the part of him that I'm sure is Latin. But I still believe he has some European descent because his other features are more prominent and almost graceful. Even his hair is soft and fine. It's cropped shorter in the back, but the front is longer, creating a disheveled fringe near his eyes. It makes him look kind of boyish even though the maturity of his features should put him at least in his late twenties or early thirties. A light sheen of sweat makes his skin shimmer, and his mouth has a perfectly kissable lower lip—just full enough to be inviting but not so much that it makes him look odd. I bite my own lip and hold my breath as I imagine tentatively what it would be like to put my lips on his. My heart beats so rapidly that I place my hand on my chest to calm it.

Forcing my attention away from his lips, I look at his hands. His lean fingers bear some evidence of callousing; he writes often, indicating he's a scholarly person.

Well, duh. The guy knows Russian and who knows what other language. He talks physics and he speaks like he's memorized the dictionary.

His intelligence only makes his looks that much more exotic and tantalizing. A genius who is *also* a hottie? It boggles my mind. He's been gifted in *every* way from what I can tell.

Gabriel likes to wear t-shirts and jeans, both fitted in exactly the right places. I've caught myself several times looking at him, just waiting for him to move the right way so I can see his lean but muscular chest. It's frustrating to only get a brief look here or there. But now that he's stretched out on a rock, I can see his chest plainly. It's well-toned in an understated way that's just right. I know I shouldn't… But I allow my imagination an audience, fantasizing the curve and heat of his chest under my bare hands.

I inhale sharply and then swallow without thinking—I hope he didn't hear that.

I should be ashamed for pettily lusting after a man whom I have no right to, but I've managed to achieve the same level of awareness of him I did last night that allowed me to see his life force. If I want the same results, I have to repeat the process. So what if I enjoy it?

Gabriel breathes low and even finally, and I think that means he's in a trance. When I step closer to him, his placidity confirms it. I stretch out my hands, hovering them over the tempting curves of his chest, giving my cursed gloves a dirty look before closing my eyes.

I breathe deeply and imagine the gentle pull of the flowing river. I let my fingers dangle in its imaginary current, and the natural smells of the forest complete the authenticity of the river in my head. The sound of our matching respirations puts me into a daze.

When nothing happens, I wonder what I'm doing wrong. Then I remember Gabriel, lying just inches from me. Anticipation kicks my awareness up a notch, and the would-be river flows, its pulse testing lightly against my fingertips.

The suddenness of the tug against my fingers startles me momentarily, but I maintain my stance, eyes closed, so I can explore the sensation.

I worry that I'm hurting him but then remember that I *will* be certain if I'm sucking at his energy. That comes with awful feelings...

To be sure, I listen for his heart. It beats steadily. All is well.

I focus on what I can feel with my hands, and when I do, it moves sharply into focus. It's not a stream, I decide. I think of it as soft fabric, or strands of hair, thousands of them, brushing along my fingers like long tresses. But they are more soft and supple; they glide past my hands with a different kind of friction than hair.

Louise described the pull of a current, but to me, the strands seem magnetic. They cling to me when my hands are at rest yet release easily when I move my fingers through them. It could be perceived as movement but I think that's a crude description. It worries me when they adhere to my hands, but I listen once more to Gabriel's heart and find it beating as steadily as ever.

I hear a sound, similar to the resonance of a violin—strings across strings. I wonder if it's the movement of the strands I perceive gliding against each other. It bears no melody, but neither is it discordant. The sound is beautiful, striking my very soul—perhaps literally—and giving me goosebumps. My chest throbs with a longing for something that I can't place.

And then I become aware of a new sense: smell. The best way to describe it is clean. Not detergent clean, but like the smell of hard rain, every trace of aroma swept up into the raindrops as they rocket through the atmosphere until the concoction becomes a symphony of a thousand scents of the earth and its inhabitants. They explode as they hit the ground, sending up a mist of one singular flavor: life. Something about the rain can make a myriad of scents, whether made up of awful odors or perfumes as sweet as flowers, seem like the most pure smell in the world.

As I submerge into the incense, I lean in, picking up on the strain of a more concentrated scent. It is the smell of Gabriel, not exactly like, but related to his smell that I already know. It's purely him; unique and inherent. It's similar to the surrounding clean aroma in that it's like inhaling a million scents in one; I'm unable to pick out one single unit of its composition. But it's definitely earthy and natural, like fresh sod maybe, or wet metal.

The aroma isn't so telling, but it floods me with an acute perception. Much like how smells tap into memory, this one imbues me with the sensation of flying through the forest, the desert, the sea—it doesn't matter. And I instinctively know I'm pursuing something; I don't know what, but I don't care. The simple act of the chase thrills me.

This journey of his soul fills me with so much love for him that it spills over, flowing right out of my head and down my shoulders, trickling in warm currents down my face and arms. It envelops me both inside and out. I think I'm crying. He's magnificent and beautiful in every way.

I don't know how long I immerse myself in the experience of his soul—I know that's what it is—but at some point, my goal comes back to me.

I take a breath, preparing for the blinding light that will appear. I tilt my head up slightly to avoid the glare and then open my eyes.

What I see can only be described as an aurora borealis in broad daylight, only magnified and intensified and spread over the huge expanse of the heavens above me. The colors are of a spectrum both familiar and unfamiliar. The sky is not one singular color, but a constantly undulating mosaic. The spectrum seems infinite and it fluctuates continuously. At first I think it's doing the changing by itself, but as I shift my position ever so subtly, I realize it only changes as I move. A millimeter's variation offers an entirely new perspective like the iridescence of gasoline floating on water or the surface of a soap bubble. It's a psychedelic experience which, after focusing on it too long, disorients me. I have to look away from it.

We're surrounded by woods, so the trees, by their sheer number, grab my attention next. It looks like I'm on another planet; the shapes are right, but the colors are all wrong. Here, leaves and needles are blue and they *glow*. Each tree is a different shade, varying from violet hues to icy shades that are nearly white: Glittering Cerulean, Grey-toned Beryl, Aquamarine, Steel Blue, Periwinkle, Cobalt, Sapphire. The trunks glow in the same way but they are a lighter hue than their respective leaves. In fact, the leaves themselves are outlined in the same shade as the trunk. The outlines are more like auras than solid lines though. It makes the trees look like they are backlit.

I shift my eyes lower to the field of rocks and boulders... I gasp in awe. Even though I know their composition must be the same—granite predominates in this area—none of the colors are exactly alike. One may be green, another pink. Like the sky, the spectrum is full of colors I recognize and also those I don't. What's more, each rock fluctuates in hue. One might appear burnt orange at first, but even leaning forward the tiniest bit changes it to a lighter orange. Like the sky, I can move my head to the left an inch and it alters the shade I perceive. It fluctuates along a scale of similar oranges, appearing peach-colored one second and more salmon the next.

I shift my eyes to the ground. Here in the clearing it's hardened clay with rocks and tufts of grass interspersed. From what I can tell, different sections of ground are different colors. Loose dirt on the surface seems more like multicolored glitter. And again, the colors fluctuate as I move. So because the ground is not one uniform substrate, looking at it is like looking through a kaleidoscope. The constant change all around me is too much to process at once, making it difficult to look at for long. The only way to prevent this effect is to hold perfectly still.

Or look at the trees... They appear to be the only things here that remain static no matter how I view them. In the face of so much inconstancy, the trees are like grounding forces—they hold this world together. But the sparsely distributed grass and undergrowth is like that, too, I notice. It ranges in yellows mostly, but only from one clump to the next. I guess vegetation is static and inanimate substances are dynamic.

The one thing all the sights have in common is a definite luminescence. Everything glows from within, inexplicably alive with an intelligence that makes me perceive that I'm in a room crowded with present but peaceful inhabitants. Tears flow from pure, joyous awe.

I have not looked at Gabriel yet. My peripheral vision has already told me he's far brighter than anything else here. So when I look down, I am prepared for not seeing anything distinct at first. When my eyes adjust, his color starts to materialize: purple. It doesn't change, just like the trees. But this is not his body I see. Unlike the trees that seem to *be* the color, Gabriel is *shrouded* in purple. His body, that is. His life force, his soul, or whatever it is, is actually *separate* from his body by my estimation. I only know this intuitively as I don't actually *see* his body beneath his purple mass.

Gabriel's life force reminds me of a cocoon wrapped around him, a beautiful gleaming purple cocoon. I examine it closely to figure out what it's made of, confused that it *feels* like strands, but actually *looks* like water swirling around him: a luminous purple liquid that appears reflective at times. I can't make out what exactly it constitutes. But I wonder if the strands are just infinitesimally small and that's why I can't see them. His life force doesn't behave quite like water either. When water flows, it always seeks continuity. If two clashing flows meet, water bubbles up; the flows quarrel for control. No water bubbles here though; the currents coordinate seamlessly. If it's really made up of strands, there must be billions of them. It frustrates me that I can't tell, but then I realize that *everything* here is like that. It's a world of color and lights, not detail. Ironically, it makes me feel like my vision is bad.

After a while, my eyes get tired from the strain and I blur them to rest for a moment. As soon as I do, his life force disappears from my view and I'm seeing Gabriel's body beneath, no swirling purple cocoon, just his body as I would see it in the regular world. Focusing even a little, however, brings his life force back into view. I look up at the scenery to see that the same thing happens there as well. Unfocusing my eyes makes the strange colors disappear and the dimmer natural ones of the regular world take their place.

Once I've thoroughly absorbed this strange phenomenon, I examine Gabriel's life force again. My own moves around my hands and arms, just like his. It's purple as well, probably the exact same shade, and where our purple swirling masses meet, they flow together, clinging to one another. As I gently lift one hand up, our life forces grasp each other as if reluctant to let go. The sight of it is completely mesmerizing. For several minutes I gently knead his life force with my own just to see them interact.

When I move my hands back and forth I realize that the stringed instrument sounds I hear are not the movement of his strands moving against each other, but the sound of our life forces *meeting* each other. Maybe it truly *is* like a violin—my strings moving against his.

My body interrupts the dazzling sensations to tell me it has been standing for too long in the same place. After a while, I can't ignore it, but I'm afraid to move. I don't know what will happen when I step away. Delicately, I pull my hands from the flow. Our life forces, which look like gravity-defying water as they reach for each other, disentangle as easily as intertwined smoke wisps.

The lights and colors fade completely from view. I blink my eyes, realizing that *that* world was far brighter than this regular, visible world. Even with the sun high in the sky over our heads, darkness hangs over the wide-open space as if it's about to rain though the sky is cobalt blue and cloudless. It's a curious sensation.

I look down at Gabriel. He breathes evenly, exuding serenity. I remember what he looked and smelled like.

I touched his soul.

The intimacy of the encounter feels like a breach of privacy. I could have seen and caressed his naked body and still not felt that it was as much of a violation as this. The depth of experience I have had with him just now makes me feel like I've known him far longer than a day. That I have no right to Gabriel's body or soul in that way makes me ashamed and uncomfortable. What do I say to him?

I clear my throat loudly, unable to speak.

His eyes pop open, a look of utter contentment on his face. "That was positively the most relaxing energy touch session I have ever had, and I was lying on a rock. What did you do?"

Nice to know it was good for you, too.

"Nothing special," I reply, shuffling my feet awkwardly.

Gabriel raises an eyebrow. "Your cheeks are flushed. Let me guess, you molested me while I slept! Dang nabbit, I missed it!"

I shake my head. He's trying to alleviate my embarrassment, so I can't be upset at him for the flirtation. But it's painfully close to the truth, exacerbating the discomfort.

"Well then? What did you see?" he asks, sitting up and piercing me with gleaming eyes.

I draw my lip into my teeth and wonder how I can skirt the issue of experiencing his bare soul. There were certainly many other things to see, but none stood out like that.

He doesn't have to know anything about how intimate that felt, though.

I can be clinical about this, right?

So what did I see? Every description seems inadequate. I saw colors I've never before conceived of. Everything was alight with flourishing life.

Gabriel is bursting with curiosity, so I say the first words that occurred to me when I saw the incredible world of color and lights. "I saw... a colorworld."

22

"So? What's it like living with a millionaire?" I ask, winding the antiquated spiral phone cord around my pinkie finger and leaning back against the wall, my legs extended out in front of me. There is no cell phone service where we're located, so I'm using the phone in the recreation common room.

"I don't know... He's not here much," Ezra replies over the phone. "I work every day at his office, running mail and making copies and stuff. He works way later than me usually, and he's out of town for a few days right now. He's got a maid though, so that's pretty cool. I don't have to clean up after myself."

"He's not there?" I ask, irritated. "He's supposed to be looking after you, not running off doing whatever it is he does."

"Looking after me? I'm not a toddler. I think I can manage to feed and clothe myself just fine."

"But... you're *fifteen*," I protest. "If I wanted you to stay by yourself, I wouldn't have asked him to let you move in with him for the summer. I would have left you at the apartment."

"You think someone has to be babysitting me all the time? Even *you* didn't do that."

I sigh in irritation. "The point is you need an *adult* around, Ezra. Someone to make sure you don't do dumb stuff."

"Like what?"

"Like, have parties... or... or vandalize property!" I sputter. "Or drive a car without a license! Or have a girl over! You know what I'm talking about! You're a *teenager*! Teenagers need supervision."

"If I had a girlfriend, she would most *definitely* be over... maybe I should go get one," Ezra muses. "And this house is so big she could probably live here without Uncle Rob ever knowing. Come to think of it, that party idea seems really great. I bet if I called Nate he could—"

"Ezra!"

He hoots with laughter. "Wen, it's *fine*. He calls every day, sometimes twice a day to make sure I'm okay. He even has someone drive me to work... It's crazy. I ride to my job as a copy boy with my own chauffeur, and in an *Audi*. I'm a regular Pebble Beach preppy."

"Fabulous," I grumble. "So what you're saying is no supervision, a fancy car, spending money, and living in the most elite neighborhood in Monterey. Sheesh, you're going to end up being one of those spoiled kids like the ones on those TV dramas featuring privileged teens living in fancy neighborhoods and sleeping with each other and having drug problems. What will I do with you then?"

"Whatever, Wen. You *know* that is not me. Stop being dramatic. Anyway, he's also getting me accepted to a school near San Jose. Some mathematical engineering school. He said I should talk to you about going there next year."

My heart catches in my throat. This is exactly what I dreaded. Only more subtle and sneaky. Robert is trying to win Ezra over little by little. Buying him things, giving him autonomy. Sending him to some fancy school that I could never, in a million years, afford. How am I supposed to compete with that?

"I think you should do whatever you want," I reply evenly, digging my heels into the carpet to push myself harder against the wall. "I'm sure it'd be a great opportunity for you."

An awkward pause prevails as I try to guess what Ezra's thinking while he measures my words. I suspect that he's read into them.

"Wen, it's not that—"

"Ezra, it's okay with me. It really is great. I'm glad you're doing so well. Don't feel guilty about being happy—although I still don't like the lack of supervision."

Another pause. Then Ezra says, "Wen, I'm not interested in living with Robert long-term. But I don't want to be a burden to you either. You should be able to have a life too, you know. Did you know Robert asked me if I thought you'd be okay with him paying for the rest of your degree? You might actually enjoy college if you don't have to work your ass off all the time. I'm sure, if you wanted to, you could transfer schools so we wouldn't be separated. Uncle Rob has been really clear that he wants to help us. Stop stressing so much. You don't have to do everything yourself."

He's Uncle Rob now?

"I know that," I reply, biting my lip to keep from crying. "All I care about is that you're happy—and that you don't say the word 'ass.'"

He chuckles. "Yeah, I promise. Never again. And yes, I *am* happy, except that I worry about you. Are *you* happy?"

I sigh. "Well, not really, but I'm working on it. It's hard to be happy when you know you might kill someone if you touch them. I have a hard time making any concrete plans in my head not knowing how long I'll be stuck like this. I'm hopeful that we'll see results, though. And Randy and Louise have both been working with me a lot," I say reassuringly. I don't want him to worry about me. Which he would if he knew how selfishly driven Louise has proven to be.

The truth is that I've been working in hypno-touch the last few days, sneaking looks at the colorworld without them noticing. I've been searching for clues, but so far I have no idea if anything I see is helpful in the least. There's just too much to absorb. I know I shouldn't expect some kind of miracle cure so soon, but it's still disheartening that nothing has stood out to me, pointing me in a direction. When I'm not doing this, Louise is teaching me how to discern energy variances, which *also* doesn't seem very helpful. What's more, *nobody* has an ability even remotely as powerful as mine. The most impressive thing I've seen is Kaylen's telekinesis. The least impressive thing is Gina brightening a light bulb by a few watts. What do you even *do* with an ability that weak?

"All right," Ezra says warily. "But you know, Uncle Rob seems pretty even-keeled about stuff. I bet if you told him about your problem, he could find the right people to help you. Money talks."

"Right," I say, rolling my eyes. "I'm sure we can just put up want-ads for a 'lethal touch cure' and then throw money at whoever shows up claiming to know how to fix me. That would solve *everything.*"

"Well, you never know," Ezra replies. "Uncle Rob is *very* connected."

"Yeah, well in case you weren't aware, these people *specialize* in life force abilities. It's what they do. And guess what? It doesn't cost me a thing. So you just work your office boy job, keep girls away from the house, and no parties. I'll be back in no time."

"Oh trust me. I have no intention of disobeying a member of the *Communal Cohorts*," he sniggers.

We both laugh then, and the sound of it consoles me. All I want is Ezra's happiness, right? Why am I getting so worked up over Robert treating him well? Ezra isn't the one who needs help right now. I am. So I move past anxiety and resolve to be happy for Ezra, whatever his happiness entails.

***

My determination doesn't last long. I knew it wouldn't. Being happy for Ezra just means I can't guilt him over what he wants to do. And I *won't* do that. But that doesn't mean I can't mope about it when he's not around. And I do for the entire walk to the research building where I'm slated to perform hypno-touch with Louise this afternoon.

When I get there, Gabriel lies before me on the raised futon. The sight of him causes my chest to cramp. I swallow a lump in my throat. Seeing him, the other person I want in my life but can't really have, makes me feel as if everything has been ripped away from me.

"Hello, Wendy," Louise says, placing her hands over Gabriel's body. "Gabe's already in a trance, so we can get started."

I pause where I stand, the knot in my chest getting tighter. I don't think I can keep it together. "I'm sorry Louise," I croak. "I don't feel well right now. I'll take a rain check, okay?"

Not waiting for her to answer, I bolt for the door, careful when I descend the stairs since there are other people here as well, some going up, others going down. I don't want to cause a fatal accident in my rush for fresh air.

When I burst outside, my first instinct is to go find a place to sit on the ground against the side of the building where I can't be seen. But at the moment I feel resentment toward the building itself as if it has a direct hand in keeping me so unhappy. I spot a tree off the gravel path. I lean against it, sucking in air as the tears begin to fall.

This is ridiculous. Get a grip, Wendy.

I sink to the ground, putting the tree between me and the path in case anyone should walk by and see me losing it.

"Wendy?" Gabriel's voice sounds from behind me.

Too late. Crap. "What?" I ask, not turning because I don't want him to see my wet cheeks. I pull my jeans-clad knees up and wrap my arms around them, doing my best to hide my face.

Gabriel, however, isn't fooled, and he comes to sit near me, directly across from me actually, about ten feet away. He is very careful to avoid my range as often as possible. "Bad day?" he asks.

I nod, trying over and over to swallow the lump in my throat.

"You didn't kill or injure anyone, did you?" he asks, his eyes glinting with mischief.

I roll my eyes, unable to help smiling. "No."

"Well *that's* a relief," he says, throwing up his hands. "So what then? You saw a ghost? I figure if anyone could, *you* could. I can see how that might be disturbing."

"No, Gabriel," I say, rolling my eyes, happier already just in hearing his voice.

He smiles gently now and tilts his head to the side as he looks at me. "So what's got you so depressed?"

I sigh. "I just talked to my brother. I really miss him."

"Is that *all*?" he asks skeptically.

Scowling at him, I say, "No, but it's not any of *your* business."

"Of course not, but I know how it is. Family is like love and madness all rolled into one," he says. "I spoke to my mamá earlier today. That woman nags worse than Randy when someone's tracked dirt in her office. If I don't call my mother at *least* every other day, she thinks I must have been abducted and she's ready to file a missing person's report. Last week I didn't call her for four days. That put her in a real fix."

"What happened?" I ask, curious about this part of Gabriel's life that I'm not privy to.

"'I'm twenty-seven, Mamá,' I told her. 'Not seven, remember?'" Gabriel shakes his head. "'Eres un hijo terrible!' she cried. 'Mijo, I gave birth to you. Even when you are one hundred and seven, you will still call me and I will still want to know what you are doing and who you are doing it with. And don't remind me how old you are! My son is twenty-seven and still I have no grandchildren! If you want me to stop bugging you, you ought to get married and have children of your own so I can call my nietos instead of *you*, you ungrateful niño.'"

I smile at him as he rolls his eyes. "She then went on and on incoherently in Spanish about all the ways I'd wronged her as a son—she only reverts to Spanish when she's really upset."

"Well in her defense, my friend Letty says Spanish is 'the angry language,'" I reply. "She always speaks in Spanish when she's passionate about something."

"That's an apt observation," Gabriel agrees with a grin. "So you know what I'm talking about. When my mother finally concluded her tirade about how it was my *duty* to give her progeny, I asked her, '"What do you want me to do, Mamá? Have a mail-order bride sent over just to branch out the family tree?' And do you know what my own mother said to me? 'I think that's a *great* idea. And pick one that speaks a language you *don't* know. Because that's about the best chance you'd have of someone marrying *you*, Mister Know-it-all. Be grateful I'm not taking you down to Mexico to arrange a bride for you myself!' And then, after all that, she had *Dad* call me."

"So what did *he* say?" I chuckle.

"Oh well, he knows how she is. Hispanic women can be *so* dramatic, simply on a whim if it suits them, especially *her*. He always pretends to give me a lecture on respecting my mother. Usually we just end up discussing the philosophy of Emmanuel Kant or Friedrich Nietzsche in French, though. She has no idea—she doesn't speak French. I'm always grateful when she turns our correspondence over to him."

I laugh openly as I picture Gabriel arguing with his mother in broken Spanish. I don't feel like crying anymore. "Your dad speaks French? What's he do?"

"He's a lawyer," he replies, smiling. "He was born and raised in France, but he studied at Cambridge. He came to the states for an internship afterward and met my mother. I guess she was a change from the stuffy British academics he was used to. Married her six months after he met her. And they've been together ever since."

"Ahhh," I say. "It's finally starting to make sense now... You're like a Hispanic French guy. No wonder you speak like you could be Shakespeare's descendant."

He chuckles. "Well, technically Shakespeare was English, but I see your point. I probably could have ended up a vociferous Latino like my mother, but I was literally surrounded by her relatives and friends growing up. I just wanted to hang on to the other part of my heritage and also form my own." He shrugs. "It started out as a way to bug people, but it grew on me. And now here I am and I don't think I could break the habit if I tried."

"I doubt even French guys speak with the same decorum you do. So you get a kick out of making people uncomfortable… why?"

"Of course I do. For one thing, I *look* Hispanic, don't I? That comes with its own stereotype. If people saw me, they liked to think they knew who I was. I strove to be well-spoken so that when I opened my mouth they'd be shocked into rethinking their assumptions. I enjoy making people wonder and question their personal philosophies."

"That *is* a pretty unlikely heritage." I shrug, smiling. "Why *not* freak people out with it?"

"Precisely." He winks at me.

"I was just upset because my uncle is spoiling my brother," I blurt, leaning back against the tree again. "It's stupid and petty, but I just feel really lonely right now without him, and the thought that he might be at some fancy math genius school being driven around in my uncle's *Audi* while having a maid clean his room just makes me want to punch my uncle in the face."

"That sounds dramatic," Gabriel says, a corner of his mouth curling up.

"Yeah, I know," I sigh. "Like I said, stupid."

Gabriel looks at me critically. "So you're afraid of losing him then."

I wrinkle my nose. "I am not afraid of losing him. I just don't like that my uncle is worming his way in through extravagant gifts. *Buying* my brother's loyalty—"

Gabriel raises an eyebrow.

"Okay fine, I don't want to lose him," I grumble, crossing my arms. "But really, it's just not a good time for him to be asking me if I think it's okay if he goes to some froufrou school next year in San Jose. I already worry I won't be able to be there for him ever again. Not like I was before. And can you believe that my uncle is hardly even around? Who's going to look after Ezra? He doesn't have any supervision there whatsoever. There's nothing I can do about it either. I'm not helping him at all and I'm not even helping myself. Here I am, able to see life forces and it's completely useless. I'm not making any progress. All I'm doing is watching my brother get taken away from me and he's the last person I have left. If I lose him…" My words catch in my throat and I look away and take a calming breath. "This is killing me not to be there for him."

Gabriel sighs and looks at me with compassion. "You *are* making progress. Being able to literally *see* life forces has got to be of use. Have some patience with yourself. It's only been a few days."

"What if it's not possible to reverse this?" I nearly whisper, looking up into the leaves above me. I can't speak the words any louder because just saying them fills me with the most incredible loneliness.

"Can I ask you a question?" Gabriel says.

"Of course." I shrug, glancing at him briefly. "But it doesn't mean I'll answer."

"Fair enough," he says, smiling vaguely. "Do you always imagine the worst-case scenario is reality?"

"No," I say defensively, scooting more upright against the tree trunk and extending my legs back out. "But if I don't even *consider* the possibility that I might not—"

"Did you envision it would be easy then?" he interrupts.

"No, I—" I stop when I really think about his question. "I just want to see some progress is all. I hate to think that I might be wasting my time."

"What does progress entail then?"

I open my mouth to speak but no idea comes to me. I wrinkle my forehead, realizing I haven't imagined what a cure actually looks like. I've been too busy looking at what it's *not.* "I'm just upset that Louise and Randy don't know as much about life forces as I thought. Louise keeps talking about *flows* and *energy kinks* trying to point them out to me—you know what I'm talking about. I don't feel *or* see what it is she's describing. I swear she's making it up half the time. What's more, I don't *care.* I don't *want* to manifest abilities in people. I *want* to fix myself. And nobody here seems to be helping me do that."

Gabriel bites the inside of his cheek. "Will you allow me to be candid?"

"Why not…" I say in exasperation.

"Well first of all, from what I've seen, your brother is loyal to a fault when it comes to you. I very much doubt he wants to leave you and become your uncle's adopted child or whatever the case is that you imagine. That said, I think he only brought up all of the ways he's being spoiled because he was trying to dispel the pressure you feel to get back to taking care of him. My guess is that he has no interest in going to this school he mentioned or in being carted around by a chauffeur with servants at his beck and call. I'd gather that he'd rather be with you, doing whatever it was the two of you were doing before all of this happened.

"You need to stop and ask yourself where Ezra's loyalties really lie and if you truly believe that something like a privileged lifestyle would really tear him away from the only person who has given him love and stability for the last year. Probably this school would be good for him, you can't deny that. But fifteen-year-olds don't tend to look that far into the future. They are more interested in the here and now. Ezra's here and now is you, the center of his universe. All he's going to care about is helping you. And by his reasoning, helping you means eliminating himself as a source of stress."

I blink in surprise. I hadn't looked at it that way.

"As for your other problem, I'll offer some of my own experience, as a scientist," Gabriel continues. "Answers don't come as linearly as you imagine they ought to. Solving a problem involves heading down many wrong paths, false starts, and eventually arriving at a solution in a place you never expected to find it."

I wipe a few tears from my cheek, disliking the sensation of my gloves now being damp. My gloves are always either dirty or wet or both, though. I just haven't gotten used to it. I look at them now, wondering what path I'll have to go down to eliminate them from my life.

"Thanks for being a good friend, Gabriel," I say, although at this moment I wish more than anything that he wasn't just my friend. I imagine scooting next to him and having him put his arms around me while I rest my head under his chin, inhaling his scent which has now become a kind of refuge for me. His smell is the only part of him that I can experience without too much guilt. Other than his words of course, which are addicting enough.

He looks back at me with clear eyes and a soft smile. "Anytime," he replies. "I aim to please."

Just having him look at me like that makes my heart race. Ever since my first encounter with his soul—I've had a few since then because he's my subject when I work with Louise—I feel like I know Gabriel better than anyone. It's like that experience of touching his life force squeezed the months-worth of time that it usually takes to get to know someone into 15 minutes. I still haven't told him *everything* about that first view of the colorworld, specifically not how I felt like I'd violated him by experiencing his very essence, or how I felt consumed by him as I touched his soul with my own. Gabriel seemed completely oblivious to the possible implications of what seeing his soul might mean on an intimate level. To him, I described a sensory experience, when in fact, it was so much more.

Even though Gabriel didn't reciprocate that experience with *my* soul, he often demonstrates how well he knows me as if he truly had. He has the uncanny ability of being able to guess my motivations in the same way Ezra, who has known me for years, does.

"Gabriel, what *is* your ability?" I ask, leaning forward.

He sighs, his face faltering a bit. "Well, I suppose someone will tell you sooner or later if I don't."

He points to a small patch of flowers growing on the side of the path. "There are sixteen flowers there, three-hundred and twenty-four petals total." He looks up at the tree I'm sitting under, leans his head one way, and then the other, and says, "That tree has forty-eight thousand five hundred forty-two leaves."

Then he scoots closer to me, very close, his heart speeding, but his thoughts controlled as he works to squelch release and contentment at finally being next to me rather than ten feet away. He does a good job because his warm lightheadedness transforms into careful reserve. Then, he raises his index finger as if petitioning patience, but in this case, I think he means for me to be still.

My body goes rigid in fright as ever so carefully he sweeps my hair to one side, lifts it up, and then lets it fall through his fingers as if he is combing it with his hands. The sensation makes my heart beat so fast it chases off the fear entirely until I'm drunk with the near-contact, but Gabriel is intent on my hair, staring at the flow as he lets it spill over my shoulders.

When the last strand falls, and chills cover every inch of my skin beneath my clothes, he says, "You have one hundred and nine thousand, two hundred and fifty-four hairs on your head which are at least shoulder-length." He shakes out a few strands that have shed into his hands and says, "Make that one hundred nine thousand, two hundred and fifty-two."

"What the—!" I exclaim, not bothering to be irritated by his obvious attempt to be close to me. Then I frown. "You get Rain Man counting abilities, and I get the Touch of the Grim Reaper?"

"Actually," he says, matter-of-factly, "I don't believe Rain Man could count strands of hair. I also have an excellent sequential memory. I can memorize blocks of text quite easily. It's photographic in a way, but not like Jimmy's. He can memorize things in a three-dimensional space as an overall picture. I memorize it character for character, in a sequence, and then recall it by reading it from my head. That particular part of my ability emerged with hypno-touch, although I've always had a fairly good sequential memory. The counting is natural though."

My mouth hangs open. "Gabriel, that's incredible! The counting is *natural*? Geez! No wonder Louise calls you an anomaly. How did I get so sheisted?"

Gabriel's eyes sparkle with delight. "I'm an aficionado of dictionary reading, and I have never seen the word 'sheisted.'"

I roll my eyes. "It's taken from 'sheisty' meaning shifty or untrustworthy. So when I say 'I got sheisted,' it means that someone sheisty pulled one over on me."

Gabriel's eyes laugh, but he's a puddle of woozy contentment inside. "'Sheisty' isn't in there either. Do you like to make up words for fun?"

"Smarty pants," I say indignantly, crossing my legs and leaning my elbows on my knees. "I can't believe you've never heard the word sheisty. You need to go memorize the Wiktionary."

Gabriel roars with laughter. "'Wiktionary?' I didn't know there was such a thing."

I grin. "Yeah, all the kids are using Wikipedia and the Wiktionary. You might want to read up on modern slang if you're going to hang out with someone from *my* generation."

"Hmm. The Wiktionary. Is that something on the computer?"

"Yeees," I say tentatively, wondering if he's joking. "Actually, you *use* the computer to access it on the *Internet.* You *do* know what that is, right?"

He rolls his eyes. "Yes, I know what the *Internet* is. I just don't use it much. I don't like those thinking boxes. What ever happened to paper and ink? The soul of humanity went right out of society as soon as those thinking boxes came onto the scene."

I laugh. "*Thinking box?* You are *hilarious.* How did you manage to get through college without using a computer?"

"By using it as little as possible," he replies simply. "I like libraries where *real* people work and you can hold *real* books. I have quite a collection, actually. None of my possessions are quite as beloved as my books. Nothing beats holding the weight of knowledge tangibly in hand."

"But a computer puts information at your fingertips instantly. I'd think *you'd* love that," I reply, baffled that someone as smart as Gabriel has made it this far in his life by avoiding the Internet. I consider it nearly as essential as breathing.

"What use is all that information if you don't have to do anything but click a button to get it? How is *that* satisfying?"

If his angst over the information revolution wasn't so real in my mind, I wouldn't believe it. But Gabriel *actually* feels that way. It shouldn't surprise me. To Gabriel, it's all about the challenge. The hunt for the unknown. Of *course* he would see computers this way. They eliminate the chase.

"You are something else, Gabriel Dumas," I say, leaning back against the tree once more.

He immediately suppresses the words he intends to say, which I suspect would be dripping with suggestiveness. I long to hear them anyway. Feeling him choke off the free and vivid expressions of his mind may be as bad as when he's used my emodar to manipulate my feelings. There doesn't seem to be a middle-ground in this case, no way to satisfy both of us. Or even one of us.

I really am torturing him. I'm torturing myself. I hate this, yet I love him. Desperately. As someone who has looked into the soul of another and found goodness and beauty, kindness and honesty. I've had an unobscured view of what motivates and moves him. How, if I am ever relieved of this curse long after we have gone our separate ways, will I be able to give myself to anyone else, knowing how intimate I've been with this one man? Knowing him that honestly, I wish I could reciprocate, sharing my soul with *him* in the colorworld. But I can't even hold his hand. There is no way I could ever give him what he deserves. Intimacy that is that one-sided will never sustain a relationship.

23

$\mathcal{K}$aylen chatters happily at me about our upcoming ride while we work together in the kitchen. Whenever I have kitchen duty, I wash all of the produce myself because I'm tired of tasting pesticides in my food. It's bad enough that I have to eat anything with preservatives, but a little extra time under the water helps the pesticide problem a lot.

Gina's with us, too, and when Kaylen isn't naming all the horses or talking about which trail we'll take, Gina's explaining her ability to direct electrical currents. I don't care, really, but I smile at her during the important parts.

"I'm ready to bring these to the counter," I warn, waiting for Gina and Kaylen to move a safe distance from me. My hands aren't gloved which always makes me anxious. I feel naked whenever I have them off. It reminds me of a time before my mom died when Letty and I went to a club. I'd gotten bad news about my mom's cancer progression and I just wanted to get lost entirely in the emotions of others. Going out was the best way to do that, and I did it all the time during that low point in my life. My ability might have been limited to touch before, but in a crowd I could easily pick up on the general vibe of the people around me without touching them. That night I guess I was feeling especially vindictive, because I dressed to the hilt: stilettos, shorts, and a halter top that was so low it didn't leave much to the imagination. I definitely got the reaction I was going for. I felt like I could have had every fawner kissing my feet if I'd asked. The control I had over their minds was... frightening. And all because I'd uncovered more skin. Strangely though, it made me uncomfortable. Self-conscious in a way that had me looking down all night to be sure my breasts were still covered and my butt was still in my shorts.

That shameful behavior aside, I now feel provocative in a different kind of way—as if I might be brandishing a rifle.

Work resumes once I've shifted carefully around to the long counter, re-gloved, and taken a chopping knife in hand.

"So do you want to take Chancy?" Kaylen asks me, assuming that I've memorized all the horses' names and personalities and am ready to make an informed selection.

I shrug. "As long as it has four legs and a mane and tail, I'm good. I just want to get on one."

I take a whiff of the vegetables I've washed to make sure I've done a good job removing the residue. They smell fine, but I consequently smell everything else in the room. Kaylen smells like she's been in the woods. Well, everyone here has that scent, but she's been hiking in the thick of it; it's the heavy aroma of underbrush. I know she didn't go riding today. She was complaining about it earlier. There are no stable smells on her either.

"Did you go hiking, Kaylen?" I ask.

She looks startled and then turns a little pale—it's probably only noticeable to *my* eyes.

"Um," she says as she glances over at Gina who is actually silent for once, spreading a marinade on some beef tips and not really paying attention to us. She's thinking about something technical, maybe more about her electric currents.

"I took a long way to the research building. Sometimes I like a little bushwhacking," Kaylen says finally. Then she bends down to retrieve a large bowl from under the counter.

I wonder at her willingness to lie though I'm right next to her. Maybe she doesn't want Gina to know. Lying to me is a hopeless endeavor. She must know that.

I mark it as odd, assuming she'll talk about it if she wants to. But what was she doing in the middle of the woods, if *not* hiking?

***

The following morning marks a week since I came here. I've been developing what Louise calls my 'energy awareness.' *I* call it imagining things that aren't there. Where Louise sites 'an amorphous anomaly in the flow,' I just feel those strands creating music against my own life force as they move past my hands. The energy near the foot is the same as the energy near the chest or anywhere else. The only progress I've experienced during the week is that I can now go into the colorworld in under a minute.

Gabriel has suggested that the only reason I can't feel what Louise does is because I can see. He says if I was energy blind like her, my hands would be more sensitive to what I'm feeling. I don't know if I buy that. I think I feel more than her.

"Okay, I think you're ready to start trying some manipulation techniques," Louise says, her hands moving in a circular pattern through Gabriel's life force. "First, we'll do spread-finger rowing.

This is very simple; you start with your hand at the flow anomaly like this," she says, holding her hand perpendicular to Gabriel's chest and spreading her fingers apart. "Then imagine sweeping the water in smooth but firm motions outward from the chest."

She demonstrates one sweep, and with it, a kind of high-pitched ringing fills my ears. I don't like it and I shake my head slightly to dispel it.

Louise doesn't notice; she's intent on what she's doing. "Then move back to the chest. Before each sweep, let your hands rest in his life force for a moment. Energy attracts energy. So if we're going to get a grip on it to iron it out, you need to take advantage of the natural gravity between your life force and his."

She demonstrates another sweep, and I close my eyes to the sound. She does it several more times as I watch her movements while at the same time pushing away the keening ring by focusing on the sound of water running in the bathroom to drown it out.

"You try," she says, moving her hands away.

I follow her exactly, holding my hands in the flow of Gabriel's life force for a moment, watching the strands swirl around and grasp at my own. Then, in one firm motion, I sweep down toward his legs.

I don't get far before the most awful sound fills my ears. Like striking the wrong chord on the violin over and over, intensified times the number of strands I must be grasping in my hands. It's agonizingly discordant in a way that reminds me of scratching nails over a chalkboard. I gasp and cringe, pausing my hands where they are. As soon as I stop pulling, the sound stops. I sigh with relief.

"You want to carry it all the way down," Louise instructs, noting my hesitation.

I nod, copying her once more. Again the sound pierces my ears and I stop. "It feels wrong," I say.

"Wrong how?" she asks, looking at me with the flicker of flame in her eyes I remember from the very first time I did hypno-touch.

I struggle for a description that won't give me away. "I don't know. Like I'm pulling too much. Like maybe I'm damaging his life force. Let me watch you again?" I suggest, thinking I would much rather endure the eerie ringing brought about with *her* hand motions as opposed to mine.

"You can't *damage* a life force," Louise says, moving her hands into place and pulling downward again. Yes, that ringing is much more tolerable.

I repeat the request for a demonstration over and over until Louise starts to get suspicious. Reluctantly, I move my hands into position again, but this time I watch what I'm doing, making sure that none of his strands have time to entangle with mine before pulling downward all the way. It's difficult, but I manage to make the motion without too much of the jarring sound.

"No, no," Louise says patiently. "You have to spread your fingers like this." She demonstrates. "If you don't, you won't have any effect on the life force. I told you. Energy attracts energy. Letting your hands rest is how you *grip* it."

I sigh. *Yeah, I figured that.*

I try again but stop once more. My motions are far too short and quick, I know, but I can't take hearing that noise.

"You have to carry through," Louise says, patient still. She demonstrates again.

This time, when I copy her, I let my hands rest and then literally shake them free of Gabriel's life force before sweeping them down. The effect isn't as good as I'd hoped because I don't think I got my hands completely free of him. But it's still better.

"What are you doing?" Louise says, starting to reveal signs of irritation. "It's a smooth motion. Not an erratic one."

We carry on like this for a while. Louise has to demonstrate over and over, and each time I follow her I have to figure out a new way to *not* copy her exactly. I note at one point that Gabriel is fully aware and paying attention to all of our exchanges. He's practically burning with questions, and when Louise and I are done with the thirty-minute session, he hops up like a jack-in-the-box looking from Louise to me.

"We'll try again on Monday," Louise says as Gabriel and I leave. Usually Gabriel hangs back so that we don't walk together, but this time he's right beside me.

"What was all that?" Gabriel asks once we reach the path outside.

I relay the experience to him while he launches into complex acrobatic reasoning. I'm impressed that he can both listen to me and think that hard at the same time.

"So you seem to have a greater manipulative effect on the life force than she does…" Gabriel muses. "Does it *look* different when she does it?"

"I don't know," I reply. "I closed my eyes every time I actually copied her—the sound was too horrible. The rest of the time I was trying to get your life force to stop sticking to me… Although… When she moves them around without pulling at anything it does seem different. Like what she's touching is more like water. To me it seems more viscous—but maybe that's because I can feel and see what's happening."

"Well that's certainly something to chew on, isn't it?" Gabriel says thoughtfully.

"Yeah," I say drily. "While you chew, I've got to figure out how I'm going to get around looking like a hypno-touch flunkee with Louise. I can't copy her. I just know I'm going to cause damage to the strings if I do."

Gabriel nods absentmindedly as he returns to his mental gymnastics. The twists and turns and flips are too swift to follow.

"Well I'm supposed to go riding with Kaylen, so I'll see you later," I say, when we reach the split in the path that leads to the stables.

"Of course," he says, not wavering from his line of reasoning. He waves at me without really looking my direction, leaving me in wide-eyed surprise as I watch him retreat. I smile though. He wasn't kidding about having something to chew on. My amusement is overtaken by whimsical desire as imagining what it would be like to knock him out of his trance by running up and kissing him. I sigh as I daydream. I would be ashamed lusting after him like this only I know he'd enjoy it just as much as me.

***

During dinner that evening, I'm filling my plate at the long stainless-steel counter, leaning against it as I pick leaves out of the salad serving bowl that have the least dressing, when Celine comes up beside me. She scoops pasta onto her plate.

"Hello, Celine," I say cordially. She has shoulder-length dark brown layers and semi-attractive features. I'd call them graceful except that her mouth always seems to be screwed into an uncomfortable position. I'd probably think she was prettier if she didn't openly dislike me. I don't think I've ever seen her smile, although Gina has told me she's actually pretty nice if you get to

181

know her. Celine never bothers hiding her grudge from me, nor does she conspicuously avoid being in my vicinity. Mostly she just stomps past me haughtily, full of some kind of jealousy whose origin I can't place.

"Wendy," she acknowledges, a pang of her grudging irritation sitting uncomfortably in my stomach. Then she goes to sit as far away from my usual seat as possible.

I plop my plate down across from Gabriel and next to Kaylen. "Will someone *please* explain to me why Celine hates my guts?"

Kaylen giggles, and Gabriel immediately backs into a mental corner.

I glance from one to the other with a questioning look.

"She's just jealous," Kaylen says.

"Yes, I know that," I say impatiently. "Emodar, remember? Maybe you want to enlighten me as to *why* she's jealous?"

"Her ability is to enhance plant growth," Kaylen says, as if that should explain everything.

"Oh wow," I say. "Now I *totally* get it. No *wonder* she's jealous. Thanks for clearing that up, Kaylen."

Kaylen rolls her eyes. "She's jealous of your ability, you half-wit. She wishes she was the grim reaper like you because she thinks her own ability is lame. She hates that you get all Louise's attention. But that's not the only reason." Kaylen looks intently at Gabe now.

"Are you kidding me?" I ask, dumbfounded. Then I shake my head. "Well she can have mine. Geez. So what's the other reason?" I look at Gabriel now because Kaylen is watching him expectantly.

"Let it not be said that I didn't warn you that this treads quite close to breaching our agreement," Gabriel replies matter-of-factly. "Are you certain you still want to know?"

"How could the origin of Celine's jealousy breach our agreement? Wait... did you *date* her? Is she...? Is that why she...?" I don't want to embarrass myself by making assumptions, but what other reason could there be?

Kaylen giggles and Gabriel watches my face with a bit of haughty satisfaction, but he also searches my expression for an indication of how I feel about that prospect.

"Yes, I dated her," he says finally. "She was quite a delightful person when I met her, albeit a bit disgruntled about her lot in life force ability."

"How does this relate to me?" I ask.

"I broke up with her right after I met you at Pneumatikon. I think she blames you," Gabriel says, spearing his salad and taking a bite.

"We aren't even dating. What's there to be jealous of?"

Gabriel remains silent, taking in another mouthful. He distracts himself with some analytical line of reasoning to suppress some burgeoning of emotion.

Kaylen rolls her eyes. "Oh *spare* me, you two. Wendy, Gabe was talking about you nonstop when he got back from LA. He had the hots for you from the start. And that coincided with breaking it off with Celine. So it totally *is* your fault if we're going to get technical about it. Anyway," she says, standing up and picking up her plate, "I've got homework. You two have way too much drama."

Then she leaves and it's just Gabriel and me at our corner of the table. I would usually take the opportunity to leave with her so I don't have to be with him one-on-one, but that would be way too conspicuous given that the conversation doesn't feel done, not to mention the fact that I just started eating. I don't want to shirk any discussion that might make our interactions easier. But I don't know what to say.

I don't have to think too long, though, because Gabriel resigns himself as he comes to some decision about what is acceptable to say. "The breakup didn't really have anything to do with you. Meeting you was a convenient excuse to do it anyway."

"Why would you need an excuse?" I ask carefully, hoping this doesn't threaten emotionally-rife territory.

"Because I don't handle breakups well, usually. It doesn't matter if the woman and I fight like cats and dogs, I still get depressed and melancholy. So meeting you ensured that I'd have another pursuit so I wouldn't have to spend any time feeling sorry for myself."

"Feeling sorry for yourself?" I ask. "I cannot *imagine* you doing that. That seems like it would go completely against your nature."

Gabriel sighs, unclenching his restraint a bit. His exposed and frustrated pain upsets me. I don't like him suffering that way. I lean forward, crossing my arms on the table in front of me, waiting.

"I feel sorry for myself because women, they don't—" he starts and stops, looking at me for permission.

"Well you can't very well stop talking *now*," I say. "I'll be up all night wondering what you were going to say."

That lightens his mood, and he continues more confidently, "Celine would have broken up with me whether I did it or not. She already had that look in her eyes. That, 'Gabe, you irritate me into irrationality' look. The look they *all* seem to get eventually. The night we broke up we were having a late dinner which she insisted on making. She made tamales, trying, I think, to warm to some part of my Hispanic background. Anyway, when she asked how they were, I had to be honest: I thought she'd made a worthy attempt, but they could use a few adjustments. Then I started to explain what she'd done wrong. I told her next time we ought to just make them together and I would happily show her. I guess that was the wrong response because she became completely unglued and red-faced, telling me I couldn't just be grateful for her efforts and that I was always so critical."

Gabriel's indignation causes me to squeeze my hands into fists as he says, "I tried to explain to her that if she didn't want an honest opinion, she shouldn't ask. And that I was very much grateful that she would be so thoughtful. I just thought if she really cared to ask what I thought about them, it meant she was open to critique. I'm only critical when I think my criticism is asked for. But it doesn't mean I'm not grateful."

He huffs. "And then she said something like, 'Oh, and I suppose if I ask you if I look nice, you'll tell me exactly what I could do to look better?' To which I replied, 'If your overall appearance is pleasing, why would I not say you look nice if that's an accurate assessment? If you ask something like whether I like your shirt, I would be more critical since you're asking about something specific. Then I would tell you that the shirt is nice but I really love seeing you in red.' And then she just lost all semblance of practicality. And that's when I broke it off. It was quite exhilarating, actually."

I start laughing because what Gabriel has described is just so *him*. And then I sober when I imagine how the situation would have gone so differently if it had been me and not Celine... How his responses during an evening meal of tamales would have made me fall even more in love with him. In fact, just listening to him give an account of it infuses me with so much frustration over not being able to tell him what I think of his story that I fidget my hands under the table as a distraction.

I try to look away, but his eyes have locked on to mine and he's searching again. I give up resisting and try to say, without words, that all I've ever wanted is someone just like him, only I never knew such a person existed. He can tell me my tamales stink all day as long as it's exactly what he's thinking. He stares back with such exposed depth that the nakedness of it makes me want to protect him.

I easily get lost in the raw and expressive contemporary steps of this latest revealing performance happening in his head. It speaks of weakness and insecurity—something I so rarely feel from him. I forget every reason I am supposed to keep my distance. Who needs touch when you can connect so thoroughly?

I want him. I don't care about having his body if I can just have him nearby and be party to his words. Why am I resisting? I'm going to be heartbroken either way; why not eke out some happiness now?

Just when I'm about to tell him so, Gabriel, surprisingly, breaks our connection. And he does so abruptly, stifling his thoughts so thoroughly that it's like being physically strangled. He scoots his chair back and says, "So now you know. I've got to be going. I'm sure I'll see you tomorrow."

When he leaves, I expect the intensity of my feelings to change, but they don't. I thought the momentary break in my resolve was due to his pleading for acceptance. But I didn't lose my defenses out of pity. He became even more real and human by exposing his weakness so openly; it made me love him more. I think he got up so he wouldn't breach our agreement.

If I were to guess at precisely what he was saying to me mentally just now, I'd say he asked me if I'd like him to teach me to make tamales. I think he even got my mental reply. I can't be sure, of course, because I can't read minds completely, but I imagine it.

24

"By the way, I invited Gabe to come with us," says Kaylen. My heart leaps but is quickly followed by my stomach churning uneasily. I say nothing. I can't stop Kaylen from inviting Gabriel anywhere she wants. That would be childish. She's taking me on another ride today and insisted she be part of my wardrobe selection for the outing this time. Who knew sitting on a horse required special attire?

Kaylen tries to sneak a good look at my reaction before she leans into the closet and pulls out a pair of jeans, testing their stretch. "These will do better than what you wore last time. You can wear my extra half-chaps, too. Now, shoes. You can't wear those sneakers again. What size are you?"

"Eight," I reply, pulling off the offensive tennis shoes so I can take the jeans and change in the bathroom, the only place that ever sees any large amount of my bare skin these days. A strange mix of elation and melancholy settles over me. Ever since my conversation with Gabriel about Celine and tamales a week and a half ago, he's done a fair amount of avoiding me outside of hypno-touch. I miss hearing his voice.

"Could you manage a nine?" she asks.

"Probably."

"Perfect, you can borrow my extra pair then—just wear thick socks." Then she bobs out of the room to get the boots.

I close the bathroom door and remove my gloves to test my glucose. I stare down at my hands, which, because I rarely see them, look foreign and strange. I've lost count of the number of days since I killed Dina—a month maybe?

I wonder whether I'll eventually forget what my hands look like. That makes me sad. I shake the thought away as I splash water on my face and try to make sense of my hair. Is it curly? Is it straight? Giving up, I secure it with an elastic band atop my head.

I lean against the door and look in the mirror, mentally preparing to be near Gabriel. This is something I do practically every day. I remind myself that he *wants* to be around me despite not being true to himself—although this past week seems to be proving otherwise. I can't force him to leave. And I shouldn't influence him to stay.

Nevertheless, his internal struggles continue during the times I *am* around him. We are never together just one-on-one. Being across from each other during meal times is bad enough. Oftentimes, in the middle of a meal, he will get up abruptly and sit elsewhere—out of range. It always stings. I wish I could figure out a way to make it easier on him. I can't decide whether his struggle is easier to endure than his unchecked thoughts. I wonder what *he* would think is easier. I should broach the topic with him. Maybe. Talking to Gabriel about anything is wonderful and horrible at the same time.

After putting on the boots that Kaylen left outside the bathroom door, I go into the hall to find her.

I knock on her door, and when she doesn't immediately answer I open it carefully. "Kaylen?" I say, peeking around the gap.

I glance around, realizing that I haven't been in Kaylen's room before. Her obsession with anything horse-related hits me full-force as every available section of wall space is covered with either horse posters, pictures of Morgan, or competition ribbons. Her desk and shelf space are occupied by pictures of horses, pictures of her *on* horses, model horses, and horse magazines.

One group of photographs captures my attention. Some of them include her with a group of younger kids all in riding attire. Others are of her with different individual children and a horse. The group photos are labeled *Sheli Autistic Riding Academy.* It's clear from the pictures that Kaylen is not one of the students. My heart hiccups with love for this girl who continues to amaze me at every turn.

Curious about her awful father that has stranded her here, I look around for a photo of him. I'm surprised to find not a single one… It makes me both sad and angry that Kaylen's 'family' isn't part of her life enough to warrant a photograph.

I turn to leave and am startled to find Gabriel, not Kaylen, behind me in the hall.

He looks uncomfortable. "She said you were taking an unbearably long time in the bathroom and told me to wait for you while she goes ahead to catch the horses for us."

"Is that right?" I ask skeptically, certain I did *not* take a long time in the bathroom. Kaylen is just manipulating me by giving me alone time with Gabriel. She sees how much we avoid each other, how awkward the space is between us when we are together, and also the way I look at his retreating figure when he leaves the room. I've told her, point blank, why Gabriel and I can't be together.

"Yes, well, I didn't want to contend with her. Kaylen is fierce about anything horse-related." His apprehension skews my agitation, making me sad once again for stifling him this way. I can tell he's questioning whether he ought to have just refused Kaylen anyway instead of risking upsetting me by subjecting me to his feelings.

I sigh heavily. "Don't overthink it, Gabriel. I'm not going to bite your head off."

My heart sinks as his now repentant thoughts nag at me. He can't decide if he should apologize for allowing Kaylen to manipulate him. He's probably worried that I'll accuse him of letting her have her way because it was what *he* wanted, too.

We start walking down the hall while Gabriel's indecision ping-pongs in my head. "Just let it go. Okay? I get it, you're sorry. But if anyone should be sorry, it's Kaylen. I explained the situation, but she thinks she's being a good friend by forcing us together."

His bafflement clouds my thoughts, and then he chuckles. "A body might think you were a mind-reader the way you answer un-asked questions. It's downright suspicious."

"A body?" I laugh. "And what would a body say if I said it wasn't that hard to figure out?"

"A body would be of a mind to compliment a lass on her mental agility."

I smile. I can't help it, and I don't know what else I *should* do. Smiling at Gabriel comes so naturally. Friends smile at each other, right?

"If you'll allow me to guess at *your* thoughts," he says, "I'd offer some consolation by saying that I won't misinterpret it if you were to allow yourself to smile if that's what you feel like doing."

I look over at him in surprise.

"Your mouth looked like it wanted to grin but your face was kind of rigid. I've seen you do it before and I've been trying to decipher it. I think I just now figured it out. I imagine you were determining the best course of action just as I was."

I nod. *Well, here's as good an opener as any.*

"That reminds me of something I wanted to talk to you about," I say carefully. Uncomfortable anguish stops up my throat. I'm about to reveal some aspect of my feelings for him and verbally acknowledge that I cause him pain—which makes it all the more torturous.

His thoughts pop hopefully but quickly slump back to resignation.

"Let me have it," he says apprehensively.

I cross my arms and bite the inside of my cheek. I should have thought the words out ahead of time, probably when I was in front of the mirror earlier. "I'm not quite sure how to say this right," I say, grimacing.

He stops in the middle of the gravel path and looks at me with unmasked concern. "Then close your eyes and forget you're talking to me. I'll move out of range so you can be alone. It'll be one regular person talking to another regular person, no emotions attached."

I look at him skeptically, worried that this is a ploy. But he bares nothing but careful regard, and an edge of dread—he's afraid of what I'm going to say.

So I close my eyes, and he retreats until I'm alone. I pretend I'm back in the bathroom, considering this very conversation. Sorrow strangles my heart again as I picture my face in the mirror. All I can think is that I want him to be happy, and I have to figure out how to act in a way that will make this easier for him—and consequently easier for me.

"I've never told you the effect your emotions have on me," I start. "They are stronger and more intense than anyone I've felt before. I think that's why I pick them up so far out. And they are so *easy* to translate. But I think that's because you never hide anything. Not from yourself or anyone else…"

So much open space around me makes me feel too exposed. Afraid I won't be able to get the rest of my words out, I crouch down, placing my hands on the gravel path for support.

"Because of that," I continue, "I have to mentally prepare every time I'm going to see you. I have to predict your behavior so that I don't unwittingly trample on your feelings. I also have to navigate the guilt I face when you struggle. I *hate* making you feel that way…"

I take a few deep breaths to calm down but lumps begin to build in my throat anyway. "I'm selfish for letting you stay here with me. I know you do it for *my* benefit. I let you because I need you for your ideas and your friendship—so I won't be alone. I know I'm using you and that just makes me sick inside… Every time you fight back your own thoughts, I ask myself if it's easier to endure your struggle, or easier just to feel *you*. I can't give you much, but I *can* give you that."

I exhale my fear, finally getting more comfortable with the darkness behind my eyelids. "I want to let you be yourself. I wish I could give you the privacy of your mind at least, but I can't." I pause, biting my lip, deciding whether to say the next part which will leave me entirely vulnerable... Do I trust him not to use these feelings to manipulate me?

What if I *don't* tell him?

Then I may give in to his advances—I don't know that I have the power to resist him. I would give part of my heart only to take it back... I can't toy with him like that. It will only make this situation more wrong.

He *has* to know. I trust *him* even more than I trust myself.

That realization amazes me. I've known him little more than two weeks yet it feels as if I've always been committed to him and never knew it.

"I'm *so* sorry for putting you through this," I say, pressing forward with the assurance of what I know about Gabriel. "I really am. I don't want to stifle you anymore. But I'm afraid that if I have to endure your true emotions whenever they strike you, I'll end up hurting you. When I experience the real you I don't want anything more than to be closer to you."

Insecurity stifles me once more and I struggle to imagine I'm alone, that I'm just in front of my mirror. I can't get a hold of the vision though so I sit down on the ground entirely, exhaling with the security of the rocky but hard surface holding me up. "I knew from the first conversation we had that I wanted more of you. And after the second conversation I knew without a doubt... that I was in love with you. I'm *so* in love with you." I gasp at the sound of those words reaching the open air. Heat floods my face and I bring my shaking hands up to my cheeks and then to my forehead.

I squeeze my eyes tighter, an edge of fearlessness leaping forward now that I've told him that. My admission seems so weak as I play the sound of my voice over in my head. The words, 'I'm in love with you' are too trivial. They aren't enough. Their meaning is so limited. 'In love' has been used and misused so often by people that it has lost its power. People fall out of love as easily as they fall *in* it. Even *I* am guilty of that. But what I feel for Gabriel... The force of it is so sharp and sure that it leaves me breathless. I want to go wherever he's going—that's where life is. Every other path now seems meaningless by comparison.

"I think of you constantly," I continue, driven by a need for him to get exactly how I feel about him. "I dream about you. I miss you when you aren't around. It feels like someone has deflated me inside when you move away from me. You are... more than I thought I wanted. I imagine you touching my face over and over in different ways and I never get tired of it. If I could just have one moment of that..."

You can't have him. It will never work.

The thought is excruciating. I hate this. I hate it so much. I need to get this over with before the injustice of it all gets me sobbing. I rub my eyes because tears are already spilling out. "When you're around I forget why we're apart in the first place. Once I'm alone though, I remember. I can *think.* What if I send you the wrong message in a moment's weakness? I would only take it back because neither of us can get what we really need. I don't want to lead you on. I know either way I'm being unfair. But I want the choice to be yours."

I want him so badly... *so* badly. But this is doomed to failure if I pursue it. I truly do not think I can endure the heartbreak. I repeat this in my mind over and over.

Silence ensues long after I finish speaking, and I wonder if I truly am alone. I listen though and find his respirations and heartbeat. They've accelerated.

"Oh... Wendy," he says finally. That's *all* he says. But the way he says it dissolves my clenched heart. Maybe it's the darkness that has me honed into his voice so precisely but he intonates the 'Oh' with understanding and warmth and an edge of desperation as the word cracks slightly at the end. It's amazing the emotion he can infuse in that one syllable. My name he says with a deeper tone that conveys esteem—with adoration and purpose as if saying my name can convey the depth of his feelings.

It works; I have never felt so cared for simply in the way someone says my name.

I have to retreat my senses because the sound of his heart is beating insistently against the last of my defenses. I need to separate myself from him so I can get a grip, and he deserves as much privacy as I'm capable of giving him. He should have a moment to digest everything before making a decision.

I inhale heavily, eyes closed, trying not to dwell on the memory of his voice wrapping around my name. I wait with a vulnerable heart, fighting to regain my footing in resolve. I press my hands harder to the ground next to me until the rocks stab my palms painfully.

When I finally find a piece of courage large enough to stand on, I start to wonder why he hasn't said anything else. And then I can't figure out what I expect him to say. Either he'll decline and continue suppressing his feelings as best as he can, or he'll take my offer knowing what's at stake. That sounds ridiculous, I realize, to think that I should expect him to somehow *resist* me if I get out of hand. Or worse, he would have to endure my apologies for words or actions delivered during a chemistry-driven moment. It's even more unfair than asking him to inhibit his thoughts. I hang my head, ashamed of even asking.

I definitely should have thought this through more.

My eyes have been closed this entire time and now I put my hands over them in shame, gritting my teeth against the enormous knots in my throat. I want to curl into a ball or lie on the ground, but I feel idiotic enough. And the damage has already been done…

Gabriel clears his throat, but I don't look up.

"I'm sorry," I reply softly, hopefully loud enough that he can hear. "That's unbearably, horribly, terribly selfish of me to even bring up. I just didn't think it through. Of course I don't expect you to—"

"I'll do it."

I look up into his composed face. The sight of him brings another wave of indecision. I have never fought against my emotions so forcefully. It's hard to even get words out amid my internal battle. "You'll what…?"

"I'll exchange freedom of thought for never making assumptions about the intent of your words or actions. Even if you plead with me to satisfy your romantic wants, I will resist you and never take them as a promise of fidelity or romantic intent. But with one condition, which you must promise me with your whole being you will uphold."

"What's that?" I ask, hardly believing that he's actually agreeing to this.

"We have a trigger word—a code word or phrase if you will."

I look at him with confusion.

"Should you ever wish to nullify our contract, you give the trigger word, and I'll know you are not just giving in to your more primitive desires."

I stand up. "You would do that?" I ask.

"Without a doubt," Gabriel says dismissively. "As I told you, I'm not good at stifling my thoughts. The past couple weeks have felt like trying to thread rope through a needle. I'll exchange that for pretty much anything, including resisting the possible advances of an alluring woman whom—" He stops. Looks up. Swallows. I don't have to have him in my emodar to know that he's holding back words. He looks at me finally. "I'll deem it a challenge. I never fail at self-imposed challenges." He stares into my eyes with definite intent. "In fact, I *love* such challenges like no other, Wendy."

Something is wrong. I think I just made a grave error, but I can't think properly with the flood of warmth pulsing into me at his words. It doesn't matter that he hasn't said it precisely—probably he is still sticking to his promise to watch his words—but I know with certainty what he just told me: *He loves me.* And my name again... He says it submissively. With unafraid tenderness. I can't find coherency and tears spring to my eyes—happy tears. Tiny explosions of euphoria burst within me and they dull any inkling of self-deprecation over the situation. His voice has drugged me, burning out the intelligent part of my brain.

I have to look away from him to calm my breathing and stop up the bliss that's going to entirely consume my sensibilities if I don't get a handle on it quick.

"I'll agree to your terms," I manage finally. "As long as you understand 'an unchecked mind' the same way I do."

Gabriel has been watching my reaction carefully and he doesn't hesitate to reply, "Of course. It means I can do whatever in tarnation I want to with my own mind, and nothing else." He crosses his arms and grins at me expectantly.

"And you still have to watch your words. And no touching-but-not-touching me with your breath on my neck or your hands in my hair or anything else," I reply, thinking I get now why he agreed so readily. He'd probably *like* it if I lost control even if it meant I'd take it back later. I think he'd enjoy having that kind of hold over me. Well I like a challenge, too. I think he underestimates me.

"As long as *you* understand that I can do whatever I will with my own brain waves," he says. "I can woo you into oblivion with my thoughts if I want to."

"And I can get away from you whenever I feel like it."

Gabriel sniggers. "Whenever you want to."

"Then you have a deal," I say, knowing that sooner or later I'm going to figure out the error of my ways.

"What word would you like to use?" he asks.

"I don't know. You're the master of obscure words. You tell me."

Gabriel thinks briefly and then smiles softly. "I think I'll opt for a phrase. How about 'gild the lily'?"

"What does that mean?"

Gabriel looks at me pointedly. "You don't know?"

I shake my head.

"Well I'll let you figure it out on your own," he replies, raising an expectant eyebrow.

I don't know why he's being cryptic. But since I never intend on using the phrase, it doesn't matter *what* it means. "Whatever," I reply. "'Gild the lily' it is—Wait, I'm not saying the phrase, I'm saying I agree with it—No, I'm not saying I agree with it. I agree with its use! That's the phrase we'll use!"

"Oh don't worry," Gabriel says, mocking. "When you actually say it, I'll know you mean it… But you can't be too careful. I can't promise I'll be able to control myself if I hear it again—even accidentally. Your admission has me inebriated at the moment. I'm at my limit of temptation with you. Don't say I didn't warn you."

I roll my eyes and we start walking once more toward the stables. I gather up the competitive part of myself. The only way this is going to work is if I treat it like a game. I have to prove to myself and to him that I have self-control. But my thoughts keep getting hazy and love-drunk with Gabriel dancing in my head with the dizzying rapture of abandon once more. No sooner have I thought that than he mentally embraces me with sudden passionate craving. My limbs feel like jelly and it's hard to imagine that I'm still several feet away from him. I still don't understand how he can touch me so directly with just his feelings.

I suck in several breaths. This is definitely not a fair match. I move to the other side of the path and fall back to get away, but even distance can't erase my own yearning. I hug my arms to myself just to give my aching hands something to do. I settle on a reasonable distance from him and concentrate on putting one foot in front of the other.

Gabriel just laughs at me joyously, and I smile because his buoyancy is like a balm to my soul. All I ever want to do is make him this happy and carefree.

25

As we approach the stables, Kaylen eyes the space between Gabriel and me with disappointment. "What took you so long?" she chides. "I nearly left without you."

"Don't get your horseshoes in a bend, Kaylee. We just had some business to attend to," Gabriel says cheerily.

His tone surprises her, and she looks over at my sullen expression with what I imagine is confusion. I'm not close enough to know for sure.

"What could possibly be more important than riding, Gabe? Anyway, I've got you both tacked up already. You can thank me now."

"Sorry you had to get them ready by yourself," I say, my excitement growing. This will only be my third time riding. We would have gone more often, but scheduling has gotten in the way. When Kaylen wants to ride, she waits for no one.

"Before we go, I think you should take your gloves off and touch Chancy," Kaylen says like it's the most practical idea in the world.

"No!" I protest, shocked that she would even think of putting up one of her precious horses for an experiment. "What if he drops dead?"

"You've touched a cat, haven't you? He should be fine," she replies.

"You should just tap him on the nose once, like Louise said she did with you. That way the most you'll do is knock him out," says Gabriel, agreeing enthusiastically.

"I still can't believe she did that," I mumble. "She could have killed herself."

Gabriel shrugs. "She must have been confident enough about what she thought would happen."

Confident *enough*? How exactly do you get confident *enough* to touch someone with lethal skin?

"Come on, now," says Kaylen impatiently. "Tap the sweet horsey on the nose so we can go."

I look into Chancy's big brown eyes. I do not want to see the intelligence there extinguished. But I resolve to try; knowing the outcome might give me another clue. And I'd like to feel something living against my own skin.

I remove the glove from my right hand. "Stand back," I command Gabriel and Kaylen. They lead their horses several yards away.

I back up until Chancy is just an arm's reach. I don't want anyone to have to pull me out, bare-armed, from under a fallen horse.

I hold my breath, bringing my hand out and extending one finger until it hovers six inches away from Chancy's face. His breath is warm and moist on my skin. He smells like onion grass and hay. Then, before I can close the distance between his nose and my finger, he tosses his head, shoving my hand with his muzzle, as if to say, "Get on with it already!"

And nothing bad happens. Chancy just stands there and lets out a snort, wetting me with horsey snot.

"Gross," I say, wiping my hand on my shirt.

Kaylen laughs, Gabriel smiles, and I reach my hand out again to stroke Chancy's nose, relishing the vibrancy of life beneath my fingertips. I move my hand over his face to his head, scratching between his ears and then down his neck, enjoying the sensation of hair and dirt and sweat sticking to my skin.

"Well, let's go!" says Kaylen, interrupting my contentment.

We mount up, and I notice that Gabriel handles his horse with practiced agility. I didn't know he was adept at horsemanship. He is a continual surprise.

We plod off in the direction of the woods, Kaylen repeating the instruction that she delivered to me the first two times I rode with her: how to turn, how to stop, how to go, how to hold the reins, how to put your feet in the stirrups, how to hold your posture, where to position your legs.

It's a lot to remember, but Kaylen does it so naturally that I have assumed copying her will be a good way to make it come naturally to me, too. Gabriel trails behind us, a slight smile on his face as he watches Kaylen directing. "Give her a break, Kaylee," he says. "She doesn't need to win an equitation class."

"Hmph," says Kaylen disdainfully. "Equitation is more than just *looking good* on a horse. It helps maintain proper balance for both you and the animal." But she lets up anyway. I don't care. I think her bossiness is funny. Kaylen on a horse is as lethal as me with no gloves on. I wouldn't cross her.

I turn to look at Gabriel. "So where did *you* learn how to ride a horse?"

"I just picked it up when I came here. Kaylen taught me, and I did a lot of reading. It was something I'd always wanted to do, and this was the perfect opportunity."

"Just picked it up?" I shake my head. "I guess that crazy memory of yours also includes perfect muscle memory recall?"

I'm joking, of course, but Gabriel looks thoughtful.

"An interesting idea. I'm not sure," he replies, completely serious. I can see I've stimulated his thought processes, so I turn back around.

Chancy is content to follow Morgan, Kaylen's horse, dutifully, so controlling him takes no effort whatsoever on my part. Gabriel brings up the rear, lost in thought, not nearly close enough to start manipulating me.

I still have one hand ungloved, and I run my bare fingers through Chancy's mane. I breathe in his animal smell, thinking that even with all the dirt and perspiration, the mix of his odors is pleasant overall. My body eases into the rocking motion of his gait which puts me in a relaxed daze. No wonder Kaylen is doggedly determined to be on a horse as much as possible. Being carried by an animal has a way of transporting my imaginings to a time when things were a lot simpler. Reflecting on that tricks me into thinking my current life is a lot less complicated. Riding is Kaylen's escape from a situation that she doesn't have control over either. It must be working because the only time I can tell that Kaylen is unhappy is whenever she's spoken to her dad or when she is forced into hypno-touch with Louise.

"Kaylen, why do you hate Louise so much?" I ask.

She looks back at me briefly and grits her teeth before turning away. "She doesn't care about anything but hypno-touch. She calls my dad and tells him how much progress I'm making, how I'm a prodigy in need of a direction and all that bull crap. Then my dad tells me I have to stay. '*Just one more month,*' he tells me. Every time it's the same. I've been put under hypno-touch on and off since before I can remember. I'm tired of it. I just want a life."

"I'm sorry, Kaylen," I say. I may have gotten the short end of *someone's* stick with my ability, but at least I have the freedom to leave if I want. Kaylen doesn't even have that.

"Let me know if you ever want me to bust you out," I add, only half-joking.

She shrugs. "I would if I thought it would change anything. I'd have to go right back to my dad though, and then right back here. What good would that do? He was here for a little while, but he left just before you arrived. I can't believe he hasn't visited me at all since then. He used to visit all the time. He claims he's busy with work, but..."

Kaylen sighs and in the sound I can hear the pain of being abandoned. "I wish he'd come back so you could zap him and make him worry that maybe it's not safe for me to be here."

Then, thinking maybe her words have bothered me, she turns around in her saddle and gives me an apologetic smile.

I smile back at her. "If only my ability could be that useful. If you want to invite him out here, I'll chase him around like a zombie with my hands out. That ought to scare him into taking you away."

Kaylen just laughs. "So how's your brother doing?"

"He's good," I say. Then I roll my eyes. "Actually, Ezra is doing fantastic. He's already been promoted from mail room boy to a mathematical consultant."

"What in the world does a mathematical consultant do?" she asks.

"Well my uncle owns a software firm, and when you're writing code the hardest part is planning it out so that you can come up with the best algorithm," I explain. "There are multiple ways to get the computer to do a job, but not all of them are efficient. The CPU needs to be utilized economically because it makes things run faster. Math helps figure out how to organize code so that you can do that. My brother doesn't write or understand much code, but he can look at the problem—say the best pattern for stoplights to move traffic through a busy intersection—and translate it into mathematical form. It's easy to write the code then. Numbers are a lot easier to deal with than abstract ideas."

Kaylen looks at me in wide-eyed wonder. "Didn't you say he was *fifteen*?"

I nod. "I told you he was smart, though."

"Yeah… but you said he wasn't supernaturally smart. But he obviously *is*. He's like Einstein."

"He's not Einstein smart," I say. "I doubt he's doing anything too hard. My uncle's probably just trying to nurture his natural talent."

"Wendy, what company does your uncle own?" Gabriel asks from behind me.

"Qual-Soft," I reply.

"Qual-Soft?" Gabriel says in a stunned voice.

I turn to look at his surprised expression. "Yeah. He's totally loaded. The guy owns a private jet and a *huge* home in Monterey. I told you he was having my brother chauffeured. I wasn't kidding."

Gabriel shakes his head. "No, I didn't doubt you on that. I'm more surprised by the fact that your brother is *consulting* for that kind of company."

"Uh, what do you know about it? I thought you hated computers."

He looks at me critically. "Qual-Soft isn't just some run-of-the-mill software firm. They work for government contractors. They specialize in surveillance—I read an article in TIME magazine about it a while back. One of their big projects is improved satellite surveillance. They basically *own* intelligence technology because of their market-share. If your brother is actually consulting in any useful capacity, I'm sure it's not anything mundane like devising algorithms for search engines—although that would still be impressive in itself. I hardly know how to *use* a search engine let alone program one. But my point is that I think you're discounting just how bright your brother is."

"Einstein," Kaylen says. "Told ya."

I had no idea what kind of software my uncle's company did. When I looked it up, I only wanted to figure out where it was and see if it was a legitimate place. You'd think I'd know more about Qual-Soft because of my degree, but I was always too busy studying to keep up with current events and Fortune 500 software firms. I know Ezra is smart, *really* smart, but code for satellites? There are only a million programming constructs that would have to go into something like that.

"Well I…" I want to defend my ignorance and say that there's no way that Ezra is involved in stuff like that, but the reality is I don't know for sure.

"Has he ever been tested in any capacity?" Gabriel asks. "If he was, he would have drawn someone's attention before now if that's what he's capable of. Maybe you're right. What do I know about programming? I'm sure there are plenty of other everyday programs they do that he could have a hand in..."

"Well my mom... she never wanted him *exploited*," I say, feeling stupid for not having seriously considered that Ezra's smarts might be phenomenal. "She said that kids should lead regular, stress-free kid-lives. She always refused the school's requests to have him formally tested or to have him skip grades. She said school was about a lot more than learning math. That he'd have to grow up too soon anyway. That's why we..." I trail off. I remember what Robert said about someone out there who has been looking for us. That's the reason my mom changed our names and never left a paper trail. I couldn't imagine what anyone would want from us, but... "They want Ezra," I whisper.

"What?" Gabriel asks, not having heard me.

"They want Ezra," I say more loudly. "That's got to be who has been after us all these years. That must be why my mom did it. She knew he was what they wanted!"

"Who is 'they'?" Gabriel asks, confused. "Someone has been after you?"

The words spill out of me as I recount what Robert told me about my mom and dad, getting more excited and more anxious to get on the phone with Ezra and my uncle so I can tell them.

"If your brother is truly that brilliant, I can see how he would be considered a valuable asset to any number of people and organizations," Gabriel says. "But there has to be more to the story. You said this person was after you before your father died. Ezra was not even born then. How would they have known he was going to be born let alone have that kind of intelligence? It's more likely that there's another reason, and your mother keeping Ezra out of anyone's sights was simply because she didn't want any attention, period."

My countenance falters. He's right. But I'm still going to tell Ezra and Robert to be careful. Thank goodness my uncle has money. I'm comforted knowing that Ezra is in the safest place he could be.

But uneasiness won't go away and an explanation is on the tip of my tongue. "Well my uncle did say that my mom was a math prodigy, too," I say, thoughtfully. "She worked everyday jobs to keep a low profile. What if it was really *her* they were after? What if they're *still* after her only they don't know she's dead?" I wrinkle my nose. That doesn't sound quite right. "But if Mom was gifted, it seems like Ezra's talents could be genetic... So if someone knew what my mom could do, they might assume her children would have similar capability. I'm just saying, that's the *only* reason I can think of that someone would be after us."

"That sounds more reasonable," Gabriel replies.

"Geez, Wendy," Kaylen says. "You have a pretty talented family."

I guess I do. And I'm just *sure* I'm on the right track with Ezra and this supposed threat pursuing us.

A memory surfaces of my mom once when she was having a conversation with Ezra's guidance counselor over the phone. It was before she was diagnosed with cancer, and I was in the kitchen making something to eat, listening to her.

"No, Mrs. Logan, I don't want him in the gifted program. I've told you this before," Mom says, leaning against the counter and looking exasperated. Her hand grips the edge, and her knuckles look kind of white. Mom's been really stressed lately, so her behavior isn't especially odd.

A pause.

"Yes, I know he's gifted. But are you telling me that the students in your remedial program have inadequate teachers? That you reserve your 'gifted' program with more exceptional teachers only for those blessed with a high IQ?"

Another pause, but I can hear the drone of a voice on the other end of the line.

Mom rolls her eyes. "So it's wrong to segregate people based on race but okay to segregate them based on their intelligence. That's what you're saying. I know better than anyone how smart Ezra is, but I also know that some things are more important than test scores and AG programs. Humility is something I'd much rather see taught Ezra. He'll have time enough to develop his talents, but children should be allowed to live and relate to other children without the pressures of the future adults want to place on them."

Mom inhales and exhales slowly. She turns her back to me. "Ezra needs to know that math problems aren't the solution to everything, namely people. He will have to grow up soon enough, and taking away his experience with 'the less gifted' will only hurt him later. There is time enough for math, Mrs. Logan."

Mom hangs up the phone.

Impressed with her lecture to Mrs. Logan, I walk up behind her. "Congratulations, Mom. You win the Nobel Prize for most backward mom ever. Y'know, most moms jump at the chance to prove their kid is the smartest. Not you," I say, squeezing her arm playfully. "You value mediocrity like it's some rite of—"

I stop because Mom is not indignant as I expected. Instead, she's unbelievably sad. Mom doesn't reply or look at me. She shakes her arm away and walks out, and I'm left staring after her in bafflement.

Mom was diagnosed with breast cancer four months later. And she died a year after that.

26

"*E*zra, just what kind of programs are you being consulted on?" I demand over the phone after telling him about my semi-epiphany.

"Oh you know... space shuttle auto-pilot, that kind of thing," he replies nonchalantly.

"What!" I yell into the phone.

"Yeah, what did you think I was doing? Helping them plan webpages? It doesn't take a genius to do that, Wen. So why would they waste *mine* on it? *Gawd*, Wen," he scoffs.

I narrow my eyes. He is totally making fun of me. I know my theory doesn't add up, but I just know there's *some* truth to it.

"Funny, Ezra. For real, what have you been doing?"

He laughs and then says, "Okay, well right now I'm trying to come up with a more efficient formula to decipher commands in a voice-recognition system."

"Who is it for?" I ask.

"I'm not sure. I just get the data and then I come up with a formula. I don't understand most of the words involved in the voice recognition, and because I don't know the context I had to ask for more data about the more common order of commands. Could be government. Could be anything."

"So space shuttle voice commands, then," I say.

"Who knows?" he replies, chuckling. "I just do the math."

"And just how smart are you, Ezra?" I ask.

Silence. And then, "What kind of question is that? How am I supposed to know? Smarter than a lot of people, I think. But your friend Gabe is right, it doesn't add up that I would be the target in whatever Mom and Dad were involved in."

"Mom was talented, too," I snap. "So it *does* add up. Where is Robert? I'm going to tell him."

Ezra sighs. "Hold on, I'll get him on three-way."

Once Robert is on the line, I have to endure small talk, which wouldn't be so bad except that I have to maintain the lie that I'm in San Diego doing an internship.

"So Ezra says you've got him working on some pretty high-tech stuff," I say finally.

"Everything about software is high-tech," Robert replies. "So yes, I guess you could say that. He was getting pretty bored in the mail room. I wanted to make sure he'd stay out of trouble. An idle mind is never a good thing."

I have to remind myself that Robert is really helping me out, he's taking really good care of Ezra, and he's not against me. Despite my conversation with Gabriel about Ezra's motivations, I am still uncomfortable with relinquishing my responsibilities toward Ezra to Robert, who can give Ezra so much more than I can. It makes me want to blame Robert for things that are not his fault. I'd like to rail at him about leaving Ezra alone so much—I learned that he took *another* business trip for four days a week ago—but I can't make an enemy of him. I need him, as much as I hate to admit it.

"It got me to thinking," I say. "Ezra's capability is pretty amazing. And I remember Mom being really protective of it. I kind of wonder if she wasn't doing that because whoever was trying to find her would have wanted Ezra. I know it doesn't align with Ezra not being born when Dad died, but I can't let it go. I just wanted you to know because I don't know where you are on figuring out who's looking for us. I want to make sure Ezra's safe."

A long pause. *So* long that I wonder if he hung up. "Robert?" I ask the silence.

"Yes, I'm here, Wendy," Robert replies. "Your concerns are valid. Ezra *is* more than just exceptionally bright. I had no idea how bright because he was never formally tested when your mother was alive. I agree, it's telling that she worked so hard to protect him. I'll keep it in mind. Ezra's safety has been my priority. You don't need to concern yourself with the time I spend away. I don't leave him unattended. Someone is constantly checking that he's accounted for.

"As for who the person who accessed your credit report, I've not been successful in figuring out who it was. Tracing it just takes me in circles. But what you've said makes me more concerned about *your* safety. After all, you were around when your father died. What if it's you this person is ultimately after? Will you allow me to have someone monitor you? Just to make sure we have *you* accounted for as well as Ezra?"

"What...? No. They aren't after me. I'm not super genius. I'm not valuable to anyone out there. Just keep Ezra safe. That's all I'm asking."

"Wen—" Ezra says.

"Ezra, I'm fine," I say quickly. I know what he's thinking. That I've been gifted in other ways that might make me valuable.

How, I can't imagine. I'm kind of a good lie-detector, but they have polygraphs for that. I'm now a good candidate for a contract killer position, but nobody knows that but the people here at the compound. Plus, no one but Mom and Ezra ever knew about my talents growing up. And I am definitely not ready for Robert to know about them.

When I get out of here, I think, *then I'll tell him.*

Originally I'd hoped that when I left here, I'd be back to normal. There's a real possibility that I'm going to *have* to spill to him before then. Progress is slow going here. I can't take care of Ezra in my condition. I hate it, but I need Robert more every day.

"All right, Wendy," Robert concedes. "But if you change your mind, let me know. In the meantime, I hope you're enjoying your summer. I know Ezra looks forward to seeing you again."

My heart reaches across the miles. I want to see Ezra, too. But I feel further than ever from having my life back. I think I see it fading to a pin prick on the horizon.

***

I'm with Louise the next day, practicing hypno-touch on Gabriel. I've had a few other subjects in the past week as people became convinced that I wasn't going to kill them by touching their life forces. But it didn't last long once they realized I'm inept at the technique. I've heard them talking about me when they think I can't hear. "She might read minds, but she can't wave her hands to save her life," is the common jibe.

I *have* learned one thing, however, from being exposed to a number of different life forces: Louise's is different from everyone else's I've seen. I assume this is a result of her being the only one here without manifest abilities, but I still think it's noteworthy. And I can't help spending time wondering at the differences.

Louise's life force swirls inward toward her chest, unlike everyone else's which flow aimlessly and willy-nilly. Of everyone I've seen, Gabriel's is the closest to looking like Louise's. His definitely tends toward the chest, but it's less obvious than hers. I wish I knew what it meant.

"Your poor efforts will never get you what you want," Louise says after explaining the 'parting' technique for the twentieth time. She looks at me with the most serene expression imaginable. She places her hands in Gabriel's life force once more, massaging the flow. What it looks like from my end is that she's caressing water,

206

and it gives easily to her touch. I look down at my own hands. They bond more solidly to Gabriel's life force, like getting your foot stuck in the mud. The longer you stand there, the more the mud sucks at you when you try to take a step. Water versus mud. *What does it mean?*

Louise watches me move my hands. I think I sense a pang of jealousy from her, but Louise is still, after so much time of being around her, indecipherable. I think the reason she seems to be off in a daydream all the time is because she spends most of her time immersed in a self-imposed trance. Essentially, she's keeping herself in the heightened sensory state that's required for hypno-touch even when she's not practicing it. It allows her excellent control over her emotions pretty much all the time. I think it's no lie that Louise is the most adept at sensing energy. I've watched some of the others do it, and none of them have the continual focus that Louise does. It's a struggle for them to maintain the mental state required for hypno-touch. Louise, however, slips in and out of it seamlessly.

"Are you ever going to follow my instructions?" Louise asks after yet another poorly-executed round of the parting technique. "I know you aren't stupid. So there must be another reason you choose not to. Maybe you don't want to cure yourself as you so adamantly claim. I know how hard you worked before all this, just scraping by. Maybe you see staying here as the opportunity to hide from your obligations. Probably you don't *want* the responsibility of taking care of your brother. Well I'm done with you. I have others more worth my time." She pulls her hands away and takes a step back.

I grind my teeth, glaring at her. While her presumption about my motivation is the worst kind of offense, at the same time her dismissal of me sends me into a panic. I'm not done here, am I? Is she going to send me away? Back out *there*? I'm not even *close* to a cure. She can't give up on me; I have nowhere else to go.

"It feels like strands of hair, not water," I blurt.

For a moment, Louise feels like she'd like to devour me whole. Her switch from bored disinterest to locking me in her sights and hurling fireballs at me with her eyes infuses me with adrenaline. My heart accelerates and my ears burn. I take an unconscious step back, too intimidated by her expression to move my eyes away from hers.

"*Feels like hair?*" she seethes.

I nod, taking another step away from her.

Louise wraps up her intensity nearly as quickly as she unleashed it. When she's done, she stands casually with her hands clasped behind her back, rocking slightly on her heels. The person standing before me could be someone else entirely.

"Why haven't you told me this before now?" she asks, as detached as ever.

"Be—Because I thought you were feeling the same thing, only you described it differently," I sputter. "It didn't occur to me that it mattered that much. But I don't like to copy you because the strands feel delicate. I don't want to break them."

Louise moves to sit at her desk, and Gabriel, whose alarm has been pounding insistently at the back of my thoughts, sits up. I know he's looking at me, but I don't look back.

Louise watches the window and says, "You're dismissed. We'll resume when I figure out whether working with someone unwilling to be honest is worth the effort."

* * *

"Wendy! You can't tell her!" Gabriel exclaims once we're outside and moving toward the lodge.

I stop, putting my hands on my hips. "I *didn't*. But I *had* to tell her *something*. You heard her. She's getting way too suspicious."

"No, she was pushing your buttons," Gabriel says. "It's one of her more underhanded skills. All that talk about your brother and responsibility. She was playing on your struggles to get you to do what she wants."

"What does it matter?" I ask, frustrated. "I'm not going to manipulate the life force the way she wants. So either I give her something to distract her, or I risk having her kick me to the curb."

He rolls his eyes. "She is *not* going to kick you to the curb, Wendy. You are far too valuable to her. And now that you've told her that you feel something different than she does, your status has been exalted. You could feign motor control issues for the next three months and she'd still want to keep you around for study."

"Gabriel, you were right there when she said she was ready to wash her hands of me. There is no reason she'd want to keep me around if I'm blundering through hypno-touch like an idiot. I'm not ready to leave yet, so I had to tell her something so she'll let me stay."

He looks at me critically. "You know as well as I do that she wants you here; you aren't a run-of-the-mill case for her. You know

208

how completely barmy she gets about you sometimes. She has never reacted that way to *anyone* else here."

"I thought that, too," I say. "But what use can I possibly be to her if I don't do anything she asks?"

"None," he replies. "That's why she resorts to manipulation. She's not going to make you leave, but she's going to exploit your desperation every chance she gets."

"Well I can't afford to take the risk that you're wrong about her," I say. "I need more answers."

Gabriel watches my face with confusion, and then a light bulb sparks to life in me—*his* realization. "You're afraid to leave, aren't you?" he asks.

I huff but don't answer. Instead, I start walking again.

"Chances are you're going to have to face the world in your condition before you see a cure," he says quietly, keeping pace with me. "You have to get over the fear. Embrace life as you are."

"Easy for you to say," I snap. "*You* don't have to worry about accidentally killing people. You shouldn't be passing judgment on me when you have no idea what it's like to live this way. I can't touch *anyone,* Gabriel! And every moment around people is terrifying!"

Just thinking about leaving has my stomach squirming, but his compassion envelopes me, relaxing the knots. "It's not my right to tell you how to live," he says gently. "And I've never killed anyone, that's true. But you say I don't know what it's like to be restricted from touching the people I want to? You'll have to explain that part to me further one day, so I can *understand* exactly what that feels like."

27

"*What* are we making?" Kaylen asks from where she sits on the long counter.

Gabriel, Kaylen, and I are assigned to dinner duty. Gabriel is behind this. I just know it. After weeks of careful avoidance, now, only three days after our agreement was struck, we end up together.

"I have to see what's available first," I say, pulling open the walk-in fridge.

Gabriel hasn't arrived to help us yet. Overall, since our new agreement, he has been elusive, avoiding my emodar unless absolutely necessary. I expected him to flaunt his feelings around me every chance he got, but I guess Gabriel's plans are never as obvious as they first seem. I haven't had to worry much about skirting his advances in between hypno-touch sessions though, because Louise was serious about dismissing me. She hasn't kicked me out or anything, but she turned me over to Randy who has little enthusiasm for working with me. She only has me doing hypno-touch once a day rather than twice like Louise did.

I turn my attention to the well-stocked shelves of the fridge. When we saw the freshly-posted assignments yesterday, I insisted on being in charge of the menu. When I've been on meal duty before, I've conceded the decisions to someone else because I didn't want to step on any toes. But Gabriel and Kaylen won't take offense to me bossing them around the kitchen, so I am not sticking to the menu plan even a little.

For once, maybe I can have a meal I don't have to pick through. There's always something served that I won't eat because it smells too funny to ingest without gagging. I know I look picky, but no one else would eat the stuff either if they could smell like I do.

I move my hands over possible ingredients, looking for inspiration, when all of a sudden I'm drawn to the bunch of artichokes in front of me; I have to have them. I don't want anything else for dinner but artichokes. I blink my eyes, confused by the sensation.

A familiar smell fills my nose, and I become aware of another heartbeat in the cold, tight space.

Gabriel.

I close my eyes, and the need to reach out and touch something—or some*one*—overwhelms me. I grab the shelf below the artichokes to relieve my aching hands.

My head spins, and my heart beats wildly. My mouth goes dry, and I struggle to push Gabriel's seductive hunger aside.

I consider making a quick exit, but I can't move. I don't *want* to move. And a defiant part of me doesn't want him to think he's gotten to me this badly. Or is this just him? I can't separate our thoughts. He must have been biding his time to make me want him that much more.

He is not going to win this.

I don't know what he's doing behind me, but I bet if I check he'll pretend he's searching the shelves for something himself. But the depth of his pining for me aches painfully through my chest. I'm desperate to relieve it.

My heart throbs, flushing my face and making the refrigerator far too hot. I can't imagine how anything survives in this climate.

"Do you like artichokes?" I croak, trying to break up the stifling heat in the air.

"I *love* artichokes. Are you thinking spinach and artichoke dip? There's some fresh spinach here," he says brightly.

How does he stand this?

I bite the inside of my cheek, fighting the craving in my mouth that has nothing to do with food. My lips part on their own, and I envision Gabriel stroking the length of my arms. I think I can almost feel it, but the sensation fades as a wave of acute desire ripples over me. I cringe, gripping the shelf to remember that I still have control of my limbs.

"No," I reply when I find my breath again, "Artichokes don't always need to go with spinach. I think I just want artichokes."

Amusement tickles the edges of his strain for control. The slight break in his concentration allows me to recover some much-needed oxygen with a few breaths.

"Are you certain?" he says. "Artichokes go so well with spinach. It's a match conjured in heavenly realms." I hear him step closer.

I can't find my words then. I'm consumed with the thrilling relief of having him near. I can't think anymore. My body is submersed in tingling anticipation that excites my every thought, making me jubilant. I can't remember what I'm doing, but I don't care. It's the feeling of being in love. He's telling me he loves me. My eyelids are heavy with the contentment of it. But I still want more of him. I want nothing else in the world but Gabriel. I'd give up the breath in my lungs for just a moment of his hands on my bare skin. I think it's only my grip on the shelf that keeps me from falling into him. I think I could eat, sleep, and breathe Gabriel right now.

"Hmm," he muses in an ethereal voice, "it's such a shame, when we have both ingredients, that we can't combine them and make something magical."

"That doesn't mean they have to be together," I say, unable to resist carrying on the banter riddled with metaphorical undertones. I just want to talk to him anyway. I've missed his voice. There's nothing wrong with listening to his voice, right?

"But I agree," I continue, managing to turn around and look into his eyes which are fraught with agonized focus. "They would be perfect together. But spinach and artichoke dip is an hors d'oeurve. You eat it in a restaurant before a meal. It's warm and messy and delicious, but sometimes you don't want an appetizer. Sometimes you're trying to lose weight. Sometimes it's too hot out for something as heavy as spinach and artichoke dip, or maybe you're concerned you'll spill it because you're wearing your new cashmere sweater. In that case, you should choose the simpler way to eat artichokes, boiled with a little butter to dip, something less serious and difficult to make."

Gabriel's delight at my willingness to continue the exchange interrupts his focus again. And just as quickly, fondness gushes within him so heavy that I can't properly breathe through it. Starved of air, my head clouds into dizziness, and I lean against the shelf behind me for balance knowing, once again, that he's declaring his love for me, and it's so much more pointed than words.

Gabriel sighs. "Butter is nice, for now, but eventually you have to eat them together. Life just wouldn't be the same without it."

He looks at me pleadingly, and his heart reaches out to me before he turns and walks out of the fridge, a stick of butter in his hand.

I half-collapse against the shelf, sinking to the floor for a moment. My hands are shaking again. I would have thought the heat wave would leave with him, but it doesn't. My insides have been erupting with their own version of longing, but mine are tinged with sadness. The difference is striking. Gabriel just *feels* without imagining anything *beyond* feeling. I feel while confronted with the things that inhibit my ability to express myself the way I really want to.

I breathe through my volatile thoughts, evening out my heart rate and focusing on finding a calm haze to recover in. I survived encounter number one. And I never even *thought* the trigger phrase. *Because you couldn't think at all.*

When I exit the fridge, Kaylen is nowhere in sight. Gabriel tells me she had to go to the restroom.

Sure she did. I am going to have a talk with that girl again.

"Why do you think spinach loves to be with artichokes so much?" I ask. I know as soon as the words come out that it's reckless. But they're already out there. Gabriel just won a small victory. He's probably smug, so I steer clear, searching for a sauce pan and skillet in the cabinet.

Gabriel takes the artichokes from where I set them on the counter and begins washing them. "At first I thought it was inexplicable," he replies. "Someone just randomly combined them, probably by accident, and found that the two together were better than having them separate. But when I think on it further, I believe it's because most people find spinach unpalatable. They find the texture displeasing and difficult to swallow. Spinach is often discounted because it is so disagreeable on its own."

Gabriel shrugs. "Spinach is pretty straightforward. It only knows how to be itself. Sometimes spinach tries to make itself likeable by combining with other ingredients—different textures, contrasting flavors—but people still resist the truthful necessity of it. Oh they flirt with it of course. Spinach is healthy, isn't it? They imagine that spinach is what they want. But they can never stick to a regimen. Daily spinach is too much to take. Most diners prefer a lot less honesty in their food. They just want it to taste good and nothing more. They want to be wined and dined and romanced with perceived agreeableness, never wanting their food to tell them just how unhealthy it is."

Then Gabriel looks at me squarely and I realize I've stopped what I'm doing to listen to him. I fumble in a drawer for some measuring cups and he continues, "But the artichoke knows better. She knows how to use the things that most people find unpleasant about spinach. In fact, she loves it to just be itself as she has figured out exactly how to master it. The texture and color and flavor of spinach is transformed when the artichoke is around. Delivered alongside herself, not many can resist it then. The spinach feels appreciated for the very things he has always been despised for."

He turns back to washing. I stare at his back with my mouth slightly open, amazed at the beauty of his words. If I was expecting to hear anything even remotely revealing by asking that question, it was certainly not this.

I want to say something, but I don't know what. I want to tell him that I want spinach and artichoke dip, but I can't. A beautiful metaphor doesn't erase the reality that, right now, I can't give him what he needs. He can't deny that.

***

When people start coming into the kitchen for dinner, I watch their appreciative looks as the smells greet them. I've been nervous. I've never cooked for anyone other than my mom and my brother, and certainly not since my senses have vastly improved. I worry that I might have made things too bland since I pick up nuances of flavor with no trouble. Normal palates will not be so acute.

Nevertheless, when people start into their food, enthusiastic exclamations abound.

Gabriel looks at me from across the table with an air of 'I told you so.' He watched me with rapt attention, surprised and enthusiastic about what I wanted to make even though I fretted the whole time that it wasn't going to turn out right. He didn't realize I had cooking skills.

"I know Gabe doesn't cook this well—I've worked with him before. And Kaylen can barely hold a knife," Chloe says loudly. "This has got to be your doing, Wendy." She forks another bite of her cinnamon beef and béchamel filled pastry. Artichokes always make me think of Greek food which is why I went with a pastitsio inspired twist on empanadas.

"I had help," I say happily and tap my nose so that only Gabriel and Kaylen can see.

"Don't sell yourself short," says Gabriel in a lower voice. "It takes more than a sharp nose to put ingredients together artfully."

"Have you cooked a lot?" asks Corinne. "You should do cooking school and be a chef. I would *definitely* frequent your restaurant."

I feel especially pleased by Corinne's compliment until I remember her gift of being able to schmooze people.

"Thanks, Corinne. I do it for myself mostly. I'm not interested in climbing that ladder."

I like to be useful, I decide, as I watch people devour their food. Gabriel excuses himself to get seconds and I sigh. I want to enjoy this easy moment. I wish I could get out from under the huge weight I feel. I should be able to relax, I think, at least for an hour or so. Can't I let my problems go for one hour?

I push at the borders of the grey cloud hanging over me, but it doesn't budge. My thoughts just get lost in its abyss. I close my eyes and imagine blowing it out of the way. I practice some of the breathing techniques Louise has taught me for meditation and my body begins to relax. My mind is an empty bowl; no dark, opaque water sullies it. If I open my eyes, my calm will fall apart. So I keep them closed, and decide, since the skies are clear, I can take a moment to daydream about Gabriel without guilt and frustration. I think about the moments in the fridge, but imagine that he really *had* caressed the length of my arms. I shiver, and my heart rate hikes up a notch.

The clean smell hits me just then, which is strange. I know it immediately and wonder why it is that I remember it now. I only smell it when I'm in the colorworld.

Slowly, I realize that it's not a memory. I *actually* smell it. Right now.

I open my eyes to blinding lights. I look around in wonder, amazed. I just came into the colorworld without the aid of a subject. I squint for a few moments, allowing my eyes adjust like always. The lights are too bright to look into at first, but gradually things tone down a bit and I can actually see things without feeling like I'm staring directly into a light bulb.

"I wonder, are you watching the colorworld?" whispers Gabriel's voice next to me.

I jump slightly.

"What are you doing?" I hiss without turning, his direction. His voice is so close, and I don't want to accidently bump him with some exposed part of my skin.

Mild confusion passes from him to me. Then recognition.

"Kaylen took my seat. She thinks it's funny to watch you squirm around me," he whispers back.

I wonder how I'm seeing this but then, with a quick glance down, I realize that Gabriel's arm is only inches from my own gloved one, our life forces reaching for and touching one another.

Invading my thoughts with impatient curiosity, he whispers, "You see the colorworld? You have that look, like you've just been blinded, and whenever you're there your eyes are unfocused like a blind person—seeing but not seeing what's right in front of you. You *must* be in the colorworld."

I smile, still not looking his direction. "Yes. You know, we'd have trouble on our hands if *you* were in my shoes. You're ridiculously observant, and that combined with incredible eyesight, hearing, and smell? You would be a force to be reckoned with. I obviously don't know how to use my talents very well."

His immediate shock stuns me, and I'd like to look at his face to figure out where this sudden amazement has come from, but I'm afraid to move with him so close.

Then he becomes tentative and testing. "You're wrong about that. I'm *too* observant," he whispers back, still dangerously close to my ear. "Your ability to turn off your senses is impressive and necessary. I'd be an ADHD squirrel on heroine looking for a single nut in a cornfield. I'd never sleep."

I can't help giggling, and I reach up with my free hand to stifle it.

My amusement becomes quickly overshadowed by Gabriel's thoughts, which are utterly mystified. He somersaults nimbly through several ideas, becoming more excited upon each landing until the intensity of his final conclusion ping-pongs impatiently inside my head.

The colors fade just then, and in my peripheral vision I see that he has removed his arm from its place next to mine.

Assuming he's still unacceptably close to my ear after whispering into it, I lean to the opposite side to get away from him. I turn to scold him with my eyes. But to my surprise, he's leaning away from me. And what's more, he's springing lightly through a thousand possibilities, thoroughly amazed.

"That was odd," I say quietly, as his waves of awed enthusiasm swell.

"This *is* a fascinating development," Gabriel says quietly, propping his elbow on the table, chin in hand, staring at nothing as his mind swims past the breakers of his own marveling to engage in critical thought once more.

I can't imagine why it's as fascinating as he seems to think it is. It doesn't change much. It just allows me to view the colorworld whenever I want, no hypno-touch subject required. Just someone's arm, apparently.

"Uh huh," I say, unimpressed. He must be trying to confuse me with emotion to distract me from his breach in our agreement. "You know being that close to my ear wasn't necessary. Don't tell me you did it so I'd hear you. I can hear you even if you whisper from the other side of the room."

He glances over at me, suppresses a retort, and then breaks off in mid-thought. He vaults through several analytical combinations too fast for me to keep up.

Maybe he wants to punish me for calling him out, or maybe it's a random emotion floating through his head, but desire pulls me in suddenly and passionately, as if grasping me in a robust tango hold, and then sweeping me toward the floor in a sensual dip before pulling me back up. It dislodges my heart and I cross my arms to hold myself together, breathless with the sultriness of the movement.

I hate that I don't have more self-control. If he can directly experience such all-encompassing feelings without so much as shifting his feet, surely *I* should be able to do the same. I wonder if the simple fact of catching me off guard is what makes them so forceful. Or maybe Gabriel is just used to feeling things this intensely. Whatever it is, he has mastered the skill of discharging them on command.

Strangely though, Gabriel's thoughts take a drastic turn in the middle of the pangs. He touches down on an idea which sends currents of gleeful possibilities down my spine.

I look over at him. "What?" I ask. "What did you figure out?"

My question only seems to excite him more, almost like I've confirmed his conclusion simply by asking.

"What did I say?" I scowl at him, willing that he tell me exactly what's got him so excited.

He refuses. I huff with frustration, listening to his silence so hard that I think my face turns red.

"Don't burst an artery," he says finally. "It's merely a theory. I'd tell you, but I'm afraid such topics are against our agreement."

I grab my plate and cup and glare at him with aggravation as I rise from my chair. "And artichokes and spinach and breathing down my neck are totally okay?" I hiss.

He grins at me. "What do vegetables have to do with our agreement?"

I stalk toward the sink with my dishes and wish I didn't have to stay to wash them as part of kitchen duty. I lean against the counter with my arms folded, fuming. Gabriel probably has a new way to torture me.

"Wendy," Gabriel's voice whispers from across the room.

I look up to see him staring at me.

"There are other ways to eat spinach and artichokes together even if you don't have the ingredients for a dip—and they are all positively wonderful," he says softly.

My lips part, unbidden, and I snap them shut. When will his words stop surprising me? He has no limits on what will come out of his mouth—or his mind. I don't think I can handle any more of Gabriel and his 'other ways' spelled out in food metaphors and strangling emotion, so I make a quick retreat from the room. He and Kaylen can handle the dishes without me.

28

$\mathcal{G}$abriel has decided to avoid my emodar once again. I wonder what he's up to. I want to ask him about his absence, but I don't. It's not my business if he decides to help me. I want to explore this new ability to enter the colorworld at will, but I need him to be the subject. He is the only one who knows what I can do. Without him, I feel like I'm not making any progress. To keep from sinking into depression, I've spent my spare time riding with Kaylen. Sometimes we go twice a day.

Randy always goes about our sessions with her eye on the clock as if she's charging me by the hour. She watches my face a lot. Louise never cared what I was doing with my face, just my hands. Ironically, when I blur my eyes in the colorworld I look like I'm focused to everyone else whereas *focusing* there makes me look *un*focused in the regular world. When other people reach their energy perception, they maintain it by closing their eyes to avoid distracting stimuli. I have no problem staying in the colorworld once there, but since working with Randy, I spend most of the time with my eyes closed, too. I also pretend that I'm feeling the life force when I'm not doing anything at all so I can endure my thirty minute session without incident. I wonder why I didn't do this before with Louise. I could have copied her hand motions without getting hounded all the time.

Desperate to see the colorworld, I sit in my room one morning trying with all my concentration to enter it by my own volition, imagining the inanimate objects can take me there. But it doesn't work.

On the third day after my conversation with him at dinner, Gabriel lies on the hypno-touch table for my appointment with Randy. I try to keep from beaming with excitement. It doesn't work so I hide my smile by pretending to retie my shoe.

"He's ready if you want to jump in," Randy says, placing her hands in Gabriel's life force.

I practically skip to her side, my hands at the ready. I'm going into the colorworld with Gabriel this time; I haven't seen him in so long. I want to experience *him*. I know that using him this way is wrong, but I do it anyway.

I have trouble concentrating at first because of my anticipation. But once I settle my thoughts, I access the colorworld easily. I sigh with the smell of him, inhaling to take more of him in, his unadulterated essence cleansing me inside and out with each breath.

"Let's start with well-digging," Randy instructs, referring to a motion reminiscent of digging a hole in the sand at the beach. I actually don't mind this motion as it doesn't have the ripping or straining effect on the life force strands that the other ones do. I know this is merely a warm-up for her though.

I pinpoint what I guess is a strong flow and begin the slow methodical massage of the life force. I keep my eyes closed because I want to focus on his scent. I paw carefully through the strands—I'm not going to damage Gabriel's soul just because Louise is misinformed about the nature of life forces.

I hear Randy huff, and her annoyance invades my bliss. But she remains quiet. Typical Randy. I've told her before that I like to ease into it, so she knows to keep her mouth shut for at least the first 10 minutes. I push Randy's mental presence away. This is my alone time with Gabriel, and I won't let her ruin it.

My heart warms with the love I have for him. I experience this whenever I take him under hypno-touch. Time has not dulled the feelings I have; the three-day absence has intensified them. I sink into sensation, into a daydream maybe. An image materializes slowly. It's a little fuzzy and disjointed, but I realize I'm remembering the kitchen, which is weird... Why am I thinking about the kitchen?

Everyone from the compound is there. They are eating and talking and I turn to see myself sitting at the end of my usual table. The scene unfolds like a movie, but fragmented and blurry. A voice whispers while the disjointed memory plays before me:

I have been waiting over a week to see her again. I've dreamt about her so often I can't properly remember what she looks like— except her eyes. But when I come into the room full of people I spot her immediately as if she is haloed in light. I want to approach her, but she's surrounded. I need to find a moment I can get her all to myself. I bide my time, even when Jimmy asks her possibly the most boorish question I can think of. I envision slugging him. I'm even more smitten when she handles the question well, sidetracking

Jimmy with an insult on his intelligence. She needs no rescue from me.

But then I see the discomfort distorting her features... I want to punch Jimmy so badly, and I just know the brute is not going to give up interrogating her. I am just about to get up and manhandle him away from her when her eyes finally meet mine. My heart gallops away from me and I can't remember what I was just doing. My intellect dissolves under her gaze until she looks away. I pacify myself with the memory of her saying, 'Thank you,' which is the only thing she has ever said to me. I've repeated the sound of her voice saying that in L.A. over and over in my head all this time. Even then she got what I was trying to say without words. I want her to read my soul again.

I stare at her longingly, begging her to find my eyes again. She looks so classy in those gloves. I need to kiss the top of her hand, presenting myself as a gentleman, willing that she might let me enter her court. I wonder what she'll say? I have to know.

Jimmy is getting impatient with Kaylen's salt shaker antics and he keeps looking at Wendy. I don't think I can stomach him talking to her again. I spot an opening: she's going to get up to put her plate in the sink. I hop up and dash over.

"Allow me," I say as I take the plate from her hands. I wish I could see her reaction.

When I return, I smile at her, get down on one knee, and take her hand... Oh that hand. I touched it in LA, but this time it's different.

That glove just begs me to kiss it, so I do, looking up to her face which is a shade lighter with surprise. I revel in that. She doesn't hate me as I worried she might after our first meeting. Her mouth softens after a moment; her eyes sparkle with amusement.

I am elated.

I don't have the willpower to let go of her hand. I want to turn it over and kiss her palm as well, but I fight the urge. I settle for just melting into her eyes. They watch mine with what I think is the slightest hint of openness and regard.

Needing to hear her speak, I find my words finally. "Gabe Dumas. A pleasure, Miss."

Her eyebrows draw together for the smallest moment and I wonder if I haven't pushed my boundaries too far. Before I can decide what to say to put her at ease, she pushes her chair back, pulls her hand from mine, and curtsies! "Dear me! Thank you kindly, good sir!" she says in the most exaggerated genteel accent she can muster. It takes me completely by surprise and it may be the cutest thing I've ever seen.

She has the room in stitches. Oh my stars. I think I love her.

She smiles at me. I think this is the first time I've seen a real smile, meant precisely for me.

Yes. I love her.

And she probably knows it. And what will she do now that she knows?

I awaken briefly from the dream. How is he doing this? I open my eyes and look down at Gabriel through his life force. He looks exactly the same as he did when I came into the room. Did I just tap into a memory? What about the voice? It was speaking to me...

Oh my...

Is he *speaking* to me with his mind? He's a telepath. I *knew* it!

Before I can think further, the kitchen scene demands my attention again, pushing itself into my mind's eye.

I tell Jimmy he's an inconsiderate cad and force him to move over. I know he's irritated at me, but I don't care. The prig doesn't deserve her attention.

"Don't mind Jimmy. He's wasn't raised properly. It's no fault of his own," I say, willing her eyes to stay on me.

"I'll make a note of that. And what should I note about you? Obnoxious honesty?" she asks, raising an eyebrow at me.

My, her wit is addicting. And the way she sees right into my soul...

"Most indubitably," I reply.

Jimmy tries to insult me, but I only have eyes for her. In fact, I don't even process what he says except when he tells me I'm impossible and leaves. Thank heavens. That was easy. And now I have her all to myself. Well, except for Kaylen. But she doesn't count.

"And he says I'm impossible. What say you? Impossible or tons of fun?" I ask her, wondering if I have communicated my meaning adequately. I would just out with it, my entire heart for her to survey, but I bet she'd be uncomfortable in front of all these people. She seems private about her feelings.

"I haven't decided," she replies, a corner of her mouth drawn down. She must still blame me...

222

"Would it help if I apologized for playing a part in violating your privacy not so long ago? I've been feeling ghastly about the whole event all this time, just itching to get in front of you and make amends, as well as find out if you truly are as spirited as you seemed that day—I'd say that question has been answered. But I am sorry. You won't hold it against me, will you?" I plead with her, desperately hoping she will accept an apology.

She looks surprised, and dare I say, appreciative?

"Probably not," she says. *"I'll let you know once I decide what to make of you."*

My heart sinks. She's not made up her mind. No wonder she doesn't want to acknowledge my feelings.

"How can I help you figure it out faster?" I ask, hardly able to keep from reaching out for her hand across the table. Her eyes have me intoxicated. I think it might be painful when she finally looks away.

"I don't know," she says. *"But I'm pretty sure it takes more than five minutes to get an accurate impression of someone."*

I think she's deflecting me... which is definitely not the same as rejection. *"Not in your case, I would think,"* I reply. *"I could be wrong, but I'd think your unusual powers of perception would allow you to glean quite a bit of depth about a person, just by being around them."* *Or maybe it's just me who feels gloriously exposed to her gaze.*

She starts to look uncomfortable again, and that worries me until she says, *"Yes. But you're kind of unusual. I don't think I've encountered anyone before who was quite so... forthcoming with his thoughts."*

My heart soars right out of my chest. She was definitely deflecting. So I ask more questions to keep her talking, hoping that she'll reveal some part of her feelings. How long has it been? Five minutes? An hour? Everything she says makes me wish for the moment to never end. I want her to look into my eyes and read my thoughts all day, every day. What has come over me? I hardly know her, but when she looks at me... I feel fully known.

The scene fades, and Randy's voice is in my ear. "Wendy? Are you going to dig all day long?"

I pull my hands away from Gabriel and look at her, disjointed as I'm pulled between reality and daydream. I don't know what I'm supposed to be doing. How long have I been pawing at Gabriel's life force?

What just happened?

Does Gabriel know that just happened?

I look down at him, then over at Randy who stands in front of me with her arms crossed and her nose wrinkled, her annoyance fighting its way past my bafflement.

How am I supposed to think when I just sank leagues into what has to be Gabriel's memory?

"I'm done for today, Randy," I say. "See you tomorrow."

I don't wait for a response. I turn and stride quickly from the room.

***

"How did you do that?" I ask Gabriel, my hands on my hips.

I just sat in my room for an hour, trying to figure out how he put thoughts in my head. All I kept thinking is that he must be some kind of telepath. He lied to me about his abilities... Only I don't think Gabriel *does* lie. But I couldn't guess how he did it. Desperation won out and I've now cornered him in front of his room.

"What are you referring to, Wendy?" he asks.

"You know. Putting *memories* in my head. *Speaking* to me in my head! How... I mean what...? You really *aren't* a telepath?" I ask, flustered because he's always a step ahead of me. Just when I think I can manage being around him, he does something like this. I think I will never catch up to him long enough to predict what he's going to do next.

"So it worked?" Gabriel says excitedly. "And you got the images, too?"

"Of course it did. Come on. Stop playing dumb."

He balks at my words, affronted. "I do *not* play dumb. I had a theory. I acted on it. And you have now confirmed my theory with exactness."

I sigh. Gabriel is honest. That's what he always is. That's why I haven't seriously considered that he lied about his abilities. I'm just being confrontational to keep from being impressed.

"I know," I reply, slightly apologetic. "You just caught me off guard. I want to know how you did it."

"I should think that would be simple enough to guess at. Do you mean how did I devise that I might be able to speak to your mind?"

224

"Yeah, sure," I say, impatient for him to spit it out.

"Do you remember three days ago, after dinner, when you entered the colorworld while I was sitting beside you?"

"Yes..."

He nods with enthusiasm. "I'm sure you remember my astonishment. You asked me what I'd discovered. Well that was it. Do you remember when you thought I whispered in your ear, asking if you were seeing the colorworld?"

I nod.

"I didn't. I was *thinking* it. And when you answered my mental question, you can imagine my surprise."

"No way," I breathe.

"So that's when I tested it. You remember the drugged squirrel reference?"

I smile at the memory. "How could I forget that?"

His mouth forms a half-smile. "I thought that, too. But *toward* you, to test if you could really hear my non-verbal words. And when you laughed, I knew you could... but only the words I directed at you."

"So how did you know you'd be able to send me images, too?"

"Oh well that was merely a guess. I didn't see why it *wouldn't* be possible. If I could send you words, I didn't see why I couldn't send you images as well."

"Whoa, that is *crazy*," I gasp.

Gabriel grins. "It would appear that in the colorworld you can hear thoughts—but only the ones intended for you. Otherwise, you would have heard me contemplating your reactions and deciding to test you."

"Are you sure that's *my* ability?" I ask skeptically. "Are you sure it's not you?"

"It is definitely not me," Gabriel disagrees. "And anyway, it makes sense that your empathic ability would allow you to 'hear' with your mind things in the colorworld that you can't otherwise hear. The same thing applies to all your other senses. We've always said your emodar is akin to mind-reading. It would appear that even *that* sense has special capability in the colorworld. I'd say it's simply strange that we discovered it in the way we did."

I exhale slowly. I feel like crying. Being around him makes me deliriously happy. Every time I let him in like this and just have a conversation, I am wowed all over again. His intellect is like some kind of drug for me; I love to experience it in action.

He watches my face, and I deliberately look into his eyes which floods him with wave after wave of deepening serenity.

Gosh, I know this is wrong. I know what I'm communicating to him by giving him this attention, and so does he. After all, he just *told* me with his memory how I can get to him, how I can communicate love without saying it.

When she looks at me... I feel fully known...

I couldn't be communicating my love any more clearly if I were saying it out loud.

His fondness grasps me tenderly, adoringly. He's exposed to me with such raw devotion, but the familiar need to protect him takes over my appreciation of the moment. It's shameful for me to exploit him this way. I close my eyes and turn my face away.

His thoughts jump around restlessly. The gentleness that had held me so carefully retreats, leaving behind his resignation. Despite his melancholy, however, excitement begins to stew somewhere in the background. He feels he has won something, but *I* know he has just been drawn even further into this painfully prolonged brand of torture that exists between us. I have just given him hope. False hope.

I step away from him, far enough away so I don't feel him. Then I open my eyes and avoid looking at him directly.

"So you were pretending to meditate then?" I ask to change the tone of the conversation.

"No. It took a great deal of concentration. I had to visualize as well as narrate. Maintaining both at the same time is exceptionally hard work, but when you add in the necessity of *directing* them both to you, well that was quite nearly impossible... which is what I've been practicing for the last couple days. I would ask you to recall how detailed it was, but I am sure you don't want to get into that..."

I raise an eyebrow. "It was very clear. That's all I'll say."

I don't know what to say next. I don't know where we go from here. Gabriel doesn't even *need* to talk to me anymore. He can just persuade Randy or Louise to let me do hypno-touch on him and *force* his words and memories on me. He can have me living inside his head the entire time if it suits him.

Unless... I alight on an idea. The solution is so clear. He has not won yet. He thinks I can't escape him, but he is completely wrong.

"And you don't feel the tiniest bit bad about this?" I ask, barely concealing the triumph in my voice.

Gabriel looks at me quizzically. "And why should I? Have I *said* or *done* anything to breach our agreement?"

"Right," I say tauntingly. "Well, you just go ahead and hit me with your best shot."

Then I turn away from him and walk back to my own room, perfectly willing to play this game.

29

I'm not surprised to find Gabriel as my subject the next day. And I'm prepared for it, except that Louise has mysteriously decided to chaperone my session today. This will be the second time she has done so since she brushed me aside. Since I often don't go into the colorworld with Randy, I've felt free to do the hand motions without being worried about causing damage. Randy has probably told Louise I'm being more compliant now.

"Okay, let's start with hand-over-hand today," Louise says.

I cringe. She knows I hate that one. But today I am not going into the colorworld either. I'll do hand-over-hand all day long if she wants me to.

I dive in with vigor. Holding my palms upward, I row them exactly as the motion's name describes: one hand over the other. It's similar to pulling in a rope. I close my eyes to complete the ruse and relax visibly. I think of anything other than the life force strings; I don't want to be drawn into that world by accident.

"Over here," Louise says after a while, interrupting my concentration. "Do you feel this? It's some kind of disturbance in the flow. Feel it?"

I glide my hands as I would have in the colorworld, smoothing out the flow as Louise would say, up to the place she has indicated just over Gabriel's chest.

"Mmm, yes," I lie, moving my hands in a gentle circular motion over the area.

"I'd like you to do wind and drag, please," she says.

Considering what I know about life forces, and how they feel to be made up of strands like hair, wind and drag is likely the most effective motion there is. I've had a really hard time faking this one with Louise in the past. Wind and drag is done by resting my hands in the life force to allow it to 'bind' as Louise says, and then moving my hands briskly in a circular motion, just like I'm winding up the strands in my hands. Once I wind them for several revolutions, I pull down abruptly and then repeat the method without pausing. In essence, the motion pulls the strands out of their flow more effectively than anything else I have encountered. It also makes the loudest and worst sound in the colorworld when done precisely. I fake this one with Randy every time. And I am definitely going to fake it with Louise.

I stand there with my eyes closed for several minutes, winding up fake strands and yanking them down over and over. Eventually, Louise, who is normally composed during sessions, turns skeptical and suspicious. I open my eyes to peek and see that her hands are resting near where I'm working. I look up to see her green eyes staring at my face. She pulls her hands away and puts them on her hips.

"Miss Whitley," she says, snapping my last name like a whip. "I am the most adept hypno-touch practitioner there is. I am not stupid, and you ought to know better than to try to deceive me. I don't know what you think you're doing or how Randy has fallen for it, but you had better get your head in this. Really, for someone who wants to be able to touch again so badly, I would think you would be more willing to follow my instructions. In the very least you could get in touch with your energy senses while you're doing it even if you refuse to comprehend technique."

She *knows?*

Louise watches my face. "Do you think I don't want to help you?" she asks.

I blink, taken off-guard.

She answers her own question calmly. "You think all I care about is improving people's abilities, but you are completely wrong about that. I'm interested in what mechanisms manifest them. Now explain to me how knowing this would *not* help you? I know you are talented. I know that you can sense them even more than I can. I can guide you. I can help you. But you must trust me."

"How…?" I ask her.

Louise laughs lightly. "How did I know? Do you think I'm making it up when I tell you I can perceive energy movement? With a technique like wind and drag, this is especially apparent. It was *obvious* you weren't moving any energy. Did you really think you could trick me into believing you were?"

I look away from her face, feeling idiotic. I always imagine Louise is energy blind because she doesn't see the things I do and doesn't feel them the same way, but she's managed to give plenty of people supernatural abilities. She ought to know *some* of what she's talking about. And I've spent my time here doing *nothing* helpful to either myself *or* Louise. I have simply shown up, done my time, and left to wrest with my own misery. Ezra is depending on me, and I am completely letting him down. Here I am, strategizing mind-games with Gabriel, and wasting everyone's time.

I have no proof that Louise's hand motions are actually causing damage. I should do them and ignore the sound. I should try it her way at *least* this once, and if nothing helpful happens I should leave and go back to my brother. Then Gabriel will finally be free to move past me and find someone who can give him everything he needs.

I will just have to work on mental control with Gabriel. He can put thoughts in my head, but I don't have to listen to them. I have to stop playing victim to my emotions *and* his.

"Okay," I reply. "Let's do it."

I hear Gabriel inhale sharply, but I doubt Louise does. His heart accelerates at my words. He knows Louise has pushed me where I haven't wanted to go. Admittedly, I am afraid to do it, but what's the alternative? He is more intent on winning me over than on helping me. I don't have time for that. If he doesn't like what I'm about to do, he can bow out now. He, unlike anyone else here, has full disclosure about what I can do.

"Wind and drag," Louise instructs.

I enter the colorworld easily, determined that whatever Gabriel intends to put in my head will not affect me. I have wind and drag to think about and the sounds are sure to be fully distracting.

Hypno-touch is nothing more than repetitious hand motions over the body while both practitioner and subject are in a heightened sensory state. It's pretty simple, actually. The hand motions are just different ways to get a grip on someone's life force. From my point of view, Louise has definitely come up with the most effective techniques to do this. The woman definitely knows her stuff when it comes to that. The awful noise is a testament and it grates on my ears. I grit my teeth, just trying to endure it. Louise watches my technique without comment, but she's definitely triumphant that I am finally obeying her. Despite the sound, which I strive with every bit of my concentration to ignore, Louise's confidence spills over to me. For the first time in weeks I feel excited; no more passivity for me.

I see Louise out of the corner of my eye bringing her own hands into Gabriel's life force. I know she's trying to discern the effect my work is having. I know she says she perceives energy movement, but I think what she feels is just the movement of strings as they get jostled by whoever is working on them. The discordant sound still begs me to stop, and it quickly dulls every bit of enthusiasm I just had. I can no longer stand it. I work hard to push it out from my attention. I struggle to focus on something else, grasping at smells, at thoughts—*anything* but the sound.

I seize Gabriel's thoughts then. I know he's been listening and he disapproves of my decision to give in to Louise's demands. I don't care. This is his fault really. He doesn't make anything more of it though and plunges me into a memory anyway. I want to resist, but the awful sound is so loud that it demands my attention. I would rather endure Gabriel's emotion-ridden memories than go back to that.

I'm at an outdoor basketball court—the one at the compound, I think. I run from one side of the court to the other: *thunk, thunk, thunk, thunk,* the ball slaps the pavement over and over. The methodical sound soothes me as the vibration the ball makes on the pavement settles out the odd mixture of dissatisfaction and bliss going on inside my head.

I stop midstride and ease the ball up into my hands, place my feet, and shoot. *Thunk, fwish;* the ball bounces easily from the board into the basket. The *thunk* sound isn't satisfying though, so I reach for the ball again, and this time concentrate a little harder.

The ball soars upward with easy grace.

Fwish.

That's better.

I begin dribbling automatically as my mind wanders, back into the conflict that drove me here in the first place. Details of the basketball court fade into a disorganized blur, but I remain grounded by the regular slap of the ball against my hand.

I've been suffering a fog of bafflement since I met her. When she's near I know she's everything I want. And even when she's not around I know this but I remain in disbelief at how perfect she is. And she's only been here one day! So I've kept going back to her to confirm my feelings. But seeing her only serves to make me want her more.

I just met her on the path outside the research building because I couldn't stay away from her. She wowed me all over and I'd met the end of my restraint. I refused to spend forever being in love with her and trying to decipher everything she did to know if she felt the same way. So I asked her how she felt about me. But I didn't succeed in getting a precise answer like I'd hoped. At first I was confused; she has at least seemed interested. But now I know it's just that my advances bewilder her. And when I think about it, I don't blame her. I may never be able to touch her physically so how could she trust that I would always want her? And it's a valid question. If I'm going to ask for her heart, I have to accept that concern as a very real possibility. I can't win her and then leave her when the restraint gets tiresome.

Thunk. Fwish. I grasp the ball in my hand again, feeling its weight. Try again. *Fwish.*

I know about being in love. You get drunk with the need to be near someone. But eventually the dopamine wears off and you are confronted with a person whom you now see with eyes wide open. I have to question why I love her to know if this can last. I have to be very clear on that, finding a true and lasting reason why a relationship without physical contact can endure beyond mere attraction.

The answer is easy though. She sees who I am and she appreciates it. I can be wholly myself with her, and that has only ever been my greatest desire.

I return to dribbling momentarily as fondness invigorates me, loosening my movements. I make three easy baskets. I long to see the object of my affection right now.

Why *I love her is the easiest part to discover. There is still one problem, however.* The *problem.*

I must win, every day, the battle against my need for her touch.

I am sure to struggle, I know that. Just being in the same room with her nearly overcomes my faculties. And she can sense it, and as a result she will have to fight feelings of inadequacy. I must endeavor to prove to her, possibly over and over, that just because I want it doesn't mean it's necessary. I don't need more than what she can offer. I will have to make sure that she knows I am happy without it.

Can I handle that? Will frustration overtake me? Can I be happy constantly searching for new ways to express my love?

I scoff at that. I live *for a challenge. This battle was* made *for me. Just like her.*

And I know she knows that.

The basketball sounds fade and the strand manipulation racket reemerges. The tug of Gabriel's strings are on my hands once more. Louise, strangely, has not noticed my mental absence. She's concentrating fervently on trying to feel the life force as I do. I slow my hand motions to careful movements, unable to endure wrenching the strings any longer.

I sigh. I would have expected to be upset by yet another invasion of my thoughts, but instead I discover that my resolve is now paper-thin. He is stripping away my defenses. How do I argue against this?

I thought that Gabriel hadn't considered anything past his feelings. I truly did. I should have known better. I *do* know better. I wonder at his ability to be so thorough in every aspect. He is *still,* without a doubt, exactly what I need. He is exactly what I want, but I still *want* to fight against him. I don't *believe* that he will want me after being deprived of a physical connection for so long. Or maybe I don't *want* to believe it. Maybe I haven't come to terms with the real possibility that this may be my life. Forever.

I wonder if *I* can handle that possibility. Can I even imagine it?

I don't realize that tears are streaming down my face until Louise says, "Whatever is the matter, Dear?"

I look at her briefly and wipe my eyes hastily.

"Just… frustrated," I answer.

Her face softens, but she's still victorious and it kicks at my anguish anyway. She moves away, taking a bottle of water from her desk and uncapping it.

"Yes, I can understand that, especially when results have come so slowly," she replies evenly after she takes a drink.

"I doubt you have any idea what it's like," I reply, meaning my words on so many different levels.

Gabriel senses we're done and sits up, looking from Louise to me, his eyes lingering on my face, apprehension twisting a knot in his stomach. He's worried he's pushed me too far. "I guess we're done for today, ladies?"

"That will be all, Gabe," Louise says, practically shooing him out with her words.

He looks at me hesitantly, questioningly, but I glance at him only briefly before looking away. He hops down, takes his mp3 player from Louise's desk, and leaves. Just like that.

Louise waits a few moments after he's gone and then says, "Yes, that *is* difficult."

Everyone knows about the chemistry between Gabriel and me, even Louise, whose presence floats around the compound like a disembodied spirit. It would be impossible for her to miss how uncomfortable my situation is with him. She knows what I want, and she's probably going to make an emotional appeal now to ensure that I remain compliant with her instruction so that I can have him.

Instead, she says something completely unexpected, "You should tell him he ought to leave. I don't think he is good for your progress. You are awfully distracted with him around: always struggling, always questioning, always wondering. It is clear he does not have your best interests; he purposely riles you. You need some time to think clearly, to focus on yourself."

Louise doesn't look me in the face. She watches the doorway through which Gabriel disappeared, as if she's merely thinking out loud.

"I'd better get going," I reply.

$\mathcal{T}$he rich scent of decaying pine needles floods my nose and I inhale deeply. I like the smell even better in the sunlight—it's sweeter that way. With the warmth of the concrete at my back, sunbeams bouncing off my face, and the pink of the back of my eyelids to hide the confusion of the world beyond this section of ground, I wonder why I don't feel more relaxed. Coming here every other day or so for the past two weeks has become habit for me. It always irons out the wrinkles in my thoughts so I can get through another day.

But not today.

Focus on yourself.

Those words won't leave me alone, and it seems that I'm going to have to think about them if I'm going to find any peace today. I exhale with exaggeration and repeat the words aloud, "Focus on yourself."

That bit of advice finds its way to me fairly regularly. Before today, the last time I heard it was from one of my mom's coworkers back when my mom was sick. She had come over to give us a meal and saw how frazzled I looked. "Honey, take a step back from everything that's going on and focus on yourself for a bit," she told me.

I stood there with my mouth open, bewildered because I didn't understand what the woman meant. I had spent the better part of the day crying my eyes out after learning some bad news from the doctor about how poorly the chemo was working. And I had spent the night before out with my friends.

As soon as she left though, it hit me why I was so confused: I already *was* focusing on myself. In fact, that's *all* I'd been doing since… forever.

My immediate reaction was to blame the mistakes of my life on this continual bad advice. Because from where I sat, it was exactly what my mom had encouraged me to do my whole life. She spent all her energy on me and my wants and my needs. Yet for all her pushing to make my dreams a reality, I was completely broken, completely unhappy. A worthless, miserable excuse for a person.

Furious, I went on some kind of adolescent rampage, throwing every possession I owned on the floor, trying to stamp out my existence with my feet. I felt betrayed by life that had made me into a big fat nothing. Eventually I ended up in the bathroom, in the empty bathtub, *finally* facing what I had become.

I hated what I saw. For years, all I had wanted was a clean slate. I kept trying to *make* one. But it kept failing. And there I was getting the same advice that had been ruining me. And it was ruining everyone around me, especially my mom and my little brother.

So I leapt up out of the bathtub and vowed that I was done with the past and I was done thinking about my future. I would no longer listen to the voice that told me to focus on myself. That's when I started seeing those sick kids. That's when I applied for college, planning to overload on courses. I worked and gave my mom every penny of my paycheck. It all started out as a desperate act of contrition. I had to *pay* for being so selfish for so long.

Tears spring to my eyes as I remember the past year in a new light. I thought I was paying my dues all this time. But instead it's been the most incredible act of transformation.

It was hard—the hardest thing I've ever done. Every day was exhausting, full of self-doubt. I cried a lot. Regularly. It's been easy to look back on it and see it as taking daily stripes. But through it all I got Ezra.

I got Ezra.

What would I do without him? He's my anchor. I almost let him get taken away from me, but I decided he was *my* responsibility. And now I have a relationship with him that I value over all others, past or present.

As a result, I got *myself.* Ever since my mom died, I've had *complete* control over myself for the first time in my life. And all because I stopped thinking about my own needs and wants.

Now here I am hearing those same three words again, and I know without a doubt that it is bad advice. I'm only getting it because I *have* been focusing on myself. Again. I thought I made the decision to stay away from Gabriel for *him.* I thought I made the decision to pursue hypno-touch here for *Ezra.*

And where has it gotten me *or* them?

Nowhere.

I have given too much of my attention to my problem. I've stayed away from Ezra because fear told me that was best for him. It has been *easier* to think that staying away was best. But I need to cope. I *have* to cope. And Ezra hasn't *picked* Robert over me. Robert has done some great things for him, but Ezra needs *me*. And I'm here hiding from him under the guise of learning about life forces when I already know far more than anyone else. I have no excuse to stay here but to satisfy my own fear.

And then there's Gabriel. I've spent all this time insisting that staying away from him is because he *deserves* better. But it was just an excuse to justify the real reason which actually has nothing to do with him: I want to protect *myself* from future heartbreak.

If I love him, I have to stop thinking about myself and what I'm afraid of. I have to just give him what he asks for. I don't know what the future looks like for us, but it doesn't matter. Trying to protect my future has always landed me in trouble. It has always made me unhappy. And it's making Gabriel unhappy—the person I *claim* I love so much.

I sit up abruptly and squint into the sky, smiling with relief. I must be getting better at this; I didn't let this selfish downward spiral go on nearly as long as the last time.

It's time to take action. And I know exactly what to do first.

***

"Tell me what you want," I say to Gabriel who is stunned and wary. I knocked on his door incessantly until he opened it. Now here he is, in all his glory, surprised to see me.

"I'm afraid that's a rather ambiguous question, Wendy. Would you clarify?" he asks, on guard.

"What do you want... with *us*?"

His eyes widen excitedly but caution constrains him. "You know what I want. I'm afraid I can't go into it on account of our agreement."

"Forget the agreement. I want you to tell me what you want. Honestly. What do you envision? What do you think our future holds? All I want is for you to be happy. I want to do whatever it is *you* believe will make you happy."

Gabriel's gleeful hope rushes over me like a gale force wind. But on his exterior, he remains calm, composed. He closes his eyes and sucks in a deliberate breath to calm himself. "I would be thrilled to expound on it if you will use the proper language to request it."

What is he talking about?

Oh. The trigger word... No wait. It was a phrase. What is it? I can't remember it. For the life of me, amid Gabriel's rushing anticipation and my own excitement, I cannot remember anything except that some kind of flower is involved.

"I can't remember it," I beg.

Gabriel's elated expectations flatten in an instant and then jump erratically in conflict. I think he's going to tell me, but then he retreats a few steps backward. "I'm sorry. I'm afraid I have to hear it."

"Gabriel, no!" I say, pushing my hand forcefully against the door to keep him from closing it.

He pauses, visibly fighting against himself. "Wendy, I... *really*... want to tell you. But I can't! I promised you I would watch my words. I won't break a promise to you. Not ever."

I stamp my foot and think: *rose, daisy, petunia, carnation, pansy... Dammit!*

"Ugh!" I groan. I kick his doorframe with my foot.

He's amused by my tantrum, but still guarded.

"Forget this," I say, advancing on him. I'll get the phrase out of him by force.

He nearly falls over his desk chair trying to get away from me. Seeing this, I step carefully, unwilling to put him in danger, but wanting to impress on him that I mean business. I reach out for him.

This alarms him further and I smile at being the one on the controlling end for once. I've never seen him so completely at a loss.

"Don't have anything clever to say, Gabriel?" I tease. "What are you going to do when you run out of floor space?"

"I—I will figure it out when I get there," he stutters, looking behind himself now so he doesn't trip over anything else.

"Tell me the phrase, Gabriel," I say softly.

He's in the corner now, and he stops and thinks for a moment, weighing my request. Then he shakes his head. "I don't think I *can* tell you," he says desperately. "You can't even remember that one simple but monumental phrase we discussed. You can't possibly be thinking clearly. The spirit of the agreement was to ensure you didn't do anything you might later regret. I can't be sure that you mean what you're doing or asking."

When I catch up to him, I say quietly, "I *do* mean it. I've never been *more* clear on that. Hold still. I don't want to hurt you."

With everything but my face covered, I am prepared to get as close to him as possible. I take his face in my hands, exhaling with relief at being near him. I close my eyes for a moment to imagine that I really *am* touching him. His heart throbs violently, and I trail one hand down his neck to his chest, covering it, feeling his life beat through my gloves and soaking into me. I'd just stand here and revel in his contact happily if he weren't struggling for control so much.

"Tell me," I whisper, pushing him into the corner with my hand, allowing my body to come as close to his as it possibly ever will.

He relaxes at the contact.

"Do it," I breathe, reading his desires. "I know you want to. Take me in your arms, Gabriel. Please. *I want you to.*"

He tenses at my words and puts his hands in his pockets.

"Don't be that way," I pout, gliding both of my hands to the back of his neck. I put one hand on the wall behind him to brace myself for safety, and I pull him toward me with my other hand and stand on my toes until my mouth is dangerously close to his ear. "Please…" I plead softly. "I can't remember it. I want to say it, but I don't remember. It was something about flowers…"

Gabriel remains composed in tight self-restraint. He looks anywhere but at me. I have clearly unsettled him, but he is going to resist with every ounce of self-command he has.

His control frustrates me, and I push him lightly in the chest. I try thinking of the phrase again, but rather than a phrase, an idea comes to me.

I take his face gently in my hands. "I love you," I whisper. "I *know* you."

It's like my words are gravity. He can no longer control his eyes. They lock onto mine as if I am the only thing in the world worth looking at. I know Gabriel's eyes. But I've never watched them for this long. The sensation is similar to experiencing him in the colorworld. But this time I am not violating him. He is allowing me to see. He is *begging* me to see him.

I have never wanted to express myself physically with anyone as much as I do right now. Every particle of me is starved for the release that comes from physical contact. I remember a famous line from Coleridge's ballad about the sailor lost amid the salty seas: *Water, water everywhere and not a drop to drink.*

And I am so thirsty.

Just when I think I cannot stand it anymore, something clicks in me: a need beyond the physical. I want *Gabriel* to see *me.*

People don't look at each other this way very often. They feel embarrassed, vulnerable in a way that probably takes years to get past—if ever. But left with nothing else to give him, I grasp at this one last tool of intimate exposure: my eyes, window into my soul. For a moment, being this naked alarms me. But Gabriel, who has been baring his soul to me all along without regard, recognizes my hesitancy. No sooner have I uncovered myself than he wraps me up with warm tenderness. It's as if I have physically taken off my clothes only to have him pull me in and swath me in a blanket. He's considerate with his emotions in a way that brings tears to my eyes. My body relaxes into him. It makes me want to reveal myself to him all the more, so I refuse to look away, inviting him to drink up what little water I have to offer.

No one has ever expressed their love for me so intimately, and I don't think I have ever given it so fully.

When we have undressed our souls fully, I sigh in contentment. As soon as this tranquility meets my desire for Gabriel's body, colors begin to swirl in front of my eyes, growing in brightness until they blind me with their intensity. I blink to adjust my sight, and gradually Gabriel's swirling purple life force moves into focus.

I don't have time ponder how I ended up in the colorworld with my eyes wide open because Gabriel is shouting into my mind, '*GILD THE LILY! GILD THE LILY! GILD THE LILY!*'

My confusion lasts about three seconds, and then I burst out, "Gild the lily! Gild the lily! That's it!"

Gabriel throws his arms around me and pulls me in tightly. I turn my face into his shoulder, nearly crying with release.

"I love you," he gasps as if the words have been stopping up his mouth all this time. "I'm *in* love with you, Wendy Whitley. Te amo. Ya tebya lyublyu. Ich liebe dich. Je t'aime."

"I love you, too," I reply, sighing into him. His embrace is unfamiliar, but in a way that connects two pieces of a whole I never knew was incomplete. It's like putting a face with a name. Or meeting someone online and then seeing them in person. Somehow, he's just more real.

Whatever I imagined it would be like to be held by him, I was wrong. I fantasized it based on past experience with other people because that's all I knew. But the flexing curve of his back under my hand… his easy and giving posture… how he caresses my arm like he's memorizing the shape of it… or how his hand buried in ends of my hair shoots the moment with just the right amount of passion—each of these reveals a new facet of him simply through the language of movement.

"I want to answer your question," he says finally.

"What question?" I reply into his chest.

"What I want."

"Oh, that one," I sigh, starting to get lightheaded—I've been inhaling as much of his colorworld scent as I can.

"Did you ever look up 'gild the lily'?"

"No," I say, ashamed.

"It means to adorn that which is already striking," he says into my hair. "And that's what I want. I was already satisfied with what you had to give. It was enough for me to simply be around you and to know that you felt the same way. To my surprise, it was *truly* enough. Anything more would be lavish indulgence. But I wanted it anyway. I want the whole Wendy. I want your ridiculous gloves and your stubborn sense of self-sacrifice. I want your smiles and the sound of your voice every day in my life. I want your thoughts and your dreams, your desires and your complaints. I want your eyes. Oh my stars, I want your eyes. Please, let me have them forever."

His words have me in such a puddle that he may have to start holding me upright. Gabriel doesn't do sweet talk; he means exactly what he says.

"And Wendy?" he says.

"Hmm?" I say, eyes closed, melding myself to his chest.

"I *do* want your body. I won't pretend that I don't. But *you* are more than enough. That will never change."

I exhale in bliss. "Gabriel, are you even real? Oh forget it, I don't care. If this is a hallucination I hope I never find out."

He chuckles, moving a hand gracefully down my arm again to find my hand, entwining it with his own. He brings my hand up to his face and kisses my palm, holding his lips there, closing his eyes, and sighing with absolute surrender.

"You can gild the lily all day, every day, for as long as you want," I say, shivering at the warmth that emanates from his mouth through my glove.

"That's exactly what I intend to do," he replies.

$\mathcal{T}$wo days later, I go see Louise to tell her I'll be leaving in a week. She doesn't seem bothered by my announcement. Of course, not much phases her anyway. I expect that she'll try to convince me of all the reasons I should stay, but instead she smiles benignly and says, "If that's what you want, Dear."

I pause for a moment, watching her as she waters one of the plants hanging near her window. Her tone almost seemed like she didn't believe me. It reminds me of the first time I told Mom I wanted custody of Ezra. Mom said something like, 'Okay, Wen. We'll see.' I had to bring it up several more times before she took me seriously.

I nod at Louise finally and thank her for all the time she's spent on me. I leave her office, shaking my head and thinking I might have to go see Randy, too, just to make sure someone is around to drive me out of this place in a week. I head back down the path to the lodge. Gabriel is meeting me there for lunch duty. I think about Louise again on my way. I still, after all this time, haven't judged whether the woman is to be trusted or not. Sometimes she could be my sweet hippie grandmother. Others times I think she might not be sweet at all. Maybe I'm looking into the mind of a psychopath. But she hasn't hurt anyone, so I opt to give her the benefit of the doubt.

The sound of something moving in the woods reaches my ears when I near the split in the path to the stables. It's far away. I'm not sure *how* far since I haven't practiced judging the distance of sounds. But it's something larger than the wildlife I typically hear. Is it a bear?

It doesn't sound *that* large. And it moves carefully, not lumbering. The footsteps are spaced apart in a way that gives the impression it's on two legs, not four. It must be human. Why would someone be out there? Is it someone from the compound or a passing hiker?

I'm so curious that I decide maybe I can *smell* them. I know the scents of everyone at the compound—with my acute nose, knowing their scents came naturally. I stop and close my eyes, sniffing the air. I smell Kaylen, Chloe, Marcus, and Celine, but I'm unsure from which direction their scents originate. To see if I can get closer and figure out who it is out there, I set off on the stable path toward the sound. Every now and then I stop to make sure that I'm headed in the right direction, listening for the rustle of movement in the woods. When I reach the head of one of the unofficial trails, I step off the main path to follow it after I determine the course is correct. I pick up Kaylen's scent here, but I don't think much of it—Kaylen navigates these trails all the time on horseback.

Her scent gets stronger though, and I stop, surprised. Kaylen's smell leads right into the woods, on an obscure but well-travelled path. I would never have noticed it without her trail leading to it. I listen again, but no longer hear footsteps. I listen more intently.

There actually *are* still footsteps, but they must be in a place where there's less underbrush. A clearing maybe?

Is it really Kaylen I hear? Why is she in the woods on foot all by herself? Then I remember that day in the kitchen. *Sometimes I like a little bushwhacking.* Kaylen smelled like the deep woods and had been nervous about me bringing it up. I haven't thought about it at all until now.

I think about following her in. I don't want to angle my way into her business; whatever she has been up to in the middle of the woods shouldn't be my concern—she hasn't shared it with anyone for a reason. But I'm going to be gone in a week; I hate the thought of leaving her still thinking she can't trust me. I trust *her,* don't I? Well… I haven't told her about my colorworld sight, so obviously we're both hiding something. Maybe if I'd given her trust, she would have reciprocated. Well I can at least fix that misstep.

I push through low-hanging branches onto the hidden trail, carefully navigating randomly strewn rocks and logs along the way. After about fifty yards, the trees start to thin and open up into a clearing. I stop on the edge of it, hiding behind the trees that hedge the space.

I gape in astonishment at the sight. Kaylen sits on a larger boulder, her hands wrapped around her knees and a look of strained concentration on her face. Spinning around her in a whirlwind are boulders of all shapes and sizes.

I can't decide what to do with myself. I thought Kaylen couldn't move more than a plastic cup, and here she is moving things easily twenty times her weight! She reminds me of Saturn, rings of space rock circling her in perfect orbit. The sight is so fantastic that watching her is mesmerizing.

Finally compelled by incredulity, I step out from the trees. Kaylen spots me immediately, and the boulders crash to the ground in a deafening rumble. She looks frightened, but relief crosses her face when she recognizes me.

"Holy crap, Kaylen!" I exclaim as I approach her. "That's amazing! Have you always been able to do that? Why didn't you tell anyone?"

"I—I didn't want anyone to know," says Kaylen. She hops down from the boulder. "You won't tell anyone, will you?"

I have to restrain the need to hug her in assurance when I see the desperate look on her face. "Like who?" I ask. "Louise? You've got to be kidding. What do you take me for?" I grow slightly defensive. I know how much she hates Louise. Does she really trust me that little?

"Well I… There was no reason to… And you were…" Kaylen exhales dramatically. "I don't know. It's not that big a deal, is it?"

"Is *what* a big deal? That you don't trust me or that you can wrangle ten-ton rocks?"

She shrugs apprehensively. "Both?"

I inhale heavily to dissolve my aggravation. Kaylen and I are better friends than this, aren't we? "Maybe the better question is *why* you haven't told anyone."

"I didn't want *her* to know," Kaylen replies quickly. "Louise, I mean. She would tell my dad and then I'd never get to leave here! I'm sorry. I know I should have trusted you. But I didn't want to take any chances."

"Kaylen, you could have told me," I say gently when I see the distress on her face. "I would have helped you make sure your secret was safe. Wow though. That's some serious progress from moving kitchen towels around."

"Actually," she says shyly, "I've been able to do it all along… ever since I had hypno-touch years ago when I was around nine or ten. Before it, I could really only move one thing at a time, and even then nothing too big. Dad was already making me have hypno-touch all the time, saying I needed to learn how to use it, to control it. That's when I figured it would be better to hold it in."

Kaylen leans against the boulder behind her, biting her bottom lip and looking at me expectantly.

"So is part of your ability natural then?" I ask.

"I don't think so. I've been having hypno-touch since before I can remember. I have a peanut allergy, so probably not. Louise and my dad are kind of close. They've been friends since before I was born. And I've been here on and off ever since she bought the place. Before that I had a private tutor at home. I think he's afraid I'll tell people what I can do. That's why he keeps me here now."

Kaylen is usually an upbeat person, but as the words come out of her mouth, her face looks like the light has literally gone out of it. Her shoulders slump, and her hands hang at her sides, absentmindedly fidgeting with the pockets of her jeans.

"I realized pretty quick what a big deal my dad was going to make out of it," Kaylen continues slowly. "I've pretended hypno-touch hasn't done anything. I don't know if they believe me. I always avoided Dina, worried she could tell, but if she could she didn't let on."

"Oh yeah…" I reply, remembering what Randy said about Dina's ability to detect lies. "I bet keeping it from *her* was hard. How'd you manage that?"

Kaylen shrugs. "I just avoided her. I refused to work with her. Which wasn't all that hard for people to understand. She was nasty. She would use her ability all the time just to be obnoxious. Someone would say, 'Thanks for dinner' after someone else had dinner duty. And Dina would walk by all haughtily and say, 'They're lying. They think it stinks. They hope you never cook again' just to be snotty and feel superior. It made her a really good lawyer and I know Louise had her sniff out people who were pushing the boundaries of breaking her legal protections. I swear she just went around interrogating people about it when she had nothing better to do."

"She sounds like a real piece of work," I say.

Kaylen looks a little more comfortable now that we're not talking about *her* ability. "She actually stopped doing that after a while and seemed like she might actually be trying to be nice. But I overheard this conversation between her and Louise once and Louise was mad about that blabbermouth guy that let something leak. She blamed Dina. And I heard Dina defend herself, blaming Louise for her ability diminishing. She was really upset about it."

"Dina's ability *diminished*?" I ask.

Kaylen shrugs. "I don't know. I've never heard of that happening, but that seemed to be what Dina was saying. And she started going under hypno-touch *all* the time. I kind of wonder if she was doing it to get her ability back—if she really had lost it. I started to be less worried about being around her because it really seemed like she either didn't know or didn't care that I was obviously lying to everyone. She used to make it a point of picking on me until my dad told her to back off."

"Wow," I breathe. I have no idea what to make of that. Louise told me point-blank that she'd never seen anyone's ability go away. So maybe Kaylen misinterpreted things. Maybe Dina's ability just evolved into something else... I shake my head. That can't be right. Plus, Randy said Dina knew I was lying about my abilities. So Dina couldn't have lost her ability if she was able to do that.

I can't make sense of it so I decide to let it go. "So what's with the boulder whirlwind? Are you practicing for your grand exit at eighteen?" I say, smiling to lighten the air that rests heavily on her shoulders.

"Ha, ha. No," she replies, a bit more ease finding its way into her voice. "I do it here because if I don't it will come out somewhere else. When I get stressed out or excited it just builds and builds, and I have to release it or I'll end up tearing the roof off of the lodge or something. It usually happens after I talk to my dad. He frustrates me so much. I figured out that if I would just practice with it, lift objects as big as possible, wear myself out, I could go a long time without it coming out at the wrong times. It's good stress release."

"Wow," I say. "So how much can you do? Do you have limits?"

"Oh yeah," she replies. "I can only lift things as long as I have energy built-up. The more energy, the more stuff I can move. And the bigger the object, the closer I have to be. Fifteen or twenty feet out, I can't move a thing. And I can't move water or anything that contains a lot of water—like people. That helps, because I swear I imagine throwing Louise into a wall on a daily basis—I would have done it accidentally by now. Probably the most impressive part is how much I can control at once. I have to focus on objects individually, so what you just saw with all those rocks took a lot of concentration."

Kaylen's youth strikes me just then. With her thick hair pulled tightly into a high ponytail, and the uncertainty in her face, she looks so much like the child she is. She's Ezra's age, only she's all alone with this monumental secret. I hate leaving her here. But what can I do?

"I'm not going to tell anyone, Kaylen," I say. "And to put you at ease, I'll tell you something about *me* that only Gabriel knows."

Kaylen arches her eyebrows and pulls herself back on the boulder. "Really? What?"

"I can see life forces when I do hypno-touch," I say casually.

Her mouth falls open in disbelief. "No way!"

"Yes way."

Her face pales. "And you *haven't* told Louise or anyone else about this, right?"

"Of course not," I reply, feeling conspiratorial. "Gabriel only knows because apparently he's a genius and he guessed it. I haven't told Louise because I'm not entirely convinced she's not a sociopath."

Kaylen hops abruptly off of the boulder and comes to stand near me, her eyes frantic. "Wendy, you can't tell her. Not *ever.*" Kaylen looks at the ground and furrows her brow. "Wow! I thought *I* had it bad. If she found out about you? Oh man. That's what she's been *looking* for all this time. Person after person has come through here, and she could care less about any of their weird abilities. She's looking for something in particular. And now you… and she… This is crazy, Wendy." Kaylen rubs her forehead with both of her hands. "Do you get what I'm saying? You joke about her being a sociopath, but she's got drive like nothing I've ever seen. She walks around, looking all harmless, acting nice, calling people *Dear* and all that crap. She is *not* nice. If she found out that you have what she's been looking for all this time…" Kaylen shakes her head again, and her desperation seeps into me to form a heavy rock of dread in my stomach—I think she might be on the verge of tears. She looks at me intently. "You have to get out of here. Like yesterday."

"I already told her I'm leaving in a week," I say, confused that Kaylen is getting so worked up about this.

She gives me a hard look. "And you're *sure* she doesn't know what you can see?"

"How could she?" I ask. "Like I said, you and Gabriel are the only ones that know. I haven't even told my brother because I don't know how much she monitors communication."

Kaylen closes her eyes and I can feel her thinking. She opens them and shakes her head. As if to herself, she says, "I get it now…

how much attention she's given you. I was confused by it at first, but I never suspected you could…" Then Kaylen locks her eyes on me. "Wendy, I am pretty sure she knows what you can see. Louise has *never* been so involved in anyone's case like she is yours. I'm sorry. If I'd known before I would have made the connection sooner. If she doesn't know outright, she at least suspects it strongly. That has to be why she's been so patient with you. Anyone else she would have dropped after one week."

"Well she can't possibly know. She probably just thinks my death-touch is cool. Like you said, it's the most bizarre powerful ability anyone has seen yet," I reply, getting disturbed by Kaylen's intensity. "And besides, if she's as bad as you say, why wouldn't she have put up a fight when I told her I was leaving?"

Kaylen plops on the ground, agitated. I copy her.

"I'm not sure," Kaylen says. "It doesn't add up, that's true."

"So say she did know," I reply. "Do you really think she's capable of something *violent*?"

Kaylen looks up. "Yes."

"Why are you so sure?"

She sighs. "You remember that guy I told you about that Louise sued because he started getting too talkative about his abilities, the blabbermouth that Dina missed?"

"Yeah."

"Well, she sued him all right. But right after that, before it ever went to trial, he disappeared."

"Disappeared?"

Kaylen nods. "Call it coincidence if you want, but that guy is *gone*. Nobody has heard from him or been able to find him since."

"There could be any number of explanations for that," I say skeptically. Kaylen sounds overly paranoid.

She crosses her arms defensively. "Of *course* there are plenty of explanations. That's how she got away with it. I saw her right after he ratted on her. That woman was livid, like someone had sold her only child into slavery and she was going to get revenge. You want to take chances, fine. But Louise will stop at nothing to get what she wants. And if she knows that thing is you, watch out."

I purse my lips, deciding how seriously I should take her. "Okay," I say finally. "I'll believe you on that. But I don't buy that she somehow knows already since Gabriel has been the only one aware of it. And I trust him. Anyway, I'm leaving in a week. And she can't stop me. And when I do, I'm going to figure out some way to get you out of here, too."

Kaylen nods, satisfied that I'm going to at least be cautious. We both stand up and begin walking back through the woods toward the main path. As we trudge over rocks and through overgrowth, Kaylen's worry lifts and she returns to the buoyant exuberance I'm used to.

"So you and Gabe…" she says, nudging me with her elbow and grinning. "I am *so* relieved that you guys are boyfriend and girlfriend finally."

I wrinkle my nose. *Boyfriend* sounds so trivial. Like I'm taking him out for a test drive to see if I like him.

"I guess you could say that," I reply.

Kaylen looks at me critically. "You *guess*? What does that mean?"

I sigh. "It means… that it's not a trial. I think of him as more than just my boyfriend."

"Okay, whatever," Kaylen says, rolling her eyes. "So what? You want to marry him then?"

I bite my lip. Do I? I honestly haven't entertained it because of… my situation. We've been officially together, as a couple, for a few days—the best days of my life—but that kind of commitment is not something I can possibly expect from him so early.

Besides, marriage is not something I have ever considered with any seriousness. My mom was always single and she said marriage was nothing more than a piece of paper. I can't disagree. It always struck me as something you do for legal benefits or maybe when you want to have kids. It's something you do to make your relationship legitimate to other people. What's more, my limited experience with married people has told me it's a contract born out of necessity and not really something people *like* let alone do *well*. Given the failure rate, it's pretty much meaningless.

I sigh. It doesn't matter what it is. It's not something I have the luxury of thinking about. I cannot even *imagine* marrying Gabriel in my current condition.

"*That* sounded unsure," Kaylen says after watching my expression.

"Of course it's unsure," I reply. "I haven't even been with him for a week. Give me a break. Marriage is not even in my vocabulary right now."

Kaylen's amusement bounces lightly within me. "Well maybe you better add it to your dictionary."

I give her a look. "Why?"

"Because I am pretty sure it's in Gabe's."

"Just because it's in his vocabulary doesn't mean he's considering something that serious right now."

She laughs. "Wendy, did that just come out of your mouth? You know Gabe considers *everything.*"

Good point. But it does *not* mean he actually wants to marry me. "He may consider everything, but he's also smart enough to know that our relationship doesn't have a precedent. It'd be stupid to jump into something like that so blindly."

Kaylen turns speculative. "That's probably true."

Beyond the blissful memories of the last couple of days, however, I can't help but wonder past the endless tomorrows I promised Gabriel. I'm striving to let it go, but I'm still frightened by the ambiguity of each of those days. I may have accepted him in my life, but that doesn't mean I believe he can foresee that he will still want me years from now. I'm willing to ignore uncertainty for Gabriel though. After all, this is just like dedicating my efforts to taking care of Ezra. I have to focus on nothing but making Gabriel happy. And I can't think of a better person to do that for.

32

"And just what is this?" Gabriel asks from behind me.

I turn around in my chair to see him holding the Superwoman costume Ezra gave me. I laugh. "Just a good luck gift from my brother. He thinks I've been inducted into Xavier's School for Gifted Youngsters. So he thought he'd send me with a uniform."

"Xavier's School... I assume that's another comic book reference? Well, anyway, I bet you'd look smashing in this." Then he tilts his head mischievously. "Perhaps I'll get to see you in it someday?"

"Maybe," I say, turning around to hide my blush. I concentrate on typing my email to Ezra letting him know about my return in a few days.

"Well, when you're done with that, I think we ought to have another private session," Gabriel says. "There's something I want to try."

"Okay. I'm almost done," I reply. Normally I'd be excited about *any* of Gabriel's experiments. Just yesterday he suggested I look in a mirror in the colorworld to see if I could spot anything different about my own life force. Unfortunately I didn't see anything unusual. My life force looks like everyone else's on the compound—except Louise's. That was disappointing. I let it go more easily than I expected though. Probably because being with Gabriel has had me on cloud nine all week. Gabriel didn't pause in disappointment at all. He was immediately caught up in amazement that a mirror works just as well in the colorworld as it does in the visible world.

But leaving has me anxious. For one thing, it will solidify my failure to find a cure here—or anything close to it. For another, I have to face people. All kinds of people who have no idea what I can do to them. What will I do? Go back to school? Get a job? How will I do those things safely?

When I'm done, I hop up from my chair. "Let's go," I say, moving to take his hand.

My muscles tense as I approach him and I pause, unsure. In only a second I realize that this is Gabriel's apprehension I'm picking up. "What's up?" I ask.

"I almost *never* wish you couldn't follow my brain waves," he replies, closing the space between us to take my hand, "but the rare occasion *does* happen that I do."

I look over at him in confusion as we walk down the hall. "Since when are you so reserved?"

"When I'd rather reveal my thoughts at a later time?" he suggests.

"Okay," I shrug. "I'll pretend your nerves are really just my indigestion."

He smiles. "Thank you."

And so I let Gabriel lead me along in silence, hand in gloved hand, until we reach the spot in the woods where I got my first uninterrupted view of the colorworld.

Once we get there, Gabriel's nerves peak to nearly unbearable levels. But he hops onto the rectangular rock and takes a cleansing breath. "I want you to touch me," he says lightly.

"Come again?" I ask. He must be using some obscure metaphor.

"With your gloves off. Just a tap. But I want you to be watching in the colorworld."

"*That's* your plan?" I ask, dubious, confused, and hurt by his suggestion.

"Wendy," says Gabriel, sitting up and looking into my eyes. "Louise did it, and she was fine. Derek was fine. *I'll* be fine."

"No," I say folding my arms, painful self-doubt constricting my lungs. I thought he was okay with what we have. We've been together less than a week and he's already hopping at the chance to risk his life just to inch us closer to a cure?

"It's the only way to see what interaction your life force has with another during physical contact. It could tell us what's happening. Please, Wendy. There's no reward when you don't take risks."

"There are too many unknowns, too many questions that we don't have answers to," I say, holding the lump in my throat down. "How can I take that risk with you?" I knew it. I knew he couldn't handle a relationship with me.

"How will you ever know if you aren't willing to try? You can't go on this way... protecting everyone and everything, not willing to put anyone in even a hint of danger. And this isn't an unknown; it's simply taking an experiment that's already been tried and putting it under a microscope."

He says it with such sincerity that I bite back a scathing remark and start crying instead.

Gabriel stands up and moves closer to me. His confusion clouds my pain for a moment but then he understands.

"Wendy," he says softly, pulling me to him. "I am so sorry. You've misconstrued my request as... as rejection, but I don't mean it that way at all. I was only trying to help... I didn't think it through—how it would sound to you when I asked. It was just another experiment to me. I know how much touch means to you, and I want to help you get to your goal if I can."

I analyze the sincerity of his words, hoping that I will find nothing there but earnestness, that I truly have misinterpreted his motives.

He senses this. "You tell me you never want to look into a cure again, and I'll never mention it. I'll never think about it. I'll never push you to find answers. Just tell me. I'll do it because I want you, forever, just as you are."

I know he's telling the truth; that was *not* a platitude. Sincerity, as always, is ever-present in his every word. It amazes me that Gabriel would do something like that—literally give up hope of ever touching me just to be with me... My heart clenches because I can't wrap my head around how I could possibly deserve that kind of fidelity.

"No," I reply, exhaling and feeling ridiculous. Why do I do this to myself? "I can't figure this out on my own. I need your head in this to help me make the connections I can't. *I'm* sorry. For doubting you. I should know better. I'm just... insecure."

Gabriel grasps my hand in his and kisses the ends of my gloved fingers and then my palm. "We perhaps both made a mistake today."

"Your reasoning makes sense though. About touching you..." I force the words out. Maybe they will give me courage to take a step in a scary direction. And Gabriel's logic is sound. There is no way to get anywhere if I'm not willing to risk a little bit.

He's so hopeful that it obscures my doubts. "Only if you want to," he says. "No pressure from me."

"You touch me," I say. "That's how Louise did it... and Derek. We want to make sure it's not concentrated in the hands or something."

Gabriel smiles, his anticipation making me even more optimistic. He steps closer to me, pulling my body toward him until we are standing face-to-face; our hearts beat wildly.

He looks purposefully into my eyes, the love I see and feel there enfolding me and evening out my creases of worry.

"Let me know when you're in the colorworld," he says.

As soon as I realize the next move is mine, my conviction crumbles. He's so close to death, and not even his utter calm can break through my nerves. I try to swallow, but my mouth is dry. I close my eyes, hovering one of my hands over his arm while casting a haze over the fear. I don't need anything other than the vicinity of another life force to enter the colorworld and stay there, but I need to feel for the strings this time because I'm too rattled.

I thought it would be impossible, given my state, but I feel the strings quickly—coming here requires so little effort now.

Gabriel is very still when I open my eyes. He watches me from beneath his swirling purple life force, waiting.

His heart beats erratically, and his excited expectation interrupts my concentration. If the moment wasn't so serious, I would grin at his uncontrollable curiosity. Even when the situation could possibly lead to dire circumstances, Gabriel still suffers from that insatiable need for discovery. It's one of the many things I love about him.

Fondness overtakes me as I think of this, as well as the other qualities about him that are so unique. They come easily to me as I experience his life force so close to mine. The smell of him infiltrates the many rooms in my brain until his essence inhales and exhales through my whole being—just like always. The scent dislodges my soul from complacency, from stagnancy. He searches, and I want to be searched out. He is so beautiful, so perfect, swirling to some unknown wind. It *is* him. I am looking at his *soul.*

"Okay," I whisper.

Gabriel raises his hand slowly. As he does, the memory of Dina presses into the moment suddenly. I have not dreamt of that day in a very long time, but recalling it is far too easy, like it was just sitting dormant for the right moment to spring on me. I don't want to feel that again. And this time it will be Gabriel experiencing the eradication of himself.

I push forcefully away from the thought. I can't imagine it, let alone go through it.

And what if Louise lied? What if Derek was just a fluke? What if the time it takes to die is different for everyone? Do I want to place my trust in Louise when Gabriel is in the balance?

I can't do anything to harm this beautiful being; I will die a lonely touch-less life before I see him hurt. I won't take the risk. I don't have it in me.

"Stop. No. I can't do this," I say, catching his hand only inches from my cheek.

I pull away, but he holds me to him. His body is unyielding, his stabbing disappointment only outweighed by indecision. I know what he's thinking: he wants to touch me anyway, without my consent.

Terror grips me immediately when I realize what he wants to do, and tears of desperation stream down my face. "Gabriel, please," I plead. "I don't want to do this." I'm afraid to struggle—I might touch him in the process.

Gabriel battles himself, and then his eyes find my face, spotting my tears.

His guilt hits me like a punch in the gut and he releases me, stepping back.

I bend over with my hands on my knees, nearly hyperventilating. My body shakes, and I let my legs collapse to the ground where I sit, hugging myself as waves of relief flood over me.

When I recover enough to look up, Gabriel's back is toward me, too far away for me to read him. He doesn't *want* me to, I realize.

I start to cry again. "I'm sorry. I'm so sorry. I just couldn't."

He turns around instantly and comes to my side, crouching down next to me and placing his hand on my back. He's upset and it quickly builds to anger, his thoughts completely stymied by it.

I look up into his face with shock, devastated by what I'm feeling from him. "I'm sorry," I say again, hanging my head.

"For what?" he asks. But only seconds later, his understanding clicks into place. "I'm not upset with *you*, Love," he says. "With myself, for putting you through that. Frustrated maybe, with your self-sacrificing nature that keeps you trapped. But even that's not something I can be frustrated with for long. I fear I would cease to love you like I do if you ever lost it. Thank heavens *that* will never happen. You are obviously committed to it lock, stock, and barrel." Then he smiles tentatively at me, taking my gloved hand. He kisses my palm.

He reaches toward me for just a moment before stopping and looking forlorn. "Would that I could wipe your tears away. But I can't even do that."

"I wouldn't blame you," I blurt, putting my free hand on the ground next to me and pressing down to find the courage to speak the doubt in my heart. "If you change your mind ever, I wouldn't hate you for it. I wouldn't even be surprised. I'd just be grateful I had the time with you I did." My words sound so childish, but they *are* honest.

He takes both of my shoulders in his hands and shakes them gently. His sudden indignation halts my misgivings where they are, making me catch my breath. "Don't you ever say that again! Don't ever doubt me. You know my thoughts. You know my feelings, Wendy. You will *not* doubt my commitment to you!"

I absorb every part of him, searching for the conviction to believe what he says. But investing my heart to the point of banking on his words would be fording a river whose depth is unknown.

"Why?" he asks, searching my expression. "Why can't you believe me?"

"I *want* to," I reply softly. "But... I only met you a month ago, and we've had weeks of push and pull between us. We've known each other apart more than we've known each other together. Just... give it time."

As much as I want to believe him, I cannot fathom how he could want to be with me in the same way I want to be with him. He has so much to offer. He's brilliant and talented. He's full of vitality and confidence. I am none of those things. And I can't even touch him. I have nothing to offer someone like him. The more I think of it, the more foolish I feel about being with him at all.

I draw strength as I imagine absorbing the solidity of the ground. I already vowed I would give Gabriel what he asked for. I will stay with him as long as he wants. I know I will never want anyone else, and instead of wondering if one day he will no longer love me, I will eke happiness out of the moments. The future will take care of itself.

Gabriel, meanwhile, thinks in rapid speed, pausing at intervals to consider an idea before accelerating ahead. Then he gets caught up with something and his resignation comes to rest like a weight on my heart.

I open my eyes, expecting him to tell me I'm right, that he needs more time to assess our relationship, but he doesn't. Instead, he says, "One day, you're going to tell me what you're really thinking. For now, I'll have to work harder to decipher you. Am I being too intense?"

"No," I say, shaking my head. I hope he's not going to continue this interrogation. My heart is too fragile. "I just need reassurance, that's all," I say, desperately hoping he'll let this go. "My doubts are not your fault or a result of anything you did wrong."

He comes to some conclusion, brushing off my words and taking my hands in both of his, holding them up to his face. "I love you more than life itself. And I'm going to prove it to you one way or another."

He doesn't wait for a reply, which is strange until I realize that his words were intended as a challenge he issued to himself. He pulls me to my feet, links his arm with mine, and we walk side-by-side back to the lodge.

How do I deny words like that, backed with his brand of conviction? I cannot ignore how they pour over me like warm water, soothing and rapturous. I want to hear them over and over, all day. But how do I accept them in such a way that I no longer constantly doubt myself as *enough* for him?

257

33

"*I* have something to tell you," Gabriel says after we've finished eating. We're sitting at the picnic table behind the lodge—it's become our place together since I gave Gabriel the trigger phrase.

I can't help that my first reaction is alarm, thinking that I won't like whatever it is he's going to tell me. I suppress it though. For one thing, he's watching me from three feet away with that look of adoration in his eyes—the one that always makes me look away in embarrassment when other people are around. For another, he's *excited* about whatever it is he wants to tell me. So it must be good. Or interesting in the very least.

But the smell of peppermint on his breath distracts me. I close my eyes and breathe him in. His fingers brush through the ends of my hair. He sweeps it carefully around to one shoulder, and I remain completely still, too magnetized by his nearness to care about the risk he's taking.

Goosebumps dot my arms, but then dismay stops up my contentment. I open my eyes. "What's wrong?" I ask.

"One hundred and nine thousand, two hundred and four. You've lost fifty strands of hair. You're stressed, and I don't like it."

I laugh. "Most girls just get a 'Hey honey, you look really stressed.' Me? I get a hair strand count."

Gabriel tilts his head. "Would you rather I said that?"

"No, of course not," I scoff. "I prefer my men intelligent and original. I also like them to have an excellent memory and the ability to count to outlandishly large numbers in seconds... Know anyone like that?"

Gabriel smiles widely, leans in close to my face, and whispers, "If you chance to meet someone like that, you be sure to let him know you're already taken."

"Um," I say, muddled by his closeness.

"Were you even interested in what I have to say?" he says softly. His breath blows across my cheek and he tugs gently on my hair.

I close my eyes and swallow. "You had something to say?"

He chuckles and leans back.

"What is it?" I ask.

"I believe you're a hypno-touch prodigy," he replies.

258

"Okay… Why?"

"Because ever since you performed hypno-touch on me—the real kind in which you followed Louise's instructions—my sequential memory has expanded exponentially," he replies, watching my face for a reaction.

My forehead wrinkles. "How exponential?"

"Just this morning I memorized *The Great Divorce* by C.S. Lewis. It's not nearly as long as something like *The Brothers Karamazov…* but I memorized that one a couple days ago."

"You *memorized* an entire book?" I ask, agape.

He nods enthusiastically. "I could only memorize about a thousand words at a time before, and it took me about a minute to do so. But I can now memorize a page in about five seconds. Times that by the number of pages, and you can imagine how quickly I can commit an entire book to memory. I memorize each page one by one until I've memorized the entire thing, and I can still recall page one."

"No way! You're like an e-reader!" I exclaim. "Download it instantly and read it anywhere!"

"I've heard of those reading devices," he says thoughtfully. "I guess it is like that. It's been quite convenient. I'm not sure what my capacity is... I'll have to experiment more to test it out."

"That is unbelievable," I mumble. I've turned Gabriel into some kind of full-fledged superhuman. Not like the rest of the people here whose abilities aren't good for much more than parlor tricks. I wonder what Louise would think about this. That leads me back to my conversation with Kaylen and what she said about Louise's goals: *That's what she's been looking for all this time... She's looking for something in particular... I am pretty sure she knows what you can see.*

I look up at Gabriel in alarm. "And you *didn't* tell Louise, right?"

He shakes his head. "I told you I don't trust her. I'd never give her that kind of information."

I relax in relief, but for the first time since my conversation with Kaylen, I consider that she might be right about Louise suspecting what I can see. And if Kaylen is right, *how* does Louise know? The only answer is that she has been withholding information from me. She knows more about my condition than she's saying.

"We need to get into Louise's office and look at my file," I say suddenly. "That woman is hiding something, and I want to know what it is."

Gabriel looks at me with confusion. "I say you have magic hypno-touch fingers, and the conclusion you draw is that Louise is hiding something? I agree that Louise has always been less than honest, but help me out with how this relates to our previous conversation."

I tell him what Kaylen told me about Louise being on the hunt for a specific ability. I leave out the part about the extent of Kaylen's abilities—I forgot to ask her if telling Gabriel was okay. When I'm done, I say, "Now that we know I can probably boost life force abilities into superhero dimensions, I'm starting to take Kaylen more seriously."

"Ahh," he says. "That does make sense. I can't imagine how Louise would know anything helpful, but it wouldn't be a good idea to leave without turning over every possible stone."

"Yeah, and what about this: Kaylen said she thinks Dina's ability diminished. That she lost part of it or something. And she blamed *Louise* for it. So to me that means Louise must know something about how to reverse an ability. Only she won't tell me because she doesn't want mine gone."

"Dina lost her ability?" Gabriel says skeptically. "Then how did Randy know about your natural ability if it wasn't Dina?"

I sigh. "I don't know. But it's still suspicious."

Now that I've accepted Kaylen's warning, other things are taking on new meaning. Like the look on Louise's face the first time I did hypno-touch and felt the life force so quickly. Or like the time I told her it felt like strings, not water. It wasn't that she was surprised; instead she was angry at me for not telling her sooner. And then there's Louise's daring. How in the world did she ever have the courage to touch me—even briefly—after I'd killed someone unless she somehow *knew* what would happen? And how would they have considered *latex gloves* safe to use to touch me without some kind of knowledge to test it out?

I nod. "She has *got* to be hiding something."

"Okay, I'm with you," Gabriel says. "So what's the plan?"

"Well… I know she has files and a computer. Chances are the files are old. Which means she probably keeps the newer stuff on her computer. That's probably where mine is."

"And what if she has a password or some kind of security on it?" Gabriel asks. "Won't we need a computer hacker? I can't do it. I make it a point to know as little as possible about computers."

"I know a bit," I reply. "I was majoring in computer engineering in college."

"Computer engineering?" Gabriel looks at me with astonishment. "I supposed I might have guessed it when you started explaining algorithm theory to Kaylen, but what other skills do you possess that I don't know about? Usted nunca dejará de sorprenderme."

"I have no idea what you just said," I say, propping my chin on my hand and admiring his torturously kissable lips. "But it is so hot when you speak to me in Spanish."

He grins at me and raises an eyebrow. "Significa que voy a hacer lo que quieras si vas a estar conmigo para siempre," he replies in a low voice.

"What does that mean?" I sigh.

"Esto significa que voy a hacer lo que quieras lo que estarás conmigo para siempre," he says, leaning in closer. "Cásate conmigo."

I close my eyes. "No really. What are you saying?"

He chuckles. "Perhaps you ought to invest in a Spanish-English dictionary."

I open my eyes. "Really? Well that wasn't very romantic."

"No, that wasn't a translation," he laughs. "What I said was actually quite romantic." He gives me a challenging grin. "If you want to know what it was, you ought to look it up."

"Stupid bi-lingual boyfriend." I grumble, crossing my arms.

"Multi-lingual, Love," he says. "Zhyenityes' na mnye. Heiraten Sie mich. Watashi to kekkon suru. M'épouser. Mujhasē śādī. Kuoa mimi. I know others. Would you like to hear those as well?"

"How many languages was that? How am I supposed to be irritated with you when your ridiculous brain makes you hotter by the second?" I whine. "Well I'm done with you and your feats of intellect trying to distract me. We have to figure out how to get into Louise's office."

"Me encanta cuando me das órdenes," he says, winding a finger in my hair again.

I wave him away playfully. "Focus, Gabriel. Stop trying to seduce me. We have to figure this out."

"I love when you order me around. You should do that more often," he says dreamily.

I move decidedly to sit on the ground. Then I lie back like I usually do, only this time I shield my eyes from the sun with my hands so I can look at Gabriel. "Okay, so breaking into Louise's office. Any thoughts on that? In *English*?"

He tilts his head at me curiously from where he sits. "I noticed you do that a lot. Why?"

I shrug. "Lying on the ground helps me think."

He raises his eyebrows and stands up. He sits down on the concrete nearby and lies down.

I laugh. "I don't think it works for everyone. My brother tried it once and said it gave him a headache."

"I find everything about you intriguing," he says. "And sitting on the ground appears to be one of your idiosyncrasies. How else will I understand why you do it if I don't try it out myself?"

I laugh again. "Okay. Well, is it at least working for the current problem of figuring out how to get into Louise's office?"

"We could figure out a way to swipe her keys," he suggests. "And I recommend we carry out this plan tomorrow night. Randy will be gone overnight on a supplies run. Best to have less people that might stumble upon us."

"Okay. Then let's get Kaylen to take your place as my hypno-touch subject tomorrow. While she's under I can pick a fight with Louise about her technique. She always gets testy but she eventually gets into it, trying to feel the energy like I do. Once I get her eyes closed, you sneak in and snag her keys. She always puts them in her bag and puts the bag on that end-table by her desk."

Gabriel hesitates. "Won't she be suspicious if her keys mysteriously disappear?"

He's right. I huff in frustration. "How about you snag them, run back to the lodge, and get her spare from her room? Then you can run back and return them."

More skepticism. "That may take a while since I don't know where she keeps her spares. You're going to be able to distract her that long?" he asks.

"I can come up with something."

"I'm sad I'll miss it," he says. "I'm sure it will be quite a show."

I turn my head to find his face. "Just get the keys, and then I'll put on a show, just for you."

Gabriel's heart accelerates and he clears his throat. "Duly noted. Pero primero voy a poner un anillo en tu dedo."

"So you're never going to translate your Spanish for me, are you?"

"Never?" he says mischievously. "Oh don't worry. I think you're right about the benefits of lying on the ground. I think I'm getting closer to translating *you*. Once that happens, I'll say those words to you all day long in English."

34

9 exhale with impatience, making sure it's loud enough for Louise to hear.

"What now?" she asks, setting her jaw and pausing her hands that are buried in Kaylen's life force.

"More gently. You look like you're scratching someone's eyes out, not combing out tangles," I reply, demonstrating the technique for her.

"I don't see how this will accomplish anything substantial. You're caressing it, not influencing its flow," Louise says, defending herself. As I suspected, she's been laser-focused on me since I told her I want to do things my way today.

"Maybe so. But from what I can see, *your* method hasn't accomplished much either. Twenty years is a long time to spend when the most you have to show for your work is a girl with a death-touch."

Louise squints at me, wondering where my sassiness has come from. She straightens and says in a perfectly delightful tone, "Well if you think my method is so ineffective, then I'm sure you'll allow me to perform it on *you*."

I think about that a moment. I've yet to gain Louise's concentration long enough for Gabriel to sneak in. Maybe a little hypno-touch session with me will capture her attention long enough… But I don't want to do it. When faced with the serious possibility, I'm terrified of what might happen. What if thirty minutes of Louise's hypno-touch makes a big difference rather than an imperceptible one… like making me lethal *beyond* just skin contact?

"I don't think that's a good idea," I reply.

"Then what *is* a good idea, Wendy?" Louise says and starts bringing Kaylen out of hypnosis.

My heart seizes in fear. Louise has decided to cut our time short.

Crap. What can I do?

"Fine," I reply, ignoring my concerns. We really need those keys. They could lead to actual answers. I look at her sternly. "But I don't want you messing with anything. Just see if the string analogy lets you learn anything new about my life force."

Kaylen's eyes widen slightly in alarm at me before Louise says, "That's all for today, Kaylen, Dear."

Kaylen hesitates. She knows the plan, so she knows it's just been side-tracked.

"Run along, Kaylen," Louise insists. "Don't you have some lessons? I believe your father said you have a history exam coming up."

I give her a little nod, and she turns to leave. "See you later, Wendy."

"Let's have Randy come in. I can tap your skin again briefly and Randy can feel your energy as it happens..." Louise suggests.

"Maybe next time," I reply, probably too quickly.

I'm drawn by that idea, but if Randy comes in, there will be *two* people that Gabriel has to get past.

Louise sighs as I lie back on the table.

I don't think she'll notice anything different in my energy, dull as her senses are, but I have to give her *something* to do while she has me under. Who knows? Maybe she'll actually be able to feel something while I'm under hypnosis. The idea excites me. And Gabriel will be around, so if she does anything invasive with her hands, he can intervene.

"Louise... Promise you won't manipulate my energy." I say.

Louise strides confidently into my emodar. She knows I want confirmation.

"You have my word," she replies calmly.

Her emotions—or lack thereof—remain steady. She's being truthful. I think. I'm not sure I'm a good judge of Louise's honesty, but I don't have any other way of being assured.

I'm so apprehensive for Gabriel that it takes immense concentration for me to allow Louise to hypnotize me. I would pretend but I know she'll be able to tell. In the weeks I have been here, she has tried to demonstrate over and over the difference between the energy of a hyper-alert person and that of a person merely relaxing on the table. But I think they both feel the same. I guess the subtle distinctions elude me.

Louise's method of hypnotism uses only her voice, no focal point like Dina's pen. Once there, I'm so relaxed that I think Gabriel can't possibly fail. I'm overcome with contentment and wonder why I didn't suggest this to begin with.

"Okay, Wendy, I'm going to feel your energy now. But I want you to do something for me. This will help you. Concentrate on your own life force. You know it's there. You've felt others'. Try to bring it into focus. Reach out to it. Bring it in. Help me perceive it with you."

I do as Louise instructs, imagining the stringed sound generated between Louise's life force and my own. If I can perceive life forces so easily, I bet I can help her better examine mine.

The idea excites me just enough to give me the right awareness; the colorworld moves into focus. I hear Louise's hands moving through my life force. I smell the clean purity of the colorworld. I just let the menagerie of experience weave in and out of me, feeling part of it, like I might be fluid rather than solid. I don't think I have *ever* been this relaxed. I've never been so fully aware of my own life force; I feel it flow through me—like a warm wind gusting from the top of my head and all the way down to my fingers and toes. I swear if I look down I'm going to see my life force blowing right into my open chest cavity. My body is merely a vessel; the feeling is transcendent—being aware of my life force and body as two very separate things.

"Are you energy aware?" Louise asks, interrupting my quiet wonder.

"Yes," I reply, pondering the light musical sound of Louise's life force moving against mine.

"I'm feeling your energy now, so keep it in focus."

Louise doesn't realize that my energy perception involves *all* of my senses and she definitely doesn't know it takes zero effort to stay in the colorworld. So I don't have to focus on anything if I don't want to. And breathing has caught my attention. I inhale and exhale, amazed each time at how I can infuse my breaths into every cell. Respirations ebb and flow that with a pulse of life so compelling it's almost frightening. I am so *powerful* that I can push energy and life into myself simply by breathing.

A sound moves into my attention then. Some quiet warbling pervades the background of the colorworld and it seems to move in tempo with my breaths—like poetry. As I listen to it, I begin to think it might be voices. I think I've never noticed it before, but it *is* very quiet. When Louise moves her hands through my life force and generates the string sound, I can't hear the quieter sound at all.

Louise lets out an audible sigh now. I can feel her working through something.

"This just isn't going to work. Let's try something else," she says after a while. "I want to talk with you about something, Wendy. Just remember, you are in a safe place right now. Nothing can happen to you here. In fact, you've never felt more safe in your life. Your loved ones are safe. You feel completely relaxed."

I wonder if she's going to try and get me to reveal something under hypnosis. That's funny. I know exactly what I don't want her to know. And right now I don't think I have ever been more clear on things. And part of that is just *knowing* that I should not tell Louise about my colorworld sight.

"Let's talk about how it felt touching Dina," she says.

My body seizes up. That was unexpected. I definitely don't want to talk about it, and she can't make me.

"Yes, I know it's scary. But you need to confront it. You know that, don't you?" she asks.

I nod, resigned. She's probably right about that. Understanding what happened that day is probably critical to understanding how my ability works.

"We can overcome it together. Imagine the room where you first worked with Dina. What are you doing?"

I can't decide if this is a good idea, but the contentment of being in the colorworld calms my conflict. If ever there were a time to talk about that day, it would be right now. The colorworld renews and invigorates me; fear doesn't last long here.

"Lying on the table," I reply.

"Who has come in the room?"

"Derek. I like him already because he makes me feel relaxed. He turns on music."

"Yes, Derek. He *is* nice. Now Dina begins to speak to you. What does she say?" Louise asks, her voice taking on a musical rhythm.

"She's telling me to relax. She puts a pen in front of my face and makes it disappear..."

"Hypnotism is so calming," Louise breathes.

I couldn't agree more with that.

"You're calm now, aren't you?" she asks.

"Yes."

"Now skip ahead. You've just come out of hypnosis. It's very confusing, isn't it?"

"Yes, I don't know what's going on. It's so loud. And I can see too much," I reply, mirroring the confusion in my head, slightly frightened by it.

"Okay, you're overwhelmed. What does Dina do?"

"She grabs my arm," I quaver.

"And what do you feel? Remember, you are safe here. Tell me what you feel."

"Terror," I whisper.

"Of what?"

"Nothing. It's suffocating me," I whimper as the memory rears up too strongly. I push it back. "I don't want to talk about this," I say forcefully. I was wrong. There is *no* good reason to relive that moment.

"Of course not. Let's talk about something else. Tell me about Gabe. What is your favorite feature of his?"

I breathe a few times to cleanse away the fear. "His eyes," I reply.

"They are quite something, aren't they? Such an animated brown. Do you think you will ever touch him, Wendy? With your bare hands?"

I think for a moment, anxiety catching in my throat. I haven't confronted that question before.

"I don't know," I reply in a small voice.

"You've imagined him in Dina's place, haven't you? The feel of her dying? You've imagined that happening to Gabriel, haven't you?"

"Yes," I reply, my heart picking up pace.

"It's so sad. You must always be afraid of that happening to him."

"I don't want it to happen to him," I plead.

"I know. That is so impossible to deal with. You always worry. You're always careful. You worry that you're not careful enough. You worry you'll harm him without meaning to."

I exhale in sadness. She is exactly right.

"Doesn't that just wear on you?"

"Yes, it does," I reply.

"You've often thought that the best way to keep him safe is to tell him to leave you alone. That way there's no chance your skin will ever touch his. Isn't that right?"

"Yes."

"You're frightened of feeling him die. You dream about it at night. You wake up in a sweat, your hands shaking, because you *know* how easily it could happen."

I *have* dreamed of that, especially in the week following my arrival at the compound. I'm so relieved to have someone to tell. In fact, it was the main reason I was able to keep my distance from him so well. Fear is a powerful motivator. Louise is so intuitive.

"I worry every day," I say, accepting the truthfulness of my own words.

"I know you do."

"He's so sad when I push him away. He hates seeing me struggle," I say.

"You feel guilty every time *he* struggles. You consider breaking it off with him every time, in the back of your mind."

I think I must be crying. How does she know this?

"You are so miserable and distraught over it. Every day. The same question. The same worry. Every moment with him you are burdened with the need to be careful. You know one day you won't be careful enough."

"Yes," I reply sorrowfully.

"And then there's your brother, Ezra. You'll have to be careful around him, too. Which one will it be? Gabriel or Ezra? Which one will fall victim to your carelessness first?"

"I don't know," I moan.

"Well, you're in a safe place now. Don't worry. You're safe. I'm helping you, aren't I? Helping you come to terms with your fears? This will make it better, won't it?"

"Yes," I reply, grateful to be able to share this fear with someone. Gabriel never takes it seriously. Neither does Ezra. No one really understands what it's like. Except Louise. I never imagined she had this kind of empathy in her.

"I will help you be careful. Don't worry. I won't let you forget how dangerous you are. Nothing will happen to Gabriel or Ezra."

"Thank you," I whisper.

"I know how hard it must be to worry all the time. But do you think that worrying helps you keep them safe?"

"Yes."

"And you know that as soon as you stop being afraid, you'll slip up, don't you?"

"Yes," I sigh, hating that I have to admit this. The fear, while it crushes me slowly, is the only thing that separates other people from death by my hand. The irony is so perversely unfair.

"Do you want to remember the danger? So that you never become complacent?"

"Yes."

"Okay, I can help you with that. Whenever you come close to another person, you'll remember what it felt like when Dina died... not all of it, just enough to remind you to be afraid. Because really, keeping them safe is about remembering, isn't it?"

"Yes," I reply, excited. Forgetting that I'm lethal is what has haunted me all this time. It's the reason I've not wanted to leave the compound. I'm afraid a normal life will cause me to be careless.

"Can you help me remember?" I ask, thinking that allowing her to hypnotize me actually *was* a good idea. If the knowledge can be just as fresh as the day I killed Dina, I'll never slip up.

"Of course," she replies. "You have the power to remember anything you want to. So I want you to pick something about that day with Dina that will help you remember. Just one thing. Nothing too scary, but enough of a reminder."

Dina's eyes are the one thing from that day that continues to remain. They were completely empty. Like an inanimate object. Her mouth was left in an open circle of shock. Petrified in that moment of terror.

"Do you have the memory?" Louise asks.

"Yes," I reply.

"Good. Now hold on to that memory. Recall every detail: shapes, colors, feelings. Whenever you are too close to someone, you will remember that moment, and it will remind you of what you can do. You will never become complacent."

I balance on the edge of distress and gratitude. I want to erase all remnants of that day. But fear of hurting someone is a tool I can use to keep the people I love safe. I don't know why, but Louise is actually *helping* me with the one thing that haunts me constantly.

"One other thing," she says. "Whenever you're afraid, if you remember your gloves, you'll feel safe again, even with the memory. You'll feel in control. You'll be reassured that you *are* being careful.

Your doubts will ease, but your wariness will not. Do you understand?"

"Gloves equal safety," I reply, warming toward Louise, which makes me both confused and relieved. I guess I'll get more out of today than just her keys... I hope Gabriel was able to get them.

"I want you to remember to relax now. I'm going to feel your energy again to help you relax. Is that okay?"

"Yes," I reply, feeling safe from myself finally.

A few minutes pass while I focus on intentional breathing, soaking in each inhalation and exhalation, a sense of being unburdened pervading my being.

"Wonderful," Louise says after a while. "Is there anything else you want to talk to me about, Wendy? About your energy? About your abilities?"

"No," I reply. Yes, she was definitely trying to gain my trust by that move.

"Are you certain? I can help you. You know that."

"I know," I reply. She's only further solidifying my theory that *she* is hiding something.

"What's going on, Louise?" Gabriel's voice demands from nearby.

I smile at the sound.

"Talking to Wendy, Gabe. I don't believe you knocked. She asked me to perform some hypno-touch on her." She pauses before saying, "I think we're done now, Wendy. As you hear the sound of my voice, you will wake up from your trance feeling refreshed."

I open my eyes.

"Are you all right, Wendy?" Gabriel asks.

I look up to his face and remember that I have just undergone hypno-touch for the first time since I killed Dina. Her eyes flash in front of my face and I cringe away from him.

"Don't come near me. We don't yet know if the hypno-touch affected my ability," I reply.

"Don't be silly, Dear," Louise chides. "I didn't manipulate your energy, remember? I made you a promise."

She did promise. And I didn't hear that piercing ring that I know comes when Louise manipulates a life force. I'm still worried, though. There are so many reasons to worry.

"Look," Louise says, grasping my gloved wrist in her hand and holding it up to show me. *In the exact same place Dina did.*

I gasp a little as the déjà vu causes me to recoil.

"Don't worry, Dear. I suspect you'll be slightly jumpy, as your previous experience left a bad taste in your mouth. Just remember: you have your gloves on. They are still effective. I'm still standing, aren't I?"

"Yes. Sorry. I'm okay," I reply as alarm releases its hold on my gut. The gloves still work. I'm safe.

Gabriel's suspicion tries to push through my calm. He watches my face intently.

"I'm fine," I assure him. "She didn't manipulate my energy. But unfortunately, she didn't sense anything odd either." I look at Louise. "Did you?"

"Unfortunately not," she says, moving to the side-table and grabbing the small backpack I've seen her carry. My heart jumps as she reaches into the bag. But then she pulls out her keys. It was all worth it.

"I'd like to keep trying, of course," she says, "But with you leaving so soon, that won't be possible. There are other options, you know. I could get someone new for you to work on... someone who hasn't had abilities manifested."

"For one thing, why would I ever want to risk giving someone else a death-touch like me? For another, how would that help me?" I ask, incredulous that she'd even suggest it.

Louise looks at me patiently. "You keep talking about a cure, but you don't seem to have any idea how such a thing might come about. Have you not considered that if you could feel a before and after state, understand more clearly how abilities come about, maybe you could undo it? Re-kink yourself?"

My brow creases as I contemplate the field of possibilities from that experiment. But I take a subsequent breath. "I would never want to risk cursing anyone with what I have."

"Even if it was the key to a cure?" she asks as she holds her door open for us.

I inhale sharply, imagining that a cure is really only one hypno-touch session away. I close my eyes, resisting the lure of something that seems so harmless.

"I can't take that risk with another human being," I say, walking past her with Gabriel behind me. He might be silent verbally, but his wariness has been in line with my own; it's making it easier for me to refuse Louise.

"I've never seen two people have abilities manifest exactly the same way," Louise says, locking the door behind us. "The chances of someone being endowed with an ability like yours are slim to none."

"There are plenty of other ways to kill people," I say, looking her in the face. "Forget it. I'm not doing it."

Louise straightens her shoulders, sighing in resignation. She doesn't bother looking back at me. "You're going to change your mind eventually," she says, turning in the opposite direction from us, toward Randy's office. After only a few steps she stops and turns. "Let's keep in touch, Wendy. I'll be very interested to know how things turn out for you."

Gabriel and I head for the stairs in silence. I reach for his hand only to jump at how casually I did it. I snatch my hand back, adrenaline shooting through me as blank eyes float in front of my mind's eye.

He looks at me carefully and reaches out for me. I take more care this time, watching the ground in front of me so I don't trip and cause some kind of inadvertent skin contact. I'm thankful Louise made me aware of how casually I've been interacting with him. The gratitude is strange given the fact that we'll be breaking into her office tonight.

35

*G*abriel and I walk quickly through the darkness. We avoid the direct beam of the lights that illuminate the path on our way to the research building.

"Wendy," Gabriel whispers from behind me.

I told him I wanted him to follow me because my vision is better in the dark, but really I want to avoid holding his hand. He's so intent on doing that all the time, and it's just stupidly dangerous. Especially in the dark. He conceded without much argument though, more eager to grill me about what Louise said and did during my hypno-touch session.

"What?" I hiss back.

"I do trust you. You know that, right?"

"I know," I reply, wondering why we are back on this topic once again. It's irritating that he doesn't believe me when I tell him Louise didn't do anything.

"I just know how hypnosis works," he explains. "She could have said something to you—something seemingly harmless—that was really just an indirect suggestion that affected you without you realizing it. That's why I don't like hypnosis, you know. I'm highly suggestible. With the right words, anything sounds like a good idea to me."

That's news to me. I had assumed Gabriel would be *less* susceptible to hypnosis, but I guess I was wrong.

"Interesting," I reply, reaching the door to the research building and trying one of the keys.

Gabriel comes up beside me, and I startle.

"You are awfully excitable today," he notes, watching me carefully.

"You just make me nervous sometimes, being so close," I reply. "Do you realize I am millimeters from killing you when you hold my hand?"

The next key I insert rests satisfyingly in the tumbler, and I turn it, grateful that barrier number one has been breached so easily.

Gabriel's confusion interrupts my relief though. After a moment of reflection, he says, "Why would you choose to dwell on that? A millimeter is still just as effective as a foot."

He's right about that. I really should calm down. There's nothing wrong with him standing next to me when the only thing exposed is my face.

"I know," I reply. "I'm just on edge about doing this."

I step carefully up the stairs, making sure I don't slip and fall backward into him. Gabriel follows my careful pace, his intellect doing several backflips through some line of logic. I wish he'd pay more attention, or at least walk farther behind me.

"Here goes nothing," I say when we reach Louise's office door.

Once inside, I bring the computer to life and sit down in her desk chair. "You go through the paper files," I instruct Gabriel.

He moves to the filing cabinets as I confront the operating system password prompt. I hold my breath and press enter, crossing my fingers that Louise is lax on her security, that it isn't password protected.

No such luck. Exhaling, I restart the computer. If this password is the only security I have to bypass, it will be easy.

"Here's your file," Gabriel says. I turn around to look at him. "But I don't see anything here that's different from when I saw it... Nothing you and I don't already know. I'll keep looking though."

That's disappointing. I had really counted on Louise having some new information in my file. Hopefully she has something more on the computer, so I turn back to what I'm doing.

"I've never seen this tech savvy side of you," Gabriel says, completely distracted from his task as he leans over my shoulder. "Despite my distaste for technology, I can't help but be impressed."

"Don't be yet," I reply, making quick work of Louise's poorly protected administrative account. I chuckle. "Well, she isn't as smart as she thinks she is. That was way too easy. I bet her files aren't protected either."

"Easy?" he says as Louise's file directory appears on the screen. He has finally gone back to perusing the filing cabinet. "All I know how to do is point and click."

"I have to say it's both bizarre and slightly gratifying to know that I can do something you can't."

"I will gladly leave the thinking box knowledge to you."

"Thinking box..." I mumble, chuckling again as I read through her filenames. Nothing seems helpful or useful. Maybe Louise doesn't keep electronic records at all. I decide to look into her software to see if I can tell whether she has some kind of spyware that she uses to monitor Internet communication on the compound.

Sure enough, she does. And it's complex. Not only does it flag certain words and phrases for outgoing communication, but it blocks it completely until it can be approved by the administrator.

"Wow," I say. "No wonder they don't worry about—"

"Wendy, does the last name Haricott mean anything to you?" Gabriel interrupts, confused but pensive.

"Yeah," I say, turning around to see him pull a dark brown folder from the filing cabinet. "That was my dad's last name. Whitley was just a made-up name my mom gave me when she went on the run."

Gabriel raises his eyebrows in surprise. "So you're a computer hacker with a secret identity and super-senses. And someone has been trying to track down your family since you were a child. Anything else I should know about you, Miss, Ah, Whitley-Haricott?" He laughs.

I roll my eyes although I *am* a little nervous at the question. There certainly *are* things Gabriel doesn't know about me, but what's past is past. And right now isn't the time. "Yeah well, I didn't even know Whitley was made up until I met my uncle. I thought it was my mom's last name. As for computer hacking, I am *not* that skilled. I just know basic stuff. Anyway, I'm more interested in where you *saw* the name Haricott. Is it that file you've got?"

"Yes," he replies. "It looks like Louise keeps two separate files on you: the one I saw under Wendy Whitley, and this one under the name Wendy Haricott. Don't ask me how she knows your real name. But there's quite a stack in here. And a compact disc."

He looks down at the file while I look for some blank discs to make a copy of the CD he has. I don't really want to sit here and look at it. It could be a lot of data. And it's clear from the fact that it's labeled Wendy Haricott that I was right about Louise. She knows something about me she hasn't said. And the woman is strange enough that I don't put it past her to take random midnight walks to her office.

"Wendy, it says here your father's name was Carl Haricott. And your mother was Regina Walden. You're sure you never mentioned your parents' names or the last name Haricott to her?"

I shake my head. "Regina Walden?" I say, confused. "My mom's real name was Sara Rowan. I mean, I guess she could have had more than one alias, but that's kind of extreme…"

"The rest of this is your information, your test results..." Gabriel looks intently at the file. "Wait a minute. Here's a chart describing your life force absorption ability. It's very thorough."

He spreads the file out on the desk in front of me and points to a chart with handwritten notes. "Look, it catalogs your ability. It says, 'Time to take complete effect varies. From five seconds to an hour once skin contact occurs. Period of skin contact has no bearing on survival. Coma precedes non-instantaneous death.' And look here, at the bottom." He moves his hand down and reads, "'Derek: death occurred forty-six minutes after contact.'"

I freeze in place. "Derek's dead?"

"If this file is correct," Gabriel says, still looking intently at the paper.

"But… Louise said she touched me. How is that possible?"

"It looks like she lied. It looks like death happens no matter how long the contact is."

The air is suddenly stifling. Gabriel's hand braced on the desk next to me is dangerously close. As he moves it to turn the page, I flinch and then ease away from him slowly.

He doesn't appear to notice my retreat.

"Gabriel… you almost… you would have… I can't believe… Why would she have kept that from me?! I would have killed you!" I exclaim, suddenly terrified of being in the same room with him.

I feel as if we are standing on the edge of a platform with a train approaching. Killing Gabriel would be as easy as nudging him forward. The possibility saturates me with so much dread I can hardly breathe. I push my chair even farther away from him until I am next to the wall. I have been so stupid to think this would ever work. I need to be inside an impenetrable bubble. I need to get away from this place. From Louise, whose lies could have killed Gabriel when he almost touched me that day in the woods. From Gabriel, who is so fragile compared to me.

"Why?" I ask as my eyes burn with tears. "Why wouldn't she tell me? I don't understand. Just one brush. That's all it takes. Why would she lie to me about that? Why?"

I look up at Gabriel who is now across the room from me. His eyes are wide as he examines the page before him, oblivious to me and my questions.

And completely oblivious to how much danger he has been in all this time.

He glances up then. He has so much excitement on his face he could be glowing. It contrasts my own turmoil so much that I can't process it.

He glances around, only just noticing how far away I am. "What are you...? Wendy... you... You have to see this!" he exclaims.

He starts to move over to where I am.

"No," I say firmly. "Just hand it to me. I'll look at it myself."

Confusion shadows his features, but he hands me the file anyway. I take it carefully, eying him to make sure he stays where he is.

He can't wait for me to read it, though. "The bottom of the page," he says. "'For unknown reasons, subject number three suffered no deleterious effects, even with prolonged exposure. Subject was unaffected entirely. Examination of subject's energy field revealed no anomalies to suggest an explanation for immunity.'"

"Subject three?" I ask, scanning the page. I must be misunderstanding him.

"Yes," says Gabriel enthusiastically. He clears his throat and sobers his voice before continuing, "But it would appear that Louise tested your abilities on four other subjects. The notes mention four plus Derek."

"She *tested* my ability on people?" I say, horrified. "And the others? Did they die too?" I ask, frantically searching the page for evidence of what he's telling me. I'm so flustered that I can't concentrate on the words.

"No. No other survivors," replies Gabriel solemnly. "They appear to have all died after different time periods.

I can't think. I have to remind myself to breathe.

Breathe.

Breathe.

Breathe.

Gabriel starts to approach me again.

I hold up my hand. "Stop," I whisper. The unconsciousness for over twenty-four hours... the horror that couldn't be escaped, even during sleep. She was *experimenting* with me!

Breathe.

"Put the disk in the computer," I command. I'm not waiting to see what else Louise is hiding. If she shows her face in this room, *she* will be the one in trouble, not me.

Gabriel hesitates but does as I ask, glancing at me periodically with worry in his eyes.

The CD contains video data. There are five files altogether.

One for each death.

Well, one for two deaths, three with one death each, and one miraculous immunity. *Such fantastic odds.* I have around an eighty percent chance of killing whoever I touch.

Might as well be a hundred percent.

A room appears in the frame when Gabriel starts the first video. I immediately recognize it as the one from Pneumatikon. And there, on the exam table, is me. Dina comes into the frame, and then Derek. It's the video of my initial hypno-touch session.

"Skip ahead," I say.

Gabriel moves the progress bar.

"Skip," I keep saying when he stops it farther along. I don't want to watch this over again, but I don't want to miss anything important either.

The video ends with me crumpled in the corner.

Gabriel goes on to the next video file. It begins in a slightly different room—the one I remember waking up in. I'm unconscious on the bed.

A man walks in. His clothes are shabby, his hair unkempt, his beard flecked with gray. He walks slightly hunched and wary, like he might try to make a quick escape. My impression of his clothing and demeanor is that he's homeless.

He spots me lying on the bed, and walks over and stands next to me. He tugs on the sleeve of my shirt.

"Hello?" he says, grabbing my shoulder then and shaking it. "Wake up!" he says loudly.

He checks over his shoulder briefly before taking my wrist as if to take my pulse. He freezes where he stands, his hand still on my arm. Then, after a few moments, he collapses nearly on top of me before slumping to the floor.

Another man enters the room. I can't see his face because he's turned away from the camera. He turns the fallen man over and holds a stethoscope to his chest, and then the frame goes blank.

"Next," I say, unmoving.

Gabriel sighs and clicks on the next one.

The same scene appears. A woman walks in this time. She wears an outrageously short miniskirt and silver stiletto heels along with a halter top. I think she's wearing excessive hairspray as her hairstyle seems to be plastered in place. Her face, or what I can see of it, is heavily made-up. She walks a little more confidently than the last man, not even hesitating to put her hand on my shirt over my stomach, cocking one of her hips as if she's bored.

Like the last man, she turns toward the doorway for a moment, raising her eyebrows expectantly. Then she turns around again and places her hand on my forehead. Like the man before her, she pauses in place for several seconds, and then collapses.

I'm in shock.

Where is my horror? Where is my *anger*?

I can't find it.

Those people on the video had no idea what they were getting into when they entered that room. To them, I was just a sleeping girl. And they were murdered, one by one.

The hardened reality slices through me mercilessly: I'm entirely and irreversibly lethal. My heart races so swiftly that heat builds in my arms and legs, moving up to my chest and then to my face even though I'm sitting still. I have never felt panic so sharp that it leaves me stunned into immobility like this. There is no way I can prevent this from happening to Gabriel. To Ezra. It's not *if*. It's *when*.

Why has it taken a video of people being mercilessly killed for me to get that? I must not have fully believed it. Why else would I imagine a romantic relationship acceptable?

Denial. That has to be it. Well, I believe it now. And with it, I find a well-stocked supply of fury.

I want to kill Louise. With my bare hands.

"Wendy?" Gabriel says. "Look! The third one is a woman. She survived when she touched you. Don't you want to see?"

I jump, startled by how close his voice is. This alarms him in return, and I think he understands my state for the first time. But his concern is nothing more than a phantom from a past reality. It has no place here.

"Get away from me," I say quietly, standing up. I don't care about the woman who lived. It's irrelevant. And I don't want to deal with his ready worry. He *should* be afraid, but not *for* me, *of* me. He hasn't been afraid enough. And he probably never will be. I know he'll never accept the danger for what it is.

So what do I do?

Leave. I just want to leave.

Where do I go?

I don't know. But anywhere is better than here, so close to Gabriel, to Kaylen, to *people.*

"Wendy...?" he says softly.

"I can't watch any more. I have to get out of here," I reply. I run from the room.

"Wendy!" he shouts after me. I hear his footsteps rushing around Louise's office, probably closing file drawers and shutting down the computer. But I don't wait.

I run.

36

$\mathcal{T}$wo thoughts push past my instincts as I flee. The first is nothing more than a whisper: *You're running from Gabriel? Why?*

I ignore it. Adrenaline animates my limbs with an unstoppable urgency to get away from everyone and everything.

The other thought is that I need my diabetic supplies before I go anywhere. Every day, three or four times a day for years, I have pricked myself, run a glucose test, and injected myself. Forgetting that I need to do this to stay alive is as impossible as forgetting to breathe.

So I have to stop at the lodge. I won't survive without my insulin, and if I take the chance of leaving it behind, I don't know when I will be able to get my hands on more.

This complicates the quick escape I want. I had planned to take Louise's car and drive away—I still have her ring of spare keys. And Randy is gone, which means that Gabriel won't be able to follow—there are no other vehicles at the compound. Now I have to figure out how to get my supplies and then get to Louise's car without Gabriel following me.

But first I have to get to my room. Right now I am running for my life. Well, for Gabriel's life really, and for everyone else's.

I hear the door from the research building slam after a couple minutes and then Gabriel's feet as he pounds the ground farther behind me. Even though I am way ahead, it drives me faster so that my muscles scream in protest. I know he's much faster than me. We've gone running every day together since I gave him the trigger phrase. I think if he wanted to he could catch up before I reach the lodge. But I want to leave without tears or negotiation or emotional appeals. I just want to protect him without guilt. I push harder.

The lodge appears in my view, and I glance around for Louise's vehicle, confirming that it's there. Then I barrel onward to the door.

I almost ram into it, jerking it open and struggling awkwardly to put myself through it as quickly as possible. My room is not locked, and I burst into it in one motion, slamming the door behind me just in time to cringe at the thunderous sound it makes.

I turn the deadbolt frantically, jittery but relieved to have the thick wooden door between Gabriel and myself. I want to stay here forever, safely isolated, but I can't.

With heaving breaths I stagger around the room, throwing my belongings onto the bed. I grab all of my insulin out of the mini-fridge and shove it into my purse after making sure the keys to my apartment in Pomona are accounted for. Of course I can't stay there, but it will be my first destination. And once I'm there, amongst familiar things, I can think. I can figure out what to *do*.

I hear Gabriel's labored breathing and runaway heartbeat outside my door now. I struggle to focus on the sounds outside my window instead.

Once I have everything I need, I lug my things over to the window. I reach for the latch on the sill, but the door behind which Gabriel waits pulls me with magnetic urgency. I want to say goodbye to him, and I want him to accept it. But I know that if I speak it will break the silence, releasing the anguish I've shoved aside to deal with later.

I move carefully to the door and place my hand on the wood. His heartbeat is lower. He must be crouched, or sitting in front of it. I let my hand brush the surface as I kneel down to mirror him, leaning against the door itself as if it is a last embrace, imagining that somehow my love will translate from the skin beneath my clothes, through the wood, and into him.

My adrenaline rush is wearing off, making me aware of my stifled pain. I've also discounted my emodar. Gabriel's confused desperation and concern is so foreign to my frazzled state of mind. But they are familiar in how unfettered and open they are—just like *always*. It feels like he's trying to project himself into my room. He's stopped up with frustration, too, undecided about what to do. But he strikes at it over and over with the force of his determination. He reasons quickly through possibility after possibility, unable to settle. And there's a touch of amazed disbelief there. I can't figure out what it means.

I press my hand to the door for a few more counts, breathing deliberately, wishing more than anything that eventually he will really get why I'm doing this. It would be easier if I could erase myself from his memory. If I only knew how.

And then, just as silently, I move fluidly to the window, wincing at the sound it makes as I open it. I hope only *my* sensitive ears can hear it slide up. I maneuver myself through it, step lightly to the ground, and steal quickly to Louise's car.

***

It doesn't take me long to figure out how to get to a familiar freeway. A couple weeks ago I discovered that I could literally smell Big Bear Lake on the air if I really paid attention. I also heard low-flying planes that made me guess an airport was nearby. Looking at a map, I figured that the compound was just northwest of the lake. Big Bear is less than an hour from San Bernardino, the perfect place to get lost in throngs of people.

You're escaping less than twenty people to protect them just to get lost in throngs of people? So logical.

"What else am I supposed to do?" I moan aloud, gripping the wheel of the car.

Yes, what are you supposed to do?

I don't have an answer, and I worry I've just made a horrendous mistake. With every mile I put behind me, I become more and more indecisive.

I just totally flew off the handle.

Then I remember the report: I killed five people just by *touching* them. And I wasn't even conscious for three of them. It could so easily be Gabriel. So *easily.* I shake my head. I am *not* overreacting. I just miss him. I hate what I am doing to him.

Gabriel is not oblivious to the risks. He's probably even more aware than I am. The problem is that he is committed beyond reason. Knowing him, he would still choose to be with me even if my death-touch evolved into a death *presence.*

How will I live with myself when something happens? *How?*

But how will I live without him? Sobs flood my chest, and I force them back, hardly able to breathe past the stabbing pains they cause.

This argument cannot be won, I realize. I am equally torn between running as far away as I can and going back and begging forgiveness. I simply drive on because I'm already moving; my foot is already on the gas pedal. Momentum wins; my hopes of seeing Gabriel again fade into the darkness behind me.

What will happen to him when Louise wakes up and discovers her car missing?

Gabriel is smart. He'll figure it out. He'll also search for me, so I'd better figure out what I want before that happens.

284

When I reach San Bernardino, I'm not tired, only desperate to get home. I drive on, arriving in Pomona in less than thirty minutes. I stumble up the stairs and literally collapse on Ezra's empty bed. I feel like I should be crying, but my eyes are empty now, and when I search for my heart, it feels very far away.

37

*C*learly, I cannot avoid *all* people. Unless I kill myself, which is one thing I am certain I do *not* have in me. Paradoxical as it seems, I am grateful to find that somewhere in the dark recesses of my mind, I have something to live for. I just have to figure out what it is.

These are my first thoughts when I wake up in the morning, fully-clothed and tucked against the wall in Ezra's bed. The scents inherent to Ezra and me are aged, and the air has settled in the room so that everything smells stale and lonely. Maybe it's this lonely smell that has me admitting that I need other human beings in my life. Plus, I'm practical; a girl's gotta eat, right? I'm a city girl. I wouldn't know the first thing about living in the middle of the woods and hunting wild animals or growing my own food. That option is out.

I look groggily around the room which really doesn't feel like home at all. Probably it's just Ezra's absence. My eyes rest on the desk where my computer sits; a sheet of creased white paper rests there. Robert's letter. I should go there. I should figure things out there. And I miss Ezra so much. This apartment isn't safe anyway. Louise knows where I live, and I did steal her car. She's probably just discovered that it's missing.

I cannot even begin to guess what Gabriel will do from here. His logical processes are such complex, unorthodox patterns that predicting his actions would be a shot in the dark. I will have to ignore that part of the problem right now.

Being away from him has given me confidence in my decision to leave. This shouldn't be so bad. If I'm away, it will force him to reboot his life from here.

Fat chance.

I brush my hand at the invisible thought, swatting it away like a fly. But the problem with flies is they keep coming back unless you really smash them.

I test my glucose and begin packing. Once I have everything I need, I make sure I have my own car keys and grab as much stuff as possible to take down the stairs.

I open the door and have to brace myself on the frame.

Gabriel is standing there in front of me with a haggard and relieved look on his face.

I can't speak, and my heart leaps toward him. I can't help my smile either, until he reaches out to me and I look down to my own hands, which are completely exposed. I forgot to put my gloves back on... I guess a break in my routine must have caused me to skip over that vital piece of clothing. But how could I forget after what I learned last night?

I stumble several steps back into my apartment. The force of instantaneous joy followed so quickly by all-consuming terror is physically painful. I imagine his dead, empty eyes. I grasp at my heart instinctively to get a grip. Tight cords of anxiety begin to wrap around my mind and my body recoils; my limbs begin to twitch.

I gasp several times, working to breathe normally again.

I don't see what Gabriel does next, but his voice is farther away than I expect.

"Wendy, please, just listen."

I don't think I can talk. *What is wrong with me?* I cannot control the tremors in my arms and legs; I sink to the floor. Why am I so terrified? Is it just because I have so much skin exposed?

"I'm afraid," I whisper. "Please, just stay away so I don't have to be afraid, Gabriel."

"I know, Love. I know. You won't want to believe what I have to tell you. You'll fight against it. But please remember that you trust me. You trust me, don't you?"

I nod, finally looking at his face.

"This is what Louise did to you yesterday when you were hypnotized: she played on your fears. She's using them to control you. She wants you to believe you are dangerous, that you shouldn't be around people. She wants you so desperate that you'll turn to her—that you'll trust her. But this isn't *you*, Wendy. This is *her.*"

I shake my head and sit up. "No, Gabriel. It's not. Whether she told me to or not, I still *feel* this way. I still *feel* like a weapon. Now I know that even the slightest touch can kill...? How can I take that risk? How can *you* expect me to take that risk? Don't you understand? That's not fair to ask of me..."

Gabriel nods impatiently. "Yes. I know it is. I know you're afraid. I know that you've always *been* afraid. I know you dream about it. I know you think about it all the time. But so does she. She's fed you a post-hypnotic suggestion, a clever one, knowing that the only way she could control you is with something you are *already* controlled by. And as for the information about Derek and how lethal you can be? I think she didn't tell you as another method of manipulation. I'm certain she held it back because she *hoped* you would slip up and hurt someone. Because then you'd turn to her out of desperation. And yes, we both got really lucky. We found out before someone got hurt. But Louise, in turn, got lucky because you found out at just the right time to make the effect most potent. It was exactly when you were the most susceptible to that fear. She couldn't have planned it any better herself."

I shake my head again. He doesn't understand. "Gabriel, you can't control anyone through hypnotism. Not really. You just *want* this to be something Louise has done. I get that. I'd probably want it too if I were in your place. You're looking for someone to blame. You want to find a way to fix it. But it can't be fixed. It's not going away. Don't you get that? The longer I'm with you, the easier it is to ignore. And one day I'll forget. And that's the day I'll kill you."

I've never seen Gabriel cry before, but tears wet the corners of his eyes now and he crouches down, putting his head in his hands. I look away, wishing I didn't have to endure his pain. He is out of my emodar, but seeing Gabriel cry is maybe worse than enduring his desperation.

"She's not controlling *you,* Wendy," he pleads as I stand back up. "She's controlling your *nightmares.* She's feeding them. You're right. She can't control you with hypnotism. But it can accentuate things you already feel... like a fear of killing those you love. Who *wouldn't* feel that in your position? It's perfectly logical to be afraid. But it's not logical to let it control you this way."

"I need to put these things in my car," I reply, ignoring his words which only demonstrate how desperate he is to get me back... so desperate he would try anything to get me to stay. I wonder for a moment how he got here, but knowing Gabriel, it was creative and I'll be impressed by it. I don't need him to impress me. I just need him to let me go.

I move robotically back into my apartment to get my gloves and put them on. When I return, he's still there, standing in front of the stairs. He won't move. So I ease carefully past him, pleading with my legs to work, assuring my shaking hands that soon they will be safely alone.

His anguish brings tears to my own eyes now that I'm close to him. It's also stained with a layer of guilt.

"I love you. I don't want to live without you. I won't," he

says, staying where he is.

I sigh and pause a few steps down the stairs and look back at him. I wish he hadn't said that. It's going to make this harder for both of us.

"You have to," I reply before turning away again.

I wonder at his guilt though, as I walk down the stairs, but it's forgotten when I reach the parking lot.

Louise is there.

Footsteps shuffle around me, and it doesn't take long for me to see that there are two guns aimed at me. Louise smiles lightly but I can't process it. My head is spinning at the utter betrayal. Gabriel has turned me over to her. *Why?*

My brain stutters, trying to comprehend it. Disbelief is the only thing I can discern with certainty. *How could he do this?*

"I'm impressed that you at least adhered to our agreement," Gabriel says as his footsteps approach from behind me. I don't turn to look at him. I can't. I want to pretend it's not him.

"I know you're an honest negotiator," Louise replies.

"Yes, and you'll uphold the other condition to our agreement?"

"How could I forget?"

"You underestimate her," Gabriel warns.

"My dear, you give people far too much credit. In any case, I'll even forgo demanding payment until we arrive at our destination… Just call it an act of good faith," Louise says with more excitement in her voice than I've heard in a long time.

"Let's go then," he replies.

I don't understand their conversation. But I don't really care. Whatever it's about, I don't need the specifics to judge that I was somehow completely blinded by this man. He may not be on Louise's side, but he is certainly on his own side altogether.

I am completely alone.

***

Dwelling on the unfairness of my life for the entire trip, I endure the minutes by spotting every single slight that the universe has served up to me in the last month, thinking that this must be how sociopaths are created. Betrayed by every single shred of hope they have, reality turns upside-down and right and wrong weigh in on different sides. I wouldn't even be surprised to see Ezra here, working a deal with Louise, finding out that he was the one who made sure the flyer was in my hands that fateful day.

Not Ezra.

Oh yes, I argue. If Gabriel, why not Ezra? Didn't I trust Gabriel just as much? Didn't I think I knew him?

I *do* know him, don't I? Why doesn't anything make sense?

I wonder if I'm going to be like Louise now. Pneumatikon seems to be the only place I might belong and have some kind of purpose.

I balk at that picture. I am not Louise. It takes some kind of evil to do what she's done. Just thinking about how she's floated around the compound for a month, looking like she's reached some kind of transcendent state while at the same time harboring the knowledge that she's murdered people mercilessly gets my blood boiling. The woman even lied to me with her mind. Who can *do* that? Someone like her doesn't deserve to live. She better hope she's not around when I figure out a way to escape.

We head back into San Bernardino, passing through regular, suburban housing developments of stucco homes, not one more notable than the last. It's completely ordinary here. So ordinary, in fact, that it feels alien. I've been living on a compound for a month, dabbling in the supernatural and killing people with my bare hands while people like this have gone on to live regular, unceremonious lives.

We reach the northern side of the city in the foothills of the mountains. We drive into a neighborhood where the homes rest on lots that are a couple of acres—definitely a wealthy area. Our destination is a one-story home and Louise leads me around the side of it. All the while, her two gun-toting lackeys keep their weapons trained on me. I know Louise doesn't want them to kill me, and I weigh trying to make my escape now, but I don't really want to be shot even if it *is* non-lethal. That would be annoyingly painful.

Instead, I follow along, arriving at a pool house behind the home. We go inside and Louise turns around with one of her weird ethereal smiles. I glare at her.

"Well, the floor is yours, my dear," Louise says, not to me but to the set of footsteps behind me. I turn slightly. It's Gabriel.

I still can't look at his face.

"Not only can Wendy *see* life forces, she can likely manifest abilities that are far beyond anything you have ever done," Gabriel says. "Since she did hypno-touch on me, I can now memorize, as yet, unlimited strings of text and recall them with ease."

I whirl on him, eyes blazing, hands clenched. His betrayal is complete. My head spins. How could he? How have I been so blind? I thought I loved him for his honesty, but it turns out that he's simply an expert at making me believe he speaks nothing but truth.

I hate him.

I don't know what to say to him. I don't know that it matters if I say anything at all. And his face is hardened; he's deliberately avoiding me.

"A liar *and* a coward? At least look at me when you betray me," I seethe between clenched teeth.

Louise laughs a high, tinkling laugh, completely off of her usual character. I don't know what it means. What did she make of Gabriel's news? I wasn't looking at her face when he said it.

Gabriel says nothing and still won't look at me. I don't know what he's feeling either. He's just out of range.

"Well let's just get on with it then," I growl, turning back to Louise, determined to ignore Gabriel entirely. "Whatever it is you brought me here for, let's do it."

"I love the enthusiasm, Dear," Louise says brightly. "But I'll need some time to get things in order. We have a lot to do!"

She leaves me in her thugs' well-armed hands and glides up the stairs.

38

Lying on the bed in my assigned room in the pool house, staring up at the popcorn ceiling, I chastise myself for probably the twentieth time since I met Dina. It's a mindless task. It doesn't require much mental effort on my part to pinpoint all the places I went wrong in the last month.

I'm utterly bored. There's nothing to do. There's nothing to see or hear or smell. There is one window but they boarded it up when we got here. I could probably exert some real force and break it, but they've got this macho dude outside my door to babysit me. I might opt for the window if I get desperate. I've also pondered hiding behind the door when they bring me my meals and jumping them with my bare hands, but that would probably end up with me getting shot.

If I'm really honest with myself, I don't really *want* to leave. In the three days I've been here, I have never been more at ease in my own skin. Chalk that up to having little to no human contact. And I'm also really curious what Louise wants with me.

I also wonder about Gabriel. Maybe his job was to gain my trust. He didn't seem *friendly* with Louise, but maybe he was just contracted by her. I remember what Robert told me about someone running a credit report for Wendy Haricott. It had to be either him or Louise. And Gabriel has some additional ability that allows him to gain people's trust. And I fell for it completely. But when I think of what I've felt of his mind, I can't fathom how he did it. Whatever it is he's capable of doing to manipulate me, he is *very* good at it.

I push away the veil of sadness that has been hovering over me for the last few days. It only makes itself known when I acknowledge his deception. I'm only motivated by one thing now: information. I was at least right that Louise knows more than she's said all along. And Kaylen was right that violence is not beneath her. If all of this can result in some kind of useful information, I'll take imprisonment. Besides, if I really want to get away, I think I can manage it. I am a weapon after all, not some shrinking violet. I don't think I'd have any remorse if Louise fell victim to my hands during my escape.

With nothing else to do, I've become preoccupied by one thing: Gabriel's smell. I wish it didn't still have the same effect on me. He's been around quite a bit. I smell him every time I'm outside this room, which is whenever my guard takes me to the bathroom. It's mixed with lots of unfamiliar scents, too. I hear people at the main house all the time. No one has any conversations worth mentioning—I guess because they know I can hear everything. I can't make anything noteworthy of the regular, everyday sounds. I have no idea what Louise's plans are for me.

I never hear Gabriel's voice amongst them—which is best for my mental state anyway. Every time my tears break free over him, I always cork them up quickly. Instead, I turn my sadness into anger at myself; I shouldn't be hurting over someone who never really cared about me anyway. So I'm glad the only reminder I have of him is smell—which is bad enough.

I've analyzed the past weeks, trying to spot where I should have seen this coming. But every moment with him felt so *genuine*. I remember wondering if it was possible for someone like him to really exist—someone capable of being *that* honest. And that's the only red flag I've come up with. My emodar is definitely fallible. As for the connection I felt with him in the colorworld... Well everything in that strange place must be an illusion after all. I don't know why I ever assumed the colorworld told the truth about *anything*. It's invisible for goodness sake.

There's another mystery: someone is staying in the room next to me. I can't imagine why, but I could swear they are being held prisoner, too.

They rap on their door and the guard opens it and says, "Bathroom?"

The mystery person goes to the bathroom and then returns to the bedroom without a word. I think it's a man. He spends time doing exercises: jumping-jacks, lunges maybe, push-ups. His breathing accelerates and sometimes he grunts with exertion. Sometimes he clears his throat. Other times he throws himself on the bed. He paces. But he never speaks, which is absolutely the strangest part.

While my neighbor is docile and agreeable, I'm obnoxious in my requests. I get a kick out of intimidating the gloved guard who's in charge of keeping me holed up in this room. He's a balding, well-muscled man with tattoos on his arms and he wears a mustache. He's pretty tall, which makes it even funnier to watch him scramble for his gun when I make a little jump at him when he brings me my insulin or when I go to the bathroom. I laugh delightedly; it's the one form of entertainment I have.

If he was really smart, he'd change out his t-shirt for something with a little more coverage; I never wear my gloves anymore. But I guess he wants to feel like a badass who doesn't need to protect himself from a five-foot, six-inch girl. Whatever. I could take him down if I really wanted to, gun or no.

Even with my confidence at an all-time high, I'm especially lonely today. I consider going to the bathroom again so I can startle Mister T-shirt, but I know even that's going to get old if I do it too much. And I really need to stay patient and wait for Louise to see what she's planning.

I hop up and pace back and forth across the room, shaking the restlessness from my limbs. I could run ten miles with all the pent up energy I have.

After twenty or so dissatisfying laps around the bedroom, I lean against the wall and sink down to the floor, extending my legs.

I nearly jump out of my skin when the sudden erratic thrum of despondency agitates my body. It's not mine. I look frantically around; who has managed to sneak up on me in an enclosed room?

Then realization hits me: the emotion is familiar. It's not mine. But I know it. I know whose it is.

I don't move. I don't even breathe. I listen for the heartbeat from the room next to mine. It's not quite on the other side of the wall, but I think he's sitting on the floor. Maybe six or so feet away?

Gabriel is in the other room. I'd know his emotional patterns anywhere.

He's thinking with the purposeful acrobatics that I know as well as my own brain waves. And he's plagued with doubt, questioning and re-questioning. He's running the same scenario over and over, testing the outcome to be sure it's satisfactory. When he's done, he tests it again, the same, but maybe slightly varied scenario.

I've always been so preoccupied with the incessant magnetism between us. But this is a Gabriel who is oblivious to the fact that I'm listening, so he isn't distracted by my presence. That's never happened before. Although these are his very private ponderings, not intended for me or anyone else, they are not unlike his more public ones. The openness of his mind now feels no different than when he knows I can 'hear' him.

Maybe I can learn his part in this if I soak him in for a while. I tell myself the reasons are merely practical, but I easily get lost in his forceful and painstaking line of reasoning. *What is he thinking so hard about?* For a few minutes, I forget how badly he's hurt me. I only want into his mind again. I haven't heard it in so long and I realize, despite what he's done to me, I haven't let him go. Whatever blinding effect he has on me, it's still present even in the face of his obvious lies. But I don't know how to escape it.

I should pull on my coat of anger again. I should protect myself from caring. But my mind is eager to dance with his again. I meld with his movements determinedly, gratified with how they relax me so easily as if they're a drug I've been in withdrawals over.

After several runs through his mysterious scenario, he changes gears, settling into satisfaction. His mental experiment has had positive results.

Now he thinks of something else which slows my mind with the weight of sadness. He reassures himself, gives himself a pep-talk maybe, and then sinks into a more hazy daydream. Whatever it is he's imagining or, more likely, remembering, it makes him happy and content. It starts as a low burning fire, comforting and peaceful, and builds slowly in force until it becomes a bit hotter. It contorts my insides, because as much as he wants to get away from the heat—or quench it maybe—he can't. He's left on the edges, staring into the fires of desire, drawn to them, unable to turn away. I press against the wall as if I am pulled into the invisible flames, too. But I know it's him I'm drawn to.

I know he is thinking about *me*.

But I don't understand. How can he have all these feelings for me when he has put me in this situation?

"Gabriel?" I say loudly without thinking.

My stomach lurches with his alarm.

"Wendy?" he asks softly.

"Yes," I reply loudly, knowing he can't hear me clearly if I don't speak up.

His delirious happiness flutters insistently until my chest threatens to burst. I hear him move closer.

"Why?" I beg with my cheek pressed against the textured wall. I mean why in so many ways. Why did he betray me? Why is he being held prisoner? Why does he still have feelings for me? I'd like to ask them all, but I'd have to shout to make myself understood, and Mister T-shirt isn't far outside my door.

He gives a long sigh. I curl up, leaning into the wall as one might fold into a couch with a blanket and a good book. I want to soak him in, and right now I don't care that he has betrayed me. I just want to hear his voice and feel him close.

He summarizes the story up front with a dance that begins with the pendulum motion of indecision. Heartbreak comes onto the scene, throwing him to the floor where he spends some time fighting to regain sure footing. He finds it, however, and begins exercising the complex sequence of mental stunts that he so often demonstrates when he thinks really hard about something. As he thinks, his confidence builds.

"You left," he says finally. "And I only saw two choices: let you fall into Louise's hands without me or do something drastic and put you there on my own terms. I picked the only thing that would allow me to live with myself."

He spends several moments reliving the agony of that choice.

I want to ask him how he was so sure Louise would get a hold of me, but I can't do it without shouting.

He whispers quietly, "I remember that evening you woke up at Pneumatikon after you'd come through hell. I was inescapably drawn to you in just those few minutes so I worked to find out everything I could about you: your mom's death, taking care of your brother while going to school and working full-time. I didn't hold anything against you, you know, for keeping me at arm's length all that time. Your determination to take care of your brother is one of the most beautiful things I've seen. But that's how I knew that wasn't you in Louise's office. I knew that was *part* of you, but you are much more rational than that."

His admiration warms my chest and I brush my bare hand against the wall's surface, closing my eyes and imagining his face. I have never had anyone esteem me the way Gabriel does. It's physically invigorating.

"I am convinced your reaction was the product of Louise's post-hypnotic suggestion. I don't know, Wendy, whether I have made the right choice in letting Louise have you. I gambled, I'll give you that. But it was with purpose. I needed some way to break you out of the spell Louise had put you under. I wish I could undo that day. I should never have accepted that you were allowing her to hypnotize you. I should have seen this coming. But I didn't. And I forgot that despite how strong you are, you're still susceptible to your insecurities like the rest of us. But Louise didn't forget. She knew exactly what those were, and exactly how to prey on them."

I wipe a tear tickling my cheek. He was trying to protect me. Why did I not once consider that? Gabriel never goes about things in the traditional way. Forget *thinking* outside the box. Gabriel *lives* outside the box. I knew that. I *know* that. I should have just *thought* about it instead of dwelling on my outrage over being betrayed.

"The only way to undo what she'd done was to put you in a situation that would free you from your fears," Gabriel continues. "The best way to cure a post-hypnotic suggestion is to separate yourself from the trigger. In this case, I knew the trigger was people—especially me, the one person to whom you are the most dangerous. Your brother would be another immediate trigger, and you were likely going to go back to him, hitting that trigger over and over. You would never be free of it unless you found a way to have it empower you."

He sighs, his intellect backtracking through his previous scenario as he second-guesses himself once more. "I realize there were other options. But I just didn't know what to expect from you—whether you would *ever* let me near you again. You might have never paused to listen or considered that your fear was unhealthy. I really believed I'd lose you, Love. I wasn't willing to relinquish you."

He holds trepidation at bay over that possibility and I know his sincerity just as surely as I always have. Still, his methods seem extreme to say the least, but then Gabriel doesn't do anything halfway.

"I know the risk I've taken," he says, as if answering my question. "But... I had to go on what I knew about you. You needed to be in a place where you would be motivated to take back control of yourself. I needed you incensed. It brings your fighting spirit to life. And as much as it crushed me to let you believe I'd forsaken you, I knew if you got angry, you would no longer be afraid. I've kept aloof over here so that you could be free of me. You needed time without me in your head, without me near. Honestly, that was the one part of this whole plan I doubted. I really thought you'd see through my betrayal. I—"

He stops and heaves in several painful breaths. "I thought you'd realize what I was doing. But then you didn't... And all this time I've had to gag myself. I've had to stay on the other side of the room. But I've projected my love for you across the wall a thousand times. It's been torture. But I had to let you heal. I just needed you to be able to... *think* without me in your head. And I am *so* relieved to be able to tell you all of this finally."

I sigh, wishing more than anything that I could tell him all the ways he amazes and inspires me. His thoroughness blows me away at every turn. And now that I'm using my brain, I can see that he was right. I remember the panic of seeing him on my doorstep. Fear was running away with me, and I couldn't find the reins to pull it back. But somehow, as soon as I met four walls and a locked door, I was ready to face anything.

"I don't know..." I say loudly, trying to figure out how to say what I want him to understand without a long-winded explanation.

"If you're recovered?"

"Yes."

"I guess if you finally believe that Louise used your fear against you, you're on the right track."

I hope he's right. I *feel* recovered. In fact, the last time I remember being truly afraid was when I saw Gabriel outside my door. I've been going gloveless, ready to use my hands instead of hiding them. But then the only person I've been in contact with is Mister T-shirt who brandishes his gun at me every time I see him. Who knows how I'll react when I'm finally facing real people not bent on imprisoning me.

"And *you*?" I ask, hoping he gets my meaning.

"Why am I here at all if you are the one Louise wants? I made a deal with her. Knowing how afraid you were, I worried you would take for granted how motivated Louise is when it comes to you. I was worried that without me in the picture, she'd use someone else to control you. From what I have seen of your file, Louise knows a *great* many things about you. If you weren't cautious, she would easily find a way to get to you. I couldn't stomach that person being Ezra. I knew the person had to be me."

I let out a prolonged sigh. I intended to let Louise play her games with me, but I didn't imagine she'd use others to make me do it—I have no idea *why* I wouldn't have thought that. I watched a video *proving* the lengths Louise will go to. But instead of recognizing that the real danger was *her,* I saw *myself* as the danger. Why do I let my emotions run away with my brain?

"What is *wrong* with you, Wendy?" I mumble. Then, more loudly, "Sorry."

"You have no reason to be sorry, Love. Louise manipulated you so that you couldn't see. And sorry for putting me in this position? You didn't. I put myself here."

Gabriel sacrificed himself. For me.

I close my eyes and finally get how profoundly Louise's hypnotism affected me. Three days ago I couldn't see *anything* beyond getting away from Gabriel. How did it seem so logical at the time? How will I know when I'm thinking clearly?

"I can't trust myself," I say, as loudly as I dare. Mister T-shirt sounds like he could be sleeping, but the TV is on, so he might be watching it. And listening.

"Yes, you can. You just have to know what to look for. Fear makes you believe you have no choices. When you see only one possible path in front of you, reject it. Reject the reasoning that brought you there entirely. Fight against fear, not circumstances, and you won't fail."

I wipe my eyes, ashamed at how quickly I doubted Gabriel.

"I know you're upset that I told her about your abilities," he continues. "I made a deal that if she'd let me talk to you alone for a minute, then I would tell her something I knew she wanted to know about you. It was a bargaining chip. I had hoped we could avoid all this. But I couldn't convince you of anything, so I failed. I had to tell her. Even if she's dishonest, I'm not capable of that. If I didn't think she already knew about your sight and about your hypno-touch ability, I would never have made the deal. But I'm certain she did already know. And her reaction when I told her was not in the least bit surprised."

"How?" I say to the wall.

"Because of your file. After you left, I had to formulate a plan. Louise was going to wake up, see her car missing, and come after you immediately. I had to get to you first, and the only way to do that was to insert myself in the equation. The question, of course, was what she might want you for. I needed to know her intentions so I wouldn't unwittingly put you in a position where you might be harmed. So the first thing I did was read every word in your file—

you and I only saw the first few pages. And now I know *exactly* why Louise has wanted you from the very beginning."

39

"Spit it out, Gabriel!" I yell when he leaves me hanging. He knows I can't really talk back to him. He knows I'm waiting for him to tell me what he knows. What is he waiting for?

He chuckles. "Sorry, Love. I guess sometimes I just like to rile you. It's so cute."

I huff, disgruntled.

"Yes, yes," he says. And then he sobers. "According to your file, your father, Carl Haricott, was gifted with what was called 'energy world sight' and also 'life energy absorbing skin."

"No way!" I shout.

"Yes. I wish it had described his ability more, but it didn't. It simply made a comparison of your vision tests and his. Your eyesight is far better than his so that may mean you can see more of the colorworld than he could. What's more, your mother supposedly possessed long-range empathy skills just like you. Although apparently hers were more general—she couldn't read people as accurately as you can but her range was something like fifteen feet."

"That can't be…" I say, trying to remember *any* point in my past in which Mom might have taken a read on me or anyone else. The number of times I lied to her when I went out with friends or came home late…? If she could read emotions then she *had* to have known I was lying. There was *never* an indication she knew anything beyond what I told her. But if her ability wasn't as precise as mine… Then maybe she *couldn't* discern lies? I don't know that I buy that. But maybe… Well, maybe she lost that ability. Like Dina?

The idea that my abilities might one day fade seems almost too good to be true. Plus, my death-touch came about by hypno-touch. It wasn't natural-born. So what does that mean? I am so confused.

When I don't reply, Gabriel says, "Learning that information about your father is what sealed my plans. This astounding memorization capability I now possess must be because of your hypno-touch skill. And since your ability is like your father's, we can assume *he* could manifest powerful abilities as well. And since Louise knew about him then it's safe to say she knows what you are capable of with hypno-touch. And *that*, I believe, is why she wants you. She *knows* what you can do, and she intends to use it one way or another. I suspect when you see her again, that's what she'll have you do, but in the meantime, I do have one trick up my sleeve. Before I woke Louise to tell her you were missing, I emailed your uncle."

"How?" I say, growing excited. Gabriel doesn't have a computer at the compound, so I'd been half-wondering if he even had an email address.

"I used Kaylen's computer," he replies. "I had to look him up and email him at his work address, but I'm sure he'll get it. I told him everything I knew about the compound's location. If he finds the compound—which I think he can do easily enough given his resources—then that should give him a lead on Louise. So he must be out there, looking for you right now."

My smile falters. Didn't I tell him about the monitoring? Louise's computer would have been the only way to send an email through the spying software. Now that I think about it, he interrupted me when I had started to tell him.

"Communication monitored," I say, crestfallen.

"Monitored how?" he says, alarmed.

"Software. Blocks flagged stuff," I reply.

He sighs heavily. For a long moment he tries to think his way around the problem, but then his spirits sink when he reaches the disheartening conclusion. "Soy un idiota arrogante! I am sorry, mi amor. I take computers for granted because I don't like the idea of using them. But I forget what they're capable of. What a terrible oversight on my part."

Silence settles the space between us for a couple minutes as we each search for a way out of our predicament. I'm sure *someone* is looking for us. My brother expected me a couple days ago, so he's got to be worried. That means he must have told Robert... But Ezra only knew the compound was somewhere in the San Bernardino mountains. I don't think he knew anything else about Louise. And Ezra's going to be hesitant to get help from the authorities given my condition. Unless he tells Robert, who may or may not believe him. Did Robert know about my dad's abilities? They *were* related, after all. So he had to, right?

"*Damn!*" I hiss far too quietly for Gabriel to hear. I remember Robert looking at my gloves that day I met him. He was really confused by them but then seemed to accept it. If my dad had the same ability when he was alive, I bet he wore gloves, too. I bet

Robert was used to seeing them on him. And then when Robert saw *me* wearing them, he must have been reminded of Carl. He must have wondered if I was wearing them for the same reason...

My eyes flash in surprise as I realize that Robert might actually be able to help me with my condition. My dad managed to father two children. So obviously he could touch people, right? My heart leaps buoyantly, but I temper it. There's no proof Robert knew about Carl's abilities. And there's no telling if the file was even accurate. We don't know that Carl's condition was exactly like mine. I can't get my hopes up. And right now, I need to spend more time figuring out how to escape Louise.

Even though knowing this information about Robert doesn't really help my current predicament, it does mean he'll likely believe Ezra and hopefully do his best to find me without involving the police. Still, a rescue scenario looks pretty bleak.

Why didn't I email Ezra while I was using Louise's computer?! I groan at that massive failure on my part.

"I agree with that sentiment," Gabriel says. "My intellect has failed me miserably this time. I tend to overlook the most obvious things sometimes... I just never imagined Louise *needed* monitoring like that with how thorough she is about legally protecting her research." He sighs, aggravated with himself.

"Not your fault," I say, although I *am* surprised by Gabriel's oversight. He's usually so thorough. But it's really *my* fault. This whole situation has resulted from nothing more than my own irrationality. Gabriel did what he did because I gave him no better choice.

I can tell he disagrees, but he says brightly, "Regardless of sent or unsent emails, I never intended for us to wait here like damsels in distress to be rescued. The right set of circumstances will come along, and we'll get out of this. To my estimation, that's exactly what you intended as well. That ugly vientre amarillo is perfectly terrified of you... Quite a show you give me every day hearing you wag your hands at that man. I'd like to witness such highsiding with my own eyes."

I laugh out loud. I'm so relieved to hear him using obsolete words. His thoughts, now that he's told me everything, begin their lithe dance once more.

Even though I have no idea how we'll get out of here, and I know that I'm in a compromised position—possibly the most dangerous situation of my life—laughing comes easily. My world makes sense again. It's hard not to be completely carefree for the rest of the day as Gabriel gets three days-worth of talking off his chest. I get three days-worth of hearing him speak to me in that unmistakable cadence. I fall in love with him all over again. My heart slowly untangles into a loose puddle.

He tells me stories of his college days—which were not too long ago—his boyhood, and more about his overbearing Hispanic mother, to whom he gave one thousand one hundred and ninety-seven grey hairs in a single summer.

My favorite story he tells is of when his parents went on vacation and left him and his brother with an uncle for a week. When his parents returned to pick them up, they found both boys out on their uncle's stoop, shoes on, bags and pillows tucked under their arms, and ready to leave. Apparently Uncle Al and Aunt Lydia were ready to dispose of them at the earliest possible second after enduring a week of boyish shenanigans.

"When my mother confronted us about just what crimes we'd committed," Gabriel says, "I graciously informed her I couldn't be held accountable for my Uncle Al leaving a ladder out where I could find it. I'd even asked Uncle Al beforehand if he believed it was possible to perch oneself comfortably on the top of a palm tree. He had fair warning.

"My mother would have known and taken evasive measures. But the old codger told me he imagined you could! What was I supposed to do? Ignore the fact that Uncle Al had a palm with such voluminous fronds situated just next to his second-story roof? He all but gave me permission, I told her. Then Mamá stared at me open-mouthed, examined my extremities for fall damage, and then said, 'Sí, I imagine he did, Gabriel. *Santo cielo!* Even I know better than to argue with *your* logic.' We never went solo to Uncle Al and Aunt Lydia's again."

I burst into laughter, which warms him with pleasure. How incredible it is that my talents allow me to connect so thoroughly to a person even when they're on the other side of a wall.

40

"*D*id you ever look up any of the words I spoke to you in Spanish?" Gabriel asks later that evening. It's late but neither of us has wanted to go to bed. We lean against each other, a five-inch barrier of drywall and insulation between us.

"No."

He's grateful.

"Why?" I ask.

"Because if you had and still thought I'd betrayed you, it would mean I truly have done a terrible job conveying my commitment to you."

That's hardly clear. Frustrated that I can't say more words, I hit the wall once. "What?" I demand.

He sighs. "Nunca he sido corto de palabras como ésta," he says softly.

More Spanish? I don't understand a word of what he just said but his anxiety gives away far more information. "Nervous?" I ask.

"Yes."

I wait, but when he doesn't elaborate, I say impatiently, "Why?"

"Because I still never really know what you're thinking and what you're feeling. For someone so attuned to others, you are incredibly guarded."

Guarded about what?

When I don't respond, he says, "I know you love me. I know you intend to give me a chance. I even remember you saying I could be with you as long as I wanted. But every time I remember those words, they just don't sit right with me. *As long as I want?* I feel foolish having accepted that kind of ambiguous acceptance from you. I don't remember you saying even once what *you* wanted except that you demanded I put my arms around you. But that's hardly a confession of commitment. All you've said is that you want to make me happy. But I'm not happy unless you are. How do we remedy this?"

He knows I want him. What more does he need to know? "Don't follow?" I plead.

I sense him getting frustrated as well.

"Spit it out," I say.

305

"Si sólo fuera tan fácil para ti! Tomaste mi corazón y nunca me has dicho el valor que esto tiene para ti!"

I get up and groan in impatience, flopping on the bed. Gabriel is so transparent most of the time. But then he starts off with another language and expects me to follow him.

"Meaning?" I say loudly, not caring now if Mister T-shirt wakes up and hears—although it sounds like he's out cold.

"Tell me exactly what you are thinking right now," he replies.

"Frustrated," I reply. "With you *and* the wall."

"When we get out of here, what do you intend to do? About us?"

Okay. Slightly less confused. But it's still a vague question.

"I just want to be with you," I reply. "You?"

"Whatever you'll allow. But I still don't know what that is."

What I'll *allow*? What does he mean? "Be with me," I insist.

"Let's try this: do you think you'll ever get tired of eating spinach and artichokes together?"

I smile at the ceiling. "No."

"Then why have you never told me that? Spinach gets insecure, you know. Artichoke goes with a lot of other things."

I get up and put my back toward the wall again, sitting on the floor once more. The flitting of Gabriel's playfulness puts my confusion to rest for the moment. I can talk spinach and artichokes all night.

"Spinach and artichoke dip is my favorite artichoke dish," I reply. "If I had to choose one, that would be it. No question."

His heart pools in warmth. "Then why is the artichoke so indifferent?"

"Because spinach would be great with other things. Why just spinach and artichoke dip? Spinach doesn't know what it's missing." I think I should always speak in metaphors through a wall. It's a lot easier to get things off my chest this way.

"What's it going to take for you to believe me that I don't want anyone else?" Gabriel moans. "Not ever?"

"The dip is best when it's heated," I reply, biting my lip.

"Of course it is. But there's more than one way to heat things up. You think you need the ingredients in the same bowl to make it a success?"

I laugh nervously. "Yes," I reply, not sure if I want to go into how nonexistent sexual intimacy is in our relationship. It smarts too much to think about what we can't have.

"That artichoke is *muy caliente* all on her own! And she doesn't need to be in the same bowl to heat the spinach up."

"If you heat spinach up too much, it wilts," I reply.

He laughs. "Not *this* spinach. If you need heat, there are plenty of ways to do it that don't require physical contact. That's what ovens are for. And stoves. And campfires. And jalapeños. Dress that artichoke up and spinach is going to be happy just being in the same room. And you know, if we're dealing with something hot like a jalapeño, and the artichoke is nervous, I'd recommend we use gloves so we don't burn our skin."

My jaw drops in surprise. "Spinach is getting really forward."

"Well are we in a relationship or aren't we? You want to talk about the stuff that scares you or just think about it all on your own and draw the wrong conclusions?"

"So dangerous..." I say. "What if the jalapeño is too much? It might be better to keep that artichoke more mellow so the spinach doesn't get overwhelmed."

"You doubt my self-control? Is that what you're saying? I'm going to risk death for a passionate moment?" Gabriel scoffs. "I have to say, I'm a little offended by that. But in any case, it really won't matter unless you've decided to commit yourself to this more than you evidently have."

I have to admit I hadn't really considered there were other ways to satisfy intimacy with Gabriel. It's a whole new realm of possibility I never explored because that closet was shut long ago.

"How do I do that without being afraid?" I reply.

"I'm not saying you have to jump right in. You're going to establish habits that will make you feel more secure. You'll find new ways of expressing yourself if you'll just be open to it. It's like any handicap, Love. We'll have other ways to make up for it."

I sigh. As usual, I have no argument. And knowing Gabriel, of course, has delved into every dark corner of our future and hashed it out is a relief. Why do these things never occur to me?

"What does spinach need now?" I ask.

"For artichokes to be completely and uncomfortably honest."

"You know how I feel about you. What am I not honest about?"

"No, I don't. You *assume* I do. Just like you've been assuming things about our prospective future because you thought you knew what kind of intimacy was possible and what I wanted. It's like you expect I should know your thoughts as thoroughly as you know mine."

"I told you I want to be with you. I love you. We're dating. What is unclear about that?"

Silence passes between us for several moments as he works on gathering his impatience. I don't understand it and it makes me defensive.

"I don't care if you tell me you love me a hundred times," Gabriel says finally. "I don't care if you flirt with me all day, every day. It doesn't hold value if there is no commitment spelled out."

Now I'm *really* confused. "Did you want to spell out the rules for dating or something? Well here it is: I'm not going to be seeing anyone else romantically and you shouldn't either. That's my expectation and that's my commitment. Is dating defined differently in your book?"

Gabriel groans in exasperation.

The feeling is mutual. "Spit it out, Gabriel!" I exclaim. "If you want something more from me, just ask! I can't read your mind. And I know better than anyone that emotions don't last forever!"

"Oh, I see. We're back on *this* again," he says. "You are just *positive* that I'm going change how I feel about this whole touch-less relationship, back out, and leave you heartbroken. Why did you even give me the trigger phrase if that's what you believe?"

I bow my head in shame and a few tears squeeze out. I did it because I wanted to make him happy. But he obviously isn't...

"Hijo de un sacerdote casto! You are so frustrating sometimes!" he says when I don't reply. "It's like my words are meaningless to you! Why do you even want me if you don't trust anything I feel or say?"

My hands ball into fists. "You assume my emodar makes my judgment about people infallible!" I accuse. "You think I can just taste someone's mental flavor and wham bam thank you, ma'am, I know them inside and out. Well I've got news for you: feelings change. So *forgive* me for not holding you to your current mental state. I believe you when you say you love me. I love you, too. I admire you. I want to be with you. I love the person you are. But crap happens. Life gets crazy. It would be stupid for me to assume that what you want right now is what you're going to want years from now."

Gabriel regards what I say carefully and then says deliberately, "Of *course* things change. How can they not? You don't stay in a relationship based on circumstances or *feelings*. You stay based on a commitment you made. And it's becoming increasingly clear that you have no commitment to me whatsoever."

"I *am* committed!" I snap. I turn to glare at the wall, thinking it's more than just a physical hindrance right now. I'd like to give it a few hits to vent my outrage.

"No, you're not," he replies evenly. "Because your so-called commitment is based on conditions that may or may not change. Mine is not. Mine is immovable. The only person who will get in the way of my commitment is *you*."

I lie back on the floor next to the wall, drained by what feels like a lecture. He's treating me like a child and I don't like it. It also seems like he's picking a fight with me; he may be speaking English, but I don't understand him. I reach out to touch the barrier between us. It now feels thicker than a mere five inches.

The sensation of the wall against my hand reminds me of a thousand nights that I did exactly this. When I was little, I always had Mom put my bed right next to a wall as soon as she moved us to a new place. I liked to be able to reach my hand out at night and touch the surface. It was the only thing that stayed the same from one place to the next. Even now it's slightly comforting because it keeps me from having to see the disappointment on Gabriel's face. His emotions are bad enough.

"*Zhyenityes' na mnye,* Wendy," Gabriel whispers, interrupting the silence between us. "*Cásate conmigo...Ti prego, dimmi che mi vuoi per sempre.*" He pleads every syllable. I wish I knew what he was saying.

"I don't know how to give you what you're asking for," I say.

"What am I asking for?"

"For me to believe you when you say you will always want me? But promises don't last, because people change. What you're asking me to do is ignore everything people have taught me simply because you tell me to. That's not reasonable when I've only known you a month."

"Then what *is* reasonable? Is there a set time period I have to meet before you will trust me? If I am still by your side in a year, *then* will that be enough? When will 'I want you forever' be more than just a conditional time period to you?"

"I don't know," I say, shaking my head as tears spring to my eyes again.

Yes you do.

"When I stop being afraid that you'll leave," I say before I can talk myself out of it. I hate admitting that, but he ought to know the truth. It's easier to say it and endure his reaction while the wall separates us.

"That's unfair," he replies softly. "You are setting arbitrary conditions. How can I ever meet them?"

"They aren't conditions for *you*. They are conditions for *me*."

"So your love is conditional."

"That's not what I meant."

"Yes it is. What is it you think love is anyway? A *feeling*?"

I open my mouth to say yes, but then shut it. If that's what love is, then mine *is* conditional because I know without a doubt that feelings change…

My brain hurts. As I verbalize my thoughts to Gabriel, I realize I am trying to live a contradiction. I want some kind of guarantee that Gabriel is going to want me forever yet I can't pinpoint how I'll get that. I feel like convention dictates that I should need more time with him to know but… why? I'm certainly not held back by a lack of knowing him well enough. My emodar and the colorworld have taken away that objection.

"I always demand too much out of relationships…" Gabriel says, partly to himself, I think. His dissatisfaction sways fitfully before reaching a hardened stop of resignation. "Maybe now is one of those times. I've tried to temper myself by speaking my heart to you in other languages, but even that doesn't seem to be working. I can't help always wanting to gild the lily. It's my curse to endure…" He sighs heavily.

"But I *want* to gild the lily with you," I plead. "Whatever my hang-up is, it has nothing to do with *you*. It's *me*."

His heart sinks into deeper sadness and he struggles for the right thing to say.

"I *always* want to hear what you're thinking," I say. "Since when do you agonize over words?"

"When what you say is the exact opposite of what I want to hear. I have no idea what you want out of this. For all I know, I'm just some infatuation that will come and go. And everything you've said implies that's actually true. I want to meet your conditions so I can be *more* than a fling. Just tell me what they are."

"Gabriel..." I say, hating that he thinks that. "You are *not* an infatuation to me."

He releases a portion of his insecurity but says, "And so what am I? Where do you want our relationship to go? Because it's either moving forward or it's standing still. And I am not interested in that. Standing still is nothing more than a slow death."

"How is it standing still? We just got together less than two weeks ago."

"Again, are you saying there is a specific time that a relationship should sit still before it can move forward?"

My shoulders slump. He's right again. But his demands that I *feel* differently are not reasonable. I don't have control over that. I can't *make* myself more sure of Gabriel's commitment to me. Heaving in several irritated breaths, I keep my cool—which is easier with his depression weighing so heavily on me.

If time isn't what I want in order to trust him, what do I really need?

I have no answer to that.

How can I have no answer?

As I rewind the last week to find clues, I recall the sting of certain betrayal I felt when he turned me over to Louise. I'm puzzled again by how easily I accepted that Gabriel had been nothing but a good liar all that time.

Because I wanted him to be.

I wanted to end it. The uncertainty has been too much for me to bear. Despite *wanting* to give him what he asks for, *I* still want nothing to do with a relationship like this—one strangled by deprivation.

Yet I know I want him. *Always.* Not just because I am in love with him, but because being around him inspires me. Even now, when he's exhausting me with his confusing demands, I'm blown away by the depth of his consideration. He doesn't ever settle for even the most obvious assumptions. And he's managed to push me into analyzing myself more deeply than I think I ever have.

I must have some issue with commitment. But how? I was the girl who always demanded that every guy I dated give me the depth of their soul, the honesty of their every thought...

I must have never actually *expected* commitment like that. I subconsciously pushed them away by setting unrealistic demands.

But now I'm getting exactly what I asked for with Gabriel and I am terrified because it's unknown territory. I only know how to end a relationship apparently. Nurturing one is completely foreign to me. Which means I have to ignore what comes naturally. And what *does* come naturally is analyzing Gabriel's emotions. Looking for a change in his feelings. Waiting for it so I can jump ship before it hurts too badly. I have to stop that. I have to stop leaning on emotions…

I snort softly and shake my head. I'm doing it again. I'm *waiting* to feel differently. Just like before I got my act together and started taking care of Ezra. I can't just sit around *waiting* to feel better about this, *waiting* to trust Gabriel. I have to *do* something to change how I feel. But what?

"I don't want what we have right now, Gabriel," I say, hoping that if I start with verbalizing my weakness, the answer will come. "Worrying that one day I will lose you is too much to handle."

Gabriel, who has been sprouting weeds of melancholy all this time, now falls into roiling misery. I hear him shift to get up.

"Stop!" I insist, coming to my knees and turning around. I put my hands on the wall as if I can stop him. "But I *do* know I want *you*."

He pauses, confused. "That doesn't make any sense, Wendy."

"I know!" I say. "It doesn't. I'm just thinking out loud. Hoping it will help me figure it out."

"Is there *anything* I can do?" he asks.

"Probably… Maybe you can get a tattoo of my name so you'll remember who you belong to when you see it." I laugh. "I know it's silly, but I want to *do* something. I want you to buy a boat and name it after me. Buy an island and name it 'The Isle of Wendy' and live there with me. That's stupid and cliché and not really practical, but I guess I'll settle for writing my name in every one of your precious books. Then you'll read my name before you ever read a word of them." I grin even though he can't see it.

"That's all?" he asks, slightly incredulous.

I laugh again. "Probably not. I just know you're right. 'I love you' isn't good enough. It never has been for anyone. And especially not for us. I want to find a way for us to… *be stuck together*." My eyes widen in surprise as I finally wrap my head around an idea that has shaken the confusion right out of me and replaced it with the unbearable excitement of understanding. *How* on earth have I missed what a relationship really is all this time?

"Stuck together?" he asks when I don't continue.

"A group assignment," I say excitedly. "Like in programming class."

"Can you elaborate?"

"Everyone gets frustrated with the group projects," I explain, speaking loudly to be sure Gabriel can hear me. Mister T-shirt is obviously a heavy sleeper. "Because each person in the group has a separate part to code and once it's done you have to come together at the end and make it all work together. It's a pain in the ass, actually. Because where programmers lack confidence socially, they make up for in arrogance about their computer skills. Code is beautiful though, in how it allows people to solve the same problem in different ways. It's definitely an art. But none of them see that because they're too busy comparing their techno-manhood all the time."

Gabriel chuckles. "Techno-manhood? I'm exceedingly curious where *this* is going."

I smile. "Sorry. I got a little side-tracked. But it *is* kind of relevant. Anyway, you show up to your group meeting to integrate your code. To sum it up, getting a working end-product that integrates all the parts is like watching your work being burned in front of you. You're thinking about all the time you put into your beautiful algorithms and hating how they're now being cut down or expanded to fit with everyone else's stuff. You do this multiple times when it's a big project, going back to the drawing board to adjust your code or write new code, coming back as a group again and trying to make it work. It's exhausting emotionally. Sometimes you hate your teammates. Sometimes you love them. But inevitably you start dreaming of a world where programmers never have to work together. The only thing that keeps you at it is the promise of a grade. But when you finally see the end product working seamlessly, it's like magic. And you realize it was all worth it and you're really, really proud of yourself for sticking it out."

"Fascinating," he says. "I admit I've never expended my brain power on wondering how programming gets done. But you do make it sound lovely… But where is this going?"

"Well that's what I want with you. A group project—for two."

"Oh now you're just making me blush with all that computer nerd sweet-talk," Gabriel laughs. "What kind of project are you thinking?"

I pause nervously because I realize what I need now and I hope it's what Gabriel needs, too. "I guess I just… never thought of relationships before as projects in progress. I figured people got together because they were compatible enough to work together over the long run. The benefit was never being alone and always having someone to come home to… But now I don't think that's right at all. And in fact, that sounds boring. I just never realized it because I never met anyone that inspired me to want to be better like you do. That's why I want you. When I think about being with you, it gives me a glimpse of that magical end-product. I've never seen a relationship for what it could *be*. I always saw them as they *were*. And they were never enough."

I take a few breaths to gain courage. "People in relationships don't have grades to motivate them to stay stuck together, but they do have contracts that help them stay together during the moments when they really don't want to…"

"Wendy," Gabriel says in a low voice, although I can feel him bubbling with tempered anticipation. I think… I *hope* it's a good sign that we're on the same page. "Are you saying you *want* a contract?" he asks.

I bite my lip and then force the words out. "I always thought those contracts were meaningless because people always screw them up and don't respect them. It always confused me that people still wanted them. But I get why now. Because it's the biggest project there is and everyone wants that magical finished masterpiece. And if I know you, you won't settle for less. And you'll refuse to fail." I take a deep breath. "And that's why I want you to marry me, Gabriel."

As the word 'marry' is on its way out of my mouth Gabriel jumps up, not just physically, but internally as well. The force nearly knocks me off my knees. His excitement is unable to find an outlet, turning frantically this way and that, spilling over and warming me. It puts a huge smile on my face. Thwarted by his inability to express himself, he pounds the wall a few times.

"Relax," I say, shaking with relief. I shouldn't be surprised by his exuberance, but I am anyway. It's clear that this is what Gabriel has been after all this time. But Kaylen *did* try to tell me, didn't she?

"I can feel you," I laugh. "So… is that a yes?"

He crouches down again and snorts. "That was *not* you proposing to me. That was simply you telling me you'd *like* me to propose to you. So let's do it proper, okay?"

I giggle. "Okay."

I hear him changing positions. I wonder what he's doing for a minute and then I say, "Kneeling?"

"Of course. You ought to stand up, you know. Otherwise it'd be odd for me to be kneeling while you're lying on the floor or something. I can't hear as well as you so I don't know what you're doing."

I stand up and place my hand on the wall. I knock twice to let him know where my hand is and he brushes the surface with his own. It comes to rest near mine. I close my eyes once more and visualize him on the other side, on one knee, his hand against mine.

He clears his throat and speaks slowly, "Wendy Whitley, I have loved you since day one. And I will love you forevermore. I'm not promising you a perfect life. In fact, I'm promising you this will be terrifically hard. But *nothing* worth having or wanting is easy. And *everything* that's good and right in this world came about by hard things. I want you and me to undertake those hard things together, no matter what they are. I want you as you are now and who you will be in a hundred years. For always. Zhyenityes' na mnye? Cásate conmigo? Will you marry me?"

I rub my teary eyes. I forget to answer until I become aware of Gabriel's bubbling anticipation. "Yes!" I exclaim. "Yes, I will!"

There's a bit of awkwardness for a moment as we both wonder what to do with ourselves. Being separated by a wall complicates the moment but not for long. I lay my cheek against it and say again, "I'm here. And I have never been happier."

This sets him at ease and we both rest there. No touch. No sight. No smell. Nothing to bring us together in the moment. For Gabriel anyway. My emodar makes it hard to feel too distant from anyone.

When we finally get out of here, I doubt I will be able to remember this room as a prison or this wall as an unrelenting barrier.

I don't think I have ever felt so free.

41

Someone is jabbing me in the shoulder with something hard. I roll over to get away only to suffer a sharper jab. The pain pushes consciousness at me more insistently and I force my bleary eyes open. Mister T-shirt is standing over me, poking me with the barrel of his rifle.

"What the...?" I say loudly. I'm having trouble finding coherency because I'm so tired. Gabriel and I were up clear into the morning hours talking across the wall after his proposal. Mister T-shirt never even stirred.

"Up," he says gruffly.

I glare at him. "You couldn't just yell for me or something? Don't you know it's not safe to point loaded guns at people?"

"Gloves," he grunts, pointing at the dresser where my gloves have remained since I arrived.

I roll my eyes and sit up. "I understand full sentences, you know. I'm starting to think maybe you don't know how two string two words together. I think I'm getting dumber by the day listening to you order me around like a cave man."

Gabriel must be awake because I hear him chuckle. Mister T-shirt raises his gun at me for real this time. Then he presses himself to the wall and waves it toward the door before training it on me again. I listen and hear commotion from the main house as doors open and close and feet shuffle. I guess I've been summoned finally.

"Right," I say, "I'm sure Louise would warrant you shooting me because I insulted you. But go ahead. Maybe you'll incapacitate me enough that I'll be useless to her. I think I'd enjoy seeing her reaction if you did that."

"Just shut up and get moving. And put your gloves on first."

I clap my hands. "Oh, look! You *can* speak English. Very well, Jane put gloves on so big man not so scared now." I move to the dresser with my hands held up like a surgeon and make a great show of wrenching the gloves on and holding them up for inspection. "Okay master, my weapons are sheathed."

"Your name is irrevocably written on my heart, Wendy," Gabriel says, so that only I can hear. "You'll still marry me?"

I smile. "Always," I reply loudly, confusing Mister T-shirt. I scoot uncomfortably close to him on purpose, but he remains steady, his gun between me and his body.

Once we're upstairs, Louise directs me to an unfamiliar man lying on a hypno-touch table. He's under hypnosis or maybe unconscious. I can't tell. I'm sure she's going to have me do hypno-touch, and I gather my nerves preemptively.

"Just start off by looking at his energy," Louise instructs without so much as a hello.

I eye her suspiciously.

"Hop to it, Dear. I'm sure you don't want to see what will happen if you refuse."

My eyes bulge in fear and I step forward, putting my hands over the man's chest. I inhale and exhale several times to calm myself. A couple minutes later, I'm in the colorworld. I open my eyes to see Louise's life force standing on the other side of the man. Her hands are behind her back and she's watching me.

"Well?" she says. "Tell me what you see."

I look down. The man's life force is beautiful. Purple, luminous, swirling rivers encapsulate his body.

"It looks like yours," I reply, noting how the man's life force swirls characteristically and purposely toward his chest.

"How, specifically?"

I continue begrudgingly, "Well yours and his are tighter to the body. And they swirl to the chest. Everyone with a manifested ability has a looser, meandering flow."

"Describe everything you see," she commands.

So for the next ten minutes I tell her the colors of everything. I've noticed, since doing hypno-touch indoors, that like inanimate objects outside, manmade objects are dynamic in how the colors vary in hue as perspective changes. I'm explaining this to Louise when she cuts me off impatiently and tells me she doesn't care what color the ceiling or the couch is. She wants to know about the life force and *only* the life force. So I tell her what I see, even indicating over the man's chest exactly how his life force swirls. I don't have much else to tell her since my eyesight is so bad here, but it all seems to interest her anyway.

When I'm done, Louise nods curtly. I hold my breath for whatever she's going to say next. Just imagining manipulating this beautiful life force makes me feel feverish. I don't want to do it, but

Gabriel's life is on the line. I'm not shirking just because I don't know what kind of ability will manifest—whether it will be as terrible as my own.

"I need you to understand why you're important," Louise explains. "You were *made* for this. It's no coincidence that you made your way back to me after so many years, and that you possess the abilities you do. There is nothing wrong with this man: no allergy, no disease. His life force is unaltered. And you are going to bring out his latent ability—something I've never been able to do."

My mouth drops open in amazement. That can't be true, can it? "My dad... He could do it, too?" I ask.

Louise smiles warmly, although her emotions betray none of that warmth. "Of course he could. Now you get to complete what he started."

"Which is what?"

Louise waves her hand. "If you become more cooperative, I'll tell you one day. What's important now is that we see what you can do."

"Are you kidding?" I exclaim, frustrated that she has outright refused to tell me anything more. "If you knew this all along, why the month-long charade? Why not just kidnap me from the start?"

Louise sighs impatiently. "In the field of energy medicine, you accomplish more with willing hands. I would have thought your... *handicap* would have better motivated you. But it doesn't matter. Either way, you will never overcome it without my help." She glances down at my hands and then back up to my face.

"You did this to me?" I ask, testing. "You made me lethal?"

"Don't be ridiculous," says Louise, exhaling with impatience again. "If I could do that kind of thing, what would I need you for?"

I frown, not sure whether to believe her. A death-touch is right up her alley.

"I don't care what you think," she says without inflection. "I only care what you can do. Now, you say the flow is centered at the chest, so you'll want to disrupt it there. Make it take alternate routes. I'll demonstrate. You copy me in his life force."

I watch Louise make hand motions in the man's energy field and note one thing that's odd: there's none of the eerie ringing that usually accompanies her hypno-touch. What's more, I could swear her hands are having no effect whatsoever on the life force she's pawing through. If awful sounds accompany life force manipulation, she wasn't joking when she said she can't manifest an ability in a healthy person.

She stops and looks at me, waiting.

At least I know this won't kill him, so I begin, pulling away from the swirl and outward as Louise demonstrates. The sound it makes is so jarring that I flinch, wrinkling my nose and turning my face away. I wish Gabriel could put some memory in my head right now so I won't have to focus on what I'm doing.

"Louise, the sound this makes is terrible," I say. "Imagine hearing music when my life force touches his, and, then as I manipulate it, one instrument plays loudly against the melody, ruining the entire piece... it's like that. It's a terrible, gut-wrenching sound. I hate it."

Louise looks at me thoughtfully and then nods. "So you hear them as well... I certainly guessed as much. Now I understand why you resisted me all that time. But you're giving it too much consideration. You're forgetting what we're doing here: unlock what humans are already capable of. Growing pains are to be expected. It's going to feel unnatural, but you'll come to appreciate how things should be. Proceed."

I copy Louise's hand motions with ease but, as expected, the experience is disturbing. It looks, feels, and sounds all wrong. But I don't hold back. I rearrange the face of this man's soul, all the while with guilt in my heart over what I'm doing. Silent tears fall from my eyes as everything I experience in the colorworld protests against me.

I have no idea whether I'm causing damage. The man still breathes; his heart pumps blood. But whatever this is, it can't be good; my instincts tell me so.

Louise is right about one thing, though. I am *good* at this. My hands... something about them connects to the life force with palpable control, so unlike Louise's fleeting influence.

My heart sinks when I think of Gabriel; I worked on him just like this not too long ago. He gave me other things to focus on instead of what my hands were doing, but I defaced his soul too. It was a bit disorderly anyway, but I bet if I'd really looked at it after I was done, I would have been horrified by what I saw.

The swirl in the man's chest slowly disappears, dissolving into the disorderly flow I am so used to seeing on people at the compound—more so. It's... chaos.

When I'm done, Louise examines my work with her hands. I hold my own hands up, a doctor who has finished surgery, keeping the wound clear of contaminants. It's too late for this man though. The damage is done. Whatever that damage is.

Louise continues to hold her hands in the man's life force and leans over to examine his body. I know she wishes she could see it like I can. I wish I *couldn't* see it, and I pull away. It's like I took an original Van Gogh and colored it with permanent marker. I hope the real painting is still underneath.

Louise's satisfaction taunts my anxiety, making me nauseated. I also pick up a hint of resentment from her.

"How exciting," she says evenly without looking at me, still staring at the man's body and maybe imagining she can see his life force. "That will be all from you today."

She nods at Mister T-shirt. "Don, take her back to her room."

I don't wait for him to poke me with his gun. I rush for the door, eager to escape. I hope Gabriel will have something to say to comfort me after that nerve-wracking, chalkboard-scratching process.

* * *

"I don't like this," I say to the wall later when it sounds like Don has gone to the main house for lunch.

"I agree. I assume she's having you manifest abilities. Did you expect anything less?" Gabriel replies.

"No. But I forgot. It's wrong. Like scratching someone's eyes out," I reply, holding my breath against the memory of the sound of manipulating the man's life force. "But Gabriel, he was healthy! I can manifest abilities in anyone!"

He inhales sharply. "Really?" he asks in a low voice. "Gads! Did she say anything about your father?"

"He could do it, too!" I reply. "She said she wants me to finish what he started! What do you think she means?"

"Selling abilities for a price?" he replies with trepidation. "I'm afraid I miscounted your value to her. This is… not good."

He spins maniacally through different scenarios. Gathering all the facts up finally, he says, "I think it's safe to assume that Louise was who your mother was running from all that time. Louise knew your father and must have known what he could do…"

He thinks again and then says, "The part I don't understand is why she had you undergo hypno-touch in the first place. Your senses

320

were tested before you ever had it done so she must have known you were who she was looking for. I think your senses were an indication that you were able to see the colorworld on some level before you ever had hypno-touch, only you were never aware of it, obviously. So why do hypno-touch anyway? And why did it evolve your ability so dramatically? Did Louise *know* that's what would happen because of your father? Why would she want that?"

I have *no* answer to that.

"The only explanation I can think of is that she hoped you would evolve it and become desperate to work with her. That's reasonable, don't you think?" he says.

"Yeah…" I run my hands through my hair. "This is nuts," I say, certain we're on the right track even though it poses more questions than it answers. "What the crap was my mom thinking not telling me about her?"

"No sense in lamenting the past, Love. I'm sure your mother was just trying to protect you in the best way she knew how. Although why it is people so often think that avoiding the truth is helpful is beyond me. It always come back to bite you in the worst way." He exhales heavily and then says, "I am sorry, Wendy. I made a deal with the devil when I didn't have all the facts. I've made a Horlicks of pretty much everything."

"Horlicks?" I ask, unable to help smiling even though the situation is nothing to smile about.

"One of my dad's favorites," he replies. "It means—"

"Yeah, yeah," I interrupt. "I can figure it out. Thanks for making me smile."

I can tell he's thinking other words that he won't say because he doesn't want to upset me.

"I know," I say, answering his thoughts. There is no way Louise will let me go now. She's going to double her efforts to keep me secure because of how valuable I am. My chances of escape are dwindling.

We both sit in silence next to the wall, wrestling aggravation, thinking about what to do next.

Finally, Gabriel says, "We need to figure out what her next move is."

"She'll move us," I reply.

"Maybe… But beyond that? Do we assume she tries to capitalize on what you can do?"

I shrug even though he can't see. "What else *would* she do?" I should have listened to Kaylen a long time ago—about pretty much everything.

When Gabriel doesn't reply, I say, "We need to escape."

"How?"

I hear a door open and then footsteps outside the pool house. "Think about it. Talk later," I say.

"You probably don't want to hear me grovel, but I can't help myself. I haven't done a thing right. I am so sorry I put you in this position. I should have... figured something else out. I was just so desperate not to lose you. I couldn't stand being separated from you. Can you forgive me?" he pleads.

"I left you no choice," I reply.

"There's always a choice," he says. "I just made the wrong one."

I slouch against the wall when the pool house door opens, exhausted by what I envision awaits me: hundreds—*thousands* of hypno-touch sessions where Louise has me turn out real live superheroes for a fee. Day in and day out: that horrible wrenching sound. Or maybe she just wants her own super-villain gang that she'll use to take over the world... Of course I haven't seen anything that seems dangerous other than what Kaylen can do, (and what I can do of course), but if Kaylen is what's possible under Louise's hands, I can only imagine what's possible under mine. Ugh. Someone should just put me down. I'm not only a weapon as myself, but in the wrong hands I'm a weapon of mass destruction.

Things are not looking good. Still, something's going to come up. I don't know whether I agree entirely with Gabriel that he made the wrong choice. He already assumed she was going to use me to manifest abilities. It's not like that has changed. He just underestimated my value. And he achieved his goal—in the most unorthodox way possible. I can handle manifesting abilities for a little while until we figure out an escape plan. And we *will*. Besides, it's not like she has me actually hurting people.

42

"Good morning, Wendy!" Louise says the next day in a cheerful voice.

I recoil. Her uncharacteristic vim has me on edge immediately. I've been woken up *again* by Don's gun in my side, but this time Louise has accompanied him. She stands in front of my door. Don stands against the wall with his rifle.

I hear a commotion of footsteps from the main house—more than yesterday. The front door opens and closes several times. Car doors open... What is going on? Is Louise bringing her new army in for me to create?

I focus my attention on Louise. She looks positively celestial in white linen pants and a purple silk blouse. Her long white-grey hair is loose and slick like she's taken extra care with it. Her small braid with its purple ribbon woven in falls over her left shoulder. Louise's hair alone is unusual enough to be a defining characteristic, but she usually completes her look with earthy clothes like faded jeans and tunics. This is different, and different worries me.

"I have a surprise for you!" she says exuberantly after I sit up.

I lean farther away from her instinctively. Whatever the surprise is, I don't want it, especially if she is this ecstatic about it.

Her smile turns into a pout. *She's pouting?* This is getting weirder and weirder.

At that moment I hear Gabriel's door open, footsteps across his floor, and someone rousing him from sleep. Then I hear a jingling metal sound followed by the distinct clicking of handcuffs.

Why are they handcuffing Gabriel?

My body freezes in panic.

"I realize the precariousness of our situation," Louise says regretfully. "You can't stay here forever, so it's time to get proactive. We've got to find a way to get along, you and I, because you have *such* a bright future and I'd hate for it to be spent like this. It's simply not practical.

"Now then, I've focused entirely on what you can do for me through your sight. You'll have to forgive me; I get so caught up in my work that I forget that there are other things out there that make life worth living. I can't expect everyone to have the same vision as me, can I?" She laughs and smiles sweetly.

I've never seen her this way. I don't know what to expect from her. Instinct tells me I should run. But Don is watching me like a hawk, and he's holding that gun even more tightly than usual. He must know what she's planning. It must be as bad as I imagine.

"I'm going to help you in the same way I helped your father," she explains. "I'm going to help you understand your other ability—the one that absorbs life forces. And there is simply no other way to do that than for you to see it at work with your second sight."

I stand up and blink at her in shock. Don flinches. Please let me be misunderstanding her.

"My father?" I ask. "He *touched* people and watched it on the other side?"

"How do you expect to control what you can do if you don't watch it?" she asks.

"What happened to the guy yesterday?" I demand, certain that the experiment must have gone awry. Why else would she be changing her plans like this? *Oh my gosh.* Maybe I killed him… That must be why she now wants me to… *kill people* so she can figure out why.

"What?" asks Louise, confused. Then realization crosses her face and she shakes her head. "Oh, he's perfectly sound. Don't you worry about *that*." Whatever she's thinking about regarding him brings a look of satisfaction to her face.

My relief is abbreviated by intense fear. I may not have killed *him,* but she now wants me to touch someone else—to kill them.

"Louise," I plead, "I'll do whatever you ask, just don't make me do this... I would rather have a death-touch forever than kill someone. Please. What am I not doing that you want me to do? I thought I copied you exactly. I swear I didn't hold back." I'm close to tears.

How does this help her?

Louise looks at me with pity. "Don't fret, Dear. This is exactly how your father learned to control *his* ability. Don't you want the same?"

"Louise," I beg, trying to convey my seriousness with my tone and expression, "if it means endangering someone, then no, I don't want that. Can't we just go back to your other plans? You want to give people abilities, right? Can't we just do that? You've already used me to murder three people. It doesn't matter if you waved a magic wand right now and cured me, I would never trust you—never be on your side. I don't work that way. You already have what you want and that's me. Let's not bring any more deaths into this, okay?"

Louise smiles at me indulgently like I'm a child. "You can't imagine how hard it was to take the lives of those *poor* souls. But we had no other way of understanding you and what you were capable of, or how safe it was to be around you. They served a greater good, which is saying something since their lives were so miserable. There's no shame in that. Sacrifice is necessary for all good things to come about."

If I wasn't already keenly aware of just what kind of heinous crimes Louise is capable of, I would swear the loose set of her jaw and the softness of her eyes conveys compassion. I can't read her right now, but her expression combined with her request... She actually *believes* what she's doing is right. She's completely psychotic.

"What's more, one subject even survived," Louise says. "And do you know why? Because you controlled your ability subconsciously. You have it in you. I have confidence this is going to be a cinch for you."

I shake my head. "You don't know that. It doesn't matter what I might have done without knowing it. I have *no* clue how to control it. There's *nothing* my sight reveals to indicate how my ability works. Don't you think I've been *looking* all this time? Whoever I touch is more than likely going to die. I can't take that risk."

"How do you propose to learn control then? There's no other way. You have to sacrifice. Isn't being able to touch people all you really want?"

"No," I say softly. "It's not the only thing. Right now, the only thing I really want is for whatever victim you've chosen to live. I don't want to be able to touch people at the cost of a life. Not by a long shot."

Louise smiles apologetically. "You say that now. But when you can touch Gabe, you won't complain again. It will be done. You won't be able to reverse it. What you'll have in return is a knowledge of how your ability works. If you can see what's happening, you *will* be able to control it. That's how all abilities start out: raw, underdeveloped, misunderstood. With your sight, you have the advantage. You'll see."

I need to give up reasoning with crazy. I look around frantically like an escape route will magically appear. Gabriel has been silent but I can hear his heart racing.

"I'm so sorry," he whispers a few beats into the silence. "I had no idea. *No* idea. I never thought... I don't understand... To what *end*? Why? Please forgive me... I have *sorely* misjudged this entire situation. I never imagined she would be motivated in this direction. But don't let her have her way. She can't force you to kill someone. You *do* have a choice. Don't compromise yourself, not even for my life... Please, I don't want to live knowing I put this on you..."

I turn back to Louise and see that she's watching me.

"Yes..." she sighs. "I know how it tears you down to be so thoroughly cut off from physical affection. You need this. It's okay that you aren't strong enough to make the necessary sacrifices alone. Your gift is enough of a burden. That's why I'm here: to help you, to guide you. You need me now and you'll find that you're going to need me later. We can accomplish great things together. I have been here before, but with your father and it all turned out just fine. You know it did. Otherwise you and your brother would not have been born, would you?"

My heart pounds in my ears, and I look from Louise to Don. He grips his weapon menacingly.

"No," I say firmly. "I *don't* need you. That's just what you've wanted me to think all this time. I don't know what your history is with my dad, but at this point I don't care. I will *not* kill anyone. You can't make me do anything."

Louise takes in my words with a hard expression, looks out the door, and nods. I hear Gabriel's door open. My heart accelerates with painful quickness.

There is a crack—a dull crack: the sound of a bone breaking—followed by a groan. Gabriel moans slightly as he breathes with staggered breaths.

"No!" I shout, launching myself toward Louise. But Don slams the butt of his rifle into my chest, throwing me back into the wall where I crumple to the floor. It knocks the breath out of me. I breathe shallowly to regain it, but inhaling causes a stabbing pain in my ribs that has me pinching my eyes shut with every breath. I don't want it to end, though. I don't want to face what is most definitely going to happen next.

"Just so we're clear," Louise says through my labored breathing, "you will go into the main house. You will not speak. You will remove your gloves and take on your second sight. Then you will touch whoever is on the table and observe the reaction of life forces, yours and theirs."

I manage to look up at her.

She notes my expression of horror. "Come now, Dear, surely you can see the benefit. But you'll have to focus if you have a hope of controlling your ability. So I would suggest detaching yourself from the act itself in favor of objective observation," she instructs.

Detach myself from killing someone? How in the hell am I supposed to do that?

"Let's go," she orders. "Now."

I stagger upright, closing my eyes to the pain in my chest, hearing Gabriel's ragged breathing beyond the wall.

This is impossible. Either way I choose, someone will die. I have no doubt that Louise has every intention of torturing Gabriel until his last breath. She will kill him if I refuse, and then she will forcibly make me kill her victim anyway just to break me.

I don't think I have a choice but to do what she says... I step forward but my head spins and I fall back against the wall.

The sound of Gabriel's gasps wrenches my heart. No one would fault me right now. Any sane person would choose the one they love over a stranger. I want Gabriel to live. Besides, whoever the victim is may not even die at all...

They are probably some vagrant. If I were to place value on a life, I would put Gabriel's even above my own. He's genuinely good and he has so much to offer the world. He deserves to live and to influence people. I very much doubt I can say the same for this person.

I groan inwardly. This isn't fair. I want to justify it so badly. But I just can't make it stick. I can't live with *knowingly* killing someone no matter the odds of their survival. No matter who I think *deserves* to live more. I've suffered so much just knowing Louise used me to kill without my knowledge. This will be a conscious choice.

But how can I possibly endure the memory of Gabriel's torture?

"No more stalling," Louise says. "You can walk or I'll have to break another of Gabe's limbs."

I look up to her stony face. She stands in front of the door. Don is next to her, his gun held in front of his chest, barring any chance of escape. I look around the walls of the room, catching sight of the boarded-up window as well. It amazes me that only two nights ago, I felt so liberated in this room. With the same wall as that night at my back now, it feels like the space has now gotten smaller.

Louise turns her head to look out the door again.

I hold up a hand. "I'm coming." I take a few steps toward her to demonstrate my compliance.

She nods at me and then goes ahead.

I can't hear anything over the sound of my beating heart as I walk to the pool house door. Don walks behind me, shoving his gun into my back to remind me he's there. I move with zombie-like strides, knowing that I haven't really decided anything. The gravity of it feels like it's going to crush me.

Once I'm outside and the smell of early morning rays filtering through the trees fills my nose, I gain confidence that this won't be so bad. I can do this. I wouldn't be here if my dad didn't know how to control his ability. And I can probably see even more than he could... If I let Gabriel die, I will always wonder if he could have been saved. There *has* to be a way to control it...

"Wendy." Gabriel's quiet voice reaches my ears. I perk up to listen to him just as we reach the patio doors to the main house. "It wasn't until I lay on the concrete with you that I finally got how you've been so resilient. It's because you like pressure. Pressure makes you powerful. I allowed Louise to have you because I knew she would put you in a box. Louise thought taking you would make you weak and unable to resist her, but she was wrong. I knew it would make you *stronger*."

Four walls and a locked door.

Gabriel is right. I'd like to stand here and marvel over the truthfulness of that statement, how I've never fully recognized it, but I don't have time. Don is poking me in the back again to get me inside.

As I step over the threshold, the change in me is instantaneous. I don't care about reasons or justification or weighing the cost. I will *not* be forced to do *anything*. I will fight. *That* is the only action I can live with. It's the only action *Gabriel* can live with. I don't have my gloves off, but I will soon. And then I'll fight for my life. And for Gabriel's. And whatever shakes out at the end, I will deal with it.

Without regret. My heart beats louder, excitedly even. It bolsters my confidence even more.

I survey the room I step into. Straight ahead, near a set of double doors that I think go into the kitchen, stands a younger guy. He's a lot less burly than Don. If he's armed, his weapon is holstered.

Another man stands off to one side. He's a lot older and looks disinterested in me or anything else in the room. He clutches a brown leather bag in front of him. I don't think he's meant to be muscle. And I think I recognize him... maybe from Pneumatikon?

A glance at Don behind me reveals that he's going to be sticking around, too. So someone else is in the pool house holding Gabriel. Fortunately, Don is still wearing the same asinine t-shirt. It will be so easy to kill him if I can just get past his gun... I have to find the element of surprise. I'll go for him first.

But what about the guy at the double doors?

I sigh. Chances are good that both Gabriel and I are going to die...

"Wendy," whispers Gabriel's voice again. I lock onto it once more. "Show Louise how much you like boxes."

His voice is clearer than I expected. A glance through the glass door to the patio and I see why. Gabriel is sitting in front of the pool house with his hands cuffed behind him. An overweight man with a bat in his hand and a gun tucked in his belt stands nearby.

The sight of Gabriel being put into submission like that makes me livid. And his words serve to inspire my defiance further. I lock my eyes on each person in the room, daring them to even look at me wrong. Gabriel doesn't dole out empty encouragement. His confidence is *real* and it infuses me with power; I feel like I could take down this whole room single-handedly.

I turn my attention to the hypno-touch table to my right. A young man lies there. He has disheveled dirty-blond hair and a filthy face. His clothes are worn and he has multiple tattered, dingy layers on. But that's not what catches my breath. I think my heart even stops momentarily.

The person lying on the table is Ezra.

43

"Remove your gloves," Louise commands, ignoring the shock on my face.

I recover from staring at Ezra and look at her, my mouth slightly open as I try to figure out what exactly is going on. Did she kidnap my brother? Why is he dressed like a hobo? If she was going to have me kill someone, why would she choose my own family?

Louise's expression doesn't reveal anything. I don't know if I should just go for Don right now or stall this a little longer.

I glance back at Ezra, who looks unconscious. I'm assured that he's very much alive by the beat of his heart and his even respirations. I don't know if he's been drugged or hypnotized. But at least he's unharmed, as far as I can tell.

"Your gloves," Louise says again, her eyes narrowing just a little.

I look down at my gloves and fidget with them, buying time so I can think. I know Louise is evil but she's not stupid. She can't possibly think I would risk my own brother's life. Unless she doesn't know he's my brother... Is that possible?

Now that I think about it, I don't think she ever met him. Only Randy did. And Randy's not here to recognize him. But how did Ezra get here?

Robert? That's the only thing I can think of. So is this a rescue operation? I can't bank on that.

Whatever is about to go down, I'll need my gloves off, so I finally start to remove them, glancing up at Louise every now and then to get a read on her. I'm utterly baffled that she might have no idea that this is my brother that she's asking me to harm.

As I get to my second glove, I visualize going after Don, planning how it will happen. I hastily construct a wall against the memory of what killing someone feels like. If I manage to touch him, I won't hang around to experience it. No matter how much I hate him, I will get no satisfaction out of his agony.

I wonder if I'll get shot.

There's no helping it if that's what will happen. No use wondering.

Whispering reaches my ears again. But I think it's coming from beyond the double doors at the end of the room. "Wendy, it's Robert. I'm trying to buy time for my men to arrive. If you can't stall, you will need to yell. I'm armed, but it's just me and I don't know how many we're up against."

I try not to react, but I guess I look at the door a little too long because Don lifts his gun menacingly.

I don't know how I can possibly suspend Louise's demands any longer. I've already taken as much time as I possibly can just getting to this point. If there are only two armed people here in this room, surely Robert and I can take them together?

I take a step forward with my naked hands clasped behind my back. Having my skin this close to my brother causes familiar anxiety to stir in my stomach. And I'm about to put him in even more danger when I put up a fight. He'll be in the line of fire.

No, Wendy.

I am not the one that is dangerous. Louise may not know this is my brother that she's asking me to kill, but she knows that he is *somebody's* brother, *somebody's* son, *somebody* period. *She* is the dangerous one. And I'm far from helpless. It empowers me. And my courage builds once more until I have no regard whatsoever for my own life. It's exhilarating.

"Wendy. The sooner the better," Louise says impatiently. "I don't want Gabe getting into a state over your absence."

She raises her eyebrows at me expectantly. But I don't move my hands. Instead, I look around. We can't wait any longer…

At that moment, I hear the grunts of a struggle and a bat clattering to the concrete. It's coming from outside. Everyone looks that direction, including me. Gabriel and his torturer are on the ground in some kind of struggle. So far it looks like Gabriel is on top, but without the use of his hands I'm sure he won't be for long. He probably only has the advantage because he took the guy by surprise.

Don makes a move for the door, but I immediately jump into action.

"Robert, now!" I shout at the top of my lungs as I dive for Don.

A loud bang happens from the double doors. Then I reach Don, who notices me too late. With a t-shirt and gloveless hands he can't go hand-to-hand. This causes him to hesitate just enough to give me opportunity. When he finally makes a decision, he stupidly fumbles for a better grip on his gun rather than running. My hand makes contact with his arm before he realizes his error.

I expect the effect to be instantaneous and the seconds of dreaded anticipation are torturous. But then it happens. Life is sucked from me. My legs collapse beneath me.

Blindness. Where is my body?

And then Nothing starts closing in.

Panic as I try to fight against it.

And then terror as I realize I can't.

Wisps of recognition as I recall being here before.

This is not me.

I turn inward.

Get away. Get away. Get away. I think it over and over so I don't lose my mind to Don's.

It works because I manage to get the message to my legs. Awareness of them lights up my mind, penetrating the darkness. I scramble backward. Something is behind me and I can't get any farther. But I think I'm far enough because my head starts to clear. Gasping for breath, I repeat: *It's not me. It's not me.*

My senses return but they lurch about, not yet able to assimilate everything. I do spot Don a few yards away on the floor. I imagine what he must be feeling right now...

What have I done?

I hear a loud splash from somewhere and it rouses me.

I see Ezra still lying on the hypno-touch table. Weakness cumbers my limbs and I can't find the strength to move. I want to go check on him but quickly remember that I'm ungloved; that is not a good idea. Beyond Ezra, I see another guy who looks like a bum. He's got a gun. He holds the weapon like a pro, which, with his filthy getup, looks odd. I look closer at his face and see that it's Robert. He's pointing his weapon toward the patio doors. I look that direction and see Gabriel's torturer holding his own gun aimed at Robert.

That's when I remember the splash I just heard. Was that Gabriel? Is he in the pool? *Handcuffed?* From what I remember, the pool didn't look like it had a shallow end.

Fresh panic shoots through my trembling arms and legs. I look around. The man by the double doors is on the floor, knocked out.

The guy with the leather bag is gone. So is Louise. I need to intervene.

Leaning against the wall for support, I push myself to my feet and say, "Put your gun down or I will come over there and kill you myself—and I don't need a gun. Just ask Don."

The man glances at me. He's got a head wound that's bleeding profusely and I can see the whites of his eyes, which reveal his fear. I move closer to him, impatient to get to Gabriel, but desperately hoping I don't have to follow through on my threat. In fact, I can't even imagine it at this point.

Thankfully he throws his gun to the floor and backs away from me. Robert steps forward and kicks it out of the man's reach while I stagger to the door.

As soon as I reach the patio I remember I can't help Gabriel if he's in the water and unable to swim. I'm about to turn and yell for Robert when I see Gabriel's head above water. I guess the pool is not as deep as I had worried. And it looks like he's making it up the ladder even with his hands cuffed behind him.

"Gabriel!" I gasp as he throws himself over the top step to the pool side. "Are you okay?"

He groans in pain as he adjusts his seat, but his eyes find me. "Wendy," he breathes. "I saw Louise run off. Is it all clear?"

I nod. "Robert showed up. Supposedly his army should be here any minute."

"Really?" he says, looking beyond me to the house. "Perfect timing. Sorry I couldn't be of more use. I almost had that ugly behemoth in the pool with me but he opted to run instead of fight…" He shakes the water from his face.

I laugh, although it's mostly a laugh of relief. It's obvious that Gabriel is in pain, but mostly he's disgruntled that he was overpowered. I'm thoroughly spent so I sit down on the cement after checking the perimeter. "Gabriel, you're handcuffed with a broken arm. I'm just impressed that you put up a fight at all."

He rolls his eyes. "A for effort? Fantastic. Thank you for thoroughly discarding my masculine need to be useful and making me feel like a toddler in a baseball game in which everyone gets a trophy. I probably further injured my arm and all for a meaningless honorable mention."

It's *my* turn to roll my eyes. "My, my, Mr. Dumas. I had no idea your *masculinity* was so vain. But maybe it will stroke your blessed ego to know that it was your attack that created the diversion that allowed me to take Don by surprise and get my hands on him. So really, you get more than an honorable mention."

He brightens immediately. "Really?" Then his eyes narrow suspiciously. "Are you just telling me that to soothe my id?"

"Your *id*?" I shake my head and giggle. "I'm inclined to say yes, just so I can keep your *id* in check, but that would be lying. I'm afraid even overinflated ids deserve the truth."

He offers me a grin. "Excellent! But for the record, you can check my id whenever you want. I'm probably going to need it. I'm certain my arm is going to call for a cast, which means I'll have battle scars to show for my valiant efforts. My id could really start getting out of hand."

I prop my chin on my knee and smile at him. "It's a tough job, but someone's gotta do it," I say. "And I gladly volunteer."

He sighs and we both long for the release of an embrace right now. But his eyes come to rest hazily on mine. We speak our embrace that way instead.

44

"*W*hat is taking so long?" I complain, pacing the front room and glancing through the window into the late afternoon light.

Robert had to stay behind at the police station for a bit longer, so he had us driven about 15 minutes away to his Redlands home—which is even *bigger* than his Monterey one. We've been waiting anxiously for him to arrive. I interrogated Ezra the entire trip here but all he would tell me was that Robert knows all about Louise and about my abilities. He refused to divulge anything else without Robert.

After Ezra woke up from his drug-induced sleep in San Bernardino where Gabriel and I were being held, and before calling the police, we decided our story would be that I was kidnapped for ransom. Since Robert is extremely wealthy, it was entirely believable. Don died from cardiac arrest—cause unknown. Gabriel's torturer and the other guy Robert took out were both arrested, and even if they decide to tell the truth, nobody will believe them.

While the rest of us were being interrogated about every aspect of the kidnapping, Gabriel was being treated at the hospital for a fracture to his arm. With Louise still at large, I nearly lost patience with the officer; I just wanted to get back to Gabriel so I could make sure he was safe. Robert's slick-suited lawyer finally showed up and got us out of there pretty quick. Thank goodness for rich uncles.

"Impatience won't get him here any faster," Gabriel says from where he's sitting on the couch watching me. "Come sit by me. I feel like I haven't seen you in ages even though we were less than a foot from each other for so long."

I smile at him, take his outstretched hand with my own gloved one, and sit down on the couch. He kisses my palm, touches the ends of my hair while examining my face. "I am so sorry," he says for the tenth time.

"If you say that one more time I'm going to punch you," I reply.

His eyes laugh at me. "Punch me? You have a bit of a violent streak, don't you?"

"Only when people annoy me, like fiancés who think they need to prostrate themselves for forgiveness when there's nothing in need of forgiving."

"Fiancé..." he muses. "I do like the sound of that."

I think I blush a little. It *is* the first time I've referred to him that way. I just barely got used to calling him my boyfriend, and now we're *affianced.*

"Ugh. You know that staring in the eyes thing is as bad as watching you make out, right?" Ezra says, walking into the room with a box of crackers and a soda. "Can't you two keep your eyes to yourselves for five minutes?"

I stick my tongue out at Ezra.

"My apologies, Ezra," Gabriel says. "But her eyes are far too bewitching." He chuckles. "Who would have thought you could be inappropriate without even touching?"

"Maybe you should wear sunglasses then," Ezra suggests, shoveling a handful of crackers into his mouth. "That way the rest of us don't have to endure your eye-groping."

"Eye-groping?" I say, laughing.

"Sunglasses. Well there's an idea," Gabriel says. "Although considering that I already have to keep my hands off of her, it's excessively vexing to keep my eyes off of her also just because it bothers you. Does it also distress you when I speak to her? Shall I stop that as well?" He looks at Ezra expectantly.

"Well it's a wonder she can even understand you, the way you talk. So I don't think it matters if you speak to her or not," Ezra retorts.

"Oh shut up, Ezra," I say, rolling my eyes at him. Then I perk up. "Hey, a car just pulled in the driveway. Is that him?"

Ezra hops up and heads for the door, pulls it open, and sticks his head out. After a few moments, he says, "Thank goodness, Uncle Rob. I can't take much more of these two love-birds. It's like indecent exposure in here with them undressing each other with their eyes all the time."

I take off my shoe and chuck it at Ezra, landing it right in the back of his head.

"Ow!" he says, rubbing the spot.

Gabriel laughs and Ezra turns around with a look of mock outrage on his face. He picks up the shoe and throws it back at me, but Gabriel catches it with his good hand before it hits me. He shakes his head. "I can't believe you're willing to physically assault your own sister."

"All right, all right," Robert says as he comes into the room, a slight smile on his face. "Do I have to start making silly rules like no throwing shoes in the house, Ezra?"

"But she started it!" Ezra protests before throwing himself back in the chair across the room.

"Yeah, but I'm an adult," I say, grinning. "That was just me disciplining you for mouthing off... You're a kid. You're not allowed to throw shoes at your elders—which reminds me of my first issue, Robert," I say more sternly. "What in the world were you thinking, involving Ezra in all that?"

Robert sits down calmly on the other side of the room, placing his leather shoulder bag next to him. "Ezra may technically be a child, but he's old enough to involve himself in your rescue. What's more, I didn't intend for it to just be Ezra and me. Our plans just didn't go the way I thought they would. But maybe you'd like me to start at the beginning rather than the middle?"

I nod. "Please. I've been dying here and Ezra wouldn't tell us a thing." I scowl at Ezra. "So Gabriel and I decided to make him equally uncomfortable by *eye-groping* each other."

Robert chuckles but sobers quickly. He looks like he's thinking through his words for about thirty awkward seconds. Moby Dick is still trolling the ocean, I guess. "Well, Ezra," he says finally, "maybe you ought to tell them what made you suspect she was in trouble?"

Ezra nods. "Well you know I've never liked you going to that Pneumatikon place so I've been suspicious all along. I got an email from you the day I was expecting to see you saying you'd changed your mind and you weren't coming back for at least another month. I was like, 'What changed?' And I get this reply from you saying they'd offered you a job. It was just... weird. You talked about how the opportunity was perfect. You said, 'I need to start earning a living again, and right now this is the best opportunity I've got.' I mean, I wasn't *really* worried about you by then, but it was out of character to have you just drop everything like that without even talking to me about it.

"So I asked you to call me. And I got a reply saying you were busy. You said you'd call in a few days and we'd talk about it. I knew you weren't supposed to talk about stuff from the compound over e-mail but I just wanted to be sure you were okay. So I sent an e-mail back to you saying, 'Is this like that time you got really pissed off at me for giving out my personal information over the internet?'"

"Ezra," I interrupt exasperatedly, rolling my eyes. "How many times do we have to go over the fact that it was not *me* that told Mom you signed up for that online comic book? I still don't know how she found out. In fact, *I* was the one that defended you and told Mom she was overreacting about it."

Ezra chuckles. "Yeah, yeah. That's why I said it in the email. But in your reply, you said, 'It's exactly like that. This place is serious about security. I swear I'll call in a few days.' And that's how I knew you were in trouble. There was *no way* you would have responded like that unless something was up. And that's when I told Uncle Rob what was going on."

"Oh," I say, surprised. The online comic book debacle is one that Ezra and I still argue over from time to time. He swears there is no other way Mom would have found out about it unless I had told her. And I hate being accused of things I didn't do, even if they are now irrelevant. He just likes to bring it up to push my buttons. "That was clever," I say.

"I know," Ezra says, tossing a handful of crackers in his mouth with a self-satisfied look.

I turn to Robert who has his hands together like he's praying, his chin resting on the top of his fingers. After a few beats, he says, "It was a good thing Ezra handled it like he did. Louise knows who I am and she knows what I can do. She knew that if I was aware that you were with her, I would waste no time in finding you. If Ezra had ever alerted her that he suspected you were in trouble, she would have gone to greater lengths to hide you more thoroughly."

"*She knows what you can do?*" I ask, incredulous. "What does that mean?"

"Wen, he's getting there. Relax, okay?" Ezra says, taking a swig of soda.

I sit back, gathering patience. Robert is so slow. He keeps pausing for a really long time. Just like when I met him. Moby Dick's sluggish communication habits are exhausting.

"I have a talent for being able to accomplish my goals. I call it being in the right place at the right time," Robert explains. "If I focus on a goal, I get a vision for where to be, and when. That's how we found you."

"So... you're like... supernaturally talented?" I ask, leaning forward, aghast.

"Yes. But I was born this way," Robert replies.

Born *with it? What is* with *my family?*

"So your ability told you where I was?" No wonder my uncle is so rich. His talent obviously gives him the edge.

"Not exactly," Robert replies. He shifts in his chair and I think he looks a little uncomfortable. He's too far away to read. "It's not as cut and dry as you would think. It takes a lot of translation on my part to know how I should go about a vision. They are completely useless if I don't get the goal right first. I'll spare you the play-by-play. Just know I was able to narrow it down to San Bernardino—to a poor area of town where there's a lot of riffraff. I couldn't get a handle on the exact time, so we went undercover with some of my men. I had them ask around about Louise, whether anyone had seen her or anyone else in the area. We spread out to cover more ground and got separated.

"When Louise showed up shortly after that, it was just Ezra and me. We had no time to wait for backup, so we decided to act the part and go with her. I was mostly concerned that Louise would recognize me—she does know me—but fortunately she didn't handle the interaction. One of her men did. So she never got a good look at me. And that's why Ezra was in the living room rather than me. We hoped my men would track us in time. But of course, that's not how it worked out. And you know the rest."

"So what about my dad?" I ask, unable to contain my anticipation. I don't care *how* Robert's ability works. I'm far more interested in learning what Robert knows about my condition. Next to me, Gabriel, on the other hand, has launched his mind into analytical super-speed like nothing I've felt yet. The gymnastics I'm used to are lost in the blur. It's making me a little nauseated and I have trouble thinking straight.

"He was born with his ability as well," Robert replies. "And I only know of two times in which someone died from Carl's touch. Usually, he just put them in a coma for a couple days, which was bad enough. He worked with Louise for years before he died."

"So... he could control it then?" I ask impatiently. *Please* let Robert know how Carl did it. I hold my breath, waiting for his answer.

Robert's slightly apologetic expression does *not* look promising. "I believe so," he replies. "And I also know that he couldn't until he started working with Louise. I think that's why he stuck by her so loyally until he died…" Robert hesitates, looking at me carefully. "Carl spent years obsessed with trying to figure out his ability. He suffered for a long time being unable to touch people. You can guess better than anyone how it affected him. But I'm sorry, Wendy. I know you're hoping I have answers, but I have *no* idea how he controlled it."

I work really hard not to let my disappointment surface. I look up at the ceiling, and then I scoot to the floor at Gabriel's feet. He squeezes my shoulder in assurance. Then he says, "So Carl was born with an ability similar to Wendy's manifested one. Can you tell us more about it? He *usually* put them in a coma? What does that mean?"

Robert sighs, definite sadness in his eyes. I think he genuinely wishes he had more useful information for me. "Sometimes it kicked in. Sometimes it didn't. If it had any effect at all, they went into a coma. And two times the coma ended in death."

"Was it different from one person to the next or did it behave sporadically?" Gabriel asks.

Robert thinks for a moment, stroking his grey-flecked goatee. "I think it was different from one person to the next. It didn't take long before he figured out the effect he was having on people. So he didn't welcome the contact after it became obvious."

"How often did it affect people?" Gabriel asks. "When did it develop?"

"To my memory, his ability wasn't apparent until he was seven years-old. But I don't know if that was because it didn't develop until then or because nobody touched him before then who was affected," Robert replies. "Because more often than not he had no effect it seemed. And the times he did, the experience was traumatic enough that he just didn't entertain testing it out at all. The first person died when Carl was only nine. It was his baseball coach. You can imagine how that impacted him."

I shudder. I can *definitely* imagine. "So why was my dad working with Louise in the first place?" I ask.

Robert measures his words carefully, as usual. "Everything Carl did until he met Louise was an attempt to understand his ability. His work with Louise was no different. But once I noticed him no

340

longer wearing gloves, Carl seemed driven by something else. Whatever he was up to with Louise, it had him obsessed and secretive. But then he died shortly after that and Leena came to me for help. She wanted to hide you from Louise. You were important to Carl and Louise and their work. I have no idea why, but it's obvious that Leena was right. And in all these years Louise has never stopped looking for you."

"I don't understand..." I say, propping my elbow on Gabriel's knee, skeptical. "Why didn't you tell me this before? You knew that the person looking for me all along was Louise? Why didn't you warn me or something? Why didn't my *mom* warn me before she died?"

Robert inhales and exhales slowly, not looking at me, but lost in some kind of memory. He looks at me directly when he answers though. "The most important thing to Leena was that you and Ezra led normal lives, unburdened by the mistakes that your father made. She didn't want you to know because she didn't want you to live while looking over your shoulder. And I was only trying to maintain that life for you as well because it was what she wanted."

"What made you decide to contact us then? Was it just the credit report or was that a lie, too?" I ask, trying really hard not to be irritated.

Robert strokes his goatee again. "No, the credit check was the truth. Louise hadn't come close to finding you in years, but that indicated she was doubling her efforts. Then I also learned she'd built that facility in Pasadena, so close to where you were living. Without Leena around to be cautious and keep you out of Louise's sights, I worried you'd be found. And that's why I decided to insert myself in your life, to protect you without you being aware."

I lay my head against Gabriel's knee, absorbing all this new information as he brushes his fingers through the ends of my hair. I've been running all my life and never knew it. And by trying to protect me, my mom totally screwed me. I want to be angry, but I did the same thing when I kept my true destination from Robert. I lied thinking it would protect me and Ezra. Lying just never works out the way you expect.

"I should have questioned you when I saw you show up with your gloves that day..." Robert says wistfully then. "I almost did, but then I wondered if maybe it was something you did to protect yourself from the emotions of others since I knew you could sense them. I figured you must not like dealing with it all the time. And I couldn't imagine how you might have evolved Carl's ability. Either way, asking you about it would have opened up everything your mother was trying to protect you from knowing. I assumed you must be doing okay if you were going to college and holding a job. And when you told me you had an internship, it sealed my peace of mind about it. It was also going to get you out of town and give me time to set up protection for you for when you got back." Robert sighs. "I'm sorry. None of this turned out how I had hoped."

"Don't sweat it," I sigh. "I could just as easily have told you. And we're all here, aren't we? It all worked out."

"Damn straight," Ezra pipes up. "But what I don't get is why Louise wanted you in the first place. How is killing people with your skin useful for her superhero-making research?"

Oh yeah, I forgot to tell them that part. "Because I can see the colorworld—I mean, I can see life forces. I call it seeing the colorworld. I never told you because I figured Louise was monitoring communication and I didn't trust her enough to tell her. But it turns out she knew anyway because our dad could do the same thing. And we suspect that I can manifest crazy strong abilities in people with hypno-touch. Louise was always trying to get me to do it, but it felt wrong so I never really went along with it."

Robert leans forward now. "You can *see* life forces? So that must mean Carl could as well. No wonder…" He sits back, deep in thought.

I frown. There is still a lot I don't understand. I wish Robert had more answers. "Louise said the only way to learn control was to touch people in the colorworld. She said that's how my dad did it. I just don't understand why she would want me to do that. How would that have helped her? Did she have some reason for *wanting* me to be able to control my ability?"

"I doubt it was for your benefit alone," Gabriel says. "And I wouldn't bank on anything she said either. It's been clear since we saw your file that Louise has been *wanting* you to hurt people, accidentally or otherwise. There is definitely a part of this picture we don't yet have."

"We have to figure out why a death-touch would help her," I say. "That's where the answer is."

"That's true, but I think you have to stop considering your sight and your touch as mutually exclusive," Gabriel says. "It's apparent that Louise wanted you to have *both* of those abilities. If we figure out how they are connected, we will be much closer to figuring out your condition." Then he rubs his hands together delightedly. "We've plenty to think about, don't we?"

"Yeah, sounds like we've hit a real mental jackpot," Ezra says drily. Then he looks at me. "Well at least it worked out. I cannot believe you are *engaged*. Anyway, it looks like your stay at the superhero cult wasn't a total loss, right?"

"Nope," I say, smiling and reaching for Gabriel's hand.

"It did work out quite well," Gabriel says, squeezing mine back.

I turn to Robert as something else occurs to me. "Robert, did my mom ever sense emotions like I can?"

Robert's eyes twitch in surprise. "I don't believe so. Why?"

"Well it's just that Louise had a file on me under the name Wendy Haricott and it talked about my dad's ability. And it also said my mom's name was Regina Walden. It said she had the ability to sense emotions within a fifteen-foot radius."

Robert's eyes glaze over in thought as he takes yet another pause before answering, "To my knowledge, Leena's name was Sara Rowan. If she had another alias, I don't know about it."

"Why would she change *her* first name and not Wen's?" Ezra asks.

"I'm not sure," Robert says. "But Leena was *very* insistent on keeping Wendy's name. Probably because there wasn't much reason to change it. They would have been looking for a Sara with a daughter named Wendy. But a woman named Leena with a daughter named Wendy would be more of a shot in the dark."

"Maybe, like Dina, your mother lost her ability and that's why you never knew about it?" Gabriel offers. "*That's* an interesting prospect, isn't it?" He immediately starts contemplating it.

"Sure would be nice if Mom would have written a manifesto," I sigh. "She probably knew exactly how my dad could touch people."

"Don't worry, Love," Gabriel says. "We'll figure it out."

I smile at him and then say, "Well I hope Louise was totally lying about why that third subject lived. Otherwise, finding a solution is pretty unlikely. Because I am *not* touching people to learn by trial and error."

"I think she was," Gabriel says. "After all, the file called his ability 'sporadic.' And it implied that Louise was interested in Subject Number Three as well. The notes described it as immunity—which implies it was something about the woman herself rather than something *you* did. And Robert just told us Carl's ability had a different effect given the person, not the instance."

"Subject three?" Ezra asks.

"Yeah. We found out Louise tested my ability on four people while I was unconscious," I explain. "One survived: a woman. So if the reason she lived was not because of some kind of subconscious control, then there's something different about *her*." I wrinkle my nose. "The disappointing part is that it looks like not only does my ability take effect far more often than my dad's, but it's also lethal no matter what." I sigh, already stressed over the huge task ahead. "Anyway, if we can find the survivor…"

"It will be a huge clue as to how your ability might work," Robert finishes. "Yes, that does sound promising. If you need help locating this person, just let me know."

"Oh, gotcha," Ezra says. "Yeah, I can see how that would be big then. So Gabe, what can *you* do?"

Gabriel gives Ezra a demonstration while Robert shows me to the bathroom. Once there, I sink into wishing I had just a minute's worth of conversation with my dad to ask him how he did it. I start getting upset at my mom again for telling me literally *nothing* about him.

But lamenting the past is useless. I have to look ahead and get to work. And this time I have Gabriel by my side. That gives me enough confidence to step into the cloudy future ahead.

I smile as I think about his proposal and how it came about. It blows me away how blind I have been to what it actually means to love someone. And how would I have ever figured it out if Gabriel hadn't pushed me? I need him. He makes me better.

How strange it is that at this moment I feel grateful for my death-touch. Despite the physical barrier it creates, it brought me to Gabriel.

It's like that wall in San Bernardino. It was intended to bar me from Gabriel and the outside world, but it brought us closer together than ever.

I laugh quietly. Walls… I think I've always had some kind of unhealthy obsession with them.

The walls in our different homes growing up were not just refuges of security for me. I used to imagine what was on the other side of them. We lived in apartments most of the time, and my wall usually abutted another unit. I could often hear the people on the other side but I spent so many nights wishing I could *see* through it as well. I was caught up in the idea that there were other people occupying the space that was only inches from me... Yet they lived a reality outside of my own that I would never know or experience. In fact, the whole *world* was full of people like that. I remember being deeply troubled by that as nothing more than a seven or eight-year-old girl...

I'm on my way back down the hall to the living room, brushing my hands customarily along the wall as I go, when the most enlightening realization washes over me and I stop. I turn to the wall I'm touching as if it has whispered to me right through my fingertips. I rest my palm on it.

I got my wish, didn't I?

My emodar: a way to live inside people from a distance. Even a wall can't stop it.

The colorworld: a place that reveals the true essence of a person—their soul. Isn't that what I have always longed for?

How many times I rested my hand on my wall or on the floor of our second-story apartment, closed my eyes, and imagined watching the people on the other side, imagined seeing what they did when no one else was looking.

I wanted to see people as they really were. That's why I was so unhappy when people didn't reveal themselves to me completely. That's why I was a skeptic and hard-to-please. Judgmental. Suspicious. Demanding. Before my teenaged years, I'd make up little stories about people I saw because I couldn't stand the fact that they existed in my world yet I knew nothing about them. Making things up was my way of filling that gap.

Looking back on those moments, all of a sudden there is a thread of understanding that runs through the chaos. Like finally spotting a gold vein in the rock face after searching in the dark for years and years. This recognition fills me with more acceptance of myself than I've felt in possibly ever. A reverent peace moves through me as this part of who I am finally reveals itself:

I was looking for the colorworld all that time and I never realized it.

Epilogue

*A*fter a week of trying to get in touch with Kaylen—including Robert's men storming the compound only to find it empty—I finally receive a phone call from her. She thanks me over and over for getting Louise into hot water. It means she's been able to return home to her father.

We exchange stories about everything that happened, and she squeals with delight when she learns that Gabriel and I are engaged.

"Do you have a date?" she demands excitedly.

"No. We've been too busy to even think about it," I reply. "New job for me at my uncle's office... Finding a new job for Gabriel up here in Monterey... Moving out of my apartment in Pomona... I need to figure out how to finish my degree—*away* from people. We've also been looking for the girl who survived my death-touch. It's been a little hectic."

"No date?" Kaylen asks in disbelief. "How is it possible that Gabe has not even *thought* about a date?"

"We've both been worried about you, Kaylen," I say. "How could we think about a date when you were out there, unaccounted for?"

"Aww. That's so sweet," she replies. "But there wasn't a need to worry. My dad was pretty ticked off at Louise. They got into a fight over the phone and I heard him tell her they were finished."

"*That's* a relief," I reply. "So what are your plans for the summer?"

"My dad's taking me on vacation!" she says. "I'm not sure where. He says it's a surprise."

"I'm so happy for you, Kaylen," I say genuinely.

"Thanks!" she exclaims. I don't think I've ever heard Kaylen so upbeat. It does my heart good.

"Shoot me an e-mail, would you?" I say. "With an address so I can send you an invite when we *do* have a date?"

"Sure thing," she says, and then we hang up a few minutes later.

Hearing from Kaylen seals my peace of mind. I can move ahead now and begin gathering the pieces of my life and, once again, search for answers about my ability.

I put the phone back on the receiver, sit at Robert's kitchen table, and absorb the fact that everyone is now safe. I need to start putting some serious thought into what I plan to do now. I've been putting off more serious introspection with the excuse of needing to locate Kaylen. I realize, rather suddenly, that I haven't gone into the colorworld since my escape. Instead, I've been relying on finding Subject Three to give me a new lead about my ability.

Robert has had his private investigator on that job. My uncle has been such a gem in all this. I truly do not know what I would be doing right now without him. I still don't feel like I know him very well, but it's hard to overanalyze his generosity when I need it so badly. And he's a busy man. He doesn't have time to sit around getting to know me better or reminiscing about my mom and dad just to satisfy my curiosity. I resolve to just be grateful for his help. He's given me a job and opened his home up to Ezra and me. The stress level in my life has sunk dramatically. I should be able to focus on exploring the colorworld now without being afraid of Louise being over my shoulder and watching my every move.

Now that I think of the colorworld, I realize that I miss it. I worry that I've forgotten how to access it. What if it's like a muscle, and if you don't use it, it goes away?

I need to hit up Gabriel for an experiment.

As if bidden, the doorbell rings. I hop up, knowing it's Gabriel.

"I was just thinking about you," I say after I open the door.

"Depending on how often you actually think about me, I am not sure whether to be impressed with that happenstance," he says as I lead him into the kitchen. "If it were me, for example, it would be entirely unimpressive since I think about you, on average, eighty percent of the time."

"I don't think I'm *capable* of thinking about you that often," I say as I reach into the fridge for the sandwiches I was making for us when Kaylen called. They still need my special sandwich sauce that Gabriel loves. "I can't think of more than one thing at a time like you can. So if I actually thought about you that much, I wouldn't get a thing done and probably be sleep-deprived."

"Good point," he says, turning his back to me. "But thirty percent of that is sleep. I dream about you. A lot."

He always turns around or leaves the room when I dress his sandwich. He says the sauce is magic and if he so much as looks at it, he's going to start guessing what's in it. And if he knows what's in it, it won't be magic anymore. Then it will taste different. I laugh at his back. "Seriously, Gabriel. Are you going to live your whole life not knowing what's in the sauce? What if I die? Won't you want the recipe so you can make it and think of me?"

"Heavens, Wendy, don't say such a thing!" he exclaims without turning around. "No, I do *not* want to know. Because you won't be dying on *my* watch."

I roll my eyes, spread the sauce, and put the bread on top. I put the container back in the fridge and hold his plate out. "Done."

He turns and takes it from me, but instead of carrying it to the table, he sets it back on the counter and comes behind me, putting his good arm around my waist and breathing very close to my neck. Close for *me* anyway. It feels like six inches or so. But it still sends shivers down my back and arms.

"I've missed you," he whispers.

I hold still with tight control. If someone is in my emodar, I don't move until I'm sure of the safety of their location. And right now Gabriel is definitely not safe. He says I'm suffering from a lingering post-hypnotic suggestion. But now that I know the briefest of touches is lethal, it's foolish *not* to take precautions.

Gabriel likes to take advantage of my self-imposed immobility—I can always count on him to make the best out of any situation. He reaches up now and brushes my hair aside carefully. My mouth goes dry and I swallow to suppress my need for him touch me.

"I just spoke to Kaylen," I croak, breathing deliberately to calm the powerful chemistry being this close to him always evokes.

"That's capital news," he whispers. "I take it she's well?"

Distress is always my first reaction to these encounters. I don't like to be afraid, but I still haven't figured out how to be careful in a way that doesn't involve fear. I have to spend some time fighting back worry, and as a defense, I always grab onto other emotions in my head, namely Gabriel's often sultry thoughts. Amid that kind of intensity, it's hard to hold onto anxiety even a little. My caution is frequently thrown to the wind.

"Yes, she is," I say. With a gloved hand I reach up carefully to find his face so I can turn and look at him. Once his eyes are on mine, I clasp my hands behind his neck enjoying the erratic beat of his heart. I move my hands down to his shoulders and back up.

I sigh. "What I wouldn't give to put my lips on yours right now..."

He takes several controlled breaths. "I can't, for the life of me, remember why it is that you can't kiss me... only I know you can't," he replies. "What have you done to my mind? I'm positively in widdendream at the moment." His need to have me even closer grows ever stronger.

"Widdendream?" I ask to keep the conversation going so that the electricity between us doesn't get out of hand. It amazes me that the enticement is so strong despite our relatively loose embrace. We're not doing much more than looking at each other and imagining a simple kiss.

"Uh huh," Gabriel says, gazing at me. He swallows and pulls me closer with his good arm

"What does that mean?" I whisper.

"Um," Gabriel answers, his breaths getting shallower.

"Um?" I say softly, laying my head gently on his shoulder with painstaking slowness. "I didn't know you knew that word."

When the tension becomes uncomfortably strained, I sigh, unclasp my hands, and pull away. He doesn't let go of my waist immediately, but instead his eyes sweep slowly over my exposed skin: my lips, my cheek, my jaw, my neck...

My regret burrows a hole into the enjoyment of the moment though as he drinks in my skin with his eyes. I want to fill the depression in with something healthier but I don't know how. I keep hoping this guilt over depriving him will eventually go away if I stop acknowledging it.

He releases me finally and smiles lazily and says, "Widdendream is a state of mental confusion and befuddlement."

"Well, you couldn't have been that befuddled if you were able to come up with a word like that on the fly." I smile back at him and lead him toward Robert's kitchen table, sandwiches in hand.

Gabriel sighs heavily. "I have all kinds of words floating around up there. It's not that hard. I'm just lucky it applied accurately to describing my state. I could hardly think straight with you that close."

"I could tell," I say, "But now that we're both back in reality can I use you to check out the colorworld? It's been a while, and now that I know Kaylen's okay, I feel like taking some action."

"I've been waiting for you to ask," he answers, sitting down in a chair and pulling me into the one next to him.

"Now, no funny business while I'm there. This is strictly for observational purposes, so you keep your hands to yourself," I warn.

Gabriel rolls his eyes. "You act like it was *me* who seduced *you* into widdendream. I was just trying to have a little fun, and you turned it into a dalliance session... Not that I'm complaining. You can seduce me any time you want."

"Dalliance?" I ask, confused, but quickly shake my head. "Never mind. Just hold still."

I hold my hand lightly on his while I close my eyes, willing my colorworld awareness to activate. I'm a little out of practice, so it takes me a little longer than usual, but eventually I perceive the strings. I open my eyes.

I squint immediately, caught off guard. It's even brighter than I remember, and I wonder if I just got used to the brilliance before because I was there all the time. Once my eyes adjust, I see Gabriel's life force next to me, purple and swirling as usual. I focus through its radiance as much as I can and realize almost immediately that I can see more now.

His life force is far more detailed than I recall: I see distinct, miniscule strands flowing around his body. Now it not only *feels* like strands, but it *looks* that way, too.

Have I just not focused enough before?

No. I've spent a lot of time before trying to see strands. I always figured they were too small for me to see...

"What is it?" Gabriel asks, noticing my confusion.

"I... don't know. But I can see more than before. I can see individual strands distinctly. They're tiny, thinner than spider silk, all bunched together and swirling. Wow!"

I stare at the microscopic strands in wonder. Each one is mesmerizing; their movement seems so... animate? Purposeful? And they glow with purple luminosity, each one astounding in its own right.

I look up and around me, noticing that the colorworld in general is more detailed than I have ever seen it. I remember thinking it was beautiful but a little blurry compared to our world. But it definitely seems like more than just color now.

Rather than just glowing with light, each object has a movement within its substance. I open my mouth to speak, but hesitate, looking harder to figure out how to describe what I'm seeing.

Gabriel's unbridled curiosity interrupts my pensiveness so I say, "I think I get why the colors of inanimate objects are always changing in hue. The texture of the object is faceted." I look at Gabriel. "Have you ever seen one of those tilt books for kids where the picture has a ridged texture and if you tilt the book back and forth, it looks like the picture is moving?"

"Of course," Gabriel says excitedly.

"That's what it's like, except the texture is more complex. I can't see the structure exactly, but there's movement that makes me think the colors change because my angle of sight allows me to view different facets of the object."

I notice something else now that I'm not scrutinizing the makeup of the gold-hued table under my hands: the air. It's shimmering subtly. It reminds me a bit of what dust particles look like in the sunlight as they shift in the breeze and sparkle.

"The air is glittering," I say. "Like I'm in a snow globe but the glitter is all different colors. It makes the air alive." I move my hand through it, seeing the particles move aside gently. It makes my hand look like it's moving through something viscous even though it still feels like empty space.

Gabriel's intellect starts to alternate between graceful somersaults and balancing as he takes in what I tell him. I continue to look around me, absorbing it all. I finally look back at Gabriel, pushing my chair back as far as I can while still holding his hand so I can get a good look at his life force as a whole. I take in the intricacy of the different currents around his body. Each strand moves in a way that never looks at odds with any other strand even though there are clashing flows. It's plain to see that his life force has no purposeful directionality, so unlike the pre-hypno-touch pattern of the man Louise had me work on. Or Louise's own life force.

Gabriel's strands still tend toward his chest. But they are in disarray. Their flow flutters to some invisible breeze that influences the variegated and inconsistent pattern around his body.

"I can see exactly where your strands are flowing... Before it was only a vague idea," I explain. "I wonder if they're attached to the body in some way—kind of like hair? But they definitely stick together, changing direction with the currents. I don't understand.

Why am I only just now seeing this?" I blur my eyes to see Gabriel's face, hoping he has an answer.

He not only looks baffled but feels it as much as I do. "I have no idea, Love."

My capability has somehow expanded to give me heightened colorworld senses. It has me worried. I look down at my hand entwined with Gabriel's. What if my death-touch has expanded along with it? But Gabriel is still alive; his heart beats regularly… I guess skin contact is still the only way it's activated.

I let go of him anyway, retreating from the colorworld at the same time. I look around, testing my ability to discern detail, realizing that yes, it's subtle, but I can see just a bit more when I really focus. Like the precise texture of the grit stuck in the grout of the floor tiles. Or the shape of dust particles in the air. So my senses overall have improved—or at least my vision. I can't as easily test my hearing and smell.

Gabriel looks at me expectantly, and I say, "I don't know if I like this. This could be really bad."

"It could also be really good," he replies. "Somehow, you've managed to improve your capability. Seeing more means understanding more. You are one step closer."

I breathe evenly to control my growing foreboding. He might be right. I hope he's right. But I wish I could have any explanation for why my ability has suddenly evolved. I only have a timeline: it happened sometime since Louise had me work on that man whose life force I defaced.

It reminds me of Dina and what Kaylen said about her ability diminishing. I've begun to accept that as true. Obviously Randy lied about the reason she knew of my natural talent. I've also been thinking that Gabriel was right about my mom: she must have lost her empathic ability before I was old enough to notice it. I admit I've been holding out that the same might also happen to me. But this is the exact opposite of that.

This means abilities can evolve one way or another.

I can't settle on hope *or* fear at that realization. They coexist right now. Gabriel is gratified, so I try my best to mimic his certainty. But in the back of my mind, the fear lingers, and doubt festers.

Look for book 2 in the Colorworld series:

Teleworld

Visit the official site at:
www.colorworldbooks.com

Acknowledgements

Deepest gratitude:

To my late father, William, whose gentle lulling voice spoke love to my sisters and me every night as he read novels to us. I will never forget the sound.

To my mom, Marie, who showed me that you can teach yourself to do anything and perfect the skill if you're willing to devote the time. It was her own stunning craftsmanship of the written word that made me want to work hard to unearth those creative genes she gave me.

To my mother-in-law, Wendy, who slogged through my junk of a first draft yet continued to encourage me in this crazy endeavor and never doubted my potential.

To my children, Novan, Beya, Iyov, and Keshet, who have sacrificed more than anyone else to put this book into the hands of readers.

To my editor, Jamie Walton, who I swear can read my mind and knows exactly where my writing is going even when I don't quite know myself.

To my photographer, Richard Heeks, who is nothing short of a genius at his craft. His incredible work for me has influenced my series more than he knows.

To my cover designer, Beth Weatherly, for coming out of retirement just for me and being such a boss at turning the images in my head into professional material.

To the love of my life, Bradley Kelly, who, before I ever conceived of writing a book, didn't just believe in me but *expected* me to live up to the potential he saw me possess long before I ever saw it in myself.

To my Heavenly Father and Heavenly Mother who never fail to put all the right people in my life at just the right times to inspire me in just the right ways.

14139625R00204

Made in the USA
San Bernardino, CA
18 August 2014